The Other Side of 30

R.Y. Swint

Angela,
Dione said I had to hurry up & sigh, so I'll keep this short!! :)
Love you for your support & encouragement. Good times working security. I miss that money.
—Regina

Copyright © 2010 Regina Y. Swint

Hardcover ISBN: 978-1-60910-233-3
Paperback ISBN: 978-1-60910-234-0

All rights reserved. No part of this publication may be reproduced, stored in a retrieval system, or transmitted in any form or by any means, electronic, mechanical, recording or otherwise, without the prior written permission of the author.

Printed in the United States of America.

BookLocker.com, Inc.
2010

Edited by: Kaytie M. Lee
Cover design by: Miguel A. Cardona Jr. (www.mc82.com)
Cover photo by: Amir West (www.photofanatic.org)

~Dedication~

This book is dedicated to the memory of my uncle, Harvey Greene "Teedlum" Penn Jr., "…with tears in both eyes…" (H.A. Penn)

~Acknowledgments~

My grandmother, Beulah M. Penn ~ My amazing grace. My keeper of peace in so many valleys. As you can see, I'm still trying to get it right, and it's even harder with you gone. Because of you, Psalm 23 and Psalm 121 remain uppermost in my mind.

My mother, Nancy D. Swint ~ No manner of expression will ever adequately say how much I love and admire you. You are one of the most beautiful and talented people I have ever known. I wish you could see what I see.

My 4th grade teacher, Mrs. Shawn Fish ~ You are unequivocally my favorite teacher in the whole world. Ever. *The Other Side of 30* would not exist without *Regina's Race*.

My friends and family ~ You are priceless. Thank you for connecting with me and keeping me connected.

Table of Contents

Prologue vii
Chapter One – Old Beginnings 1
Chapter Two – The Happening 11
Chapter Three – Red Light Runners 26
Chapter Four – Never-Never Land.. 35
Chapter Five – The Reluctant Homewrecker 41
Chapter Six – The Other Side of Thirty 49
Chapter Seven – The Other End of the Candle 60
Chapter Eight – Easy Sins 73
Chapter Nine – A Real Date 86
Chapter Ten – Girl Talk 102
Chapter Eleven – The Virgin of the Village 107
Chapter Twelve – Her Story 121
Chapter Thirteen – Merry Christmas, Baby 134
Chapter Fourteen – Just Fine, Thanks 141
Chapter Fifteen – Things on the Side 150
Chapter Sixteen – Hindsight 163
Chapter Seventeen – Reality Check 174
Chapter Eighteen – Good Intentions 178
Chapter Nineteen – A Friend with Issues 189
Chapter Twenty – Slipping Away 195
Chapter Twenty-One – Midnight and a Half 202
Chapter Twenty-Two – Missing Pieces 210
Chapter Twenty-Three – Broken Sleep 232
Chapter Twenty-Four – Conduct Unbecoming 246
Chapter Twenty-Five – Something Else 254

Chapter Twenty-Six – Messengers 265
Chapter Twenty-Seven – Misunderstandings 275
Chapter Twenty-Eight – Man Stuff 286
Chapter Twenty-Nine – Happy Hour 292
Chapter Thirty – Another Side 313
Chapter Thirty-One – Forth and Back 326
Chapter Thirty-Two – The Wake Up Call 331
Chapter Thirty-Three – Second to Last Chances 338
Chapter Thirty-Four – Figuring It Out 346
Chapter Thirty-Five – Barely Sane 359
Chapter Thirty-Six – All That I Can Be 371

Prologue

"I am having the most amazing sex...with your husband. Yes, your husband. As a matter of fact, I fuck him every chance I get." I felt my eyes draw tight as I stood there, pleased with my cool delivery, satisfied at having rendered her completely speechless.

Well, I would have been pleased and satisfied if it weren't for the truth. And the truth is that I was actually standing in the shower, rinsing the soap and Noxema® from my face, rehearsing a conversation that would probably never happen. I mean, really. Who breaks news like that, anyway?

The more I thought about it, the worse it sounded. I tried again. "I'm sorry to tell you, but he doesn't love you." I liked the image of her, hands on hips, with her mouth caved open, making that sound like something had lodged in the back of her throat.

I grabbed the washcloth and drifted back into my fantasy. "There's nothing you can do about it. Hey, this is just the way it is." Okay, that's some bullshit, but it's my shower and my daydream.

"What can I say? It just happened."

Okay, that garbage wasn't going to work. I felt like I was about to break into a rendition of "Woman to Woman" or some other 70's I-stole-your-man song, and I wasn't feeling the bitchy soap opera dialogue.

I wanted to convince myself that it would be best just to come right out with it, like it would ever be that simple. But an ongoing thing like this doesn't just happen. And it doesn't just stop.

Seven months had come and gone, and in that time, all I'd managed to do was convince myself that I was in love or something like it, with somebody else's man. Curtis is the kind of man who you'd always have to be strong about when doing the right thing is at stake, and the day I slipped and fell back into bed with him wasn't my day to be strong.

His look was not just hypnotic, it was downright poetic. I would practically gravitate toward him. And when he smiled, the two tiny dimples just above the corners of his mouth could make you say yes before he even asked the question. He's always had a gift for making me forget myself.

Just then the bathroom door swung open and there was my partner in crime.

"Sebrina, who are you talking to?"

"Nobody. I was just—singing," I told him.

He smiled. "Well, come sing for me."

I smiled back. "In a minute."

You could hardly call what we do singing. Though something about the way he does what he does makes me want to sing to him. Sing for him. Sing about him. Anita Baker said it best. He brings me joy. And if anybody could ever bring me joy when I'm down, it's Curtis. Even if he is the reason I lost my way in the first place. But that's not part of the song. Or is it?

Chapter One – Old Beginnings

I arrived in Atlanta in the fall of 1998. About a year later, Curtis and I ran into each other at my job. I'm in the Army. He's a Marine recruiter.

Ever since I joined the Army, God has seen fit to give me my share of what we call special assignments. This job is one of those kinds of assignments. I'm the first to admit that this place is not most people's idea of the "real Army". I don't sleep in the field three weeks out of the month. I don't run five miles a day at four o'clock in the morning. More on that running thing later. I've never been deployed. I don't pull guard duty at the gate and yell, "Hark, who goes there? What's the password?" or any of that stuff.

I haven't done "real Army" stuff since forever ago, when I was crazy enough to let one of my basic training buddies talk me into going to Air Assault School with her so that she could follow her boyfriend to Fort Campbell, Kentucky. Air Assault School—that's rappelling out of helicopters—is when I discovered that I'm afraid of heights, but also found out that I'm a better runner than anyone who hates running ought to be. Then came the Army's Master Fitness School, just for normal career progression. Of course, that was back when *Be All You Can Be* was still the Army's motto, its best motto in my opinion, and I was on the fast track to somewhere. A few years later came MEPS duty.

The MEPS, or Military Entrance Processing Station, is that place that every high school kid contemplates going to when the job offers and college scholarships aren't flooding the mailbox after graduation. The same place that every college student thinks about going to when they're stressed out, flunking out, or just running out of money.

It's where you go to take the test and the physical and would get sworn in if you don't change your mind first. It's that place where college grads say they'll never, never end up because they're educated and ambitious. They've got connections, friends, frat brothers and sorors, internships. And most of all, they've got a degree, like it's a magic wand.

But circumstances have a way of turning situations around. It's rude when you realize you got few, if any skills, little or no marketable experience, and you've also got loans to pay off. And when it comes time to make that first payment, your degree, internships, networking, and ambition all add up to pocket lint. The next thing you know, you're in Never-Never Land, the MEPS, and that's where I work. My particular MEPS is on Fort Gillem, just south of metro Atlanta.

Think back about that Army test that those recruiters came to our high schools and gave, that we just took so we could get out of class for three hours. Well, those people aren't recruiters. They're Test Administrators, or TA's, and I'm one of them. The recruiters are just there to help out. We call them proctors. And it's not the Army test. It's an aptitude test that tells people how qualified they are for certain jobs. We still give it at high schools, but we also give it here at my job, usually on the computer, but sometimes with paper and pencil. But I digress. Enough of sounding like a pre-test briefing.

Anyway, I usually work at night, which is a true blessing because I hate getting up early. As much as I love this job, ten years ago you couldn't have told me I'd end up here, in Uncle Sam's Army. Looking to have my own adventures, get my own stuff, and yes, pay off that mortgage called a student loan. I saw just how small the world is when I ended up stationed right back at home in Georgia.

And who do you guess just happened to be recruiting for a few good men right here in ATL? Gunnery Sergeant Kirkpatrick Mortecai Curtis. Only by then, Curtis was an ex-boyfriend who was about to be married in six weeks. His fiancé, some prude-ass looking, chunky-faced military brat who'd followed him from wherever he'd found her, was having her We-Need-Our-Space- Before-the-Wedding phase. Stupid heifer.

It was the Tuesday after Columbus Day weekend, a few days before the Georgia Student Test Day, the biggest, suckiest MEPS testing day of the year. Teachers and students scurrying around between classrooms, recruiters running amok, too many books to keep up with. Curtis came blowing into the MEPS, huffing and puffing, and just expecting somebody to fall for one of those tired-ass excuses for being late for a test.

I'd gotten up at o'dark-thirty, driven way out to some school out near Athens, gotten lost on the way, finally found it, given a test, arrived back at work just in time to do QRP—that's Quality Review Process—on records for the next day's business— and then finished that up just in time to take up my post at the front counter to check in applicants for the night test. By closing time, at six o'clock in the evening, you could say I was a little cranky, but mostly just ready to go home.

Curtis came bolting in just after six, baby-faced applicant in tow, as I was collecting the clipboards from the counter. That's what recruiters do when they're late. Bolt through the door for effect. Before he could even begin his excuse, I cut him off. I'd surveyed every inch of his body in the time it took to take one breath, even noticing that he'd fixed that once-chipped tooth, but I started my ass-chewing spiel like I didn't even know him.

"Listen here, S'arnt. The Marines don't run nothin' up in MEPS. Late is late." Late or not, he was the best looking thing that I'd seen come through that door. Hell, maybe even the best looking thing walking on two legs. I felt like I could pass out, but I hardly even blinked.

He blinked a couple of times, surely caught off guard by the fact that he recognized me. Then he started his excuse. "I know I'm a little late. We had a flat." He talked and breathed like they'd just changed four flat tires in a hurricane and barely made it there alive.

"Aw, bull—," I looked over at the kid in mid-sentence, "—loney." Recruiters and their stories.

He said, "Really," with a wide-eyed, high pitched, faked sincerity. "It was the damned-est thing." He paused and then started again in his regular voice, attempting to exert some kind of authority. "I don't need to explain that to you. I need somebody to take care of my applicant. Is that you?" His mouth was so pretty and he was really working that gum. I glanced over at the applicant again, who as if on cue, started heaving and breathing like he was out of breath, too.

"Maybe it is. What's that got to do with you being on time?"

No answer.

"What you need," I said, "is to be here by 1800. Not 1815, or even 1800 and one second. The cut off for check-in is six o'clock."

"It's just now six o'clock," he said. "It's six o'clock."

"Yeah, yeah," I said back. "'Time for Street to rock', and all that, and time for me to go home. And breathing all heavy like you just sprinted barefoot down 75 to get here don't change none of that." His eyes demanded contact, but I blinked down at my computer to reemphasize my point. "And actually, according to my terminal, you are 7 minutes and— 12 seconds late." I batted my eyes back up at him. "Sorry."

"I—"

"Must be new," I said to finish his sentence. He had his jacket on over his shirt, so to add insult to injury, I asked, "What's your name S'arnt?" I knew that Marines can be really touchy about rank, so I purposely called him S'arnt just to see how anal he would be.

"Gunnery Sergeant," he corrected me, and he meant it.

I suppressed the smirk I felt coming on and pretended to exercise some military bearing.

"Hmph. Well, S'arnt Gunnery S'arnt, excuses are the tools of the weak and incompetent." I turned my back on him as I opened door to the files room, just behind the counter. "Or don't they teach you that in the Marines?"

"You're still talking to a senior NCO," he said to the door closing behind me. "Or don't they teach you that in the Army?"

"Yep," I said, as I opened the door and returned to the counter. Then I reminded him, "Teach us how to tell time too. And you're still late." I was on a roll. "Anyway, out of time, out of luck. It's all the same."

"Just who do you think you're talking to?" The demand kind of turned me on, as if I weren't already.

I stepped back and batted my eyes again. "Just who do *you* think I'm talking to, Lateness?"

His left eyebrow jumped up like he was intrigued, or maybe starting to get a little pissed off at knowing a Marine couldn't take control of the situation from a soldier.

"Tell you what." I relented. I already knew when they came through the door that I was going to let that kid go back to take the test. I just wanted to make them sweat a little bit, but there was really no need to keep torturing either of them. "I'll give you a break. But this is the first and last time you get away with this, and only because you're new. This doesn't happen again."

He let out an unimpressed, "Hmph."

Uncalled as it was, I continued to give him a hard time for the hell of it as I took the Seven-Fourteen, the test request form, from the applicant. "Next time, save all your flat tire, got stuck in traffic, bad weather or whatever other kind of stories for your station commander when I send you up out of here."

"I am the station commander." He leaned forward on the counter, and watched me work at filling out the test form. God, I could smell him, and it was the most delicious scent of all day mixed with lingering cologne.

Then I let out an unimpressed, "Hmph." After a few seconds, I said, "Okay S'arnt, I got it. Back up, now. You're crowding me." Distracting me was more like it. I tried not to lick my lips, remembering them pressed against his bare heaving chest. Plus, I needed a manicure. I continued with, "What I need you to do is either get back to the recruiter lounge…"

He just stood there, so I stopped writing.

"Or get out," I said with a shrug, "In which case, you can take Mr.—," I looked down at the 714, "—Madison, with you. Your choice." I glanced at a bewildered Mr. Madison, who just wanted to take the test.

Curtis took a step back, braced with his arms crossed, like he was daring me to try to physically remove him. A chill rushed through me and knocked the pen right out of my hand.

He must have sensed it because he loosened up. "Okay, let's start over. How are you doing today?" He smiled and put his hands on the counter. Even his hands were still beautiful, with those long, lean fingers. Clean fingernails. Flat tire my ass.

"I'm good," I lied, tired as hell. "If I was any better I'd be screaming with my legs in the air." Mr. Madison chuckled. I smirked. Curtis' eyebrow jumped again, but I pretended not to notice. "And you?" I asked and started to look away before he had time to reply.

"I'm good and getting better," he said, starting to smile.

"That right?" I pretended to be half-listening, as I picked up the pen and kept writing, but I was absolutely hinging on the sound of his breath and the smell of his cologne. I regrouped. "Stand by Gunny, while I get Mr. Madison checked in."

"No problem," he agreed. "How about I wait over here?" He leaned his fine ass against the door.

I smiled down at the counter, fantasizing, telling myself he still has a perfect kiss and how his lips are still so soft and smooth.

All I could think was how much I missed him. Christ help me. I wanted to jump across that counter, wrap my legs around his back, and fuck him through his clothes. Instead, I just finished processing young Mr. Madison, and sent him back to the test room, where I'm sure my fellow TA was going to be pissed at me for checking in someone fifteen minutes past the cut off time.

When we were alone, I said, "Hey," still imagining my legs flung around his back and holding tight. "Oh my goodness, it's good to see you." I wanted to go in for a gentle hug, before returning behind the counter, but something stopped me.

He smiled and said, "Hey," back to me.

"About before, Curtis. Sorry I had to be so hard on you in front of the kid. We really have to put our foot down around here. You know. You have to be like, 'When in charge, take charge'. Especially when you get hard headed recruiters coming in here when they feel like it. And it's been a really long day. I was just messing with you a little bit."

"That's cool," he said, then added, "Where did you learn to become such a bitch?"

Bitch? "Watch your mouth, Marine." I winced a little. "Was I that bad?" I'll show you a bitch.

He nodded. "Somebody taught you well."

"Yeah. These bitch-ass recruiters," I said, a little defensively. "Marines, mostly."

"Calling me and my brothers bitches?"

"Mmhmm. The world's finest." I turned away for a moment to open the files room door and click off the lights.

Whether it's true or not, I have something of a reputation for favoring Marines. My coworkers seem to think the Marines put stars in my eyes. "Something about those blue pants," I always say. "You know, even the ugly ones make you look twice." If any of that is true, Curtis started all that.

"Well." He puffed out his chest. "Everybody can't wear these blue pants."

"Thank God," I answered, attempting to deflate him, but smiling inside.

"Somebody used to like them."

"Shhhh. Somebody likes them now," I mumbled with my back still turned.

"Say what?" Oh, God. He heard me.

I just said, "Hmph. These green ones fit fine." His arms and chest filled out that jacket just right, and I wondered if it all felt as good as it used to.

"Mmhmm," he said. "Filling them out a little bit too."

Now, that wasn't necessary. I did the best I could to keep from consciously frowning, but I was sure frowning on the inside. These damn pants never come back fitting the same once they go to the cleaners. Too baggy in the front, too tight on the hips, too high in the hem. I got self-conscious, thinking how he must have noticed my pockets bulging on the sides the slightest little bit, and as I rubbed down the sides of my pants, I finally came back with, "And they actually match the shirt. Imagine that." Hmph. Like your ass is as narrow as it used to be.

Now, if I'd have called him a peacock with all those damn non-matching colors, he'd have had his feelings hurt. Red stripes on royal blue pants, pea green stripes on a khaki shirt, black and white Good Humor Man cap. Leave it to the Marine Corps to put such an ensemble together. I stood there expecting his righteous indignation, feeling a little righteously indignant myself.

"All I'm saying is you look good." He sighed. "And it's good to see you, too." His teeth were gleaming.

"Yeah," I sighed back, and then I was beaming. Matching or not, he still looked good to me. Leave it to the Marines to make some tacky shit like that work.

While I was closing down the counter and straightening up, we talked a little more about his recent past, my recent past, how I'd been, how he'd been, how long he'd been in Atlanta. Then he segued not-so-subtly into guess-what-I'm-finally-getting-married.

Suddenly the smile just stuck to my face. "That's great," I said through my teeth, not making as much eye contact as before.

That's when he told me about his fiancé, Andra-Lyn, and her little phase. I tried not to flinch at the sound of her name. The hell she get a name like that, anyway? Her and her fucking stupid ass phase. I just nodded and smiled. I might as well have been The Joker, I couldn't stop smiling.

I don't know what came over me, except the little devil on my shoulder telling me that opportunity was about to come knocking. I couldn't even remember my last good sex. I had to be working on some kind of record to have gone that long.

I mean, it wasn't really as if he was a new man. It wasn't like I was adding yet another name to a list that was already getting too long for me to remember the order.

"So, what time do you leave here?"

"Now," I said, glad he asked.

"You wanna go somewhere and talk? Maybe get something to eat."

I should have been thinking, *Hell no! Don't waste a good year of chastity and clean living on his fixing-to-be-married ass. Say no thank you. Damn him.* But I said, "Okay." I smiled like the cat who was about to eat the canary.

"Okay." He smiled back. "What's up? Follow me? Or do I follow you? Where do you want to go?" I guess I never noticed how much smiling and laughing people tend to do when they're up to no good. And yes, there was a lot of smiling going on.

I must have looked like I was giving his question some serious thought, because he threw in, "Oh wait. You don't eat as much as you used to, do you?" Then he laughed.

I laughed too because at that point all I was thinking was that the chances were better than good that I was going to have sex that night.

Then I said, "Whatever, man." Thinking. "Anyway, how about you follow me to my apartment. I live near here. Just give me a minute to get changed." He smiled and nodded. I walked down the hall to the female locker room and changed into my civilian clothes before the drive home.

Chapter Two – The Happening

On the drive home, the little devil reminded me that dignity never warmed an empty bed on a cold night. And values never held me late into the morning. And if you really want to be real about it, stacking giant pillows next to you on the man side of the bed and backing up on them in the middle of the night like they're a warm body just doesn't cut it.

Yes, I was raised better than this. And I know the consequences. But my strength, integrity and moral courage all abandoned me like they were all as tired of me as I was of having them for my only company. Me and my values. My hollow values and cold dignity.

When we got to my complex and started up the stairs to my apartment, we passed and spoke to my neighbor from across the way, Elliott, who was on his way down. He was a well-groomed guy, who always looked ready to be somewhere. I'd seen him look better taking out his trash than a lot of people I'd seen going to church.

He smiled at me, then at Curtis, then at me again, and mumbled in a barely audible tune, "Mmmm, some girls have all the luck."

Curtis started a double-take. "What did he say?"

"Aw, nothing. A Rod Stewart song," I said.

"Okay," Curtis said. "Looked like he was checking you out pretty hard."

"Yeah?" I asked, more like making a statement. "Whatever. He's cool, but he's kind of flirty."

"Even when a guy is with you? That's a pretty bold white boy."

That was probably my cue to tell him that I didn't bring many guys to my place, but I just put the key in the lock and pushed the door open. "Like I said, he's harmless."

Curtis walked in the apartment behind me and stood at the door, waiting for his invitation. "So, sit down," I said. He sat down and started to unzip his jacket but stopped. "You can take it off if you want," I told him. So he did. And all he had on underneath was one of those A-line, wife-beater undershirts. Where the hell was his shirt?

"Hey," I said, "Where's—? Aren't you supposed to have on—?"

"Yeah," he cut me off. "Sometimes I cheat."

Suddenly morality, the little angel on my other shoulder, tugged at me to get a grip. The man was fucking betrothed, for goodness sake. But loneliness is the bitch that gave birth to despair and self-pity. And on the end of any day, despair and self-pity were the last kinds of company I needed. The company I needed was sitting right in my living room with his shirt missing and the kind of party I had in mind had nothing to do with pity.

I went to the refrigerator and took out a bottle of water. I untwisted the cap and took a swig of it like it was something stronger. Then I shrugged it off, refusing to feel guilty for my thoughts. He's the one engaged, not me.

I stood there in the kitchen, leaned against the bar, in my gray sweats and sneakers, contemplating my next move. So began the baggy sweatpants seduction. The same kind of sweats that in college, my roommates wanted to hide and burn because I wore them so much. They'd said the best way to get a man's attention was not to look like one, to walk the road of a much higher maintenance than baggy jeans and bushy eyebrows, and for a while I tried the path of panty hose, heels and regular make-up. Some of what I'd picked up along the way was worth holding on to, like hot waxes and hair weaves. But hey, fashion is a nice place to visit, but I don't want to live there. Home was the comfort of loose-fitting jeans, pony tails and ratty, baggy, preferably gray sweats. The down side is risking looking like this when in front of an unexpected man.

"So, show me around," he said as he leaned back on the sofa.

"This is it," I said. "It's just a one bedroom."

"So, you're saying I don't get the full tour?"

"I like how you're sitting talking about show you around, and you're all reared back on my couch, getting comfortable, like you plan on staying." Actually, I liked that a lot. I set the bottle on the bar. "This is the kitchen." He stood up as I turned and modeled like one of the *Price Is Right* girls. "Over here is the laundry, the pantry," I continued as I swayed to the left and right. "Around the corner to my left, your right, is the bathroom."

He pretended to be impressed.

"That's the living room-slash-dining room-slash-study."

"Very nice," he said, playing along. "You know, you do that very well."

"Yeah?" I smiled. "Guess I missed my calling, huh." I kept going. "Behind you is the closed-in balcony, complete with the tear in the screen that's been there since I moved in."

"Niiice." He opened the sliding door and ducked out onto the balcony and stood there with his hands on his hips. At first, I watched him, sucking my teeth, or, not so-subtly licking my chops, if you will. I walked out behind him and put my arms around him and pressed the side of my face to his back, the first time I'd touched this man in over ten years. His body was warm and welcoming, as he put his hand over mine, pressing it to his chest. Damn, he smelled good.

He turned around and held me. "So, is this as close as I get?"

"This is probably close enough," I said, not letting go. "Maybe even too close." Little angel was fighting the good fight, but losing.

"This is cool." I felt his chin touch the top of my head.

I wanted him so bad, I could have bitten a plug out of his chest.

"Um, can I get you something?" was the best I could come up with.

"Something like what?" He kind of laughed through the tension.

"Uh, juice, water, something like that." Maybe a cold shower? I sort of tried to pull away.

"In a minute," he said, holding me.

"I could show you the wrought iron bed I got made in Turkey." Okay, that was about as subtle as a sucker punch. Little devil wouldn't give up yet.

He followed me to the bed that took up more than half of the room. "Damn," he laughed. "Is it big enough?" Sure, it took up the whole room. The whole frame was black wrought iron, with scroll designs in the headboard and footboard, and the mattress was set high off the floor.

"Don't be jealous," I said. "It's a one of a kind."

"I don't doubt it. Looks, uh, good and sturdy."

"Yep. I designed it myself. Try it out. But take your shoes off."

He pulled his shoes off and sat down. He patted his hand on the bed, signaling me to sit next to him.

I sat down, then lay back across the bed, my feet dangling. He lay back next to me for a few seconds, his feet dangling a little too. "This is uncomfortable."

"Yep," I agreed. The battle between what I wanted to do and what I should do was kicking my ass.

He pulled his feet onto the bed and lay down the regular way. "Come lay next to me."

I did, counted to three slowly in my head, and then sprang up.

"All right, that's enough," I said. "Let's go."

"In a minute." He pulled me back down next to him.

At first we just lay in bed, cuddling next to each other, my back to his front with his arms wrapped around me, in that little spoon formation, sharing space and body heat. And I told myself that was more than good enough. But then I reached up behind me and rubbed his face, and then the back of his head, and then he said something sweet and stupid like, "Mmm, this feels familiar."

I replied with something just as weak like, "Mmm, vaguely." And he squeezed me tighter. After a few moments of silence, I said, "You know, you did something earlier tonight that kind of turned me on and I couldn't figure out why until now."

"Mmhmm."

I couldn't tell if he wasn't really listening or if he was just cueing me to go on, so I said, "Hey."

"Mmhmm," he repeated. "What did I do?"

Then he kissed the back of my neck. It was kind of quick, as if just to test my reaction. "Baby, you feel so good."

I used to love to hear him call me Baby. I couldn't even remember the last time anybody had told me I felt good. It was like, Strength said, *Enough already!* Integrity chimed in with, *Lighten up for God's sake.* And little devil said, *You're already laying here with him. Girl, you better get this.*

I pulled his arms tighter around me and kissed the back of his hand. "You stepped back from the counter and crossed your arms. You know, like you were pissed off about something."

He didn't say anything.

"Anyway." I kept talking, nervous about confessing and unable to stop. "It reminded me of the first time I saw you. That time in the Square that night with the DP."

He kissed me on my neck again, a little slower, a little wetter. "Is that okay?" he whispered.

This time, when I kissed his hand, I continued by taking each of his fingers one by one into my mouth and pulling it out slowly. I missed our little jokes about roller coasters and sex, how he would nickname himself The Scream Machine, The Mind Bender® and The Georgia Cyclone®. Oh yeah, and the Devil Dog, a Marine thing. I missed the way he used to drip sweat all over me. Nobody dripped sweat on me the way he used to. And Devil Dog? Let's just say most Marines don't live up to that name.

My body was screaming, all right. If I ever needed my mind bent, it was now, and if I played this just right, it wouldn't take standing in line for an hour at Six Flags®.

Before I reached his thumb he was on top of me. And the next thing I knew, we were doing the familiar thing, fast and urgent, then slowly, like we were exploring each other for the first time. I held on to him, absorbing him, missing him, trying to act like familiarity was all I was feeling. Mmmm. He was still a perfect fit, though a little tight at first. Nobody ever fit me the way he did, and I'll bet he never fit anybody else that way, either.

The sex was so good, I could've slapped him. It was that after work, *Baby, just tear my back out* kind of good. So good, apparently, that afterward, as we lay in bed, our sweat cooling, he felt like baring his soul.

"You didn't deserve all the bullshit that went down between us back then, Sebrina." Now came the things that I had never heard him say, but I'd always hoped he was thinking. "That whole thing with me and old girl," he continued. He couldn't even remember her name. Tina Jones. I haven't seen her in years, but I'll never forget her.

"Yeah, I know," I said. "Forget it." Lord knows it took me long enough to.

Tina was one of my old roommates. She and Curtis had a meant-to-be secret fling. She was a pitcher on our women's softball team. I would have called her my friend, my best friend even, until I found out that she was fucking around with the man she knew I loved. I told myself that Curtis and I would have had something perfect if she hadn't come along and ruined it.

Curtis' point of view was that I ruined it when I refused to put school on hold to stay with him.

"What would it take to make you stay?" he'd asked.

I didn't have a direct answer, but I knew I wanted to finish school. For some reason, it was so important then. A promise wasn't enough. He needed me to make up my mind and marry him before he was transferred overseas. His argument was that I could finish school anytime.

Of course, my response was that if he really loved me the way he'd said, then he'd wait. That we could make it work if we were both committed. And some other stuff about if it's meant to be it would be.

He called bullshit, and told me he had his answer. But even when he asked, "Is there anything I can do to change your mind?" my answer was no. For the first time ever.

But Tina…Tina said yes. Not to marriage, but to opportunity.

I guess the break up sex he had with me that night hadn't been enough. So he managed to get a little extra going away gift from too-happy-to-oblige Tina at his hotel room. But Tina had a big mouth. She'd told one of our other roommates, Layla, all about it. Especially about what a fool I was to throw away a man like that just because I wanted to finish school. And for whatever reason, Layla felt obliged to tell me. Just because she thought I'd want to know.

When I found out, I went some kind of crazy. Not crazy crazy, just the feeling like shit and showing it kind of crazy. Stopped going to class, stopped bathing, as trifling as that is, started sleeping on the floor because I couldn't stand to touch the bed. Nearly flunked out of school. Almost joined the army. I seriously considered mixing Nair® into her Pink Oil Hair Lotion®, while she just went on about her life. Came to and from the room every day as if nothing had changed, and when she did bother to look me in the face, it was with an air of *What's done is done. Get over it already.* That little Memphis bitch.

I'd felt like I'd been pushed off a cliff. It was like free falling for miles waiting to hit rock bottom. Some days it hurt to breathe.

I don't remember the day when I woke up and he wasn't the first thing on my mind, though I'd sworn that I would mark it on my calendar if it ever came, but by the time that day had come, I guess I'd finally resolved that it must be some kind of rite of passage into womanhood to be betrayed by friends and heartbroken by men. Or maybe there was just no calendar around. I'd like to think that only the strongest of us get that dose of betrayal and heartbreak in the same shot. If you live through that, you should never cry about anything else again.

****

Anyway, there I was, despite God's grace, in a place in my life doing things that I never said I would, with a person I'd made up in my mind I could get through the rest of my life without. I'd promised God that if He got me through then, I'd be better for it now. Now look at me.

"It was stupid, and I was wrong," he said. "I was young, dumb, and—,"

"And full of shit."

"And I never apologized, did I?"

"You know, you can really fuck up a mood." I elbowed him in the side. Lucky for me that I was still buzzing with a little afterglow. Or maybe it's true what they say about time. Funny how things that mean the world at nineteen, don't mean much of shit on the other side of 30.

"I remember being sorry about taking your virginity."

Hell, I remembered being sorry about it too, but good God, why was he confessing this to me now? Did I look like a fucking priest? Hell, we're not even Catholic. Fuck a confession.

And did I really give a fuck about what he remembered? I even remembered his exact words saying to me, *I'm the one that's going to take care of you*, and, *There's nothing I wouldn't do to make you happy*. Bullshit.

He took care of me all right. Hell, I even remembered vowing that I'd never have sex again until I got married, condemning myself for not having saved it longer. And yet, ten years and several broken vows later, there I was, laying up with the same remorseful son-of-a-bitch.

"As much as I loved you, and as hard as I cried for you, I should have cut your fucking head off." I could feel him looking at me as I stared up at the ceiling. "Both of them," I added.

He gave me the *Damn, where did that come from?* look.

Now this Miss Tender Loving Care had somehow had the power to change his ways. In the six and some odd years they'd been together, he'd never cheated on her. Was I supposed to admire that? Was I even supposed to believe that? The fuck? More confessions?

"Until now," he said.

"You're killing my buzz, man. And fast." I'm sure I rolled my eyes at that. Whatever.

So did that make me some wily seductress? A conquering hero or something? And now he was about to marry her. Shit. I did not want to hear about her. Was I supposed to feel some sense of accomplishment, having shaken his fidelity? Was I supposed to apologize? Why the fuck was he just now getting married, anyway? I reasoned that he sure wouldn't have been laying up in my bed with me if he had been already married.

"So that's it," I said, finally. "I guess I'm supposed to be the last of your wild oats before taking the plunge or whatever." Yeah, I mixed metaphors, but my sex buzz was wearing off and I was sobering up with a hella hangover. The only thing that could have made me feel worse is if he'd told me that she was still a virgin and saving it for their wedding night. Thank God it didn't come up.

He sat up and reached across my body for his pants. He took out his wallet and flipped it open to a couple of pictures of her. I took little comfort in the fact that Miss TLC had excellent potential for becoming Miss Piggy with a little effort. Probably some little princess who had never had dirty fingernails or a bad hair day. Probably never drank wine from a plastic cup. Probably doesn't even drink. Little young-ass, fat-fingered heifer. Looks like she has issues with water retention. And acne. And loads of fat girl potential with very little effort.

"Curtis." I swallowed and took a breath. "Are you in love?"

"Yeah," he said, like he needed a drink of water. Why did I ask him that? Why did I care?

"Well," I concluded. "At least we know this can never happen again, right?"

He cleared his throat. "Right."

Early the next morning, he left all warm and fuzzy inside, not to mention all cleansed and purged by his confessions. I walked him to the door and for some odd reason, offered him my cheek when he leaned over to kiss me goodbye. His lips kind of lingered on the side of my face as he breathed softly and said, "It was really good to see you, Sebrina."

"It was good to see you," I said, with poorly feigned indifference.

Elliott was up already, with "Do You Think I'm Sexy" blaring from behind his closed door. Just as Curtis was leaving, Elliott opened his door.

He flashed a smiled at us before he bent down to pick up his paper. We all said, "Good morning," at the same time.

"I just love Georgia weather in the fall," Elliott said, as stood up and took a deep breath. "Mmm."

Curtis walked away and I just shook my head and closed the door.

I didn't have to be at work until eleven, so I went and wrapped myself up in the covers and lay there with his familiarity clinging to my senses and my sheets.

I got up and went to work like nothing. I told myself it was just a thing that happened, just something I needed at the time that I needed it. No big deal. That's all I would allow myself to think of it. I came home and went to bed on those same familiar sheets, meaning to savor the scent. I was tempted not to wash them at all, like I could spend the rest of my sad life clinging to a secret memory. I dreaded being alone again. I don't know if there's ever a good time of year to be alone, but this was definitely not a good time. I guess I just didn't really know how sick of it I was until I had a taste of not being alone.

****

The fall in Atlanta is what makes people want to move to the South. The clean air, the mild weather, the genuinely laid back lifestyle. And baseball fans. Atlanta has the best, true blue baseball fans, even when they're not winning. Long past hurricane and flood season, and well before the clocks fall back, when twilight still comes after eight o'clock, and the nights are still warm and perfect for sleeping naked with breezes and moonlight coming through open windows. And whoever's not having sex is probably dreaming about sex. I tried to dream about it. I wanted to dream about it, but it was one of those times where the dream you want to have just won't come to you. About the only consolation I had was the Braves going to the World

Series.

For every breezy, naked, moonlit night going on a month I lay there, thinking, drifting in and out of thoughts, into unsolicited dreams, sleeping on stale sheets and stale memories. Yeah, stale sheets. I know. That's nasty. Most nights, I'd stare at the ceiling wondering if he held her the way he used to hold on to me. I'd lay awake thinking about what it could've been that she did to get him that I didn't do. More often, I'd have nights where I didn't even remember falling asleep, but I must have because I'd wake up cranky and thoroughly unrested.

When I did dream, it was about dumb shit like being hungry and eating something you can't taste, or riding roller coasters in the rain, or some other nonsense.

I saw them together for the first time in the PX parking lot one day, and I got that I-want-to-throw-up feeling. I was sitting there in my car, thinking and re-thinking my thoughts, re-contemplating decisions, wishing I could undo a few old ones. I swear I must have thought him up.

He was pulling into a parking space just in front of the one I was about to back out of. Our eyes met and we both blinked away, as if not looking at each other would keep a secret from spilling out of our eyes. Brief though it was, it actually pissed me off that the little bitch didn't even notice.

She got out of the black Jeep Cherokee first, walking a few steps ahead of him, wearing a busty pink top, jeans and sandals. The kind of top and the color pink that screams, and jeans not tight enough to be trashy, but just tight enough to say *I know I'm all that*, the ones with the low rise in the front that show off the navel and a flat, though not very toned stomach. And the sandals made especially for people with pretty feet.

She's the type I always figured he liked. That medium to high yellow skin, long hair, like somebody in her family was Indian, Hispanic or White.

And big breasts. At least a 36C, probably even a double C. I'm a dark brown, weave-wearing, padded 34B. We couldn't have been more different.

Her shoulders were rounded and soft-looking, and her back was a little wide. Her arms were undefined with so much room for back fat and hanging arm fat waiting to happen, I almost managed a smile. They'll eat out a lot, and she'll put on a good ten or twenty pounds in the first six months. Then again, it'll probably all go to her breasts, so he won't mind that.

I watched her walk that pretty-girl-walk all the way to the entrance. He walked beside her, putting his hand on her back as he opened the door for her. She is pretty, damnit. I sat there hoping she's a bitch who can't cook, prone to breakouts and bloating during her period.

I wished I was pregnant just then. I'd show that bitch what kind of man she really had. She might be his wife, but I'd be the mother of his child. I'd make her life as miserable as she'd made mine. And I'd flaunt my baby every chance I got. But I wasn't pregnant. I was just nauseatingly jealous. Sick with jealously, having sick thoughts.

She wasn't so lucky. After all, if he'd sleep with me six weeks before his wedding, what kind of prize could he really be? He's weak and selfish. Whoever said that sour grapes make bitter wine was right. That smart-ass would have been me before I fell off my high horse. And if anybody was ever drunk with bitterness, it was me. I just sat there, sad, small, and pathetic.

I expected that for the rest of my life the sight, sound or thought of anything that could even remotely be associated with her from her hair color to her bra size will hurt me. The longer I sat there, the more I hated her ass. What a bitch that must make me. He told me that she's the quiet type that some people might mistake for the snotty, snobbish type. Whatever.

I cranked up my car and drove off. The Class Six package store was just down the road from the PX, and if I ever needed a drink, it was today. I went to bed trying to convince myself how much better off I was without him. But who the hell is better off sleeping alone? I finally drifted into a buzz-aided sleep.

Funny how things become clearer in a drunken slumber. I didn't realize how much I loved him until he died. I inexplicably found myself sitting in the middle of the sidewalk at the bottom of the steps just crying until I couldn't see, and my chest was so full and swollen that it hurt to breathe. All I knew is that he was dead. Just like that. Not sure how it happened, I was just smothering in grief. I prayed and prayed to God to please make it go away, to make it be undone.

"Anything, anything Lord, but this."

Then I woke up. A stupid dream, thank God. And a schmidgy bit hungover. The tears shut off like a faucet, but my heart still pounded like I'd been running all night. And the truth remained: He was still getting married. But that was okay now. I sat up in the bed, thanking God and telling Him that I was all right with it.

I was all right with it for a good week. The next week I was a little less all right with it. It only took a few days more to get back that sour taste in my mouth. You know, that bitter bile taste like you want to vomit but you know there's nothing in your stomach? Yeah, that.

What was happening to me? I go years without seeing someone and then, suddenly I'm so in love with him I'm grieving? By the end of the third week, I was still getting up in the morning thinking about how the two of them were probably still in bed. Damn near every song I heard on the radio reminded me of me and him or him and her. I thought about all the things that they've probably done together that he should have been doing with me. I couldn't believe that he was going through this irrevocable thing knowing that I love him more than anybody will ever love him in his life.

The wedding day just happened to be my 30th birthday, November 27th. Who the hell gets married in November? And he should have remembered that it was my birthday. Who gets married on their ex's birthday? That…son-of-a-bitch. I sat at home alone on that joyous day drinking lots of wine from a plastic cup. But still, I'd rather see him married than dead.

Chapter Three – Red Light Runners

As much as I wanted to, I couldn't stop the way I felt when I thought about Curtis, about being with him, about us. I can think of a good three, four, ten reasons why this is a bad idea, but it's funny how commitment and temptation work on you. He's committed to someone else, and I keep yielding to temptation. I wish I had a good reason for not being stronger. I abhor the thought of being involved with a married man. A married military man, at that. That was supposed to be my never-never land. And both of us being military makes this thing a particularly bad thing, a court martial offense. But he was mine, first.

It's kind of like running a stop sign. You know you're doing something wrong, potentially dangerous. But for some reason, you do it anyway, and keep taking chances doing it. And because you didn't get caught the last time, you're thinking, the more you do it, the better your odds are of getting away with it again. You're thinking, *So what the hell? Nobody got hurt*. Not really. *I'm careful enough*. Sort of. *It's harmless*. Pretty much. And you continue being selfish like that, as if no one is ever going to get hurt. And always, always, eventually someone does, broad-sided or rear-ended, and never saw it coming. Right now, I'm the one in the driver's seat. I'm in control of a situation that should have never been. And it's just like I'm driving on through the same damn stop sign that's more like a red light. The first 30 years of my life have been sitting on red. When was it going to finally be my turn to go, damnit? I just got tired of waiting.

It was the second week in January 2000, the first year of the new millennium, or the last year of the old millennium, depending on your perspective. However you look at it, it was the year to make some changes. Another year would not go by with me in this situation, bringing in the New Year with a bunch of folks from work, or by myself, or in church, or any of the above, man-less.

One would think it impossible, but there I was, nearly two years in the Black Man Mecca of the South, and man-less. Sans man. Man deficient. Absent man-ness. Now I know how the Ancient Mariner felt. Talk about not a drop to drink. If ever there was a draught of men anywhere, it's here: Too old, too young, too gay, or too married.

So, I was sitting in the files room at work pulling records for QRP. As usual, there were a couple of records missing for the Marine applicants, so the obvious place to start looking was in the Marine counselor's office. Instead of getting up walking down the hall, I called.

When I heard, "Atlanta MEPS, Gunny Curtis," the voice jarred me a little, so I said, "Who?"

"Gunny Curtis," he repeated himself, raising his voice and sighing. You can just about guess how I liked the nerve of that bastard huffing at me.

So I said, "Gunny Curtis, please don't scream in my ear."

He answered, "I wasn't screaming, staff sergeant. You're on the speakerphone." Then he repeated, "Atlanta MEPS," and sighed again.

All I could think was, *I know where the hell I am!* Hmph. I answered with, "Can I talk to someone in the Marine Liaison Office." After a short pause, "Please," forced its way out of my mouth

"You're talking to the Marine Liaison Office. What can I do for you?" I could hear his audience's amusement in the background.

"You can bring a couple of records for QRP," I told him. I spouted off the names, something like, "Jones and Roberts are on the floor tomorrow, so we need them."

"Uh, Who? What?" he asked.

Then I sighed, "Records for Q——. How about this, Clueless? You can get me off the speakerphone and let me talk to somebody who actually works in there."

All he managed to get out was, "Uh," before one of the actual Marine liaison counselors picked up the receiver.

He cleared his throat and continued. "Sorry about that, staff sergeant. That's what we get for letting recruiters answer our phone."

"Uh, yeah." I paused for a couple of seconds, damn near forgetting what I'd called for. Finally I said, "Hey Gunny, can you bring us a couple of records for QRP?" I gave him the names and hung up. A couple of minutes later, he dropped the records off at the front counter. Then he sort of smirked as he walked away.

I was in a bad mood for the rest of the day. I felt empty and cheated like I missed my chance to say something, but what did I have the right to say? *I'm mad as hell that I fucked you, and even madder than hell that I can't fuck you again*? It was all I could do not to cuss somebody out for asking the simplest question or making the most ambiguous comment. I guess we all go through our days asking each other how we're doing, and most of us don't even care about the answer. I'm no different. Depending on the time of day, day of the week or week of the month, I could easily respond with, *I'm hungry, my feet hurt, I need a new weave, and I just started my period I'm in dire need of a bikini wax and dire-er need of a man to notice*. But I stick with the *Just fine, thanks*, adding the standard, *And you?* in passing, like it's not a question.

All that particular day, saying, *Just fine, thanks*, when I really would rather have babbled on with, *I'm tired, broke, and lonely, I spend way more money than I make, I make way less money than I'm worth, and I want a man of my own*, was really a struggle.

When I got home that night, I found Curtis' business card in my door with a note written on the back. *Sorry about today. Call me, please.*

I won't deny that I ran to the phone to call him. I took a couple of breaths and then dialed. When he answered, I told him, "I just wanted to tell you that you shouldn't be just dropping by over here, leaving notes on my door."

He cleared his throat before responding. "So what you're saying is, call first from now on?"

"You know what I'm saying. You shouldn't be coming over here, or leaving notes on my door. Or anything. From now on."

"Listen, could I come by in a minute?"

"You already know the answer to that," I said.

"So, I'll see you later?"

"You know, I'd rather you wouldn't. It's not a good idea."

"That's not a no."

I was tripping at how I was even going through the motions with this conversation. "Curtis, let's not start this, okay?"

"Start what?"

"Look," I said. "You know I need a lot of attention, and you—you just ain't in that kind of position."

"I just want to talk," he lied.

"Come on, Curtis. Don't play me like that. Give me a little bit of credit."

"Okay, Baby." I heard the smile in his voice. "What's up?"

It didn't help that he was calling me Baby, but I could listen to his voice all night. I dragged on with this bogus exchange, like I wasn't already considering exactly what I knew he wanted. "You have no idea what it's been like for me. And to be honest, I'm really just almost at the point of not giving a damn."

"So, tell me what it's like," he said, like that wasn't enough said.

"You've only been married for a couple of months," I said back. "What do you want with me?" That was a rhetorical question, and he knew it. What did he mean, so? So? "So if I see you again, I know all I'm going to want to do is fuck you." Okay, that did not come out right.

"Wow," he breathed a slight chuckle at my lack of subtlety.

"I mean, shit. You know what I mean."

"I miss you too," he said. "Really."

I just held the phone.

Then he said, "See you in a minute, Baby," as if my silence was the only real answer he needed. Then he hung up.

Awwww—shit! Shit, shit, shee-it! I stood there for a couple of seconds and just cussed myself. No. No. Don't do this. I cussed all the way to the shower. I had to shave in the shower, because I hadn't had a recent bikini wax, and I didn't have any Nair in the house. I cussed while I shaved and bathed myself in smell-good shower gel. I stood and looked at myself in the mirror while I reminded myself how wrong this was.

I went in my bedroom and turned the covers back and lit a couple of candles on the dresser. I sat on the bed in my bathrobe and then just fell back and stared up at the ceiling fan. I thought about what color lingerie I would put on. Or maybe just a bra and panties. Damn! I wish I'd bought those edible pink panties.

Okay. No. No edible panties. "Don't do this," I said out loud to myself. I sat up and swung my feet for a few more seconds. Then I went and sat by the front door, for several minutes trying to unmake my made up mind.

When he knocked on the door, I was still sitting there in my bathrobe. I stood up and leaned my back against the door.

"Hey."

"Hey," he said, his voice muffled through the door. "It's me."

"I know."

"So—what's up? You opening the door or what?"

My stomach fluttered as I stayed braced against the door. "You know this is a bad idea," I said.

"Since when is that reason enough not to do something?" His twisted logic made us both laugh. I took a deep breath and turned around and cracked open the door.

I was about to make another reasonable argument when he pushed the door the rest of the way open and kissed me. He came in and pushed his back against the door and held me and kissed me. Kissed me. And kissed me. I managed to get out the words, "I'm just saying I don't want to get hurt."

He just said something like "Mmmm," and kissed me harder and breathed harder and held me tighter.

"I don't, don't um..." My mind went blank for a second.

"Don't what, baby?" he asked. "You don't want me?"

"Um, don't want to hurt her," I think I said, which was exactly true. I didn't even know her, or care about her, honestly. But I knew what it was like to be hurt like that. Hell, I knew what it was like to be hurt by him like that. And none of that, at least at that moment, mattered one bit. What mattered is that I was feeling too good to want it to stop. Damn a red light.

He reached his hand inside my robe and whispered, "If you don't want this, just tell me, and I'll stop." And he kept saying, "Tell me you want it, Baby. Tell me you want it," all the while pushing his hand between my legs.

He picked me up off of my feet and turned me around so that my back was against the door and stayed pressed against me. And I kept saying, "Please," and breathing like I was running from something but not getting anywhere.

And he kept kissing me all over my face, my neck and shoulders, and pulling his clothes off and saying, "Please what, Baby? Say you want it. Just say it. Say you want this dick."

Hell yeah, I wanted it. I wanted to ride him raw, so hard that he'd feel like I would break it off. I wanted it doggy style and thrown up against a wall and to feel him sweating all over my back. I wanted to take it in the ass and beg him not to stop because he'd be hitting all the spots that couldn't be reached any other way. I wanted his tongue shoved so far up my pussy that I could feel it in my throat. I wanted to swallow him whole and hear him scream for me and God at the same time. I wanted all that, and I wanted to not want it, but not as much as I wanted it. "I—oh God," I heard myself about to pray for forgiveness for what I knew I was about to do. "I—can't. Mmmm. Please."

And every time I thought I could catch enough breath to say what I should have said, he'd kiss me in my mouth until I could hardly breathe. God, he was feeling good. He was smelling good. But mostly, he was feeling good. I could feel the ripples in his stomach pressed against me.

"Please, what, baby? Tell me," he said, like he really thought I could.

I couldn't tell him anything. I couldn't even think of anything but hard dick. Hard, magnificent dick, throbbing between my parted thighs, begging to go just a little bit farther, all mine, if I dared to claim it. Mmm. My dick. Long enough. Wide enough. Just the right amount of rough. Too close to pass it up. Again. Who was I kidding?

It was like I was some pothead who was suddenly consumed with a fiend's case of the munchies for forbidden dick. Or a crackhead who just couldn't resist one more hit of that sweet, smooth, slick pipe that had my jaws tight and my mouth literally aching to taste it again, calling me. "Tell me you want it, baby."

"I," was all I managed to get out. We ended up having sex right there against the front door. He had my head spinning. I could feel my body tightening, and then loosening as he slid so easily inside me, welcoming, begging, needing every thrust and stroke and motion that he put on me. I swear, I felt the walls moving and the floor about to give way.

He was exactly what I needed, exactly what I'd been missing, and I wasn't ready or willing to give him up again. It was right there against that door that I decided. Now, what we do is her problem, not mine.

He stayed all night, holding me close. I don't know what he told her, and didn't care, because it felt good to feel good, and up until now, I'd forgotten how good. That sexy, beautiful kind of good that you only get from being touched by a man you can hardly wait to touch you, and when he does, you don't want him to ever stop.

A few hours later, I vaguely remember staggering to the door to lock it behind him, and then making my way back to the bed. The smell of him was making me hot all over again, so I pushed myself out of bed and stumbled to the shower. I went into work a few minutes early. Even went to PT. On a cold ass day in January.

Just be clear, doing PT, physical training, means running at least two miles. Not only do I hate running, I hate early mornings, which sometimes makes me wonder how the hell I'm still in the Army. People on three continents know I hate PT, so for me to have my ass up and running, things have to be going way wrong or way right. What is it about good sex that makes you feel like you want to do stuff you know that you wouldn't ordinarily want to do?

Anyway, New Year, new attitude. I told myself that 2000 is the year to come up, not back up. And there's no room in my life for this second hand stuff that he was trying to get me caught up in. His clock starts ticking right now.

I trudged along the track for a few more steps and then came to my senses. What the hell was I thinking? That sex the night before would make running less of a pain in the ass the next day?

The scales were definitely tipped. I was feeling way too good for my own good. My shift doesn't start until eleven, but I got to work and was ready to rock by 10:15 or so. And that includes the time it took for me to press my skirt, using the iron and board in the vault, pin my hair up, put on my uniform and adjust my ribbons on my shirt.

I walked into my shop just like any other day except the thought of recent sex had me smiling. I'd expected that today would be a pretty uneventful day, considering the night I had last night. I was still tingling and my thighs practically burned thinking about it.

I came through the door and heard the Charlie Brown theme song playing. Residual Christmas music, I guess. I sat down to a stack of tests that came in from one of the MET—or mobile something-something—sites waiting to be coded and graded, so I dug in. A MET site is one of our remote testing locations in different parts of the state where the test administrator goes to give a paper version of the test for applicants who for whatever reason choose not to come to the MEPS to take the computerized version.

When I looked up, I saw my grown-ass coworkers dancing around, mimicking the Charlie Brown gang in that scene where they were all on the stage getting down to Schroeder playing the piano. I have the best coworkers. Silly bastards.

Chapter Four – Never-Never Land

By the time my 31st birthday came into view, I discovered a different side of myself, settling for sex on call. Seven fucking months into this, I thought I'd have broken it off by now. Or something. Something, damnit. Birthdays have a way of waking you up.

I thought it would be hard to keep Curtis a secret, but it's actually kind of easy being discreet. Just don't tell anybody. What a concept. I play it like he's just some good looking Marine who I happen to have a crush on.

I've told a few people about our initial run-in at the night test, and there were a couple of witnesses to our intense phone conversation during QRP, but no one here knows that I've known him all of my adult life. At worst, I've only implied that I'd like to get to know him in the Biblical sense.

And maybe I commented that we must have been together in a past life or something. After all, this is a whole other life. That way, if somebody happens to catch me looking in his direction or smiling at him, I've already put it out there like that.

I'm not going to say everything is great all the time with me and Curtis. The sex is great, and that's saying something. Anyone who says great sex doesn't count for much in a relationship hasn't had much great sex. Anyone who says sex isn't everything obviously isn't having sex.

But sometimes I wonder if he's so good with me because he is married. He's damn sure better than any single man I've ever been with. The way I see it, married men are probably better in bed than single men because married men just do their thing without all the worry about *what if I'm not good?* A married man won't ever stress out about trying to prove something to you because they can always go home to her. That's my take on it.

And as much as it beats the hell out of being alone, I haven't forgotten that nobody holds you like your own somebody. Somebody else's man holds onto you like he's missing something. The way Curtis holds me now. It's not like I can't tell the difference. It's not quite the same kind of touch, not how I remember it being before, but it's still good.

It's like he's coming in from the cold after being outside for a long time and warming up next to a cozy fire, just until he's warm enough to go out again. Sometimes a few days. Sometimes a couple of weeks. Sometimes a whole month almost goes by. I can't believe I'm still accepting this bullshit like it's all right. I tell myself that it will change with time. When things get back to the way they're supposed to be.

One day, after one of those stretches, he called to say he was on his way over. This was the same day that I was doing my soap opera-in-the-shower monologue. It was a couple of weeks before the infamous Mission Week, which is the last week of the month when we're all putting in longer hours at work.

Everybody's trying to make a target number of bodies before the last day of the month. That means the MEPS is open late because recruiters are working late and we're there to support their trifling asses. We should call it Mission Impossible Week, by the shape some of them are in. But it wasn't so bad for me that day since I had opened that morning, and I got off right after QRP. I was back home by that afternoon.

It was near middle of August, still a few months away from my birthday, his anniversary. It was a particularly hot day, and that was reason enough to be cranky, but I guess I was a little more uptight than usual because I'd told myself that I'd have either ended this relationship or he would've ended his marriage by now, and I hadn't made any progress in either direction.

Anyway, today it was hot, so when he asked, "Do you want me to get anything?" I thought to myself, a divorce would be nice, but I asked him to bring me an ice cream cone.

"The Mayfield® one." It should have gone without saying, since Mayfield makes the best dairy products in the world, but it didn't hurt to be sure that he'd bring the right thing.

"Okay, Babe," he said, like he was writing it down. "Be there in a minute."

He showed up with a little brown paper bag and a big smile. I met him at the door bare-footed. I was wearing a wife-beater undershirt, no bra, those old short gray PT shorts, and an even bigger smile.

I had my mouth all fixed for a Mayfield cone and what does he walk in with? Not even the Nestle® cone. Not even ice cream. Two of those damn rainbow-colored popsicles!

"Thanks," I said. I took them from him and went and threw them in the freezer. He walked over and pulled me to him, and I just stood there with my arms limp beside me as he hugged me.

"What's the matter?" he asked, apparently clueless.

Something inside me just went off. "Curtis, how the hell come did you ask me what I wanted, and then brought me something else?"

"But—"

"But why in the hell did you even ask me what I wanted if you were just going to give me what you wanted me to have? Am I supposed to just keep on settling for whatever's convenient for you?"

"Babe, calm down." He had the nerve to be smiling.

I shot him a *fuck you* look. "I 'on't-wanna-calm-down," came out of my mouth like one word. And him telling me to calm down just pissed me off more.

"Sorry, Baby."

"Don't be Sorry Baby," He tried to continue but I cut him off. "You're always 'Sorry Baby,'" I said. "Trying being 'Dependable Baby' for a change."

He let me go off on him. Then when I paused, he said, "I just thought these would work better."

"Really? I'm glad I didn't ask for lemonade. I guess you would've brought me back a fucking pitcher of tea." I snatched myself away from him and went and sat on the sofa with my arms folded. "Damn."

"Babe," he said again. His smile turned into a smirk. I pretended to be looking in another direction as he stripped down to his T-shirt and shorts behind the counter, of course placing his pants and shirt neatly over the back of one of the chairs, his shoes in a neat and orderly fashion, dress-right-dressed, next to the chair.

I shook my head as I looked over at him. I felt myself calming down against my will. "Better for what?"

He reached into the freezer, then walked over to me carrying one of the popsicles. He tore the wrapper partially off and put in my face. "Taste it."

"I 'on't-want-none-of-that," I said, again in one-word fashion. "And you're gonna make a mess." I kept pouting.

"I hope so," he said. "Please."

I licked my lips and put them on the tip where it had just started to un-frost. "It's too hard. Tastes like ice." Not only did he not get me ice cream, he brought me freezer burned popsicles.

He took it back and pushed the wrapper down a little more. Then he licked around it and pressed his lips against it to warm it up. "Now," he said softly.

I tasted it again and pulled the wrapper the rest of the way off. I started to bite it, and he stopped me.

"Hold up. This one's mine." He pulled it away from my mouth and laughed.

"Don't be stingy." I smiled and reached for it. He held it out away from me with his right hand, and then pushed me back on the sofa with his left hand. I closed my eyes as he pushed my shirt up and pulled down my shorts. My eyes popped open when I felt the popsicle on my stomach.

"Hey!"

"Hey," he said back.

"That's cold," I pretended to protest.

"Not for long." He picked up the popsicle and then kissed where it had been. "Just thought you needed cooling off there." Then he moved it lower. "And there." I smiled as he moved around to other warms spots on my body and kissed those places too, finally concentrating on a spot he'd decided was in most need of his popsicle therapy. I just moaned and purred and ooed when he touched the inside of my thigh and shuddered for a moment when I felt a cold tingle inside of me. He licked my thigh and pushed his face between my legs, gently kissing and licking all the wet and sticky spots, and working the popsicle in and out. It was amazing. He said something goofy, like, "Now that's really sweet," as I tried not to cum too fast. "Just how I like it." Goof ball.

The popsicle was all but dissolved as he hovered over me holding the stick. "Still want ice cream?"

"You know it," I said back, smirking. "But let's finish off that other popsicle first."

He rolled off of me and said, "That's what I'm talking about."

He brought the other popsicle back and unwrapped it in front of me.

"Where do you want it?" he asked, holding it to his lips.

I took it from him and slid it in and out of my mouth. Then I pressed my lips against the tip of it and nibbled around it. "This one's mine, right?" I smiled at him. "Now you lay down."

"What?" he asked. "Are you gonna put on a show for me?"

"Only if you want it," I said back. I knew he wanted it, and he knew I wanted to perform for him. I can't really explain it. I just love watching him watch me.

Chapter Five – The Reluctant Homewrecker

Sex is so much better to me when we have time to take a short nap together afterward, before he has to leave. Admittedly, most of the time, it's just sex, a shower, and then we'll talk while he's getting dressed to leave. Other times, I just stay in bed while he showers because I want to keep his scent around me a little longer. But sometimes, like the Popsicle Day, we have a little time to lie around together and talk and nap.

At every opportunity, I tell him how glad I am that God brought us back together, and for a reason. I just know it's our second chance to get it right.

He always says he's glad, too. And I believe him.

But talk is mostly about work, his or mine. Mostly his. How he can't figure out why his station can't make numbers and how I pretend that I care. I care about him, of course, but I could give a shit about his recruiting issues. Sometimes I'll stand behind him and rub the top of his head, or caress his back or massage his temples while he talks and worries.

I start out rubbing his shoulders and work my way up the back of his neck. Sometimes I notice that he gets these two big swollen knots on the back of his head just behind his ears that seem to appear out of nowhere. I didn't even know knots on the back of our heads behind our ears even existed, but he has them a lot, and they need to be worked out and that's what I do, usually obliging his request to, "Sing for me."

I guess you could say that "You Bring Me Joy" is something like our song, even though it was already a couple-few years old when we met. It just happened to be playing on the Quiet Storm in my room the first time he kissed me. So yeah. It's our song.

On a few really rare occasions, he's been able to stay overnight. His wife goes out of town sometimes to visit her parents—Mama's Girl, spoiled brat, dumb bitch—and once she was out of town for a whole week with some convention with her sorority or something. I wish she would just get a clue and stay away for good.

It's nice waking up to him when that happens. So nice, I actually get up and make breakfast. So beside myself in fact, I even serve him in bed and feed him. I don't even eat breakfast, but when he's there, I feel like making it for him. Sometimes, I'm so happy with him, it just makes me want to sing, without him even asking me to.

This day wasn't one of those sleep-over occasions, and I wasn't rubbing him down. We were just lying together, tangled up on the sofa while I listened to him tell me the same hard luck story about his recruiting station. "My guys work their asses off all month long," he said, which I've always doubted. "And we still keep coming up short." I always try to sympathize, but he's a recruiter, and I know what they're like.

I think most of them bust their asses for the numbers at the end of the month because they've skated all month long. A few of them bust their asses at the beginning of the month and get their numbers early, and they're okay, as long as they're having a good month. Some expect that they don't have to work at all, just sit back and let the applicants, the would-be recruits, come to them. And then there are the poor bastards who try to work it all month long, but keep coming up with rocks, as in dumb as rocks. Some of them just aren't people-people, and should never have become recruiters in the first place. But all of them, I mean all of them, expect that they're doing us a favor by walking through those doors of the MEPS.

I found myself only half-listening, as I lay in his arms, tracing little circles on his chest. Then out of nowhere, while we're still lying there sticky on the sofa, him buck-ass naked with nothing but socks on, he asked me, "Why do you do this?"

He shifted around to lie on his back and I straddled on top of him.

Now he gets a case of conscience? This conversation could never have come up before sex. I lay my head on his chest, listening for his heartbeat. "You know, from now on, you gotta take your socks off."

"What?"

"No more of this sock sex stuff," I said. "That's ridiculous. I've always hated that." I have always hated that.

"Okay, okay. Whatever. Now answer the question. Why do you do this?"

"This?"

I'm sure he meant to compliment me by saying that I'm smart and attractive, with so much to offer, blah, blah, blah. "Why a married man? Why me? Why not just date single men?"

Because I love you.

I want you to wake up and realize that I'm the one you were meant to be with.

I want you to leave her and be with me, like you should have never married her.

I want you bad enough to do bad things until you do the right thing.

But did I say any of that? No, I just pretended not to notice him pretending not to already know the truth. How is it that I can be so vocal at work, and can't manage to speak my mind when it comes to this man? Instead, I play along. "Who'd you have in mind?"

"Like some of those other guys from your work."

He knew I had a rule about not dating guys that I work with, but I asked, "Like?"

"I don't know," he said. "I guess like some other soldier, sailor, airman, Marine." He sounded like one of our morning briefings.

"Don't forget the coast guardsmen," I added.

"They're sailors too, smart-ass."

"Are they really?" I asked, not being a smart ass, but he didn't know that. "Are you sure?"

I found myself amused that the pace of his heartbeat sped up as he talked, so I egged him on. "You know, I didn't even know the Coast Guard was a branch of service until I started working at the MEPS."

"Me either." he said dryly. "I'm talking about like one of those guys always up in your face at the MEPS, buying you lunch or giving you his card."

Okay. That, I wasn't expecting. I raised my head up and propped my chin on his chest and said, "I mean, so what?"

"Don't play me," he said back. "You didn't really think I didn't know, did you?"

"Oh," I said, laying my head back down. "Those Barneys. Hmph." I started to leave it at that, but I heard myself explaining. "Curtis, it's just food. And it's just because they want a favor. A late tester, a walk-in tester, an early test score or something. You know how it is."

"And here I thought I was special." He sighed, finally lightening up.

"Trust me. In that way, you're all the same. And besides, what we do," I pointed out, "what we just did, is not dating."

He chuckled at my stating the obvious.

Then I said, "Baby, what if I told you all of this is just an elaborate experiment?"

"An experiment," he repeated.

"A sociological experiment. To find the man, if any," I emphasized, "who wouldn't cheat."

"Really," he said, apparently not amused. "Very funny."

"Mmmhm," I said. "What does the Bible say? 'Many a man claims to have unfailing love, but a faithful man, who can find?'"

"Proverbs 20:6," he said. "And you're twisting it."

"I'm paraphrasing," I said back. "Anyway," I said, liking the idea. "And you're part of my research."

He shifted around a little underneath me. "And how many other guys are helping with this research?"

"Just you, so far," I said.

"Whatever." He laughed. "I'd better be."

"Yeah, well that's the problem isn't it?" Then I laughed. "Like you're in any position to tell somebody what to do." I decided to take it even further. "We should've ended this shit months ago. Then maybe I wouldn't have to hide my other man when you came around."

"All right," he said, not laughing. "Don't fuck around and get somebody's ass whipped."

"Somebody like who?" I looked up at him and then rested my chin on his chest again.

"Keep playing," he said, and slapped me on my ass so hard that I jumped off of him. He caught me and held me down on top of him. "Where you going?"

He laughed again, but I wasn't smiling. Then I faked a laugh at him and cut it short.

Then I got quiet.

He nudged me. "What's up?"

I took another moment. What the hell am I doing with a married man? Is this really going anywhere? Is clearing the air at this point worth the risk of losing him before we give ourselves a chance to get this relationship off the ground? "I remember you told me that that time with me was the only time you cheated on her."

"Yeah," he said.

"That it wouldn't happen once you got married."

"Yep." He sighed hard. "So what? Now you're judging me?"

I shook my head. "I just…What are we doing?"

When he didn't have an answer, I sighed. "I'm just as guilty."

"Right," came his unsolicited affirmation.

"You don't have to right me. I just wish—"

"Wish what?"

I shrugged. About a second later I managed to say, "All this."

"This what?"

"This, this lying thing." I was frustrated at my loss for words. "Well, I just don't like it."

"Lying thing?" he repeated, as if he didn't get my meaning.

"You know." I rolled my eyes at him. "This secret shhhtuff," I said, not really sure why I didn't say *shit*. "Secrets hurt people."

To which he coolly countered, "Secrets only hurt when you tell them."

"Yeah," I conceded, and let it go at that.

"Look," he said. "Life just happens the way it happens, you know?" He sighed through his nose. "It can't always go according to your plans."

"Or expectations," I mumbled.

Then I pushed myself off of him again.

"Hey," he said, like it was a question.

"I'm gonna get a shower," I said. "You coming?"

We got in the shower together and stood face to face silent for a few seconds. Then he held on to me as I turned around from him and faced the water. At first, he rubbed my shoulders and kissed the back of my neck. Then he slid his hands up and down my arms and then just held me like he thought I would slide down the drain if he let me go. The water beat down on us for a few seconds and then we washed each other. Neither of us said anything else.

He got out first and got into bed. I stayed for a few more minutes, lathering up my face and exchanging words with myself. And singing.

When I came out of the bathroom, he was lying on his back with his arms crossed behind his head, waiting for me. Then he turned over onto his stomach. "Come on."

That was my cue to climb on his back, still my favorite sleeping position, but instead I climbed over him and slid down into the bed and looked up at the ceiling.

"Come on," he insisted, so I climbed on top of him. I thought about his question, So what?

So what do I have to show for it? Am I any better off than I was being celibate? Aw shit, never mind. What's the point? I'm fucking him and I have no immediate plans to stop.

"What's up?"

"Nothing," I said. *So what* was exactly right. *So what*, was all it really amounted to.

"All right. Cool." He agreed to end the conversation with that tone of voice that plays it like he only agreed to drop it because I insisted. Then he said, "Okay, get down. Come here."

I got down off of his back and nestled myself up against him so he could hold me.

"Sing for me," he reminded me.

He set the alarm on his watch, then slipped his arms around me. I pulled his arms tighter around me and sang the first couple of lines of "You Bring Me Joy".

"Okay?" I asked.

"Better than okay."

A few minutes later we fell asleep holding each other.

****

We spent a lot of time together in September and October, almost every day or every other day. But a relationship like this takes compromise. It means accepting the fact that you won't always get the attention you want when you want it. It means letting the other person have time and space enough to handle circumstances in other parts of their lives, and trying to keep the complaining to a minimum. That's a big one for me. I'm not normally a complainer or a nag, but I do like my time and attention. So yes, I've modified my standards and expectations a little bit since getting into this situation, but I consider it an investment in my future happiness. Funny the things that you absolutely would not put up with at nineteen that you find yourself willing to reconsider as time goes by. Seems like the more time that goes by, the more time you spend alone, the more things you're willing to reconsider.

I could tell he really wanted to be with me instead of going home to her, so what was he waiting on? I guess he just told her it was work keeping him away from home. But the closer it got to my birthday, the scarcer he became in November. That bothered me a lot, but I guess that's why it's called compromising. I told myself that God was just teaching me a lesson in patience.

Seems like God has been teaching me this lesson all my life.

Chapter Six – The Other Side of Thirty

As I turned over to the empty darkness next to me, all I could think was, *They're probably having sex right now*. I'd say it was about 2:30 in the morning, the middle of the night on my 31st birthday, and that was my first waking thought. I'm so fucking depressed.

Then it came to me, my next thought, *I know why people commit suicide*. Despair is a son of a bitch, but I've already said that. You know, homely old Despair and his ugly twin Self-Pity, the kind of unwelcome guests who like best to visit in the middle of the night, the first to come extend to me birthday greetings.

I was having that dark, whiny, teenage, nobody-understands-me, no real reason to be depressed, kind of despair, when nothing is right and no one can fix it. The kind of despair when friends and family are all useless because you've decided that no one on earth can genuinely relate to you, or they'd all just judge you. Your bad timing, bad decisions, regrets are all unique to you.

But I wasn't suicidal. I was 31. I was in bed, alone on my birthday. And it's a shitty feeling all right, but hardly unique. I lay there telling myself if only I hadn't slept with him that last time, then I would be so bad off, saying, if only, like it's that easy.

In bed until noon, not really sleeping but not wide awake, hoping the phone would ring, I felt the weight of a heavy funk all over me. I knew that the best thing that could be done for the way I felt was to get up, brush my teeth, take a shower and put on some fresh underwear. Nothing works wonders for getting you out of a funk, literally and figuratively, like a hot shower, clean teeth, and fresh underwear.

I got up, washed away the funk, piddled around the house until two, waiting for his call, which didn't come. Then I went to my hair and nail appointments and at least I looked good.

One of the best things about having a birthday right around Thanksgiving, is the after-Thanksgiving-before-Christmas sales. So for my birthday, I decided to treat myself to some good old-fashioned impulse shopping at Lennox Mall, arguably the most expensive mall in Atlanta. I'd worry about regret at the end of next month, when the bill came.

The first thing I bought, after a Chick-fil-A® lemonade, was a Coach® bag not much larger than the size of a checkbook, just because it was cute. Then I bought a bottle of Chanel No. 5® and two bottles of Happy®, as if I had anything to be happy about. Next stop was the M.A.C.® counter to buy a whole bunch of other stuff I didn't need, and also try to get in for a makeover. There was nobody there, so I took that as a sign I just needed to spend more when I made my way to Victoria's Secret®. I paused at one of the mirrors to check out my new weave, dye and eyebrow wax job, and that was a mistake.

Not that I didn't look good. That was money well spent, and I was fine to death. I must have been admiring myself too much, because I didn't even see the girl walk up behind the mirror.

"You know, you have a really pretty face," she said. I stopped checking myself out long enough to appreciate the sadness and absurdity that the best line any man has ever said to me in my life, was now reduced to a cheap sales pitch.

"Thank you." I was really thinking, *Give it a rest already. Now that you've finally bothered to show up, you don't have to try so hard.*

"No, really," she insisted. "Do you have time for a makeover?"

I'm spending money in the mall on a Friday afternoon. What else did I have except time, a new credit card, or no man? Or in my case, all of the above. I felt half a smile coming on.

Before I'd said yes, I found myself staring right into the face of Miss TLC. I had to blink a couple of times, pretending to have something in my eye. After all, I'd had her on my brain all day, so maybe I was having a nervous breakdown, hallucinating and all that.

"Not right now," I said, tried to play it off. "I'd probably better schedule another time or something." I tried to think up an excuse. "You look like the only person here and I wouldn't want you to have to keep stopping to help other customers. I hate that. I like a lot of attention."

"No problem." She smiled so sweetly it was almost smug. I could have slapped her, wrung her damn neck and then punched her square in the nose. Oh, and stomped her ass, too. "But promise me," she said, "you'll come back and let me give you a makeover when you have time. Maybe after you do some more shopping."

Bitch, I ain't promising you shit. And keep your beady eyes off my bags.

She offered her card and I glanced down at it. When she realized I wasn't taking it, she put it away. "I'm just treating myself. It's my day off. My birthday." Like I owed her an explanation.

"Girl, you don't owe me any explanation," she said, unexpectedly grounded. "Any excuse will do, right?"

Before I could catch myself, I was mumbling in agreement. "I know that's right."

"Oh come on, now. I know you got to give yourself a makeover on your birthday."

She was a pushy little thing. I checked out the rock on her left hand. Very nice. Her hands looked soft and unworked, like the heaviest thing she ever lifted was a can opener. I'll bet she can't even cook. Or she's just good at one thing, like making spaghetti or something that takes absolutely no creativity or skill. She didn't look near as bloated in person as she did in the picture or that day in the parking lot. Her complexion was clearer than I'd hoped it would be. She's probably using that Proactiv® stuff from the infomercials.

"What the hell," I half grumbled. "You're right. You sure you're not too busy?"

"I just took an hour and a half lunch-slash-break, and nobody missed me. Now you tell me."

To that I just said, "I guess." I never knew anybody who worked in a mall who had it like that. I just shrugged and shook my head.

"Girl, sit down," she insisted. "Where else do you have to go besides Victoria's Secret?"

Nosy little heifer, huh? I guess she'd surveyed my stuff for the missing bags, but I sat down anyway. Okay, so I had some kind of morbid curiosity about my competition. Like anybody else, I guess I wanted a closer look.

"Well, first of all, my name is Andra-Lyn."

What the hell kind of country-ass name is that? It occurred to me just then that I don't think he's ever said her name. Just *her* or *she*.

"Sebrina. With an *e*." Did I just say that snotty shit?

We exchanged the regular pleasantries as she talked about the different shades she thought would best compliment me. The more makeup she pulled out, the more she talked. If she didn't know what the hell she was doing, she had me fooled.

"How old are you today, Sebrina with an *e*?"

"31."

"Really," she said.

Here it comes.

"You look much younger," she continued with that surprised tone of voice.

"Thanks."

"I'm sure you get that a lot."

I shrugged. "Only now that I'm over thirty, it's actually a compliment."

"I heard that," she said. She started out with some kind of cleanser stuff and then began to put foundation on my face. "Close your eyes."

I closed my eyes and she kept talking. "Where did you have your eyebrows done?"

"At this place in Decatur. Don Janelle's."

"They look really good," she said. "Did they do your manicure too?"

"Mmmhmm," I said, drumming my fingers on my lap. "There's this Jamaican girl there who's really good. Gave me the best Brazilian wax I ever had in my life."

"Pedicures too?"

"They do everything," I said.

"You'll have to give me a card or something. Maybe I can go check them out."

"They're good, alright."

"Yeah?"

"Yeah. But I get my weave done in College Park," I said. "This shop called Perfect Ten over by the Bank of America. Off of Old National."

"Okay," she said. Then she stopped blending the foundation on my face. "Girl, that's a weave?"

I opened my eyes and rolled them at her. Bitch, you know this is a weave.

"Damn, that's good." She ran her fingers through it. "I didn't know they had skills like that on the South side. They hook it up like that over there?" She asked, not quite convinced.

And who said you could put your hands in my head?, but I let it go. "Do they," I said. "Yep. Well, it depends on who you go to. I go to a girl named Phyllis. I'll give you her card too."

"Thanks," she said. "Close your eyes."

"The shop in Decatur does good weave too, from what I've seen," I told her. "A little on the high side, but I'm sure it's worth it."

"It don't really matter to me. That's what my man is for, right?"

"That's one thing," I grumbled, not really meaning to say it out loud.

"Plus, if it's worth it, it's worth it," she said.

I just let her go on like she knew anything about needing a weave. Another one of those good hair-having heifers who act like they don't know they have good hair. "Well, if nothing else, get that bikini wax. Plus, they're pretty good about the personal attention thing. You know, not scheduling appointments on top of each other. Not a whole lot of waiting around to be seen. That's what I like about Phyllis. I like people who get you in and out."

"Yeah, I feel that. I hate when people are working on me and have to stop to keep helping other people," she said. She just heard me say that earlier. Heifer.

"Yeah," I said. "Or leave you under the dryer all day so they can take another walk in."

"Or keep getting on the phone."

"Making more appointments."

"Or just talking. Like people don't know they're at work."

"Yeah!" Then we both laughed.

She changed the subject. "Are you going on a big date or something like that tonight?"

"'Fraid not," I said, keeping my eyes closed. "This is probably the highlight of my day."

"Hmm. Don't feel bad. I know how that is," she sympathized.

"Really?" Now I was the skeptic.

"Believe it or not," she said, "I know how you feel. My man is at work too."

Too? Why did this heifer just assume I had a man, and that he was at work?

"And today is my anniversary, and I'm at work."

Aww, waa-fucking-waa, I thought as my eyes popped open.

"Unh-uh, keep 'em closed. I'm giving you a little liner right here."

I closed my eyes again. "So I might as well be at work too. They know it's my anniversary. I'm taking off early. Hopefully, he'll come home early."

"Mmmph," I said. The way she put on her wide-eyed, soft pouty face, as if there was a man around, gave me the impression that she's the type who's used to getting her way. I think she did it subconsciously, because I'm pretty sure I only do my wide-eyed, soft pouty face around men.

"Okay, open," she said. "Very nice. Look." She turned my chair toward the mirror on the counter.

"You're right," I said. I was transforming like I belonged in a M-A-C makeup ad in the middle of *Essence* magazine.

"And we're just getting started."

"I don't like it real heavy, okay."

"You shouldn't wear it really heavy. You're already pretty."

Okay, now she was embarrassing me. "You don't have to keep saying that," I assured her. "I'm here to buy you out today, anyway."

"No, really. I'm being real with you."

I was afraid of that.

"Anyway," she continued as if we were friends. "I would've at least wanted to have had lunch with him today, but he works all the way over in Douglasville."

"That's too bad."

"I know, right? I have to actually plan to pop in on him," she said, not breaking her stroke. "Which, you can imagine, doesn't happen too often."

"That's pretty bad," I said again.

"Yeah. By the time he gets home, all we'll have time to do is have sex." Then she stopped herself and kind of laughed. "You know what, I'm sorry. That's a little too much information, I guess."

"It's okay," I said. "I know the feeling."

"What does your boyfriend do?" she asked.

"More like my ex-boyfriend," I evaded the question.

"Oh, well, that's all right too," she consoled me. "As good as you look today, you'll go out and catch three boyfriends."

"I guess."

"His loss, Sebrina. Remember, this is your day." She continued with the standard girlfriend pep talk while she worked. "You know how men always like to piss you off or break up with you right before your birthday or a holiday."

"Yeah, well, we're not really broke up. It's just that we don't see each other as much as I'd like."

"Oh."

"He's busy with stuff and we've got a few issues to work out," I said. "That's all I'm saying."

She was actually a nice girl. And I'd really wanted her to be a bitch. I really wanted her to be an ugly bitch. But she was neither of those things, and I felt a little bad about our situation. A little bit.

"Well," she changed the subject. "What do you do?"

"I'm in the army."

"No kidding? Small world," she said as she sampled different lipstick shades on my wrist.

Smaller than you think. I managed to keep the thought inside my head.

She kept talking and sampling. "We'll start out with this moisturizer. You should always have one of these handy. Use this even when you're not wearing lipstick. Keep your lips conditioned." She swabbed some of it on my lips and then pressed her lips together as a motion for me to do the same. "My husband's a recruiter. He's trying to make his monthly quota."

I kept my lips closed.

"Do you know any recruiters where you work?"

I nodded.

"Hold on, I'll show you a picture. You probably know him."

"I don't work up front much," I lied, "and recruiters aren't allowed in certain parts of the building. I might have seen him."

"You probably have," she chirped. She showed me a wedding picture from her purse. Not a very happy-looking day from the looks of them.

"He's a nice looking guy."

"Thanks," she said. "I know what you're thinking."

I doubted it.

"It looks like someone forced us to stand next to each other," she attempted to pick my brain.

"A little bit," I admitted.

"Curtis never smiles in pictures," she said putting it away.

She calls him Curtis.

"He makes me sick with that 'I'm a macho Marine' shit, sometimes."

"Well, I'm sure he'd look better smiling," I said, for lack of anything better.

She continued. "So I just stood there looking just as plain as I could, right next to him." She wasn't wearing much make-up in the picture. I guessed she was just wearing it now for work. Nobody would buy make-up from the girl in that picture.

"Oh, well, that explains it," I said.

"Except now all our wedding pictures look like *American Gothic* or something." All that was missing was a pitchfork in his hand and the farmhouse in the background.

I shrugged as indifferently as I could. I really had no interest in imagining the rest of their wedding album.

By the time she'd finished, I really did look like a masterpiece.

"All you need now is to be out with your girls," she said. "You look too good to let it go to waste."

"I don't really hang out with that many females."

"So where they at?" she asked. "Leaving you hanging on your birthday?"

"I really don't have any girls," I said.

"Oh well," she said. "I know how that is. I haven't made many girlfriends since we've been here either."

"Girlfriends are overrated," I told her. "You're really better off."

"Yeah, I know. I ran into one of my sorors the other day out at Town Center. She's been living out in Conyers for a couple of years."

Conyers? People from Conyers act like Conyers is the only city in Georgia. I'm surprised she crossed the city limits, much less go all the way across Atlanta to go shopping. What the hell was she doing at Towne Center? I didn't really care enough to ask.

"I'm supposed to hook up with her and do something together sometime soon." Then she made the most horrible suggestion. "You know, we ought to go out and have a birthday-anniversary drink together."

God, no. This was already too awkward, and now she wanted to by me a sympathy drink. "No, thanks," I said. "Really, I'm good."

"Girl, you're more than good. You look damn good." She smiled. "And I do damn good work."

"Yes you do," I agreed. And I meant it. I had to give her that.

"Now we have to go somewhere and forget Curtis and… What's His Name." She straightened up the counter. "What's your ex-man's name?"

"Uh, Mack," came out of my mouth like a question.

"We'll go forget about Curtis and Mack for a minute."

Who invited you into my birthday? "What the hell. I guess." Damn. I guess was more morbidly curious than I thought. Or maybe the pushy thing just caught me at a weak moment.

"That's right, what the hell. Now let's leave before the happy hour hoochies come in, wanting a quick touch up."

Chapter Seven – The Other End of the Candle

One drink turned into a couple of drinks, and then a couple more. A minute turned into a few hours, then half of the evening. We talked and drank. The more she drank, the more she talked. The more she talked, the more I drank. She talked about how it's been forever since she went out without her husband. She talked about how he surprised her with a new car for their anniversary. A sparkling white Volvo C70, because they're smooth, classy and safe.

I wanted to be a smart-ass and ask, *What the hell is so safe about a convertible?* But I got the point. Volvo has a reputation for being safe.

I thought about my dirty blue used '89 Honda Civic. Not a smooth ride at all, but dependable. Barely hanging in there, but there when I need it. And just about used up. Was my life one big metaphor? What does a Honda have a reputation for being? Cheap? Easy to get? Used? Popular for stealing parts? What?

She talked about how she planned to leave the mall one day and go back to school. She had aspirations of being a hair dresser. Not very ambitious, I gathered.

Actually, she wanted to own her own salon. "One where people make and keep appointments on time, with no waiting," she explained.

Now, that's pretty ambitious. Hell, I had aspirations of finding a salon like that.

And she drank faster than me. I would never have figured Curtis' princess for a drinker, but she held her own.

At first we sat at the bar, passing glances with all the cute guys that passed by, scarce though they were. Then we finally got a table and ordered something to eat to soak up the alcohol. I knew right away that I liked this place because they kept the drinks coming. I even found myself sharing my suicide theory with her and she actually seemed to get it.

"So, the secret to not committing suicide is to not feel unique?"

"Right on," I said with my nose in my glass.

"As long as I feel like somebody else is feeling me exactly, I'll never be that desperate." She related perfectly.

"That's what I'm thinking," I said, feeling like a Ph.D. "Why do you think there's a support group for every damn thing under the sun?"

"There's a support group for unsuccessful suicidal folks?"

"Probably, somewhere," I said.

"Suicidals Anonymous," she joked.

"Hell," I said. "It wouldn't surprise me."

"Hmm," she said. "So if and when I'm sane and sober enough to realize that I'm not alone, I'm saved from myself. Right?" Then she drained her glass.

She was obviously patronizing me. I actually supposed that the moment at which a person decides to commit suicide is the most sober moment of his or her life, but I decided to keep that thought to myself. I just shrugged and said, "Yeah."

Maybe it was the liquor working, or maybe she sensed that I was about to slip into the Depressed Drunk role. She got us back to picturing men in their underwear. "You know, my husband looks sooo good in those boxer briefs, he should get paid to wear them."

Honey, don't I know it? "Mmmhm," I said, pretending to not really be listening, but actually in full agreement. Even though I was feeling a good bit uneasy about communing with the enemy, the urge to know as much as I could about this woman who'd obviously captured the heart of the man I loved was even stronger. Hmph. She should really be more selective about the company she invites herself to keep.

It must have been about 8:30 when her cell phone rang. She fumbled around a little bit in her Louis Vuitton bag before finally retrieving the phone.

"Heyyyy Baby," she answered.

I sucked down another vodka & cranberry while she talked.

"That's okay, Babe. I'm okay. I'm just out with a girl from work." She waved at the waitress and asked for another Cosmopolitan. Heifer would know the real name for it.

He must have asked if she was drinking.

"A little bit. Are you home? Just a couple. Are you home?"

He must have said no.

"What time do you think? I'm going home in a minute. I will. You stay and make your mission thing. If I'm asleep, wake me up. Love you too, Baby. You too, Baby. Happy Anniversary."

Before she could say, "That was the love of my life," my phone was ringing.

I'd had enough to drink by then that I couldn't tell if I was more annoyed that he called me in the middle of my attempted mind meld with Andra-Lyn, or that he'd called me at all. Low down cheating bastard.

"Hey," I answered.

"Hey," he said back.

"Hey, damnit," I repeated.

"Babe, it's me. You okay?"

"I'm half drunk, if that's what you mean. I've had a couple too." I looked across the table from me at the unbitchy, unugly, completely oblivious heifer sipping her drink, and I got a little more pissed, so I motioned for another drink, and concentrated on the melting ice in bottom of the glass of the one I was working on. I can't make sense of my feeling bad for her and resenting her at the same time. I was near drunk, but I would have felt that way sober.

"Where are you?" he asked.

"Wrong!" I said. "The next thing out of your mouth should have been 'Happy Birthday, Baby,' ya bastard, but it wasn't. It's my birthday, too, remember?"

He just repeated himself. "Where are you?"

"About two and a half sheets to the—"

"You know what I mean," he said.

Andra-Lyn interrupted, "Is that him?"

I nodded.

"Tell him you got a date," she suggested as she worked on her drink.

"I'm not home," I told him. "Where are you?"

"I was on my way to your house." He said it like we had planned it all out. "What's up?"

I almost said his name, but I held my tongue. "C— Can I call you back or something?"

"Or something?" he asked like he had the right to have an attitude about it. "Why?"

"I'm not alone, and I'm being rude. I really need to go."

"Who's there with you?"

"It's no big deal," I told him. "Somebody offered to buy me a drink, and I accepted."

"Somebody like who?"

Just say it, I told myself. Andra-Lyn. Andra-Lyn. Andra-Lyn. Your country-ass-named wife, you son-of-a-bitch. I can't believe he never told me her name in all this time. I can't believe I never asked.

"Tell him you have a date," she repeated. She was smiling at me like she and I had a secret, almost daring me.

"Aaa—, A.L.," I said finally, feeling rather clever. "I don't know how late I'll be, so it's probably not a good idea. How about, Happy—."

It must have come out slurred a little, because he asked, "Who the hell is Al?"

"That's telling him," Al said.

"How about Happy Birthday?" I finished my sentence as I hung up and turned off my phone while he was in mid-sentence.

"I can't believe this day," I said. Any other day, I'd have been tearing up rubber and asphalt trying to get to the other side of town just to meet him. I must have been feeling resentment, envy and a little sympathy. Or maybe it was a tinge of guilt-laced tequila.

"Good for you," she said. "Don't worry, he'll call back."

"Yeah."

Then her phone rang again. "Oh, hey baby," she said, smiling a ridiculous smile. "Okay sweetie. I'll see you in a bit, then."

She hung up and explained that her husband decided not to work late after all. "He said he'd meet me at the house in about an hour. I guess he just won't worry about that mission stuff this month."

"I guess," I said back, not looking her in the eye.

"Our anniversary is more important than some recruiting stuff," she said proudly.

"Apparently." I pretended to smile. "That's good."

Just then, a tall, brown-skinned bald guy passed our table and smiled at me. He had a nice smile. He was dressed really nice and had on good shoes.

He had the build of a former college athlete who probably looked really good naked about 10 years ago. Now he looked like he had a few soft spots in unflattering places.

Al noticed that when he walked past us, he was still looking toward me. She was facing his direction as he sat at his table.

"That guy back there is checking you out," she said. "Don't look."

"I'm not," I said. "I've seen enough."

I guess she noticed the lack of interest on my face meant that I was thinking about someone else. "Girl, don't let yourself start moping about that crumb."

She was right. I was moping and he was a crumb.

"You look too good tonight to let it go to waste."

"Mmmm," I said, sulking.

"Or maybe you're just so used to men falling all over themselves for your attention whenever they pass you."

I smiled up at her. "Hardly."

We laughed for a couple of seconds.

"Trust me," I said. "I'm no man magnet." Then I tried to give myself a little credit. "Unless I'm all made up. Like now."

"So you camouflage being pretty by not making up," she reasoned.

"Camouflage, huh?"

"Army talk, right?"

Okay, whatever. I shrugged and kept talking. "Guys noticing me now is not really as big as deal as it was back in the day. It's cool and I like the attention, but you know how it is. Getting the attention you don't want and not getting the attention you do want."

"All the time," she said with that *Amen* tone of voice.

"I guess I kind of figured that's the way it is. Not really minding so much that people didn't notice me. I knew one day someone would see me for me. And one day, he did."

She started to smile until I said, "But it wasn't enough."

Her smile faded as she waited for my next sentence.

"He's—been unfaithful a few times," I confided. It didn't matter that I had chosen that moment to confide in his wife. She might as well have been a bartender. Just a sounding board. "I don't even know why I'm still messing with him. We're not even together really. Just—together."

She was silent.

"And trust me. All the makeup from Max Factor® won't make him love me the way I need him to." I sighed. "So why bother?" Do they still even make Max Factor? Well, she got the point.

"It's supposed to be for yourself, Sebrina." Spoken like a true makeup salesman.

"Right," I said. "How many women do you know wear makeup for themselves?"

She shrugged and then made an expression as if to acknowledge my point. "I guess it is kind of a chore sometimes."

"Sometimes."

Man or not, the real reason I don't like wearing much makeup is because I've never been able to put it on without making myself look silly. Like I was a little girl playing on my mama's dresser. Like I was trying too hard. Too much here. Not enough there. Always the wrong colors.

"I've always hated the way I looked when I made myself up. It's a chore enough taking it off when somebody's put it on right, but at least I don't mind looking at myself in the mirror."

She smiled again and said, "I feel you."

"I still feel pretty when I'm taking off makeup that's been done right. If

I'm taking off makeup I've put on myself, I just feel like I've wasted my time."

"Anyway," she repeated, "you look good tonight."

I sort of smiled, feeling like 31 might as well have been 71. I'm gonna be alone for the rest of my life. Cue Depressed Drunk.

She kept talking about shades of eye shadow or false eyelashes or something.

I nodded toward my drink, picturing some lonely, bitter old woman with nothing to look forward to except feeding a house full of mangy cats and scratching an occasional vaginal itch from dryness.

Then she changed the subject like nothing. "How are you in bed?" she asked.

"Excuse me?" Did I hear her right? "No offense, Al, but I'm not that drunk, yet." Maybe I need to slow down on the drinks. I'd had at least six.

"Sebrina, I'm not trying to pick you up," she reassured me. "But I'll tell you this."

"I'm not sure I want to hear this," I said, taking a big swallow from what was left in my glass. Am I about to find out that she's a closet lesbian? Bisexual?

"Why not?" she reasoned. "You probably won't remember most of this conversation in the morning."

"Probably not. What's up?"

"Fuck the shit out of him."

"Come again?" I put my glass down.

"Trust me. That's how I got mine." She was proud to admit, too, and it pissed me off. As if all it took to keep a man was a good fuck. She went on with, "He loves it when I scream my head off."

"I'm not hearing this." I picked my glass back up and drained it.

Incredible. This has got to be the strangest conversation I've ever had. Maybe bizarre is a better word.

Was she actually presuming to advise me? I knew what he liked long before she did. But then, I had to remind myself that she didn't know who I was.

"I'm serious," she said. "Girl, I scream like it's the end of the world. All that screaming and moaning shit. Men can't get enough of it." She giggled and started eating a potato skin. Between bites, she added, "And it'll be really good to your man, because you made him miss it. Just try that the next time you see him. You'll see."

"I'm not hearing this," I repeated. Maybe I needed some potato skins too. I grabbed one off of her plate and stuffed a big bite of it into my mouth.

"Okay, maybe that's no big secret, but sometimes it's all we got. We shouldn't be ashamed to use it like a weapon once in a while." She turned the plate and picked up a buffalo wing. "Love is war sometimes. And war is hell, right? Ain't that what they say?"

What did she know about it? I asked myself, chewing to keep from grumbling the thought out loud. I don't know shit about war, and even less about love, apparently.

We were quiet for a few seconds.

Then I confessed, "Al, I really love him." Was I actually calling her Al? "I wish I didn't, but I do."

"I know," she said, munching and drinking.

"Nawwww you don't." I knew it was time to stop drinking, because I was starting to slip. If I wasn't careful, I'd mess around and tell her everything. "I mean I reallllly love him. I'm sorry, but I always have. There's nothing that he could ask me that I wouldn't do. I used to see my children when I looked at him."

She sat across that table from me and smiled some more. She just shrugged her shoulders and smiled. Why was she smiling at me? Doesn't she get how dangerous it is to love somebody so much you'd do anything to be with him?

"You ever run any red-lights?" I asked.

"Okay," she said. "You have had enough."

"You're probably right."

"You're gonna feel like shit in the morning." She kept eating and drinking.

"I feel like shit now."

Not only was she turning out to be a nice person, but it was starting to look like she could out drink me.

"It's okay girl. We've all been there, right? Only you know if it's worth it to keep going back to him." As disinterested as I tried to look, she seemed compelled to go on, telling me about one of her college episodes. How she thought she was in love with the first man she'd ever slept with. "He had my head all kinds of twisted."

She was a psych major and he was the department head. A psych major of all things. No wonder she got such a kick out of the suicide theory.

"It was a bad idea from the get-go," she said, sort of tapping on the napkin holder.

"Yeah, but since when has being a bad idea been reason enough not to do something?" I sort of smiled, thinking of Curtis and his twisted logic.

She stopped tapping and looked up at me for a second and then said, "Girl, he must have been playing some serious head games with me because I just kept falling back into bed with him."

"Really," I said, with a tone that most people would have recognized as apathy.

"Really," she kept on. "I mean, without exaggeration, *There, but for the grace of God,* and all that. That shit liked to have killed me."

Couldn't she just shut up and indulge me? If I was going make a confession, she just talked all over it. She had to take over the conversation and tell me a whole bunch of other shit that was none of my business. I almost smiled, at her, thanking God that at least she wasn't a virgin when they got married. Something about that was a small comfort.

Then I said, "Can you understand what it's like to have to admit that you still don't have a man out of your system? Especially when it feels so good."

"Sometimes you just can't help it," she said nodding. "And to make it worse, he was married."

I guessed she could understand. Guess she'd been through her share of red lights after all. Little Miss Perfect wasn't perfect. "Well, I guess it's just one of those things," I said, making sure I didn't sound judgmental.

"Yep," she said. "But I tell you, if I had it to do over, well, you know."

"Yep," I replied. "Me too." What the hell was I saying? I had it to do over, and I did.

"You know how that goes," she said. "Great while it's going on, but when it goes bad it's just gone."

I didn't respond. I just stared down into my glass.

She looked at her watch and started gathering her things. "You know what," she said. "I'm gonna get a taxi home. Curtis'll kill me if I wreck baby before he even gets a chance to break her in."

"Yeah, I guess," I said. I didn't mind her going, I just didn't want her to go home to be with him.

"How about you take a taxi home with me, and I'll have Curtis bring us back here in the morning to pick up our cars before he goes to work."

Now that was a shot of cold water in the face. "I promise I'm not that drunk," I said. "You go ahead. I'll sit here for a while and eat some more. Then I'll head home. Don't want to be home before midnight on my birthday, you know. Maybe I'll let that guy behind me pick me up." I winked.

"Okay," she said. "But let me get your number so I can call you to make sure you got there okay." She picked up my phone from the table and then programmed the number into her phone.

"I just got this phone," she said, holding it up. It was tiny and expensive-looking. "A little present from me to me." When I didn't say anything back, she put the phone back in her purse. "Well, happy birthday, girl. I'm going to go home and wait and see if I can get some, if he's not too tired, and I'm not too drunk." She winked as she slid out of the booth and put her purse on her shoulder. All of a sudden, she was the Horny Drunk. "Remember what I told you," she said as she walked away. "Fuck the shit out of him."

Instead of thinking about her advice, my drunken thoughts turned to Curtis. Curtis, that son of a bitch. How dare he call her first? Then call me to set up some booty call. That dumb bitch. Mission, my ass. If he'd really been planning to be with me, he should have called me first. Then maybe this night would have turned out differently.

Nope. More like he was to set up a quickie with me and then gonna run home to her and act like the happily married husband. She's so stupid. Fuck feeling sorry for her. Little know-it-all heifer. As a matter of fact, they're both pathetic. Fuck his dumb ass, too.

And what does that make me? Damn, I used to have it all figured out. Now I'm sitting here realizing that I don't know shit. I'm not handling the other side of 30 so well. I just know it wasn't supposed to be like this. So, why is it? Is this as good as it gets on this side? Hell, I guess so.

The bald guy was still checking me out. I saw him when I turned in my seat. I knew he'd still be looking. Men are so damn predictable. He took that as his cue to come sit at my table. What the hell? Flirting with him would keep me from having to go home and spend the night alone. He took Al's spot and said, "Hi."

"Hi, yourself," I said back, which for some reason, wasn't enough to run him off.

"Can I buy you a drink?" What a tired ass line.

"Look," I said. "No offense, good looking, but I got plenty of shit going on in my life right now to give me early wrinkles and headaches, without pouring it from a bottle."

"No problem, Ma," he said, still sitting there.

"My body's a temple," I snapped. "Not a still, you know." Of course I said this with a half-finished drink sitting in front of me.

"I know, Ma," he said. "Tell me about it."

And so I did. And then some.

Chapter Eight – Easy Sins

I thought if I could make myself refer to Andra-Lyn as her new found nickname, then I could regain my distance from her as a person. So I decided that from now on, she'd be Al. And of course, Al was right. When Curtis and I got together again, a few days later, he missed me something awful. It was mid-morning on a Saturday. He should have been at work, at what they call a pool meeting, one of those early morning, stay motivated, pep talk kind of days with all of his new recruits, but he handed it off to one of his other recruiters. It was the beginning of the month again. So much for working their asses off.

He showed up at my door with a bunch of flowers and a bottle of wine. Story of my life, the wrong man doing the right thing, but I accepted anyway.

We made love so hard, you'd've thought he was going off to war the next day. And I missed him so much I could have swallowed him whole.

But then after the buzz wore off, I lay there and caught my own case of conscience.

"Sorry about your birthday, Baby," he said.

"Sorry about your anniversary," I said back.

Instead of responding to my response, he asked. "Like the flowers?"

"Yep," I said, glancing over at them on the nightstand. "Thanks."

"You don't sound like you like them. Something wrong with them?" He straddled over me and kissed my forehead. "The guy said they're 'Magical Moonlight' or something like that." He kissed my chin, and then my neck.

"Yeah, they're really something."

"But?"

Why was he pushing these stupid flowers? To start with, they're over a week late. I said, "Babe, the only thing wrong with the flowers is that they came from you." I guess he just ignored that answer because he just kept kissing me. When he reached my chest, I just sighed and asked, "How do you get away with this?"

"Easy," he answered. "I'm careful. Real careful," he said, kissing my stomach and then my navel.

"How do you explain, you know, the late nights and stuff."

"Work."

"First of all, I'm sure she's not stupid, Curtis." I turned away from him. "What about when she calls? What if she just drops in the station? Then what?"

"First of all," he said, intending to mock me, "she never just drops in the station. She works at the mall, so she don't have the kind of job that she can just leave when she feels like it. And when she calls, my guys cover for me. It's easy enough to say I'm in an interview or gone to take some kid to dinner or picking him up from the MEPS. Anything. Plus, I keep my phone turned on."

He talked as he turned me back to my original position so that he could resume the path on which he'd started. "You know I keep my phone with me." He paused to kiss another spot. "And that's really the only number she calls me at."

"Good idea," I said.

"She trusts me," he said.

Bad idea. "Great. Maybe she is stupid."

"We all cover each other," he continued as he kissed the inside of my thigh.

"Each other," I repeated.

"It's not like they don't have their own stuff going on."

"I guess it's too easy not to," I said. "I get it. I'm just 'stuff going on'."

"I didn't say that," he said. "*And* I'm not saying what we do is like an 'everybody does it' type of thing, 'cause there's plenty of brothers on the straight and narrow."

Hmph. I need to get me one of them.

"Don't start tripping like you're one of those people who think this uniform is all I am. It's a part of me, and it always will be, but that don't give you and nobody else the right judge me."

"Doesn't it, though?" I asked. "I mean, you're supposed to be the most honorable man on the planet." I was kind of annoyed thinking about it.

"I am honorable," he said, as he licked the inside of my thigh, while I tried my best to be unresponsive. He paused again. "I love the Corps, and I do my duty. But I'm not perfect, and you ain't either, young lady."

"Oh, don't I know it," I said. And I know we're more than the uniform. "I was just asking a question."

I found the strength to close my legs and push him away. So he sidled up next to me and wrapped his arms around me.

Then I said, "You know what?"

"What?" He squeezed me.

"I think we need to take a break." I felt my throat getting tight and lumpy.

"I thought that's what we were doing." He put his hand on my thigh and starting moving it up.

"No, I'm serious." I cut him off. "I'm really having a shitty feeling about this."

"What can I do to make it better?" He nibbled at my ear, not really hearing me.

"Can you change the past?" I felt myself stiffening up. "Can you give me back the last year of my life? Can you fucking be somebody else?"

He stopped nibbling and sat up. He looked at me like he was actually listening, furrowed brows and all.

"Why are you doing this to me?" I asked liked he'd really have an answer.

"Hey, what's all that?"

"Man, don't you even care about nothing, except getting fucked," I asked. "Or have you even stopped to think that this is a court-martial begging to happen? Haven't you ever heard of Article 134?"

"Shhhit. A court martial? For what? Conduct unbecoming?" He didn't notice that I wasn't amused. "If the Commander-in-Chief can get away with it, why not me?"

Did he really? "Did you really just put me in the same category with *that* woman? You don't think no better of me than that?!"

His mouth dropped open. "Umm. What?"

"Didn't you fucking hear what I just said? I feel like shit." I had the instant sore throat and my voice quivered a little.

"Baby, come on now. How many times are we going to talk about this?" He was calling me Baby again, but it wasn't working.

"You ever heard of bad company? That's you," I said before he could answer. It was an odd time for me to remember what my grandma used to say to my mom and aunts about committing "easy sins" from dealing with people and situations about which she knew she knew better. But that's what popped into my head. Easy sins and bad company. And shame was all over me. "What I need is some good company. Not you. Leading me astray."

He laughed at my choice of words. "Leading you astray, huh?"

"You know? This is what they call a toxic relationship," I said, not sure where'd I heard it.

"What are you talking about?"

"I'm talking about how you make me sick." I guess that's what easy sins do. Make you sick for no reason. And he did. My stomach hurt and my head pounded and my throat ached.

"I make you sick?" he asked, sounding offended.

Maybe I didn't mean it that way, but I'd already said it. "Uh, yeah," I said, not sure which way to turn, and my voice was starting to crack.

"You're bad for me. That's all I'm saying." Come to think of it, I did get a queasy feeling whenever I thought about him, and my stomach ached whenever he wasn't around. "Yeah," I repeated. "That's exactly it."

He tried to blow it off as he lay back down next to me.

I pulled away from him. "And you've got to go. Now." I pulled away from him.

"Babe—," he started rubbing on me again.

"Now," I repeated, as my voice recovered.

"What's this about?" he asked. "Your friend Al, I guess."

"It's about me, telling you to leave."

"Naw, it ain't," he insisted. "It's about your boy, right?"

"What boy?" I asked before it registered that he was still talking about Al. "You don't know what the hell you're talking about."

"I know you need to learn to erase your messages before you try to play me," he said. He had the nerve.

"Play you?"

He reached across me and picked up my phone from the nightstand and handed it to me. "Something you want to tell me?"

I looked at the phone and saw the two text messages from the night of my birthday, *CHECKING ON U. AL* and *HAPPY BDAY. MUCH LOVE MAMA*

"There's something I want to tell you, all right," I said as I put the phone back on the nightstand. "You are crazy."

"I'm waiting," he said, like he had the right to expect something.

"Curtis, please get your ass out of my bed and out of my house."

"No," he said. "What if I don't want to? What are you going to do about that?"

"What if?" I repeated. "What if I lay my fist upside your head?" What if. What nerve. "What if I don't want you to be married? What are you going to do about it?" I threw the covers off and got up and went to the bathroom. "All I need is some married motherfucker bringing me flowers," I grumbled. Why the hell didn't he ever give me flowers before? "Men make me fucking sick! Give me my damn flowers while you're single! How about that?" I pushed the closed the door behind me and turned on the shower. I would have slammed the door, but it was one of those light-ass pressed wood doors that wouldn't slam, so I had to push it real hard to make it sound the way I was feeling. And it still had too much air in front of it. I sat on the floor with my back against the door. She gets a new car and I get fucking flowers?! What kind of shit is that? Fucking week-old flowers at that. Serves me right.

A few seconds later, he knocked. "Babe, come on, now."

I didn't move. "I don't want your old married-ass flowers. Go give them to your wife!" I buried my head in my hands trying to muffle the sound of me sniffling.

He talked through the door. "Shit. Sebrina don't do this," he said as he pushed the door, trying to come in. I wouldn't let him. "What do you want me to do?"

"How about do right by me, or do the fuck without me?"

"What the hell is that supposed to mean?"

"It means...," I paused. What did I mean? "It means, leave her or leave me the hell alone. That's what it means. You know what the fuck it means." I braced myself by pushing my feet against the vanity cabinet.

I wasn't totally surprised when he didn't have a response to that. I was a little surprised at myself for finally saying it, though. He didn't move until I screamed, "G'on and get the fuck out!" A few minutes passed, and I finally heard the front door shut. When I knew I was truly alone, I got in the shower and sat down and let the water beat down on me. Until the hot water ran out. Then I let the cold water run, hoping it would make me numb. All it made me was cold.

I went back to bed and stared up at the ceiling. What kind of man is he? The married flowers were still on the night stand taunting me. What was left of the bottle of wine was next to it, calling me. I grabbed the bottle and turned it up. In a few long swigs and swallows, it was gone. After a while, I dozed off, but it was brief. The phone rang and I knew it was him before I even looked at the Caller ID.

"What!" I answered.

"I just called to tell you that your boy ain't shit."

"Oh Lord!" I said in that tone of voice that nobody would dare address God. "Do you know you really are out of your mind?" He didn't answer.

"And he lets his girl keep his phone. He must be a kept man or something."

"His girl? Kept man?" I asked. "Curtis, what is wrong with you?"

"I was just looking out for you," he said.

"Curtis, what did you do?" I asked. Surely he didn't call his own wife's cell phone number and not recognize it.

"I told Finley to call your friend's number and a female answered the phone."

"Looking out for me? Call his? A female. Curtis, you idiot." Why didn't I just tell him then? That *female* is your wife, dumb-ass. So what if it was a new phone? A woman would have remembered the number the same minute her man gave it to her.

"Babe, I'm just telling you, so you'll know."

"Curtis, tell me you didn't call a number from my phone."

"Fin called the number and then when a woman answered the phone, he said he was trying to call Al's phone. Some woman told him, 'This is Al's phone.'"

I couldn't believe it. But I kept talking. "And did Fin tell her that her man was cutting out on her or what?"

"No," he said. "Nothing like that. All I had told him to do was call that motherfucker and tell him to stay the hell away from my woman. But Fin said some woman answered his phone."

"Your woman?" I asked.

"His woman," he corrected himself.

"His woman?" I asked again.

He didn't say anything.

"So you meant to have Finley call and threaten a total stranger?"

"Something like that."

"Don't y'all have better things to do besides calling around threatening folks and playing high-school ass games on the phone? That's why you can't make your damn numbers."

"So what's up?" he asked.

"And then you come crying to me about the damn rocks you bring in to take the test and can't score past a ten to qualify for the physical." I was just outdone. "Unbelievable," I said. "Un-be-fucking-lievable." I put the phone on my chest.

"So what's up, Sebrina?" he asked again.

I put the phone back up to my ear and started talking. "You're so damn busy scribbling down numbers out of my phone, you don't even know who the fuck you're calling."

"I don't care who it is," he responded.

"Obviously not. You can't even damn see straight for looking so hard. How would like it if I just started writing down and calling numbers from your phone without thinking about it?" I slammed the phone down.

It rang again almost immediately. "Hey," he said back. "Don't get mad at me because your boy got somebody else."

I breathed heavy into the phone, not responding.

Then he asked, "What exactly are you so upset about?" as if I were being unreasonable. "Having heard the truth or having believed a lie?" Then he added, "Don't sit there and get mad at me for telling you the truth. Be mad at that bastard that lied to you."

"You're right, Curtis," I said flatly. "Why would I get mad at you?"

He was silent. Then he said, "Like I said, I was just looking out for you."

"Save your fucking favors, okay."

"What?"

"I said, don't do me no fucking favors!"

Silence again.

Finally, I asked, "Are you finished? Can I hang up now? I'm really tired. And this whole conversation is giving me a headache." I slammed the phone down again, before he had a chance to answer back.

Less than a minute later, my cell phone rang.

"Hello!"

"Hey, girl. You all right?" It was Al.

"Hey," I said back. "What's up?"

"Girl, your boy is really tripping!" she said. "Your man just called me, looking for Al!"

"Really," I said back. "And what did you say?" I asked, as if I wasn't already aware of this conversation.

She started to repeat the gist of what Curtis had already told me and my phone rang again.

"Hold on, okay?" I said, sitting up in the bed, realizing a nap just wasn't going to happen today. I lay the cell phone face up on the night stand and picked up the other phone with an attitude.

"Yes," I answered, not really meaning to be polite.

"What's up, Ma?" said the voice that wasn't Curtis.

"Oh, hey," I said back, suddenly pleasant. "Hold on, okay?"

"No problem," he said. His name completely escaped me.

I held the receiver face down beside me on the bed and picked up the cell phone.

"Hey, I gotta let you go," I told Al.

"Don't let him get to you, girl," she said.

"It's not him," I told her. "It's—the guy from the other night."

"The cute bald guy?" she asked, already knowing the answer. "Good for you, Bree."

Bree? When did I tell her she could call me that? I rolled my eyes. There she goes, acting like we're friends. My friends don't even call me Bree. Oh hell. I guess that makes it appropriate then.

"Okay," she said. "Call me back. Bye." She hung up quickly. I clicked the cell phone off and tossed it to the other side of the bed. Then I went back to my other call.

"Hey," I said again. "How you doin'?"

"I'm good Mama," he said in what was definitely not a southern accent. "What's up with you? You get my message?"

"Oh, yeah. Thanks. Nothing really," I answered both questions at once and then used the pause in our dialogue to scramble for words to say that the other night was a fluke. That I wasn't in the habit of having one night stands, and that I wasn't particularly interested in a repeat performance.

"Look," he said. "You wanna get together later? Maybe a movie or go eat or something?"

"Or something?" I asked, thinking it was my fault for having given him the wrong idea about me.

"Naw, Mama. Nothing like that." He laughed and it was sexy as hell.

"Really," I said, still skeptical, but interested.

"Naw, naw," he assured me. "Not that I didn't have a good time. Got a brother wondering why you haven't been in touch and all that," He laughed again. "But really, you seem like, you know. Well, you seem like somebody cool to hang out with. You know. Just chill or whatever."

"You could tell all that from one night?" I said, not yet assured, but smiling. I was assured that I must have seemed like a quick hit, and he was probably trying to get back in, if I was willing.

"Uh, yeah," he said, as if he could see me smiling over the phone.

"Uh, yeah," I repeated. What the hell? He was asking me out on a legitimate date. "Okay."

"Okay, cool," he sounded pleased to be getting somewhere. "How about I come by about 7 o'clock? We can eat and catch a late movie, Yo."

So now I'm *Yo*. First I'm *Ma*, then *Mama*. Now *Yo*. I thought, *What's next?* But it was cool because I was feeling his dialect, even though I acted like it was nothing. For a moment I thought about whether or not I preferred to meet him somewhere, but I agreed to let him pick me up. It wasn't as if he hadn't been here before. Why the hell was I trying to be cautious now? And I wouldn't have to drive anywhere.

"Okay, 7 o'clock," I said.

"Okay," he said.

"Okayyy," I said again.

"Okay, Ma," he said, kind of laughing. "See you in a few."

"Okay," I repeated. If I don't say something else quick, he's going to think I'm an idiot. "Hey, I know this is going to sound really fucked up, but what's your name again?"

He laughed and said, "Whoa—Ma, it's like that, huh?"

"I'm sorry." I was embarrassed, but I didn't want to keep calling him *Hey*.

"That's a'ight," he said. Then he cleared his throat. "It's, um, Brown."

"Okay, right," I said. I guess I deserved that. "Might as well be Smith or Jones, right?"

"No, really," he said. "It's Brown."

I could have sworn it was something Hispanic.

"Raphael Brown."

"I'm sorry," I apologized again. "Now I remember." I knew I couldn't have been that drunk. But what the hell is a black man doing with a name like Raphael?

"No, problem," he said. "What's yours?"

"Aw, shit," I said back, and couldn't help smiling. "Touché," I said as he laughed that sexy laugh.

"Sebrina," he said before I could answer. "With an *e*. I was just messing with you, Ma. See you at seven, a'ight."

"All right," I said. "Bye." I hung up and looked at the clock. It was already after four. I decided not to call Al back and set the alarm for 5:30. After the day I'd had, I wanted to rest to clear my head before Raphael Brown came over.

Chapter Nine – A Real Date

Of course I didn't get up at 5:30, so when Raphael got there, even though it was a little after seven, I still wasn't ready. He was wearing jeans, a black T-shirt, and a leather jacket, looking cute to death.

I opened the door with Noxema on my face and I was still in my bathrobe with big red curlers in my hair. "I promise, I'm almost ready," I said, letting him in. "Just have a seat. I'll be right back."

I ran to the bathroom and finished my hair and washed my face and then ran into my bedroom where my clothes were already laid out. One of the outfits I'd bought myself on my birthday spree. Luckily, it was a simple casual ensemble that complimented what he was wearing or it would have taken longer to get ready because I would have had to find something else to put on.

It took me no more than 15 minutes to finish getting ready. He smiled at me indicating that it was worth the wait.

The movie was okay. Scary enough that it had a few moments that were perfect for clinging to a good looking date, but not so scary that I'd hate it. At the restaurant, he teased me a little.

"I'd hate to see how you'd act at a real scary movie," he joked.

"Scary?" I scoffed. "The book was better."

"Really?" he asked, like he didn't believe I'd read the book, which I hadn't. "The book?"

Wasn't there a book? "Hell, I don't know," I admitted. "That's just what everybody always says."

We both laughed.

The night was on a good roll, because we hadn't been seated for five minutes before the server brought our bread and took our orders. The drinks came right away. He drank his Corona from the bottle, and I sipped my mango-strawberry margarita from a straw, no hands, like a little kid would drink a slushy.

As I buttered and ate my bread, we talked about what we did for a living, where we went to school, how we ended up in the Atlanta area.

"So, tell me something," he said.

I nodded okay.

"So you've got a degree, and you're enlisted instead of an officer," he said, like there should have been a question mark on the end.

"Yep."

"And you got your reasons for that, I'm sure."

"I never planned on re-enlisting. I was only doing three years and getting out, but you know. Circumstances and situations."

"I know." He smiled. "So what has the army given you for the last six years of your life?"

"You mean, besides premature gray hair and a foul mouth?"

"Sure," he said.

"Hell, I don't know. Job security? Benefits? A free driver's license? And somehow, I've developed a talent of making friendships that don't seem to go anywhere."

"All good stuff."

"Well, look at you," I joked. "You got a master's degree. Is that all you got out of six long hard years of college? Bad knees and a job coaching college football?"

"I guess that's about it," he said. "I do a little scouting too, remember?"

"Oh yeah," I said. "That makes all the difference."

We both chuckled at that.

He sat across the table from me smiling and not saying anything for a few seconds and finally said, "What's up, Ma?"

I didn't think much about how I said it, but I said, "You know, you're a pretty big fella."

He smiled at that. "Am I?"

"What are you? 'Bout six-two, six-three, two ten?"

"Six-five. Two twenty-five."

"Umph," I said. "Yep. You're a pretty big guy, all right."

"Yeah, I guess so. And you're a pretty little lady."

"Small frame," I checked him. "Five-five, one twenty-one." Unless I'm retaining water. "Okay, one twenty-six. One thirty when I'm retaining water."

"Pretty," he said again.

"Oh," I finally got it. "Thanks." I felt myself start to blush. "Um, so let me see some ID."

"Now you want ID," he said, reaching for his wallet. He flipped it open to his driver's license and turned it towards me on the table. His birthday was in August. He lived in Covington.

"So, are you married?" I asked.

He put both his hands out in front of him and flipped them over a couple of times.

"Are you married?" I insisted.

"Naw, Mama," he said. "You don't see no rings do you?"

"Well, I prefer a verbal confirmation, you understand."

He laughed. "Yeah, I guess I do. Never can be too sure, right?"

"Right," I said. "Girlfriend? About to get married? Gay? Bisexual? Any of that stuff?"

"Naw, Ma. None of that either," he laughed.

"Well, why not?" I asked, not laughing. "I mean, what's wrong with you?"

He just smirked. "What?"

"I mean, not about the gay stuff, but why aren't you attached to somebody?" Then I broke it down. "Don't get the big head or nothing, but you look good as hell."

"Maybe I was meant to be your husband," he answered, still smirking.

"Hmph," I answered. "Well, where the hell you been?"

"Apparently, not in the right place at the right time."

Damn, if he didn't have a good answer for everything.

Why he didn't leave my bitchy, inquisitioning ass at that table as fast as he could, I have no idea, but he just sat there, looking, listening, smiling, eating and drinking. I guess I felt like if I threw as many questions at him as fast as I could, he wouldn't have time enough to throw any at me.

And for as cool as he was sitting there, looking good enough to fuck sober, for as much as he said he understood that this was just dinner and a movie, I felt the need to explain myself. He didn't ask a thing about it, but I just wanted him to know how much I really wasn't the person he'd met before. I wanted him to understand that I wasn't one of those high-maintenance, heavy make-up-wearing, hair laid every day kind of sisters. Though I don't know that any woman starts out wanting to be described as low-maintenance, I rather liked the idea. And the truth is, no matter how high-maintenance any woman claims to be, there are just some days when we all just need a little white cotton underwear in our lives.

"I'm probably nothing like the person you think I am," I said. "I don't know how to explain it, really." I took a deep breath and started again. "You know, that thing, I mean all that stuff the other night. That wasn't me."

"Damn," he said, smiling. "That's too bad. Well, where she at, now? What's her number?"

"Oh, very funny," I said. "I'm just saying, you know, that whole made-up face, and the sleeping with men I don't know. It's just—I mean, you can see I'm not a big make up person, right?"

"It's cool, Baby Girl," he said. "I got it. You know, with your birthday and being mad at your man and all that."

"Well, sort of like that."

"Don't sweat it," he said, leaning back. "We just hanging out, right?"

"Right."

The appetizers showed up as if on cue. "I'm not trying to get all heavy on you," he said. "I just want to feed you." He pushed the plate of cheese sticks and chicken wings over to me. "Now eat."

I took one of each.

"You explained it pretty good the other night," he said as I ate. "You're only wearing make up because it's your birthday. You're only spending time with me to keep from running after your boyfriend, who you're not speaking to right now. And, uh, let's see," he continued, "You're feeling a little lonely and reckless, so don't expect this to mean anything. Is that about right?"

I said reckless? I called Curtis my boyfriend? I tried to recall a few more of the details of that night, but except for the sex being pretty good, there wasn't much else I remembered. Not because I was sloppy, blackout drunk, but because I don't remember caring much about what we talked about.

"I should never have used the word reckless," I said. I should never have used the word boyfriend either, but isn't that just like what we do to describe a relationship that's not really a relationship whenever sex is involved? "I'm so not a reckless person. I wish you could know the person I really am."

He nodded as he took a drink. "I'd like that."

"And thank you so much for not being crazy," I quickly added without really thinking about it, and we both laughed. "There's no telling what you could have done to me," I said. "With your big ass."

"You're welcome." He sort of smirked.

"I mean, other than what you already did." I smirked back. "Oh, you know what I mean."

"I get it, Ma," he said. "I don't have what you're looking for right now. It's cool." He sounded convincing.

"Yeah," I said. I didn't think it kind or appropriate to tell him that he never would have, seeing as how he was the one spending time with me on a respectable date, and the one I wanted to have what I'm looking for belonged to someone else. "It's not really fair, but the truth is, the whole time I was with you, I was thinking about somebody else."

He just gave me an *I know* look and blinked down at the table. Damn, I've got to work on my subtlety. That wasn't a nice thing to say to somebody who's giving you a free meal.

The salads arrived, mine with extra tomatoes, and the waitress took away the used dishes. He ordered a second Corona. I was still working on my first margarita. I was really pleased that he had such good manners, saying "Thank you," every single time she did something, brought extra napkins, filled a water glass, replaced the bread basket.

I thought about how he sat in my living room, looking through photo albums, listening to songs that all had some Curtis story behind them. He even slow danced with me, like the romance was real, and at the time, that was good enough. I guess sometimes sex does just happen. But he wasn't the one.

I knew that because except for after I'd had too much to drink, when I looked at him, I didn't get all tingly. Didn't get a sense of need to have a certain special itch scratched. I just saw a regular guy. A nice-looking regular guy, but that's it. For some women, that would be enough. A nice-looking guy with good manners and a job. For a woman much smarter than me, I guess, that would be reason enough to latch on and never let go.

After a few more minutes, he spoke again. "So, tell me, what do you want?"

I tried to give it some thought before answering. I wanted to choose the right words. "I've been waiting for Mr. Right since I was sixteen years old," I admitted. "I went to college thinking he'd be there waiting for me. I went into my twenties ever-hopeful, optimistic, waiting, doing the right thing, or as much of the right thing as I could manage, you know?"

He smiled at that.

"Then, it was like, the closer I got to thirty, the faster the sands of time started running through that damn hour glass. And here, fifteen years and seven sorry brothers later," I paused as I recounted, "okay more like ten, if you count the ones I just let go down on me without having sex with them, and even that I regret miserably." I would have trailed off further if I hadn't noticed the blank look on his face. I tilted my head at him. "Oh, like you never let some girl you didn't give a damn about suck your dick."

The waitress arrived from behind me with the entrees just as that phrase was coming out of my mouth. She had one of those looks on her face like she wondered what she'd just walked in on. "All righty then! Be careful. These plates are hot," she said as she set them in front of us. He had a T-bone steak, with a baked potato and broccoli. I had the shrimp scampi pasta. "I'll be right back with some more bread."

As she turned to leave, Raphael added, "And A1 sauce, please." She nodded, and smiled at me and at him as she walked away.

He cleared his throat and chuckled. "I didn't say nothing, Ma."

"Exactly," I said. "You couldn't warn me the lady was right behind me?"

"But you were on a roll." He was clearly amused.

"Whatever." I scrunched my nose at him. "Anyway, here I am, looking at thirty in the rear view, still waiting, and still by myself. I don't want these to be the days of my life, you know?" It had all come out more obscure than I'd intended. "I guess I'm still waiting on the right man to come along, singing the right tune at the right time." I heard a Donny Hathaway song in my head.

"Okay," he said, clearly not getting it.

I tried to be clearer. "I just mean a guy who treats me like they do in the love songs. Like, 'Baby, this song should have been written for you.'"

"Oh yeah," he said. "What woman doesn't want a man to sing to her, right?"

But it wasn't just that I wanted singing. I needed it. I needed one of those gut-feeling, heart busted all to pieces, so glad I got you, never want to lose you, kind of song. "Hell, if he can't sing, he could just play it." I tried to sound lighter about it.

"So something like, 'You Remind Me of My Jeep' is definitely out, I guess," he joked.

"Unless you're trying to say I'm wide and heavy, uh, no."

We both enjoyed the humor in that. Some song lyrics are just so fucking stupid.

"Anyway," I continued, "I just don't see myself settling for the wrong man singing the right tune, you know?"

From the way he looked at me, he didn't know. "Sounds to me like you already got a singer in mind."

"Naw, Dawg, it's not like that at all," I lied, trying to lighten up.

"Isn't it?"

"Look, I didn't mean to get so heavy on you. It's just, well, you asked." I shrugged. It was too depressing to keep explaining.

"Yep, I did."

"It's no big deal, Bruh," I said, not quite sure how convincing I sounded. "Most of the time, I just think of him as my thing on the side."

"Really?" He looked unconvinced.

"Really," I said. "Sure do."

And he shrugged, still smiling that I'm-not-buying-your-bullshit smile.

"Aw, hell, I'm hooked."

Then we both laughed.

"If that fool called me right now and said he was in jail, I'd turn around and ask you for bail money and a ride to go get him."

"No joke?" he asked.

"No joke," I said.

"Damn, Ma. That's deep."

"Just want you to know up front how I feel." I twirled my fork in my pasta.

"Just want you to know up front that you wouldn't get none of that shit from me," he said back with a chuckle. "But I get you. You just want what you want."

"I'll probably call him as soon as I get home," I admitted.

"Probably," he agreed. "Do your thing, Yo."

Now I was back to *Yo*. "Hell, I was just getting used to *Baby Girl*."

"Hey now," he reasoned. "If I can be *Bruh* and *Dawg*, you can stand to be *Yo*, right?"

I smiled at that. Or maybe I was smiling at the way he licked his lips as he drank his beer. "So, uh, Yo," I started, "tell me how a black man ended up with a name like Raphael. Are you parents art fans or fans of the Ninja Turtles?"

He smiled back and I was glad he wasn't offended. "Actually," he said, "my pop's name is Ralph, so my moms thought it was a good name for me."

"Okay, cool," I said. "So your mom is Hispanic."

"My moms," he said, smiling, "is something very special."

"I'm sure," I said back.

"My moms is Puerto-Rican and Mexican, if you can believe that."

"Cool," I said again. Then I thought out loud. "But, hey, I always heard that Puerto-Ricans and Mexicans didn't mix with each other."

"Hmph," he said. "Well, they mixed enough to make 6 kids." And then he laughed.

"Wowwww."

"What can I say? Mi Abuelo fell in love with a Puerto-Rican cutie, and the rest is history."

"Well, how sweet is that?" I said. "Me who?"

"Yeah," he nodded. "Para perseguir las reglas del amor de otra pelsona es estupido."

I looked at him blankly. Did he just say I ask stupid questions?

"Oh, that just means it's stupid to follow someone else's rules when you're in love. He always used to say that love is love, but you can imagine that his family and my grandma's family didn't like it too much."

"I suppose not." I was really thinking about what he'd said about 'love is love'. Wise old grandpa.

"He says my grandma taught him that," he continued.

Well, okay then. Wise old grandma.

"Then, the day my moms was born, all that nonsense with the families just went away. Funny how a baby can melt away years of ignorance."

"Yep. They say a baby changes everything." I kind of slipped into wondering about when and if I'll have babies. "But hey, love is love is love. That's the way it should be. You have a wise grandpa."

"And so, she named me Joaquin after her father, mi abuelito."

"Hmph," I said. "Raphael after your Pappy, and Joaquin after your Papi,"

"Something like that, silly girl," he said.

"Aww, you like it." I found myself flirting, feeling comfortably silly. Why was I flirting with this man, knowing I don't even like him like that? I blamed the margarita.

He took a sip of his beer. "I guess I do."

"So, what's your mom's name?"

"Sabrina," he said, smiling.

I smiled back and shook my head. "So, that's why you remembered my name, huh? Because it's the same as your mama's. Now I get it. Mmhmm."

He shrugged. "Only she spells it right."

"Very funny, joker," I said.

We ate and talked. I mostly talked. He mostly ate, but I could tell he really listened to me.

"I could talk to you all night," he said.

"Hell, at this rate, you just might," I said matter of factly, "because I love to talk."

"No kidding?"

"Naw," I said. "Hell, sometimes I talk just to hear how good it sounds when it comes out." Then I winked at him. "I have some very lovely extended conversations with myself."

"Learn anything?"

"Sometimes," I said. "Sometimes, I'm just full of shit."

When my dessert came, I had a slice of strawberry cheesecake, he said, "You ain't no slouch at eating, either."

I laughed. "Yep. My two strongest suits. Talking and eating. Not necessarily in that order."

And it was a nice date, and it was nice to get out of the house, even though my mind was somewhere else. Thoughts of Curtis slipped in as the date drew to a close.

"So, you're fluent in Spanish," I said on the ride home. "That is so cool to me."

"Yep," he said, nodding. "All my life."

When we got to my apartment complex and parked, we sat in silence for a few minutes. I couldn't help smiling at him for having shown me such a good time that didn't involve sex. He was funny and easy to talk to. I was missing Curtis, but I was in no hurry to get up to an empty apartment.

"So," I said, stalling. "Why don't you say something to me in Spanish."

"A'ight, Baby Girl. What do you want to hear?"

I clasped my hands in my lap. "I don't know. Something nice. Tell me something really nice." I kind of pushed him on the knee, playfully. "But keep it clean."

"Clean, huh?" He arched his eyebrow and then looked ahead. "Okay, here goes," he said, licking his lips and then looking at me in my eyes. My eyes got wider as he prepared to speak, and I bit the corner of my bottom lip as I waited. Then he just sort of breathed the words, "me diverti mucho contigo, y me gustaria tocar tus piernas otra ves y besar tus caderas . How's that?"

"Damn, that sounded good," I said, even though I didn't understand a word. Or maybe it was just the way his lips moved when he said it. I felt a hint of an itch just then, but I shook it off.

"Thanks," he said.

"Well, what does it mean?"

He kind of hesitated as he held back what could have been a devious smile. "It just means I had a good time with you and, uh, I'd like to walk you to your door. Again."

Again? I thought. Letting him walk me to the door again might tempt me to invite him in again. But what the fuck, right?.

"Oh, is that all?" I asked. "It just sounded sexy as hell, I guess."

"Yeah, I guess."

"It was really sweet of you to offer to do that. I don't get that nearly as much as I should. Somebody taught you well."

He cleared his throat and said, "Well, I have had my share of practice."

Before the either of us opened the car doors, we just sat there smiling at each other. Then I reached for my door handle and started to get out.

"Well, I'd do that for you anytime, Ma," he said.

"Hell, you can right now." I chuckled. "Get to work and open my la peer-ness, why don't you," I said, trying again to mimic his pronunciation.

He smiled as he opened his door and got out. I smiled back at him with my head tilted to one side as he walked around to pull open my door. What a sweet guy. "Thank you. I mean, Gracias."

"De nada. Really."

"Say it again," I said as we reached the steps. "I really like the sound of that."

But now he was embarrassed, and wouldn't do it.

"I've been meaning to tell you how much I like your spot," he said.

"These are cool."

"Yeah, it's all right," I said. "Until you have to carry a whole bunch of shit up the steps by yourself. Just another peril of negotiating a single life."

He sort of laughed at that.

"And for a single somebody, I'm always buying shit in bulk. Cases of bottled water, washing powder liquid, a bunch of canned goods. Cafeteria-sized pickles. A big ass T.V."

"Yeah? Washing powder liquid, huh?"

"And don't let it be raining," I went on, pretending not to notice that he was calling out my country talk. "I busted my ass on these slippery-ass steps not too long ago trying to lug a bunch of stuff in one trip." After a pause and a thought, I said, "Pickle juice everywhere."

He looked like he wasn't sure whether or not it was okay to think it was funny.

"Oh, it's funny now," I said, laughing. "But you better believe I was pissed at the time."

"Yeah," he said thoughtfully. "I guess you could've really gotten hurt."

"Whatever, man. I think I was more pissed off about breaking my pickles than I was about falling."

When we reached my door all I had to say was, "Well, thank you for the—for everything. I had a nice time." I was definitely feeling an itch that needed to be scratched. Where the hell did that come from? That drink wasn't that strong.

"Me too," he said. "I'll call you sometime, a'ight."

"A'ight," I said back.

"Well, I'ma go," he said.

I said, "Okay," and he said, "Okay."

And we exchanged, "Okay," back and forth about five more times.

Finally, I offered him a hug good night and he was okay with that.

When I got inside my apartment, I couldn't wait to call Curtis. That night out should have made me forget him, but it only made me miss him more. It was late, and I probably shouldn't have been calling him. I decided I didn't care, so I dialed. I didn't really expect him to pick up, so I was ready to leave a really well-thought out message on his voice mail.

"Hey, Baby. It's me," I said, like he wouldn't know otherwise. "I was just thinking that maybe I over-reacted a little bit today, and that I really miss you. And I'm sorry about all the drama, so if you get a minute, maybe you could come by and we could talk. Okay. Good night. Bye." It's just like old Papi-abuelito said, I reasoned. Love is love, damnit.

I hung up and took a deep breath. I hoped he would call right back, but he didn't. I told myself it was okay. He'd call tomorrow.

Days passed and he didn't call or come by at all. I guess he was giving me that break I said we needed. I left a couple more, *Hey, it's me* messages and just waited. At the end of that week, he finally stopped by. I noticed that he didn't call before just popping up, but at that point, I didn't care.

I opened the door. "Hey."

"Hey. Something you want to talk to me about?" He sounded really serious, but he smiled as he talked. And he stood there, turning me on something awful.

I was so glad to see him, I couldn't even smile back. As I opened the door, I swallowed and said, "I was thinking that maybe I shouldn't have called you toxic and stuff like that."

"Maybe?" he asked.

"Yeah," I said. My heart was starting to beat faster and I tried not to sound anxious as I spoke, but I don't think it was working. "And maybe the reason I get so sick and achy around you is because I miss you so much when you're not here."

"Yeah," he said, crossing the threshold. "But I'm here now."

"And I do want things to be different for us, but I know it's not that easy, like I want it to be." I couldn't think of shit else to say.

He was cucumber cool and I was about to pop like corn in hot grease. I stood there at the door, in a V-neck T-shirt and panties, waiting to see what his next move would be. He walked toward the bedroom, starting to undress as he walked, drawing me right behind him.

"You still feel like talking?"

"Sure," I said. But the kind of talking I wanted to do didn't require words and he was okay with that too.

Chapter Ten – Girl Talk

Al talks to me like I'm her best friend, and I talk to her like she's my priest. And I'm still not Catholic. She tells me all about her life, her wonderful man, and I tell her I can't help falling back into bed with a man I know I shouldn't be with.

She liked the idea of me hooking up with Raphael, to whom she referred as the cute bald guy, or the cute Puerto-Rican guy. I was starting to wish I'd never told her anything about him, that I'd spent any time with him, especially that I'd slept with him that one time. Now, suddenly, she's some kind of relationship expert.

Today we went shoe shopping. The plan was to get sensible shoes. The be-on-your-feet-all-day, but professional-looking shoes, but we ended up buying shoes for show. The make-your-legs-look-pretty shoes.

"I'm getting these too," I said. This was the third pair of shoes in a row that I'd tried on and liked enough to buy.

"Good choice," she said. "You should get those in the brown too, 'cause you never know."

Suddenly, I was struck with a touch of sensibility. "I can't walk too far in these, though."

"Yeah, but they're not made for walking."

"You're right," I said. Then I turned to the sales clerk. "I'll take these too, please."

Before I could thank her for talking good sense out of me, she asked, "You know what first attracted me to Curtis?"

Damn. It was hard enough not to think about him without her bringing him up, but there she had to go fucking with my shoe high. I wasn't in the mood to guess, so I asked, "What?"

She started smiling before she spoke, like she was about to tell me a dirty secret. "His walk."

"I can understand that. Nothing sexier than a sure-footed man."

"Amen," she agreed. "That's my baby, all right."

Naw, bitch. That's my baby. "Don't you ever call him by his first name?" I was actually annoyed, but she didn't notice. I was glad she didn't notice, because there was no way I should have known that Curtis wasn't his first name. Thank God for the shoe buzz.

"Not really," she said. "That's how he introduced himself when I met him, but I don't really like it. Kirkpatrick is his first name."

"Oh." I pretended like I didn't already know this.

"But Kirkpatrick is so nerdy, and Mordecai sounds so old-fashioned to me."

"Yeah, I guess so," I said, sitting there tapping mismatched feet. "Anymore old-fashioned, his name would have been Adam, huh?"

She nodded. "Mmhm. And he'll probably want to name our first son junior."

"Probably," I said.

"I tried to call him Kirk when we first starting dating, but then I just started calling him Curtis after he took me to his Marine Corps Ball."

"Okay," I said, getting the point, already.

"His daddy calls him Junior, and they don't even have the same name." I just nodded. She just went off. "I don't know why men insist on naming their sons after them when they know good and well that they wouldn't have wanted that name if they would've had a choice."

She had a point.

"Then all of a sudden, it's a cool name," she said as she picked up a shoe from the display.

"It's a nice, eh, name," I said, putting my shoes back in the box and handing them to the lady.

"Yeah," she said. "Like I want my baby having to fight his way home from school every day." I guessed she'd had that conversation with him too.

"Or run," I said.

"Yeah. Or run," she said, and we both laughed. I told myself I was really laughing at her shallow ass. Curtis couldn't help that his name was Mordecai anymore than she could help her name was Andra-Lyn. I just shook my head and kept laughing.

My laughing quieted as I thought about the two of them having children. "You know, I could stand a lemonade right now," I said. I really could have stood something much stronger, but it was early on a Saturday.

"Me too," she said.

We stopped at Chick-fil-A on the way to the hair salon.

"You know what's really good?"

"Sex with popsicles?" I said, surprised at myself for lightening up. Must have been some residual new shoe buzz.

She looked at me kind of funny and then shook her head. "You're crazy," she said. "Raspberry lemonade."

I made an "Mmm?" sound through my straw, as I looked at her.

She nodded. "There's some restaurant downtown that Curtis took me to when we first got here."

Suddenly, my mouth was really dry. "Really," I said, right before taking a big slurp.

"I can't remember the name of it," she said. "But that's where I had it. That's some good stuff. I was thinking, Chick-fil-A would make a killing if they started marketing raspberry lemonade, like that place." She smiled like she was thinking about what a good time they must have had there, and that started to irk me again. As far as the lemonade idea went, she seemed to be on to another good point.

"They do make the best lemonade, don't they?" I said. Then I had to check myself again. I had a whole lot of nerve to have an attitude with her for being in love with her own husband. I changed the subject without thinking it through.

"You really love him too, don't you?" I asked, shaking the ice around in my cup.

"What?" she asked.

I recovered with, "I mean, the way I love—Mack." God, I hated that name. I wish I'd come up with something better, but now I was stuck with it. "I mean you talk about him a lot, and you probably don't even notice it."

"Yeah," she kept smiling as she talked. "I guess I do." Then she got thoughtful. "But enough about him. What about you?"

"What about me?"

"How'd you meet Mack?"

"A frat party," I said dryly. Sad, but true.

"Okay?" she said, expecting me to go on.

I pushed away from the table. Not something I wanted to share with her. "I'm going to get a refill." I shook my cup again. "Are you good?"

She was good. I got my refill and some chicken nuggets and returned to the table. She'd held her thought.

"So, you met at a frat party?"

"Yep. He walked up to me and said I had a pretty face."

"That is so sweet," she said with that high pitch that we use when we say something is so sweet.

I shrugged it off. "I guess."

"And what did you say to him?"

"I said thanks."

"That's it?" she dragged on.

"Well, I guess I really didn't know what the hell else to say. We talked for a good six hours straight the first night we met." Then I smiled. "I thought he'd never kiss me."

"And the rest is history, as they say," she said. She was sort of right. The rest might ought to have been history.

"Well, we sort of lost touch for a while and then—I guess." I stopped.

"And then fate just hooked y'all up again," she said.

"Yeah, I suppose it's like that."

"That's so romantic."

"Yeah, well it would be if he wasn't… If we'd hooked up sooner, I guess."

She looked at me kind of funny again.

"I mean sooner, again," I tried to explain. "Not sooner than before the first time, but sooner than this second time. I mean, again after college, but before—you know what? Never mind." I could never make somebody like her understand what it was like.

Chapter Eleven – The Virgin of the Village

I went to college expecting a crash course in self-esteem. Self-esteem and my prince would find me and make all of my self-proclaimed high school inadequacies disappear.

What I got was Facts of Life 101. Being brainy and virginal is just as unattractive to college men as it is to high school boys. It didn't help that my fashion sense was severely impaired. I practically lived in gray sweats and sneakers. My eyebrows had never been razored, waxed or plucked. I didn't wear makeup, and I was still wearing a curl, for God's sake. And not even a good one.

All of my roommates were the pretty at first sight kind of girls. We lived in a dorm called The Village, an apartment-style complex with four bedrooms, a bathroom and a kitchenette to each apartment. Me, Miss Plain, sharing living space with Miss Best Dressed, Miss Most-Likely-to-Succeed, and the ever-popular Miss Sexually-Active.

I was in hell.

To add to it, I put on the dreaded freshman fifteen and weighed more than I ever had in my life. So there I was, frumpy, brainy and virginal with a greasy, badly done curl and bushy eyebrows, spending my Friday nights at home with *20/20*.

Instead of getting that much anticipated surge of self-esteem and meeting my prince, I went on believing other people were better than I was just because they wore nicer, more fashionable clothes and trendier hairstyles. And even though I knew that a lot of them were popular for all the wrong reasons, I carried around that feeling that I was less of a person, less valuable or something, just because of how I looked, what I didn't have and the attention I wasn't getting. Good sense told me better, but I wasn't listening.

By my second semester, word got around that I wrote term papers and essays for money. I started out tutoring English 101 and 102, just sort of helping out a couple of guys here and there, the ones who didn't pick it up so easily. It wasn't long before most of my pupils decided they'd rather just pay me to do the work for them, until, finally, I was making more money writing than I was tutoring.

And that's not saying much because half the time, they couldn't even pay me. But when they couldn't pay me, they'd offer to bring me food from the cafeteria, and lean days being what they were, I took it, which in hindsight, probably accounts for the freshman fifteen.

Being a campus egghead was a not so exciting existence, but people liked me well enough. But that was far from being popular. I wrote papers and I was a virgin. Guys noticed me, and some were friendly, but my guess is that those who thought of me as anything more than a little sister probably thought I was just too damn much work for the trouble and ensuing drama of seducing a virgin. Or maybe it was the curl.

I hung out at the ball games and went to parties with my roommates, but I didn't get asked on any dates. And just when I thought it couldn't get any worse than that, I heard that they all called me the Virgin of the Village. Freshman year pretty much sucked.

In the fall of my sophomore year, I met Curtis at a frat party. His opening line really was, "You have a pretty face." He was obviously full of himself, just as you'd expect any good-looking frat boy to be.

Maybe I was just an easy mark, but Curtis was the first man to ever tell me I was pretty.

I was still pretty plain at nineteen, but thank God, I had graduated from the greasy curl to a relaxer and a cute hairstyle. I had also shed most of the freshman fat and grown into my lean, athletic genes, and on that night, I traded my daily gray sweats for some better fitting jeans.

Curtis' younger brother was pledging Omega, and Curtis, also an Omega, was in town for the infamous Hell Week. The first time I saw him, he was in the Village Square standing next to the DP, the Dean of Pledges, on top of a table, looking all stone-faced and serious with his arms folded, giving the pledges their usual hell. He had on a short-sleeved black T-shirt and gray sweats, and his brand was showing.

There was a party that weekend, there was a big party, and the newly crossed-over Omegas, were jumping around, groping girls, dancing and stepping and stumbling. I was standing with my back against the bar, basically holding down the floor. When the music slowed, I watched Curtis approach from across the room. The lights got low and there he was in my face.

"You have a pretty face," he said. Just like that.

I'm sure I looked at him like I was either confused or surprised that he was talking to me. Then I told myself, *Of course you do,* and played it off and managed to say, "Gee, thanks," like I was blowing him off. "What are you trying to say about the rest of me?"

"Dance with me." It came out more like a summons than an invitation.

I thought about pretending to have an attitude, but why bother? He could have asked anybody, but he chose me. I wanted to dance, and it was a slow song.

When the song was almost over, he leaned in my ear and said, "They call me Mack."

I just kind of purred at the smell of him. "Hmmm. Thanks for the dance." I started to walk away.

He held on to my arm, asking something like, "Where you running to?" Another song started and I danced with him again. He was really easy to hold. I guessed he must have felt the same way about me because when he opened the front of the jacket he was wearing, I reached inside his jacket and slipped my arms around his waist. I held him close to me like we'd come to that party together, like we were a couple. If our bodies had a language, they were saying, "Mmmm," to each other.

"What do they call you?"

"Usually by my name," I answered.

"Which is?"

"Sebrina."

Then he purred, "Mmmhmm."

That was the extent of the dance floor dialogue. When that song ended, he led me off of the floor back to the bar. There was one stool open, so I sat down and he stood next to me.

"Order what you want," he said. "I got it."

I remember thinking, *So, now I'm a salted peanut, to be had for the price of a drink,* paraphrasing one of my favorite Bette Davis lines in *All About Eve*. I said, "Sprite, please. I don't drink."

"Two Sprites, man," he said to the bartender. And then he turned back to me saying, "My little brother just crossed over. Jo-Jo. Number 4."

Turned out that he didn't drink either, and something about that made him even more attractive. Maybe it was the way that Sprite wet his lips, or just the fact that his breath didn't smell like all sour or medicinal when he talked. "My body's a temple, not a still," he'd said, like I'd just offered to buy him a drink. He had a small chip in one of his front teeth that I probably wouldn't have even noticed except that the way his dimples cut long and deep into his face made it hard not to watch his mouth when he spoke.

"I know Josiah," I said.

"I guess you do," he said with a laugh. "You're probably the only person besides my mama who calls him that."

"We met during orientation. He's a nice guy. We have a couple of classes together. Everybody here just calls him Jo. Or Curtis." I don't know what it is about playing sports that makes athletes call each other by their last names, but it works. "But I always liked the name Josiah." He raised his eyebrow. "I just have thing for names. Not your brother," I clarified.

"That's good to hear," he said, and touched my hair.

I thought about what I would say next and came up with, "I saw you in the Square with the DP the other night. He's my roommate's boyfriend. I asked her who you were and she told me everybody calls you Mack, but that's about it."

"You asked about me?" He seemed pleased. The bartender set the drinks on the bar.

I was sure every girl on campus had asked about him. I sipped from my glass and then admitted, "Well, yeah. I noticed that you don't go to school here. I'm guess I'm wondering why you came all this way just to haze your little brother."

He laughed again. "It's not hazing. It's grooming."

"Whatever."

"I just wanted to be here to cross him over."

Then I asked, "So what's your real name, Mack?"

"What's the matter with Mack?" he asked back.

What wasn't the matter with it would have been a more thought-provoking question. "It's—never mind." I just let it go.

He told me he dropped out of school during his junior year to play football with some Canadian league. He played for a year and then came home and joined the Marines. That was two years ago.

"One day, I'll finish school," he said, like it was nothing.

I took a particular liking to the confidence in his voice. The power and vulnerability in his eyes were mesmerizing. The strength of his jaw was probably more genetic than Marine Corps training, but the way he chewed that gum, made me envy the gum.

"My first name is Kirkpatrick," he said, changing the subject. "My mother's maiden name," he explained. "She named me Mordecai after my father."

I listened and nodded.

"My teachers used to call me Kirkpatrick until I got into sports. Then everybody just shortened it and started calling me Kirk."

"And Curtis, right?"

"And Curtis," he confirmed. "Then one of my coaches nicknamed me K-Mack because my initials were KMC. It kind of stuck until the bros shortened it to just Mack."

"I see," seemed like the appropriate interjection. Seemed like a bit of a stretch, but okay.

"You know, like *Mack Daddy*."

It figured. "You've got more nicknames than you know what to do with, huh?" Then I told him I liked the name Mordecai. "Sounds noble. You know, it's got that honorable biblical thing going." I smiled. "But Mack? Come on. Any sister with good sense would run the other way." I caught myself looking at him and suddenly felt a little embarrassed. I looked down into my glass as if I didn't know it was almost empty.

"So what are you saying? You ain't got good sense?"

I drained my glass and crunched on a piece of ice as I thought about my answer. "Apparently not." I put the glass down on the bar and looked at him. "And what does that say about you? You're still standing here next to somebody who probably ain't got good sense."

"Says maybe we were meant for each other, I guess."

"Or," I said. "It says ain't neither one of us got good sense." At that we both laughed and our laughter faded to awkward silence. I cleared my throat just for the noise.

"Mack is probably not how you should introduce yourself to someone you're really interested in," I said. "Thanks for the drink, though." I pushed the glass away from the edge of the bar and stood up to walk away. He was really cute, but he was about to play me like a game of Spades, and despite the implication, I did have good sense. I took a deep breath, proud of the way I'd handled myself as I walked away.

He followed me for a few steps. "Hey," he said, pulling on my arm again.

He'd come after me! Now I was really proud of the way I'd handled myself.

"How about just Curtis, if you like that better?"

I liked Curtis better than Mack, and he apparently preferred it to Mordecai, so I said, "Okay, cool."

So there we stood in the middle of the room again, oblivious to the party going on all around us. I took those few seconds to take full inventory of his gorgeous chocolate brown skin, dreamy eyes, perfect lips and those dimples. At that point I didn't care that he could see in my eyes that I was surveying him, because he was doing it right back.

"You know, you have beautiful eyes," he said.

"Have I?" I asked, not caring how corny he sounded. I'd never noticed anything so special about my eyes, but maybe the eyebrow wax set them off. I'd let my roommate's sister, a professional hair dresser, talk me into letting her do them. She was the one who'd straightened out the curl, so I thought, eh, what the hell? Maybe she knew what she was doing.

I remember being really impressed with the transformation and she told me then, "Ain't no trick to looking good," talking to my smiling reflection. "I knew from the first time Layla brought you in here, you had a lot of pretty potential." She'd given me one of those larger than average sized hand mirrors to briefly inspect my eyebrows and then spun me a partial turn to cue me out of the chair. "The outside is easy."

Just like something a big sister would say. What did she know about the outside being easy? She and Layla looked to me like people who'd been pretty all their lives, so what did either of them know about it? Still, I could tell she was trying to impart some free wisdom into the services rendered, so I just said, "Mmmhmm, you're right."

And Curtis reaffirmed it. "Yeah," he said. "You're real pretty."

"Thanks," I sighed hard. "Again."

He asked if we could talk outside. I said okay. And we talked for an hour about all kinds of nothing. He was easy to talk to. Then he asked if he could walk me home. The club was just around the corner from campus, so it was a short walk, and the stars were out.

He wasn't super-tall, closer to five-eleven or six feet even. He had that rugged, roughneck kind of handsome thing going for him. And when he walked it was more of a stride. And something in his stride seemed to make him walk a little taller and stand a little straighter.

It was then when I first noticed that he had that thing about him. A thing I couldn't put my finger on, just a sexy-as-hell thing. Few things look better on a man than confidence, and there's nothing more confident than a man who walks like he knows where every step will land.

Somewhere in the conversation, we discovered that one of his frat brothers, one his line brothers in fact, was from my home town. "You know Snake?" His eyes lit with enthusiasm.

"Snake?" I asked. "Back home, we just call him Floyd."

"Oh, that's my boy!" He said, like we were talking about a celebrity. "Small world."

"Apparently," I said, less enthusiastically, but amused at his enthusiasm.

"Yep," he said, still smiling. "Snake is one of my closest brothers. I was the best man at his wedding."

Small world, indeed. "I was at that wedding. I don't remember you."

"See," he said. "There you go. We could be soul mates, and you just blew me off like that?"

"Soul mates, huh?"

"There must be a reason we're meeting again, right?" He was pretty smooth. And I was buying every word of it.

"Speaking of brothers," I segued, "Is it just you and 'Jo-Jo'?" I asked. "Or do you have other brothers and sisters?"

"I've a twin sister named Esther," he said.

"Like Aunt Esther, from *Sanford and Son*," I said. "You're a twin?"

"Not exactly," he said. "And yeah. I'm a twin. But she did stay in a lot of fights in school because of that Aunt Esther stuff." He smiled. "We all stayed in a lot of fights."

"It's not a name you hear every day."

"She went by her middle name in school. She was crazy about being called Esther."

"Esther the queen," I finally got it. "That's cool."

"My daddy thought so. But I guess that's about what you get being a preacher's kid."

"Bible names," I said, thinking of Esther and Mordecai in the Bible. And Josiah, one of the righteous kings. Guess I'd paid more attention in Sunday school than I'd thought.

"You know how kids can find the damned-est shit to pick on each other about. Me and Jo-Jo used to be getting in fights all the time with people picking at us about being preacher's kids. You either learn to run or fight. You know?"

"Uh huh," I said back. "What about Esther?"

"Always running around chasing somebody on the playground." Then he laughed. "I remember one day after school she beat down two girls at one time. They tried to gang her."

"And you didn't help?"

"Hell, she was already pissed by then. She wasn't the one that needed help." He laughed again. "They had been calling her stuff like, 'You 'ol heathen' and 'fish-eyed fool,'" he said in his Aunt Esther voice, and we both laughed thinking about it. "They were dancing around the on the bus, up and down the aisle, talking about, 'Waaah! Glory!'"

"Not, 'Wah, glory'."

"No," he said. "I mean 'WaaaAaah! Glory!' More feeling in it."

I just said, "Mmph," at the way he was tripping.

"I mean they really pissed her off," he said, holding in a laugh.

"Sounds like it."

"And then, she had the nerve to threaten to beat me down if I told Daddy. Like she thought she could whip me."

"She sounds pretty tough."

"That girl." He shook his head and smiled. "She ended up going to

Tennessee State on a track scholarship." Sounds like she learned to run and fight.

"I think Esther is a beautiful name."

He glanced over at me like I was full of shit. "Well, I'm sure she'd appreciate that. But nobody 'cept Mama calls her Esther."

"What do your mama and daddy call you?" I asked, moving to the next thought. "For some reason, they call me Junior." He shrugged. "Guess Daddy wanted a junior, and Mama wasn't having it. So my nickname is a compromise. I guess."

"I guess," I said.

"Well, you know, love is about compromise, isn't it?"

Then I shrugged. "But we digress."

"Yeah."

"So, everybody else calls you Mack."

"Except you." He smiled as he talked.

By the time we'd gotten to my room, we'd talked about everything from nicknames, to Big Bird, to blue pants and blood stripes, to the Bible.

"Whoso findeth a wife findeth a good thing," he said.

"Yeah. So I hear." I was intrigued by his choice of scripture. "Are you saying you believe that?"

"I know that."

"Well, *Whoso*," I said. "Whenever *you-so do-so* find her, let's hope that you appreciate her. And obtaineth favor of the Lord, and all that."

"Oh, no doubt." He nodded confidently and winked, which made me smile. Something told me that he already had the Lord's favor and always would.

We sat on my bed and I talked and he just talked back. "Sometimes the scripture just comes to me out of the blue," he said.

"Yeah, I know," I said. "Well, probably not a fast as they come to you, but sometimes they just come out according to what's on my mind at the time. Is that weird or what?"

"Or what," he said and laughed.

I nodded in agreement.

"I must have picked it up from my daddy, I guess."

"I guess," I said. "I just read a lot."

"It's something you don't lose," he said, like he was reading my mind. "Just an extension of my own thoughts. Something that helps me through."

"You're not the only one," I said. "Jo-Jo's line name is 'Preach'."

"I know," he laughed like it had been his idea.

I laughed too.

Then he said, "Saa-Bree-Naa," sounding out every syllable.

Before I could stop myself, I said, "It's just Sebrina. With an *e.*"

"Oh," he said. "So don't tell me you're one of those snotty Smyth with a *y* type of folks that's always got to tell people how to spell your name, like everybody you talk to is going to write it down."

"No," I said. The last thing I would ever be is snotty. "I just thought you were making some kind of fun of my name."

"Never," he said, and I thought that was cool. "Come on, now. After I just told you about how we came up fighting."

He made sense. "Oh yeah," I said. "My bad."

The more we talked, the cooler he got. The cooler he got, the more I wanted to talk, no matter how late it got or how sleepy I was. I felt myself talking out of my head as I dozed in and out of the conversation.

"People ever call you Mort?"

"Uh, no."

"Never? Mort? Mortie?"

"Not unless they wanted an ass-whipping." He brushed my hair back off my forehead and thumped me. Then he ran his thumbs across my carefully manicured eyebrows and kissed me softly on my forehead. "You making fun of my name?" he asked in almost a whisper.

It was morning before I fell asleep in his arms, listening to the sound of his voice. He didn't even try to feel me up. There was something sweet about that. He just caressed the side of my face and told me how smooth my skin was. That was the night I fell in love.

I'm sure he probably could have talked me out of my panties that same night if he had half tried, but he didn't. He hardly even kissed me. Besides the kiss on my forehead, there was just one simple, smooth kiss that seemed to work its way into the conversation. It was like he was waiting for me to take a breath between the words, and when we both paused at the same time, he leaned over and kissed me. Like it was a formality to get out of the way so that we could finish talking.

I'd spent my life thinking, dreaming, writing poetry about it. Sex, love, making love, being in love, and all that. And there, when I'd least expected it, I'd met the man who was about to make it happen. Cliché, yes. But I guess sometimes the truth is cliché.

Of course if I had it to do over again, I'm sure I wouldn't have rushed it like I did. I'd only known him for about two months, and he'd been working on me hard for about a month, if that, visiting back and forth on weekends. I'd like to be able to say it was a long courtship. That he wooed me and wowed me. Wined and dined me. But it just didn't happen that way. He did bring me chicken from *Bojangles* a couple of times.

He was a 22-year old man, after all. Young and dumb. But I loved him. I'm sure that sounds incredibly juvenile and naïve, but that's what I was. Juvenile, naïve, and genuinely in love. And I've long ago convinced myself that being in love negates the fact that I didn't make him work for it the way we're all brought up to believe that we should make them work for it so they'll love us or appreciate us more or whatever.

He noticed me at a time in my life when I might as well have been invisible. He picked me out of a campus full of prissier, more popular women. He listened to me and I felt like he appreciated my thoughts. He held me like I was the most special thing in the world. Sometimes he slept so close to me that I'd wake up and couldn't move because he was sleeping on my hair. Sometimes he'd even sleep on top of me. And sometimes, I'd sleep on top of him. And I felt warm and safe and loved. We'd talk late into the night, early into the morning about the most trivial things, like they meant something.

Stuff like that convinced me that he must have loved me. Stuff like that and the rush I got from his touch was unlike anything I'd ever felt. And I didn't want it from anybody else. I'd be sitting in the middle of class sometimes and get all flustered and hot just thinking about his hands on me or having his body pressed against mine. I guess that's when I knew it would be him, though he probably knew it too long before I did.

He made me comfortable talking about and thinking about sex, making up jokes about the Devil Dog, the Scream Machine, the Mind Bender. When I'd say stuff like, "So you're going to bend my mind," he'd say, "Just let me know when you're ready to ride."

It was cute and childish and all that stuff being in love was back then. And I thought I'd left it back then until I saw him again.

Chapter Twelve – Her Story

"And the rest is history, right?"

Al's question pulled me back into the present. Of course, I hadn't told her any of the details that might have given me away. "If only," I said.

We sat there slurping and shaking our cups. Now seemed like a good time to change the subject, but curiosity got the best of me.

"So how did y'all meet? You and Curtis."

"In college," she said.

"College?" I was a little surprised. History repeats itself, I guess. Or rather, *her-story*, as it were. Here we go.

"I was a junior and he was taking a couple classes to finish his degree."

His degree?

"Computer science," she said. "Don't look so surprised. All Marines aren't jug heads, you know."

So now she's reading my mind? And it's Jar Head, dumb ass. Anyway, I said, "Please say you didn't meet at a frat party."

"Nope," she said.

I don't know why I got relief from that. "Good."

"At a probate show."

"Oh yeah," I said. "You're an AKA."

"Yeah," she said. "How did you know?"

I nodded toward her keys on the table. "One of my old roommates is an AKA. You kind of remind me of her."

"Oh. Cool," she said. "Anyway, the big sisters made me dress up in this tight leather dress and sing *Giving Him Something He Can Feel*, with my line sisters backing me up like En Vogue." Then she smiled again. "It was a trip."

This was getting worse. "You sing?"

"A little," she said, humbly, but I could tell was pleased to tell me about her hidden talent. "Anyway, you had to know me in college to get it. I was the geeky, wallflower type."

"Yeah, I know that feeling."

She stirred around in her cup before she spoke again. "I was a hot mess."

"Yeah?"

Then she had a flashback. A sullen flashback that wiped the smile completely off of her face. "I remember one night I overheard one of my roommates entertaining her company by telling him how homely I was. That hurt because I thought she was my friend. Then I heard him say, 'Damn,' and they laughed like I was Miss Jane from *The Beverly Hillbillies* or somebody."

"Damn," I said too. "Well, she was just jealous, you know. Hating and all that," I said, finding myself consoling her. Then I got really analytical. "She probably knew that her best years were already behind her."

"Right. In the twilight of her best years, putting me down was her way of making herself feel good."

"Exactly," I said.

That theory worked for the two of us. But really, who among us has the intuition to know when we are one of those whose best years are lived in high school? None of us knows if we'll be one of those who'll hit the wall by 18. And who would want to know that all of our potential and attention and adulation from the masses would be dried up before you're legally old enough to get into a club and buy your own drink?

"If that wasn't bad enough," Al continued, "I had to be kept awake by the sound of them having sex on the other side of that damn cardboard wall."

I tried to stay with her. "We had some pretty thin walls in my dorm too. Like toilet paper."

"He wasn't even her boyfriend," she recalled as she kept chunking her straw around in her cup.

Clearly, she wasn't ready to let it go just yet, so I hung on, too.

"Some of my roommates had those 'special friends' too," I told her. You know, one of those boys you couldn't call a boyfriend because all you did together was have sex. "Just creeping to and from each other's room when nobody but the roommates are supposed to know." People called it creeping before some comedian gave it a mainstream name, the Booty Call.

"When I was a freshman," she said, "I had this humongous crush on this football player. He was a fifth-year senior and he didn't even know I existed. And he had a girlfriend."

"They always do," I said.

"I guess the day I really knew I didn't stand a chance was when she walked by a table I was sitting at with a study group in the library one night right before finals. She knew one of the girls at my table, right? So she stopped and they started making all kinds of small talk. You know, talking about nothing."

"Uh huh," I said. Pretty much like we're doing now.

"When she walked away, my friend said, 'I hate to burst your bubble, but did you see that big ass hickie on her neck?'"

"Damn," I said. "Was it like all that?"

"I guess so," she said, sighing. "I didn't even notice it because I was too busy trying to figure out what she had that I didn't have."

"Been there." There now.

Did she mean to tell me that hickie girl wasn't the standard issue light-skinned, narrow-featured female that's been in since the beginning of time? Sorry, but girls like Al get only so much sympathy from me. We might have been kindred wallflowers, but here's where we parted company. If old girl had something Al didn't, it was probably because she was a darker skinned, brainy sister who had more on the ball than long hair. More power to her.

"Anyway, the bubble burst. And I fantasized about hickies I would never get."

"That's too bad," I said. "His loss."

Then she looked at her wedding ring and pepped up. "Talk about God's grace and unanswered prayers."

"Everything happens for a reason." I shrugged, not nearly as self-satisfied or peppy.

"That next semester, everybody on campus was talking about how she was going around, burning everybody with herpes."

Well, shit. Can somebody ever write me a happy ending? Now the sister on the ball had to be hot. Hell, she probably got it from the guy you had a crush on.

All I could think to say was, "Hmph. Terrible shame." Back then, we all still thought herpes was the end of the world, and that AIDS was the gay man's disease that Eddie Murphy made fun of in *Raw*.

"That's how I ended up messing around with Tony." He was the head of the Psych Department.

The fling was over almost as suddenly as it supposedly started. She'd met him for quickies in his office—there was a couch, go figure—until he finally lost interest and started screwing one of the secretaries. She glossed over it like it was no big deal, all while managing to blame the circumstances of her crushed crush for her indiscretions with a serial philanderer.

Oh yeah, blame it on the dark, brainy sister. Like she was the one that turned you into a home-wrecking hussy. The thought was barely out of my head, when I reminded myself that that situation was not completely unlike my own. Suddenly, I found myself back on the moral fence.

"And it just turned out to be a small fling."

A small fling, huh? See, this I why I couldn't stay feeling bad about fucking her man. Serves her right. Bad karma and all that. She brought it on herself!

"For him anyway," she added with a shrug. Then she said, "You know, I went home crying to my mama and she had no sympathy."

"Hmmm," I said.

"Talking about, 'a small fling just like a small box of matches. Fire is fire. No such thing as that small foolishness.'"

"Or a little herpes," I added.

"Yeah," she said. "Just like that."

We both kind of laughed, her at her foolishness, me because I was uncomfortable.

"I'd never do something like that now," she said. "You know what goes around, comes around. I was just young and stupid."

I guess that makes me old and stupid.

"You know how it is," she said. "How you go to school already convinced that Mr. Somebody-to-Do-Me-Right is just there waiting for you."

Talk about schoolgirl idealistic ways.

"And instead you just end up with Mr. Somebody-Waiting-to-Do-Me."

"Hell," I said. "Don't feel like the Lone Ranger. I couldn't buy a date."

She smiled at that.

"Our phone was always ringing for someone else," I said. "All during the day. In the middle of the night."

"During the *Young and the Restless*," she chimed in.

"The only time I got calls in the middle of the night was when someone needed an essay or a term paper written at the last minute. The only time guys came to see me at all was when someone needed help with their homework. How do you like that?"

By now, she was too busy smiling to notice my full on lament. Suddenly, I had the urge to break that smiling shit up, so I tossed out another question.

"So, how is it that a psych major ends up working behind a makeup counter?" I always figured that for the kind of field that required an advanced degree.

"I was going to be, am going to be a child psychologist."

"And?"

"I wanted to be married," she said. "School and jobs will always be there, but a good man at the right time is a matter of opportunity."

"So it seems," I said.

"My mama said to wait for the man who will love me long after the novelty wears off. And so I did," she said with a distinctive air of triumph.

Wait a minute. "You've only been with two men in your whole life?"

She nodded. "I waited for him, and he found me, just like my mom said he would."

Well, shit.

"Curtis and I agreed that we'd get married, and I would put grad school on hold until he got closer to retirement. That way, I wouldn't have to be in the middle of school, and he'd have to move, and I'd have to drop out or try to transfer credits just to be with him."

Curtis and you agreed, huh? More like he decided and you complied. It doesn't take a psych major to know that when a person says, *So-and-So and me this*, or *So-and-So and me that*, that it was So-and-So's idea in the first place.

"But you're young," I said. "And you had plenty of time to get married. Why couldn't you just finish school and then get married?"

She chuckled. "I don't know. I love him, and I guess I just wasn't willing to take the risk. Long distance relationships are hard enough, much less long engagements. I've got friends who have been engaged for years, and still not married because somebody still had something left to do before the time is right. Some of them have had babies in the meantime, and still not married. I didn't want that to be me. Good men and marriage proposals don't just come by every day for us."

I guess she had a point. Marriage proposals are rare enough, let alone marriage proposals from men who are actually ready to get married, not those proposing out of guilt or under some kind of duress from family or friends. And heaven preserve us from the ones who propose with zero intention of getting married, just to pacify us for a little while longer. Sometimes, years longer.

"That's true." I told her about a couple of guys in my past who wanted to marry me, but that I knew then as much as I know now that I didn't want to be with them. "Why marry somebody you don't love, or," in her case, "when you're not ready, just for fear of not getting married?" I can't make sense of that. Maybe she couldn't make sense of me taking that kind of chance with my future.

"Girl, of course I was ready. Women are born ready and waiting," she clarified. "School's not going anywhere, so why take that risk?"

"Well, you know what they say," I said. "If it was meant to be, y'all would have ended up together anyway."

"Maybe so. But you know how rare it is for black women to get married nowadays. I feel like if you want to be married, it's about compromise."

"I guess that depends on what you compromise," I said. Now, all of this is coming from a place in me before I became the great compromiser that I am. The person who would have said, *Naw. Naw. I can do without that for now. I want, deserve and will have this or that, and I won't be settling.* And that included love.

"We also agreed that we'd wait to have children until after I finished school and got my career off the ground," she offered up. "So he compromised, too. He wants kids, but he agreed to wait. Love means compromise, sometimes."

"Sometimes," I conceded.

"I guess Curtis just came along at the right time in my life," she said. "When I wasn't expecting, you know."

I just said, "Mmmhmm." As much as I tried to empathize about falling in and out of unexpected situations, and I could empathize, I still couldn't get past the singing thing. "You sing," I said again, my jealousy rearing its head.

"I'm no Aretha Franklin," she said, modestly.

"Yeah, well, who is?" I said. "So, you serenaded him, and the rest is history, huh?" I tried to act like I was thinking it was sweet, but it was really making me sick.

"Him and about a hundred other guys standing around whistling and cat calling at us," she said. "But yeah, I guess that's about the way it started."

What the hell was his old ass doing at a probate show anyway? He was half-way to thirty already when she was just barely twenty. I did the math quickly in my head.

"We dated for forever," she said.

Six years.

"Yeah. There was a whole bunch of stuff about how he'd been hurt before by someone he thought was 'The One'. I thought he'd never ask me to marry him, but he did. And I was ready."

"Yep," I said back. So in six years of dating, she couldn't find time to complete her masters and Ph.D? Whatever.

"And it all started at that stupid probate show."

"Amazing what a tight dress, high heels, a little makeup will do for you, huh?"

She didn't notice my insult. "Add a good weave and a little well-placed wax in a few spots and you got a super model, right?"

Or did she? Was this heifer trying to be funny?

Then she smiled and asked, "Did I ever tell you how he proposed to me?"

"No," I said. "I'm sure I would've remembered that." I tried to smile like I really wanted to hear it, because I knew it was coming anyway.

"We went to this spot near campus where they had a poetry & spoken word night," she started.

Aw, Lord. She's going to give me the verbatim version.

"He knew I liked that kind of stuff, so he took me there on my birthday, right before he got orders to come here."

"Okay," I said, resisting the urge to tap the table to say get on with it.

"Then the next thing I knew, he was up on stage, reading a poem. Well, sort of. It was so sweet I just sat there and cried."

"A poem?" I asked. He never read me poetry.

"Yeah. It was so sweet."

Yeah, yeah. I got it. Sweet.

Then she started to recite it, dramatically pausing after every few words.

I sat there with one elbow on the table, with my face propped up with my hand, my mouth partially stretched into what looked like a smile.

Finally, she got to the ending with, "'No, I did not come here to rap, act, or sing-

But I did buy a ring.

It's one carat and flawless-

and its left a brotha drawsless

but my baby is worth it.

I can't believe I'm getting down on one knee-

Andra Lyn Peggy Moore,

Will you marry me?'" She was nearly in tears then.

Peggy? Bitch, how many damn names have you got? I tried not to flinch my nose up at her, though I doubt she'd've noticed. "That is really sweet," I said, my mouth still stretched across my face. "Peggy, huh?"

"My other middle name," she explained. Something about her face struck me that she was one of those people who used to be fat as a kid, and then lost a lot of weight at fat camp, but still kept the face fat.

"Hmmm," I said. Time to end this torture. Who the hell has two middle names, anyway? "Okay, I've had enough," I said, as if I was referring to the lemonade. "You ready to go? We got about fifteen minutes to get there."

There I was, taking her to my favorite salon—actually, she was driving the Anniversary-Mobile, and I was along for the ride—to get all prettied up for a date with her husband. I must have been tripping. What's worse is that I'd gotten her started reminiscing about her own glory days of college and ended up having to hear her proposal story, on I couldn't help thinking should have been mine.

Among other things, she'd run track at USC Beaufort for three years until she tore something and missed a big NCAA meet. No wonder her legs were her best feature, though they still wouldn't win no prize, in my opinion. I can't believe she ran track with those chunky, tree-trunk ankles.

Anyway, there we were, a former Olympic hopeful, and me, the anti-G.I., who whines about running a couple of miles on a PT test. Then she came out with, "You know, I have some the best memories about college, don't you?"

"Mmmhmm," I said. Okay, Flo-Jo, a minute ago, you were ready to go crawl under a rock next to Jane Hathaway. Pledged your way to instant self-esteem, and suddenly you got great memories. Right now, my most vivid memory about college is losing my virginity—to your husband. And the more I thought about it, the smaller I felt, wishing it was a big blur. But I just said, "Yeah, me too." The truth is, I'm still waiting for the best years of my life.

She turned up the radio. "Oh, I love this song! It's so real."

I just looked at the radio and then looked straight ahead.

And there she sat, driving and singing. She would like the worst Whitney Houston song ever made. I sat there listening, or trying not to, while she sang along, "'Same script, different cast.' Oooh! Sang it y'all."

When we got to the salon, we talked about hair cuts, highlights, hot wax and French pedicures, but I guess we were both just thinking about our private college things. Her, probably thinking about serenading her prince, and me, thinking my own thoughts.

I could only speculate about how beautiful and romantic their first time was, and I'd rather not. So I just sat there with my hands in hot mittens and my feet covered in paraffin wax, remembering mine. The romantic, the unromantic, the awkward. And how much I love him. I mean, loved. I mean, loving how good the sex is between us now.

The esthetician led me away from the pedicure chair, with cotton stuck between my toes, to the waxing room. As I climbed on the table, I decided that sex is probably not what I should have been thinking about at a time when someone is so close to my private parts with hot wax. I tried to distract myself as I lay there on the waxing table getting the hair ripped from my body. It felt like I was getting hot flashes. So I shifted my thoughts to the here and now.

God, it must mean something for us to have found each other again after all that time. He told me I was special and I believed him. He called me his soulmate.

Okay Lord. What's the lesson in all this? Why did I ever bother to reflect on all this if it was just going to depress me?

I started getting mad, and that helped me concentrate on something besides whether or not the wax was warm enough or too hot. Finally, the comfort came. I calmed down and the comfort came. I'm talking emotional comfort. Waxing is anything but comfortable.

Maybe this wasn't the ideal relationship, but he makes me feel beautiful when I'm with him. He holds me in his arms while we watch old movies and TV shows. We laugh at the same commercials, because we both like them, not because he's trying to like what I like to get me to like him. We dance slow to no music. I listen to his so-called recruiting problems, and his listens to my MEPS drama, and sometimes, a lot of times, we just fall asleep talking. There's a special connection that I get from his touch that makes me melt from the inside, and that's worth more than physical contact and stimulation. Whatever is wrong with our relationship, I don't think you can fake this kind of connection. Not for this long.

Thank God that I'll never be one of those who never feels special, nor one of those who settles out of fear of being left out. Some people may never even feel love from somebody they genuinely love back. Some people go through life wishing, trying and wading through a swamp of countless frogs, waiting for and hoping for the prince to come and pull them out. I fell into that trap more than once, letting men put their hands and mouths where they shouldn't. Some give up and settle for being touched and held and physically stimulated by someone who leaves them emotionally cold, sick and empty. Dead, like a gutted fish on newspaper.

I'd rather be by myself than have hands on me that made me feel like that. Only problem was, the hands I wanted on me were reserved for someone else, or at least, they should have been. Wrong or right, anybody with any sense should know that if special comes your way, you take it.

Somewhere in the next room was that someone else, the one who had it all. She had it all. All that I wanted she had. And I would never be the one. And I hated her for it. Then I told myself, *You know what? Fuck her.* That bitch got my husband, and all this is a second chance from God for me to get him back. That must be the plan. Anything I have to do to get him back, serves her ass right.

We left the salon and she dropped me off at home. Then she went on her date. I sat in the house making some really good eggnog, which turned out exceptionally well. The more rum, the better. And if it didn't make me forget about being home alone while they were out acting like the happy couple, it was spiked enough to fool me into thinking I felt better.

Chapter Thirteen – Merry Christmas, Baby

A I must have really fucked the shit out of Curtis, because I had so much time on my hands over the next few days that I taught myself how to make Christmas wreaths. I made one for my door, and two for the double doors at the MEPS.

It was about a week or so after I'd apologized to Curtis for calling him toxic. I could feel something was going to finally change for us. I'd spent the entire year wishing for a change. Praying for it. Waiting, very patiently, for it. Finally, it came.

Or, more specifically, it didn't come. My period was two months late, and while there's definitely an upside to no period, a couple of over-the-counter pregnancy tests can add lot more weight to the downside.

I argued back and forth with myself, thinking maybe I should, maybe I shouldn't tell him. People say you should be careful what you wish for. My problem was I needed to be careful how I wished for it.

I sat on the floor waiting by the door for the twenty minutes it should have taken him to get there. Then I sat at the dining table with the phone in front of me, waiting for it to ring, waiting for Curtis to call and say he was still on his way. I thought about paging him or calling again, but then I thought not. I could think better when he wasn't there, but all I could think about was bad timing. Then again, *Anything it takes*, right? Love is love.

It was December 13th, eleven months to the day after we'd started this affair. Eleven months of messing around with a married man. Maybe this was my chance to light a fire under his ass to make that move. Damn, he just needed to get there.

Finally, there was a knock on the door. Except it wasn't just a knock. It was a KNOCK. Like three hard raps on the door that preceded a battering ram kind of knock.

Okay, maybe I shouldn't have used the words, "really urgent" on his voice mail.

I opened the door, ready to ease his mind when he just blurted out, "What the hell is this?" He barely crossed the threshold and then pushed a partially unfolded wad of paper that used to be one of his business cards in front of me. I glanced down at it. It had his wife's cell phone number written on it.

"Hey," I greeted him as if he hadn't said anything. "I need to talk to you about something."

"Talk to me about this," he demanded, referring to the phone number.

It took me a second to figure out what he was talking about. I stumbled over my words. "I—um. Babe, I don't know. Can— can we not talk about that now?" I stammered trying to stay on track.

"What the fuck are you trying to do to me?"

"I—nothing," I said. "I haven't done anything. I—need to tell you something." I pulled at him to lead him to the sofa, but he just stood there.

"Tell me how the fuck this number— Why the fuck is she calling you?"

I sat down alone and started massaging my temple and then rubbed my eyes.

"Curtis, what do you want me to say? I just—Don't—"

"Just, what? Don't, what? Say something," he said, crossing his arms.

"Don't make it into something it's not," I said. "I didn't do anything."

I don't know when I'd planned to tell him that his wife and I were friends, if you could call it that, but now was definitely not the time. Besides, we weren't really friends. "I don't want to go into it right now. It's really a long story."

"Don't play with me, Sebrina. You know whose number this is. And you know where I got it from. What kind of sick-ass game are you playing? You fucking stalking my wife or something?"

Oh, now he's calling me crazy. "No, I'm not stalking your wife," I said, but then I decided to be a smart ass. "How is old Petunia anyway?"

He looked confused at first and then figured it out. "It's Peggy," he said. "And for you to think you know so much, she doesn't go by that name anyway."

"Aw, Peggy, Petunia, Piggy," I said, getting angry. "It's all the same, ain't it?" Don't get mad at me because she's got a chunky face. And tree trunk ankles.

He squinted his eyes at me. "Look," he said, "You won't be disrespecting my wife. Get that straight right now."

"Disrespect?" I repeated. He had a lot nerve to even let the word come out of his mouth. "What do you call what you're doing? Talk to me about respect the next time you're trying to eat another hole up in my—."

"Shut up!" he cut me off, and it actually shook me a little. "What's up with this shit?" he asked, unfolding the card completely, and then wadding it back up and stuffing it in his pocket.

"You wrote it down, smart-ass" I said. "You tell me. Why the hell did it take you all this damn time to figure out whose number that is?"

Where did he find that crumpled-ass card anyway? And why the hell hadn't he thrown it away?

"Why is she calling you?"

"I don't— Look, we just talk sometimes," I said, not making things any better. "Come sit by me, baby." I patted on the sofa. "I want to talk to you, okay?"

He walked over to the sofa and stood over me and started asking questions faster than I could think of the answers. "About what? What? Y'all friends now?" He had a right to be skeptical, but he was being a jerk about it.

"Not really," I said. "Well, sort of." I looked up at him. "I wish you would stop making it into something it's not."

"Well, which is it?" he asked. "You talk about me?"

I shouldn't have answered, but I said, "Not the way you're thinking. I promise."

"How in the fuck do you know the way I'm thinking?" He didn't move.

I kept talking. "Babe, I wouldn't ever do anything to hurt you. I'd do anything for you."

"Then how the fuck do you know what she know and what she don't?"

I didn't answer.

"What the hell have you been saying about me?"

I tried to stand up in the small crack of space between him and the sofa and was starting to say something like, "Baby, I just need you to—," when he pushed me back down by my shoulder and took a step back, like he was daring me to get back up.

I looked up at him and felt my chest burning and my eyebrows wrinkling up. Suddenly I was hot all over, and my heart was beating so fast. I heard myself say, "Don't you ever put your hands on me like that." I stood up again and walked toward the door and started to open it. He walked up behind me and pushed it shut and leaned over me.

"This was a mistake," I said softly.

"Damn right, it was," he said, not moving.

"Get your paranoid ass out of my house," I said, trying to hold myself together.

"I'm telling you," he said again. "Don't fucking play with me."

"I'm not," I said. "Now get out. Now."

"Damnit!" He drew back and then slammed his fist against the door. I know his hand must have hurt, but he didn't even flinch. His eyes were red. He put his finger in my face. "Don't make me— Fuck it. Just—just move. Move!" He brushed me aside and opened the door. He grumbled something like, "Dumb bitch," or "Son-of-a-bitch," as he walked out. He didn't seem to notice the water damming up in my eyes. I'd never seen him punch anything in my life, and certainly nothing so close to my face. This was the father of my child and he'd just stomped out of my house without me even bringing it up. Oh God, please help me.

If only I had been strong enough to say no that first time. Or the second time. Or anytime. What was I thinking, sleeping with him without a condom? It was all a big mistake.

All at once, the stress was all on me, thinking about what I had to do next, or not do next to keep from losing him again, because I couldn't take losing him again.

Shit, what just happened? I just got him back, and now he was mad at me about some bullshit. Shit that I should have told him about a long time ago. It was just a mistake. I mean, a misunderstanding. Now he was really pissed at me. And my dumb ass just threw him out. What was I doing?

All I could think was, *He's really pissed at me. And it's all that bitch's fault. I gotta do something to fix this. Fast. I just got him back.*

I called him twenty-eight times and left "I'm sorry, can we talk?" messages, with the "Baby, please call me back" at the end of each one, but he never answered or returned my calls. I thought long and hard about what to do. I made a few more phone calls. You know, the one to the places that fix situations like this. Finally, I had an appointment to go fix it. Look at what this bitch is making me do.

I don't think I slept at all that night.

All of a sudden, from what I thought was a fixed state of non-sleep, my nerves started throwing me all over the house, from my bedroom to living room, and back to the bedroom. Then, from bed the floor, just trying to shake off, knock off, pray off whatever this thing was that was strangling the life out of me.

And whatever that thing was, Curtis was holding it, even if he didn't know it, like a weight pressing up and down on my chest. And every time it felt like it would let up for me to barely breathe, I would just shake, and shake. "God, get him off of me. Please, Lord, make it stop. Make it stop." But the shaking wouldn't stop and the tears wouldn't stop. "God, please, please, please!" I wanted to hit something.

My throat drew tight and it hurt to speak. "You know I'm hurting, Lord. Please get him off of me. Off my heart. Out of my mind. Lord. I don't want to want him. I don't want to love him. Lord, if you love me, please take this off of me." The throbbing in my head moved its way through my whole body. My legs, back, arms, hands and feet even hurt, and the pain didn't go away. I thought it would if I could just stop crying. "Oh, God. I want him so bad. I know it's wrong, Lord, but why won't you make him love me enough to leave her?" And I curled up into a ball, pissed off and pitiful at the same time, because God wasn't listening.

I wanted it to stop. I wanted the feelings to stop. I wanted to hit something that wouldn't hurt my hand. I got up on my knees and I just rocked for nothing. My eyes hurt. The hair at my temples hurt. "Make it stop, make it stop," I said, in little whispers. Then I lay my face on the floor and beat with my fists. "God! If he wasn't supposed to be mine, Lord, why'd you let me think he was going to be mine? Now he's gone!" Like that was

God's fault. Why wasn't He listening to me?

I know I sounded confused, but I wasn't confused about what I should have been praying, no more than I was confused about what I shouldn't have been doing.

Chapter Fourteen – Just Fine, Thanks

I had my first of two appointments scheduled for that next afternoon. It was a dismal, misty Tuesday with cold, spitting rain. This first appointment would be a consultation, an *Are you sure this is what you want to do* type of thing. Of course I was sure.

I had the morning shift at the MEPS, the opening shift, at five-thirty. Actually, I got to work closer to six and still I was mad about that. I was mad about everything.

The first friendly face I saw belonged to Mr. Allen, retired Air Force, God love him. Mr. A. has to be the nicest person in the MEPS, if not the nicest person I ever met. He was the kind of person who would graciously offer you half of his Spam® sandwich, if you liked Spam, and whenever we had office potlucks, his recipes were always Spam-inspired.

He also has that rare gift of asking you how you're doing, and genuinely caring about your answer. His voice is always warm, and his eyes are always smiling, even early in the morning. While I'm certainly no fan of Spam, I am a fan of Mr. A., and particularly a fan of the way his facial expression managed to tell you, *it's all small stuff, so don't sweat it.* Still, I replied to him with the standard line *just fine, thanks,* days. It was another one of those days.

Mr. A. worked in the Testing Section with me and three other military TAs, Sergeant First Class Bennett, the section supervisor, Petty Officer First Class Tubbs, a senior TA with the most experience in the section, and Staff Sergeant Mitchell, who basically lived part-time at the MEPS, because he was having problems with his pregnant girlfriend, who was trying to pressure him into marriage. Of course, and nobody was supposed to know that Mitch was staying at the MEPS after hours, but everybody knew except the commander and the first sergeant.

****

Two days later, I was on my way to my operation. Another cold day, with a dark sky, but no mist or rain. It usually took forever to get around that damn 285 in mid-morning, but not this time. I was there in no time. Early, even.

I went inside, checked in, sat down. I found myself sitting in a drab beige waiting room with textured wall paper, a room that even with windows and climate-control, was too small to breathe any decent amount of air. Even so, I managed to keep sitting there.

Okay, so I did entertain the thought that being the mother of Curtis' child would keep a small piece of him attached to me, but I wasn't really serious. And yes, I did get a kick out of pretending to crack Al's face with the news that we'd been sleeping together all that time. But they were just thoughts. Now I just felt sick and small, reminding myself that if she got him, it wasn't meant to be.

It's just as well. I wasn't about to kid myself into thinking that he would leave her for me just because I was pregnant. If he was going to leave her for me, he'd have done it already. In fact, he'd have never left me in the first place. He'd have never married her in the first place if he ever meant any of that bullshit about us being soul mates.

I frowned, picturing myself turning into that miserable, hurtful bitch who uses a baby for leverage. You know, one of those women always trying to move or manipulate a situation into her own selfish direction. I could see myself becoming a user if it meant getting closer to Curtis. If I had that baby, anything I would *need* for the baby, I'd have to go through that bitch to get to Curtis, and though it would be impossible for me to resent her any more than I already did, Curtis would hate me for it, and nobody who really loves their child would want to raise it that way. So I might as well be right where I was.

It was taking forever. Maybe I shouldn't have made the appointment on a work day. Maybe I should have taken a day of leave. Maybe I shouldn't be here, but then I'd covered that ground already. Anyway, they needed to hurry up.

I started thinking about girls telling stories about it in high school, saying it doesn't fuck with your mind or stay with you, or take away a small part of your sanity. If I wasn't sure they were full of shit then, I was sure now. Or maybe the tell-tale heart doesn't beat as loudly in the head of a 15-year old as it does in a 31-year old. Add to that the mind-numbing tick of a biological clock and the nerve-wrecking clamor of phantom wedding bells that toll not for thee, and you've got me, as close to crazy as I ever wanted to be, sitting here, waiting my turn.

I glanced at the woman sitting next to me, looking like she was waiting for a job interview. There I was in sweats, and she looked like she's... Ugh, God. Another light-skinned, long-haired version of that bitch, except this one had long sculpted legs that didn't look like they should be planted in Piedmont Park.

This bitch didn't look at all nervous or scared or remorseful. She's probably done this before. I couldn't stop looking at her. I remember thinking, she's gorgeous, like a model or something. And I was sure she knew it. She had that *I know I'm all that* look about her. All self-assured and shit.

Then, as if that's all I needed, Miss Universe cleared her throat. What could she possibly have to say to me?

"This is taking forever, huh?"

What a dumb-ass question. Shouldn't this be a time for quiet reflection? Soul searching? Silence?

"Uh, I'm not sure how long it takes. This is my first time doing something like this."

"Mine too," she said.

"Really?" I muttered. Okay, that was hateful.

She either didn't notice or didn't care, because she went on. "My boyfriend doesn't want children," she said. "Not yet. We made this decision together."

"I see," I said as I gave her a look like I didn't give a damn. She didn't notice that either. Where was he, I wondered.

"We didn't plan this, of course."

I still didn't care.

"I've been dealing with him for four years, and he's still not ready. I didn't think bringing a baby into the situation would help."

"Hmm," I said back. This is the part where I should have reminded her that this is really none of my business, but I let her keep going. At least her chatter drowned out the voices in my own head.

"All this time, and we're still not married. He wants to wait. I mean, what is he waiting on, you know?" Her voice was a little weaker now than when she started talking.

"I know, all right."

"Oh yeah," she said in afterthought. "My name is Sarah." She extended her hand across her lap and we shook and I pretended to half-smile.

"Okay."

Then she said, "Nice to meet you, Kay."

I didn't bother to correct her, but I thought, yeah right. Your name is

Sarah like my name is Kay.

"It's not really, is it?"

"Hmm?" I asked, thinking for a second she'd read my mind.

"Not really nice to meet. Here."

I sighed and shrugged. "Another time or place I guess."

"In another time or place you couldn't have told me that I wasn't ready to be somebody's mama," she said back. "I so wanted to have a baby," she babbled on. "But it's like what they say, right? Be careful what you ask for."

"Tell me about it," I said.

And so she did. "I used to get mad at my friends in school for playing the baby game. It never gets the man."

I thought about Floyd and Mitch. I don't guess I would really say *never*. I couldn't believe this shit. I tried to tune her out, but her voice kept fading back and forth into my consciousness.

"You'd think they didn't learn anything from the generations of women who play this game."

"And lost," I jumped in again. This babbling loser.

"I know, right? And waaay before them."

"I guess so," I mumbled. I glanced at the door that led to the operating rooms. Why didn't someone come? Where was the nurse calling my name? I just wanted to get this over with. What the hell am I doing? I am not this kind of person. How did I get here? Is she still talking?

"Then again, I never expected to be still single after 30."

"Hmmm," I said.

"Just turned 30 last week," she kind of smiled as she said it. "Happy birthday to me, right?"

"Uh, yeah."

She sighed and changed the subject. "What time is your appointment?"

"About ten minutes ago." I said. "Yours?"

"About 40 minutes from now. I needed to get here before I changed my mind."

Since when did grown people start telling time like that? Ten minutes ago. Forty minutes from now. Shit.

I had to be at work in a few hours. I'd whined my way back onto the eleven-to-six shift, but I'd swapped it today for Mitch's two-to-close, which meant I would be the late person tonight. Men are so easy, sometimes.

My leg started to twitch. "Guess we're a little behind schedule."

"Yeah. Maybe the doctor got picked off in the parking lot," she said back.

"Uh, that would be bad," I said. "What's that about?"

"Sorry," she said. Then her leg started twitching. "I guess I'm just a little, you know."

"Yes, Ma'am, I do."

We both sat there fidgeting, feeling, you know.

"It's just that, I mean, if I wasn't sitting in here, I'd probably be somewhere driving around with a pro-life sticker on my car." She sighed again. "I always believed that if I could make it through college without getting pregnant, then I was just gonna have a baby, whenever it happened. Period. Then when this happened, and I'm damn a week into 30, I felt like I needed my ass whipped." She looked down at the floor.

"Don't you trust him?" I interrupted.

"I used to," she paused, "until I told him and he said 'I hope it ain't mine." Then she looked pissed off, like she could burn a hole in the floor. "I just don't think I'm as ready as I thought I was."

I nodded and a silence followed. Finally, I added, "Well, I've always been raised to believe that this is wrong. But I just don't see the reasoning behind hurting or killing doctors when you say you want to preserve life. Now, that's kind of hypocritical, I think." Just then I felt a warm rush of something pushing the words out of my mouth. "I mean, I have values. I just think that people who go around picketing and blowing up buildings, and beating up doctors, and spending their days coming up with clever phrases to justify their actions are just as much trying to play God as the people they're protesting."

She sighed, like she was taking a breath for me.

"I mean, if you really give a damn about me as a Christian, just pray for me, and leave me the hell alone."

"Do you pray?'

What kind of a question is that? Of course I pray. "Of course, I pray," I said, half annoyed.

"Do you believe it?" Her voice suddenly changed, like she was someone else.

I didn't answer.

"I mean, do you trust him?" she asked.

"Trust who? Curtis or God?" I looked her in the face.

She suddenly had this strangely peaceful smile on her face. "Who do you think?"

"I used to," I said, not bothering to clarify my answer.

"How old are you, if you don't mind me asking?"

I did mind. "Twenty-two," I lied.

"Right out of college, huh?"

"And none the wiser."

"What major?"

"Psychology." Might as well lie some more.

"You look so young," she said, wistfully.

"Mmmhmm. Get that a lot."

"Well, you have way more time to start a family." She started to trail off as she talked.

"Sometimes, we just have to do what we have to do." It sounded like almost a whisper when she finished.

"It's not like I'm over 30 and need to worry about my chances of ever having a baby again, right?" I made a joke of myself, even though she wouldn't get it.

"Yeah, I know," she said softly.

"You know what?" I realized what I'd said. "I didn't mean that. I mean, that wasn't meant to say you wouldn't ever have babies after 30."

"No, I know," she said.

"People have abortions all the time and have healthy babies later," I went on.

"I know."

"I mean, I wanted to trust him, but I waited and waited for him to come to me, so we could talk about it, and he could tell me that I was making a mistake and all that, but he never did."

"Yes, I know," she sort of chanted, like she was having a conversation with someone else.

"I would have delivered some time around the 4th of July," I sighed again, as if she was still listening.

She just said, "I know."

"Excuse me?"

"Excuse me," she said back, as if we'd just bumped carts at the grocery store.

Just then, a stout black woman with a short salt-and-pepper afro stood at the counter behind the glass, and called me by my fake last name.

"I know," again, said Sarah, sitting next to me. Then she just jumped up and walked toward the door.

What? Where the hell was she going, after I done spent the last 20 minutes working out my nerves about this shit? I know her old ass ain't leaving, I thought, forgetting for a moment that she was actually younger than me. What the hell was she going to do with the baby of a man who didn't even care about her ass? I looked after her as she walked out. She just got up and left. She left?

The fat lady with the thinning hair on the sides called my name again. Why is she rushing me all of a sudden?

Where the hell is Sarah going? What? Suddenly, she had it all figured out and this bitch didn't bother to share the answer with me? See, that's why the heifer reminded me of Al in the first place. Selfish wench.

Again, the fat lady sang my name.

I wanted to say, *Stop calling me, you stupid bitch, and give me a minute to think about what the hell just happened,* but she just looked dead at me, like she recognized me from somewhere. Then she cocked her head to the side, like she was checking out my shoes. I looked away from her. I didn't know what just happened. I didn't know anything. How could he know me and still pick her? That son-of-a-bitch. I'm the one with his child. God, please.

Was I having an out of body experience? Was I dreaming again?

The nurse called my name again. And then I saw straight enough to do what had to be done.

Chapter Fifteen – Things on the Side

I'd like to pretend the memory doesn't stay with me. I'd like to say that it's all about lying up on a table, putting my feet in stirrups, closing my eyes and being hosed out by a giant vacuum cleaner that sucks out little clumps, clots and masses of blood until it's over. Then they give you juice and cookies until you're steady enough to leave. But this is not a Red Cross Blood Drive.

At a place like this, they might pat you on the head or rub your hand for a small dose of comfort before they remind you that they really need to free up the space for the next lamb to be butchered. First, you wait forever. Then you prep forever, as if they're giving you more time to change your mind. Then you go into it like it's nothing. Up on a table, feet in stirrups, like a pap smear. And then they vacuum you out. I guess it's not really an operation, but I think of it that way.

It's a quick, painfully painless, thought-sucking, horribly simple procedure. They let you stay there for a little while because you're weak, but I'm sure they'd rather you have someone there with you to take you away. It is rather like giving blood or plasma, except for that whole thought-sucking, feet up in stirrups thing, and the juice and cookies rip off. Just a little light-headedness. And that's about how I felt. A little lighter in the head.

I went to work and was glad that the MEPS was nearly cleared out of people who worked there. And thank God, it was a slow night for night testers. I stood most of the time, because it was less uncomfortable to me than sitting down. I felt like I was walking around in a giant diaper, because you can't use tampons right away after something like that. Even worse, I ended up having to scrub a spot out of one of the chairs in my office because the damn diaper leaked. I drove home, mad, sad and spotty. Now I know how babies in dirty diapers must feel.

I guess I'll spend the rest of my life wondering if people know. They probably do. Somebody always knows. They just act like they don't. But how could they? Nobody knows about my situation. I was just being silly and paranoid. But from now on, I'd wonder about it. And maybe one day I'd tell somebody. Or maybe I'd spend the rest of my life just pretending it never happened.

I used to tell myself that if I ended up pregnant by the time I was thirty, I was going to have me a baby, just like Sarah who'd sat next to me. Just like Sarah, I wouldn't want to take any chances, because they say it's harder to have babies after thirty. So, either way, baby. Come what may, or so I'd said. But it's just not that easy, especially when somebody else's man is involved. All this shit in my life and all I could think about was whether or not he would come back to me.

When I finally got home, I showered, put on a new diaper and for some reason, went straight to my closet. I looked down at some of the shoes and actually cocked my head to the side thinking about how some of them looked like they'd gone out of style and come back in after all this time. Others, it was just time to get rid of them. Then I thought, for what? So I can regret having done it later? My head was in some crazy place that I didn't like.

I finally got in the bed and spooned up against my stack of giant pillows on Curtis' side. I held one of the giant pillows in front of me like it was a teddy bear and lay there waiting for sleep.

"I'd be somebody's mama if it wasn't for him," I said. What was I saying? It was because of him that I would have been a mama. And it was because of him that I wasn't. I wanted my mama. Not to lecture me, chastise, or advise me. I wanted her to hold me close, and tell me it was gonna be all right, even if it wasn't.

Then, if that wasn't enough, I had to be awakened by Elliott the neighbor's pre-Christmas I-got-the-blues music. "Oh, give me a damn break!"

I threw the covers off and stomped over to his apartment and banged on the door. I stood there, thinking to myself how rude it was of him to keep up that kind of ruckus on a work night, even if it was early in the evening. "Comfort of a Man" blared through the door. He came to the door in his bare feet with no shirt on, and he was so polite when he invited me in, I could have punched him. I remember focusing on how perfectly sculpted his eyebrows were. At first I stood at the threshold with my eyes squinted and my mouth fixed to say something really ugly. "No, thanks," I said. "I just had a really shitty day. Can you give me a break? The music?"

I guess I shouldn't have said I had a shitty day, because then he became so cordial it would have been too rude to refuse. Elliott was about 6'2", athletically lean, with dark hair, chiseled features, dark eyes, a gorgeous Kennedy-esque smile, and he was wearing the hell out of a goatee. He could have been a Calvin Klein model or rock star or something, but he was just the gay guy who lived across the way.

I'd only been in his apartment once before. When he first moved in, he came over to borrow a sauce pan. He'd said he'd felt like cooking spaghetti, that a home wasn't really broken in until you'd done two things at least once in it—cooking was one of them—but he didn't have anything to boil the noodles in. When he didn't return it after a couple of weeks, I went to borrow it back, kind of like Coleman, a coworker and neighbor who lived in the same apartment complex, had to come back to my place to borrow her iron back, after I'd had it all week.

Elliott's place wasn't immaculate, but it wasn't a dump either. I thought it odd that he didn't have any pots and pans in his house, but he said he didn't believe in waste. He said the only things he really needed were a toaster, microwave and a coffee maker. Funny, the things different people consider wasteful. I was staring at about 165 pounds of tall, dark and wasteful square in his eyes.

When I went inside, the room was practically vibrating and he was playing a movie with the sound turned down. He offered me a drink and I accepted. I didn't really feel like being alone.

After about a half bottle of wine, he'd told me that the sound of Stephanie Mills' singing was soothing him after an unexpected break up, and I'd in turn, told him all about my shitty day. I found myself not caring that I barely knew him, but just glad that he acted like he wanted to listen. And that he kept the drinks coming.

"I'd be somebody's mama if it wasn't for him," I said.

"Maybe you should try not to think of it that way," he said, topping my glass off again.

"Right," I said. "It's not like they were sucking out body parts, right?"

"Right," he smiled weakly. He had a telephone work-voice, deep, but soft and silky. One of those voices that makes you fantasize about what the person on the other end of the phone looks like. And then you get disappointed once you see the person that goes with the voice. But Elliott's voice matched him perfectly. Well, almost perfectly. I know a lot of women who would be disappointed if they knew what I knew.

"I tried that too." I said. "I've been telling myself all day that it wasn't a baby yet, just clumps of blood and mush, but I'll bet we'd've made a pretty little girl."

Elliott just said, "Um, sure." If he thought he was depressed before, I'll bet he was really sorry he'd invited me in.

"A little boy would've been cute too, with his daddy's eyes and dimples, but I'll bet our little girl would've been gorgeous."

I think the wine could have been affecting me a little faster than normal, maybe because of the procedure, or because I hadn't eaten much. I'm sure I was just babbling to the tune of woe is me.

When I said, "Shall I offer my firstborn for my transgression, the fruit of my body for the sin of my soul?" he just looked at me with a blank. "Micah 6:7," I said.

He just said, "Yeah."

"I opened my Bible this morning before I left the house, looking for a sign from God," I told him. "And that's what I flipped open to. How's that for a sign?"

I know I must have sounded like a crazy person, unsure one minute, trying to justify my actions the next. I wondered if he was judging me, the way I'd probably judged him. I told him everything from the beginning to the right now, to the fight in between, to how I was trying to fix it.

"I sat there all morning," I said, "the rest of the morning, trying to figure out how to fix stuff."

Elliott just listened.

"I don't know how things got so fucked up," I said.

Elliott didn't have to say it. The gentle, nervous look in his eyes was clearly saying, *Sebrina, you're the thing on the side.*

I couldn't believe it took me this long to realize that I'm his thing on the side. He's not mine. Me and my baby were the things on the side and I had to do something about it, and it's not at all what I said I'd do back when I was wishing for this to happen. "The next thing I know, I was making an appointment, planning the next fucked up step in my life. She told me they could see me the next day to talk about it."

He sat there silently listening to me babble on about my thoughts, like how I used to tell myself that Curtis' being married was his wife's problem.

"But it's my problem more because, well, you know."

He seemed to grasp a bit of that and asked, "Um, well, what about his wife?"

"Well? What about her?" I said with a little bit of salt in my tone.

"She's not some hood rat dingbat with no clue, right? She must feel something's off," he suggested.

"Whatever, I guess," I said. "She's just one of those clueless bitches who walks around with an attitude like 'I trust my man no matter what.'"

"That doesn't say a lot for his home life."

"What home life?" I needed my glass refilled, and he obliged. "He's a fucking recruiter. He doesn't have a home life. And anyway, let's not make this about him and her. I'm the one all fucked up, okay?"

"Yeah," Elliott finally added.

Instead of lighting a fire under his ass, I let him burn me. And leave me. I felt like a gutted house.

"I guess it's like, you know what they say about the grass is always greener," I tried to reason.

"Yeah, well everything green ain't grass," he said.

"Yeah," I said. "Which ought to be enough to tell me to stay the hell out of her back yard."

"Sometimes," he said, "All people see are pretty things. And it's just not reality, you know?"

Why did I suddenly feel like he was lecturing me? "Whatever," I said.

"I'm just saying that maybe there's something to be said for the view from the other side of the fence."

I was silent for a few seconds after that and then he said, "You know, you can't help who you love, really."

"Is that right," I said back. I could tell he meant to say something thoughtful.

"I mean, look at me," he said, and I looked at him, bracing myself for what he was about to tell me.

"I met somebody online once, and fell totally in love with him. Sort of."

Sort of? I sat there, not really frowning yet. "Okay."

"It was like, everything about him was perfect until I met him face to face, but by then it was too late. Sort of," he continued, speaking of voices that don't match.

I said, "Hmmm."

"I looked at him and thought, 'You must have had a real ugly mama or a real ugly daddy or somebody cursed your mama when she was carrying you, 'cause you are not cute at all.' But I couldn't say that," he laughed.

I laughed too, and said, "No, I guess not."

"Standing before me," he continued, "was living proof, prime example number one, that love is definitely not blind. There was nothing good-looking about this man. Nothing!"

I tried to hold it in, but by the time he said, "Something went terribly wrong in his gene pool," I was laughing out loud, which made my stomach hurt, but it hurt when I held it in, too. I guess I told myself that I deserved the pain, so I laughed and hurt at the same time. "He looked like a damn smurf, dressed in blue velvet or some shit."

"Stop, okay," I said.

"I'd been having phone sex with one of the seven dwarves!"

"Okay, enough!" I said, seriously. One mental picture I could do the rest of my life without was Elliott having sex with a dwarf. "I get the point, Elliott."

"Damn, he was ugly," he kept going. "Mouth looked like he'd been opening bottles with his teeth. And chewing the glass. He gave pretty good head, though."

"Elliott," I said, trying to stop him, but he was on a roll.

"I tried to keep my eyes closed, thinking about the way he sounded on the phone, but when I opened my eyes, my feelings were hurt all over again."

After that, I just said, "Well."

"Now I know how Moms Mabley felt." He referred to a joke she'd told in an old stand-up routine about a husband so ugly he hurt her feelings.

I smiled because I remembered the joke too.

"Practically had my mouth watering," he continued. "When I laid eyes on him, I knew I didn't want to put my mouth anywhere on him, and I didn't want his stubby Barney Rubble hands anywhere on me."

That's about what you get, I guess, from the Internet.

"And he had the audacity to tell me that he was a competitive body builder and a pro football player—for the Falcons. Little shrimp."

Before I knew it, I said, "That should have been easy enough to check out, though."

"You'd think," he said. "But you know, you expect people to be honest."

Yeah, right. Where else but on the Internet can Barney Rubble pretend to be The Rock?

"Didn't you even see pictures before you met him?" I said. "That seems reasonable."

"He sent me pictures all right," he said. "Pictures with the top of his head cut off or wearing a ball cap, to hide a receding hairline, or pictures cut off from the shoulders down to hide the fact that he was a living, breathing marshmallow." He got up and went to do something in his kitchen, but he kept talking. "We met up at Bulldogs. And that's about what he looked like in the face too."

Finally, he stopped. And except the phone sex and the head part, his story did make me feel a little better. A part of me wanted to ask him how the story ended, but I was half-afraid that he'd be too descriptive about it. I told him that I didn't dare talk to my mom about my situation. "She's not the most open-minded person."

"It happens," Elliott said.

"We just don't relate too well on the subject of men. I mean maybe that's part of the reason I can't have a decent relationship."

"Maybe," he said.

"Eh, bullshit," I said back. "I don't really believe in that blame the parents nonsense. I'm just feeling a little fucked up."

I told Elliott the story about how my dad had been carrying on with the same woman since before he married my mom. The same woman has a baby with—well, not a baby anymore, but a baby at the same time I was born. The same woman my mom and one of my aunts ganged up on in an alley behind my grandma's house supposedly about something other than my dad. My mom broke her hand on the woman's nose.

I was 20 years old at the time, and found myself basically chastising my 38 year old mother about being too old to fight over a man. The best she could respond was, "She hit me first." I shrugged. "To this day, she refuses to admit that she's ever been in a fight about a man."

"Everything is about a man."

I agreed. "It damn sure seems to be."

"Just drama to spare," he smiled as he talked.

"So no, she cannot advise me on men."

"Completely understandable," he said. "Don't feel bad, though. My parents can't advise me on men either."

After a second to sink in, I smiled up at him. He told me that he hadn't talked to his father since college. "Different points of view," he said. He described his parents as conservative liberals. They'd marched with Dr. King from Selma to Montgomery, but gays and lesbians could go to hell right alongside the lawyers, mechanics and cab drivers. For the life of him, he couldn't understand how they could just, "straddle the fence like that."

"Yeah," I said, not really sure how liberal I felt about the subject. "I mean, shit or get off the pot, right?"

He looked at me and blinked.

"Never mind," I said.

He told me how he'd tried to make his parents happy, and hurt a lot of other people in the process. "I mean, I had girls doing things I know they didn't want to do, but did it anyway because they wanted to please me." He shook his head. "High school, college..."

"College Park?" I asked, with a raised brow and a smirk.

"Maybe one or two in Buckhead," he said back and winked. Then he added, "I just wanted to be normal for them."

"Normal is highly overrated," I declared.

"Yeah," he said. "Well sometimes, it scares the shit out of me not to be."

I actually understood what he meant, about that scared not to be normal thing. I fear never being happily married or having a family of my own. I'm quite literally the L-A-S-T of my girlfriends to either get married, have a child, or both. I have younger cousins whose butts I wiped as babies now having their own children. I fear that one last heartbreak will break me. I fear that I've missed my chance to be normal. But I didn't tell him any of that.

"Yeah," he said, as if he'd read my mind at that moment. "Normal is highly overrated."

We both sort of smiled. We yapped on for a while longer. Back and forth about Curtis and Andra-Lyn, and even a little bit about Raphael. Well, actually I did most of the yapping and drinking. He just mostly poured and listened.

If fucking up has shown me nothing else, it's confirmed that I'm not the type to be content to admire the view from my side of the fence. It's shown me that everything is not what it seems, on any side, and you don't know until you know. But knowing now what I didn't know then, I'd have stopped at those red lights that got me in this fucked up place, or at least at some of them.   At least that's what I told myself at that moment.

But good grief, damnit. I've been a good girl all my life. Well, up until recently. And God is still saying, *Wait your turn*, and I'm still asking, *When?* And He's still saying, *Not yet.* Maybe it was the alcohol, but my head hurt thinking about it.

"What is it that your really want, Sebrina?" Elliott asked.

Without any need to think about it, I said, "I want him to love me. I want him. But he doesn't, does he?"

"Sweetie, maybe you just need to get out more," he said. "Has it occurred to you that the only reason you've been on a decent date is with what sounds like a pretty nice guy is because you went out drinking with the wife of the man you're sleeping with?"

Actually, no. I hadn't considered the irony.

"I don't know what that says to you," he added. "But to me, it says you need to get out more. Maybe you could get out with your other friends. The girls from work"

"We get together sometimes, work functions and stuff. But not a lot lately. I've got my own situation, and they've got their own lives and relationships. And families."

At this stage in life, it takes planning and prior arrangement to do just about anything. Otherwise, it's kind of easy to miss each other, even when you live in the same city. I really don't have that much planning flexibility, operating on Curtis' schedule. But then, I guess that's not a problem now.

Near the end of the second bottle, I thanked Elliott for his ear and his wine and finally told him how much I admired his eyebrows. He said that he did them himself, and actually offered to do mine sometime, but I think he was just trying too hard to be nice without letting on that he felt sorry for my dumb ass. I said, "Maybe some other time," and went back to my empty bed with the big pillows. I thought that being buzzed would help me doze off in spite of his loud music, but the pillows still weren't working for me.

Oh, dear God. Then came the crying fit. "Oh, God," came out in a heaving sigh. "What did I just do? My baby, my baby." The tears filled my eyes and ran down face, slowly at first, but then faster and heavier as my stomach started convulsing and my nose starting running so much I could barely breathe. The more I blew my nose, the stuffier and snottier it got. Then my head and my chest ached. "Oh, Lord, God, help me."

I don't know what it is in us that makes us pray so hard when we cry, but it was working me over. As I wiped my face, I stretched my thumb and forefinger across my eyebrows and rubbed my hand up my forehead as though doing so would soothe the aching, or erase the truth, or calm the pounding in my chest. Something. I wanted to think of something else, anything else, but about what I'd done. I don't want to think about this ever again. I won't think about it. "Lord, make it stop. Make it stop." I lay as still as I could, waiting on my thoughts to refocus.

Chapter Sixteen – Hindsight

I must have been losing my mind.

I wanted Curtis next to me. I wanted his touch. His smell. His smile. His eyes. His tongue in my mouth. His dick in my hands. The taste of him on my lips.

God, I just killed my baby this morning, and I was actually turned on. But I wouldn't cry again. I wouldn't think about that baby, or this morning, or twenty minutes ago. Thinking about him should have made me sick, but it didn't.

My God, I wanted him. He loved the way I touched him. He loved it! I missed his voice telling me how good it feels and how bad he wants me.

I missed the way he would wrap his arms around my waist, caressing that place just above my navel, right below my rib cage, and that place just below my navel right where my hair line starts to grow in. I even missed the way he gets on my nerves when he says, *'Bout time for a wax, ain't it, Babe?*

I was thirsty for him, and the smooth, sweet, salty sweat from him brow, his neck, his chest, his thighs, his whole body. The thought of him made me lick my lips for any wetness that seeps from his pores. I wanted him in my face, to be in his face, all over his body, him all over my body, whispering screaming, breathing my name, his name dripping from my saturated lips. God! Why was I so damn horny?!

I lay there and thought about how he introduced me to oral sex and how I would hear girls talk about how guys like it better if you're not so fuzzy down there, and how I talked myself into getting waxed so he would like it better. And I did it for him gladly, although having hair ripped from the roots from the most sensitive area on your body in four or five different directions repeatedly is some painful shit. Hell, I might as well have been losing my virginity all over again.

The first time is definitely the worst. After that, I found that it got much better. The sex, I mean. The waxing is still painful as hell, but at least you know what to expect.

As far as losing my virginity, when that time came, I was practically begging for it. Of course, I'd expected the night to play out the way I'd choreographed it in my dreams. My dreams were always something poetic and sappy that moved in slow motion, because that's the way I expected love to be.

It was only six and a half weeks after we first met. I don't remember where my roommates were, but I had the apartment to myself. I don't know why my mind chose to torture me with this particular memory, but here it was.

It was a warm rainy October night, and I liked the way the room smelled like rain, that clean, breezy, wet leaves and grass smell. Candles on my dresser burned low as I waited. I lay back on the bed, propped up on my elbows with the sheet covering me. As the shower stopped running, a breeze blew through the blinds at the open window.

Steam preceded him from the bathroom, and I thought he looked like a god stepping out a cloud, the towel holding on to his waist until he reached the bed. Water clung to his eyelashes and glistened on his shoulders.

I closed my eyes as he dropped the towel from his waist and then straddled and hovered over me. "Hello, Beautiful," he said. I loved the way he called me Beautiful, like it was my name.

The thought of him made me wet all over. I ached to have him touch me, to cover me like a wave that rushes over my body, drenching me. Sounds a little Harlequin Romance-ish, but that's how I was feeling.

Anyway, I touched my finger to my tongue, running my nail across my teeth, imagining him. He took my hand and held it down beside me. I was boiling to the point of evaporation and scorching. When he kissed me, I caressed the back of his head with my other hand.

I said something like, "Now," in a wispy tone of voice that I'd always wanted to use. This moment that I'd rehearsed so many times was playing out perfectly.

"Uh-Uh," he whispered. "Not yet." He lay his body against mine, and rubbed my hair back and kissed my eyelids and shoulders. He pulled down the sheet and kissed my breasts and rested his head on my chest.

"I—." I felt like this was the place to say I loved him, but he interrupted.

"Shhh," he said, as if to calm the pounding in my chest. He rolled off of me onto his back. "Come out of there."

"Huh?" Suddenly, I was reduced to simmering. In the fantasy, I'm all covered up the whole time. He was supposed to get under the sheet with me, like on the soap operas.

"Come here," he repeated.

I floated toward him, my naked body now straddling his.

"Sit up for me," he said.

When I sat up, I wanted to cross my arms over my chest, but I didn't. When he said, "You have such a beautiful body," I was glad I didn't cover myself. "Don't be afraid of me, okay?"

"I'm not," I smiled. "We're about to do it, right?"

He smiled back at me. "Put your hands up there. Hold on if you need to." He bit his bottom lip.

"What for?" I asked, as I reached for the headboard and held on to it like the lap bar on a roller coaster. "What are you doing?"

"Shhh." he said as he slid beneath me. "Trust me. I promise you'll like this."

He kissed the inside of my thigh and I shuddered.

"You have such a beautiful body," he said again as he rubbed my legs and then kissed the other thigh. Long and slow and wet, he kissed me, going up, and up and up.

Is he doing what I think he's doing? At first I pulled away, but he held onto my waist and pulled me back. It wasn't much of a fight. His tongue stroked me inside and out. *He is doing it!* But he was right. I liked it so much my whole body shook.

It was like he was inhaling me, nibbling at me, almost biting me. And the shuddering got worse, and I felt myself sweating all over him. Only it wasn't sweat. I was just wet with excitement and didn't know any better.

He breathed my name over and over and his name just oozed off of my lips. I wanted to grab hold of him, but I felt like if I let go of that headboard, I would have fallen right off that bed. I arched my back and briefly fought back the urge to beat against the wall and reach for things that weren't even there. He kept pulling me back down onto his face, more and more nibbling, inhaling, sucking, kissing me all over places that would have embarrassed me if it didn't feel so good. I bit my lip to keep from begging him to stop. I heard myself making noises, grunts and moans and unintelligible words that made no sense.

Finally, to keep from biting my lip off, I screamed.

He stopped, pried my hands from the headboard and pulled me down to him. The room was dark by now, but I could see the sweaty prints of my hands staining the wall.

"I like that," he said. His face was wet.

"Like what?"

"The screaming," he said. "I like it a lot."

"Well," I said, "I mean, I'm glad." And I was shaking like crazy.

"Okay?" he asked.

I was a little dizzy, but I said, "It's not over is it?"

He laughed and flipped me over to my back. "Kiss me."

"Huh?" After that? Is he kidding?

"It's okay," he said, pecking me on the lips. "Trust me?"

"With my life," I said, almost like a reflex.

"Why do you always say that?" he asked. I guess I did always say that, and I'd never really thought much about why.

"Why do you always ask me why I always say that?"

"I asked you first," he said, smiling into my eyes.

"I asked you second." I smiled back because I thought I could see myself in his eyes.

"So answer the question."

"Because I do," I answered so simply.

"Do what?"

"I do love you. And I trust you."

I was expecting him to say, *I love you too*. Instead, he said, "So kiss me."

So I kissed him and it was really wet. I kept kissing him and soon I was bubbling over with all those poetic feelings again, wet and gushy, chills running all through me, like electricity could shoot from my fingers and toes. I pushed him over on his back and pounced on top of him.

"Whoa," he laughed. "You know once we do this, you're gonna want it all the time," he said prophetically.

"I want it now," I insisted. "I promise I'm ready." I attacked his neck, his ears, his eyes, his forehead, with nibbles and kisses. "Tell me what to do again." I wanted to know how to make him sweat.

"It'll be easier if I start out on top. If that's okay with you," he kept smiling as he wiped my hair out of my face.

So we traded places again and he slipped his left arm underneath me. I took a deep breath through my nose and closed my eyes, imagining, fantasizing, dreaming.

"Hey," he interrupted.

My eyes popped open.

"Look at me." Then he whispered, "I want you to keep your eyes open for this."

He kissed me softly at first, a few times like barely kissing me. I arched my back like before and he moved his arm from under me and put his hands just above my head.

"Okay. What else?" I asked, like I was taking notes.

He smiled and kissed me again. Then he gave me a long, slow, really wet kiss. "I want you to moan for me."

Then I fixed my eyes on his, trying to ignore the sudden quiver in my stomach. I tried to say, "Okay," but nothing came out.

He stroked my eyebrows with his thumbs as he positioned himself between my legs.

Putting his hands under my thighs, he whispered, "Bend your knees for me a little bit, Baby."

I bent my knees a little.

He sighed. "A little more."

I bent them a little more.

"Okay," he sighed again. "A lot more." It's at this point that I was finding that the real thing is a little clumsier than poetry and movies. I breathed in again and opened my mouth as he shoved his tongue down my throat.

"Hey," I turned away to catch my breath. "You're kissing me like you're mad at me."

He smiled. "Hardly." Then he kissed me softer. "Is that better?"

"Mmmhmm." Almost as sweet as the first time he kissed me. "Do you remember the first time you kissed me?" Okay. I was stalling.

"Uh huh," he said as he readjusted my legs.

I tried to stay focused. I didn't want to admit it, but I finally said it. "Curtis, I don't know what to do. Where do I put my hands? Shouldn't I be— holding something?"

"Hold whatever you want to, Beautiful."

His ears were within immediate reach, so I held on to them, tracing them inside and out while he maneuvered on top of me, kissing my neck and trailing down to my shoulder. Then he took my hands and held them down beside me.

"Now?" I tried to concentrate on this moment. He didn't answer me. He kept kissing me and squeezing my hands and dipped his body slowly, kind of rocking on top of me. Just when I felt pressure rubbing against me, he let go of my hands.

I was staring up at the darkness toward the ceiling, rubbing his ears and getting myself ready, and he let go. He turned and reached for the condom in his pants on the floor. I closed my eyes again like I didn't notice.

"Hey. Eyes open," he reminded me, as he tore open the package. Then he said, "Here. You can help me."

"Curtis, you don't have to use that. I mean, don't you believe me?"

"Yes, I do, Babe." Then he said, "I hope you won't ever—I hope you'll always protect your body." He stopped and looked at me. "Even with me."

Nobody would ever touch me but him. But I said, "Okay."

"Here. Help me." He started putting the condom on, unrolling it at the tip, and then he slid my hands down over it as it rolled on. Then he held my hands there and guided himself back to where he'd left off.

As he started to push again, he moved my hands and held them. I looked down, but I couldn't really see what was going on. He kissed my face but I didn't kiss him back. He pushed a little more and said, "Come here." This time, I didn't gravitate so easily. His arms were underneath my legs to keep my knees bent.

All I could think was, *Is he doing it right?* "It's hurting me, Curtis." I looked up at him.

He rocked back a little without pulling away. "It's easier this way, Baby. You're just a little tight. Now, come to me." So I tried to push toward him. Then all at once, he just threw my legs up with his arms and pushed really hard.

I inhaled a deep breath thinking, Oh my God. He's going to kill me. I'm going to die from sex. God, please don't let me cry. Please don't let me cry. I was squinting trying not to close my eyes.

I was holding on to and rubbing the back of his head, and his face was tucked between the side of my neck and the pillow. My face was wet with tears and tears were running into my ears. When he came up for air, he shoved his tongue in my mouth again, and then started kissing me all over my eyes, my ears, under my chin, and all over my neck. And he kept saying, "Don't run from me, Baby. Come to me."

Run from him? Where could I go? All this going on, and my legs were just sort of flung up in the air, dangling.

He was kissing me so hard and sweating on me so much, I could hardly breathe, much less moan. I was trying not to scream or cry out. Though if I had screamed, when I think about it, he probably would have just stopped like he did when he went down on me. And that would have been okay, because this didn't feel nearly as good. I tried to hold my breath until it was over, but that just made my stomach hurt. So I lay there, sucking in pieces of air, scooching away from him a little at a time.

"Here." He pulled me down to him and pushed my legs up onto his shoulders, which apparently wasn't working too well for him because then he moved my legs to behind his back. "Hold on this way. Cross your legs. Don't let go." All in one movement, he lifted me up, wrapped his legs around me, and pushed my back against the headboard. Now we're sitting up.

In the middle of all this bumping, moving and sweating, he said, "Don't cry, Baby. You know I love you don't you?" All I knew is he was pounding inside me like he was digging for something on the other side. And then I noticed he was just smiling at me like he'd been watching my face the whole time.

This was not even close to the love scene I'd pictured. "I love you, too." The words just sort of stumbled out of my mouth. Love? I felt my eyes water up and my throat got tight. I was ready to tell him to stop, but what was the point? *We're doing it now. You can't take it back. Is he trying to split me in two*? I decided not tell him how much it was hurting me, because I didn't want to mess it up for him. *Why is it taking so long?*

And I was lying there, well, actually sitting there, feeling stupid. *Everybody was right. You should have waited.* If hindsight is ever 20/20, it's at that moment when you realize you should have waited.

Just when it felt like he was about to go through me, he slowed down. He grunted like the wind had been knocked out of him, and his body jerked a few times and he held me really tightly with one arm and slapped the wall with his other hand. Then he peeled me off of the headboard, turned me, and landed me on my back again. Now our heads were toward the foot of the bed. My head was spinning and I could barely focus on his face. *I waited 19 years for this?* It's over? On the movies, it lasts all night. On the soap operas, it lasts for a whole episode. Sometimes two.

What was that? Fifteen, maybe twenty minutes? I tried to look over at the clock on my nightstand, but my eyes were blurry from sweat and tears, and I didn't even really know what time we'd started. I wanted to jerk away from him or turn over or something, but he was still on top of me.

I was wet all over, and him dripping sweat on me didn't help. He was still smiling as he wiped his face. He started kissing my neck, softly, the way I liked it.

I pulled his hand to my mouth kissed his palm. Then I took each of his fingers into my mouth one at a time. I must have seen it on a movie or something. Well, wherever I got it from, he seemed to like it as much I liked doing it.

"I did that?" I referred to the beads of water on his forehead, feeling kind of triumphant.

"Yep," he answered.

I felt him pull away and then lie back down on top of me and that was a good feeling. *It* was worth getting to this point. I told myself that *it* didn't hurt that much.

"You can put your legs down if you want," he said. "Are you cold?"

I was chill-bumped all over, but I said, "Just a little." So we got untangled from each other and got under the sheet. Before I had time to lay my head on his chest, he said, "Sit up for me."

I sat up, and he rolled out of the bed and went to the bathroom. Then he came back and lay down, and pulled me close to him. Okay, the *it* part wasn't so great, but this after *it* stuff was a real good feeling. I lay in his arms, thinking about how good I could be at *it* if we did it every day. Especially that roller coaster part. He could bend my mind anytime. I fell asleep with the taste of his sweat on my lips.

That same night, I remember him nudging me awake me saying, "Ben."

"What?"

"The other brother is Ben." We'd tried to remember the names of all the kids in *The Waltons* in a conversation some time earlier. Now he remembers Ben? And he woke me up for that?

I just said, "Oh. Thanks." And then drifted back to sleep.

Now, I tried to think and dream about stuff like that. I missed the person he used to be. Hell, I missed the person he was now. I hated sleeping alone.

I woke up pissed off about nothing and everything all at the same time. It was nothing in particular, but everything. It's more than just a bad hair day. It's bad hair. It's more than just a house with no closet space, clothes that don't fit right, chipped nails, need of a pedicure, and running out of dental floss. It's a bad house, bad clothes, bad nails and toes, and having to floss in the first place. And the phone not ringing. At all!

The days seemed to drag on forever. And the longer I went without talking to him or seeing him, the more I felt like shit. That motherfucker. And I just killed my baby. But I won't think about that.

Chapter Seventeen – Reality Check

As if I needed anything else to go wrong, a week and a half later, I failed a physical training test. I'd just gotten promoted, but still hadn't been to BNCOC, a basic leadership school for newly promoted, soon-to-be promoted, or conditionally promoted staff sergeants. I'd just had a PT test for the record in October, but I had to have a record test within thirty days of my school date, and I'd failed it good. Who gives a PT test right before Christmas? And Curtis still wasn't speaking to me.

I told myself that if I thought about him hard enough, long and hard enough, he must've been somewhere thinking about me. If I thought hard enough, he'd pick up the phone and call me. If I thought about him hard enough, he'd just appear at my front door. I missed the way he caressed my face and kissed my neck. I missed the sound of his voice and the way he called me Baby. Sometimes I missed him so bad, it was all I could do not to throw myself down a flight of stairs. I felt empty without him. I missed him more than I ever did before.

I guessed this was all a part of my punishment for coveting another woman's husband, who ended up leaving me anyway. And when I thought things couldn't get any worse, Sergeant Lopez, the Medical Section's NCOIC, Noncommissioned Officer-in-Charge, an Army E-8, turned up as my remedial PT instructor.

I can't say with any certainty that Master Sergeant Lopez is miserable, but he can certainly bring the misery. He's a former drill sergeant on the fast track to first sergeant. Recruiters and service liaisons can't stand him, because he's quick to snatch an applicant off the medical floor if they don't have the paper work or won't give a urine sample. He doesn't care about recruiting numbers. Qualified or disqualified is all he knows.

He can be kind of a jerk at work, but people seem to respect him. He makes the hard decisions and gives the hard answers and when it's time to *make the money*—that's what he tells the people in his shop the hours between 0600 and 1000 are—it's time to roll up your sleeves and go to work.

HM1 Coleman, the Navy's version of a medic, once told me that she admires that when it's time to work, he's not just standing around supervising, superintending or delegating. He's back there drawing blood, doing weigh-ins, watching people pee in a cup or whatever it takes to clear the floor. He hasn't forgotten that he's a medic too. She told me that she knew that he'd be the first in line to burn you at the stake when you fuck up, but she felt like if any NCO in the MEPS would have her back, it was Sergeant Lopez. He was the first person I ever heard say, "If I'm not getting on your nerves, I'm not doing my job. If you like me, I'm not doing my job." He's pretty young too—he turned thirty the month after I did—to already be wearing E-8 stripes.

I don't think I've ever seen him smile sober. But I saw him smile, laugh, and even tell jokes at Coleman's New Year's Eve party last year. Of course he was drunk enough to fall off of a speed bump. I admit it. We all did our fair share of drinking. Hell, I've even done a few other folks' share, but I digress.

Now Lopez' *job* was to help me pass my PT run, and keep from getting kicked off the promotion list before I could get to school. Somehow, he'd kept my PT card from reaching the personnel office with a flag action attached to it. I guess he didn't hate everybody after all. Or maybe it was Christmas spirit.

On Christmas morning, I just sat on the side of my bed and cried. Not a bawling, wailing, snot-flinging, theatrical-type funeralistic crying, but I couldn't stop the tears from rolling down my face. And not because I'd failed the PT test and was in danger of getting my rank taken. I was lonely, but didn't want to be bothered with anybody. But I would have gladly been bothered with Curtis, if he'd bothered to bother. Half the day went by and he didn't. What is wrong with him?

But no surprise, Raphael texted and called. He said he had something for me and he just wanted to drop it off if it was okay with me. Of course, it was okay. At least he'd thought enough of me to call, to stop by and even buy me a gift. It was a copy of Sam Cooke CD wrapped in a red ribbon and no wrapping paper. That was kind of cute.

"I went to two Walmarts and a Best Buy to find this," he said proudly.

I hugged him and kissed him on the cheek. "It's great. I actually don't have this one."

"Me either," he said and shrugged.

I hesitated a little bit, but invited him in to listen to a few songs. A couple of hours later we had listened to the whole CD, over and over again. It was still early in the day, and it beat being alone. God, why couldn't he be Curtis? Or why couldn't I be satisfied that he wasn't? He didn't seem to notice or mind that I wished he was somebody else. A couple hours with a distracted, thoughtless heifer seemed to suit him just fine. When he said he'd call me later, I knew he would. I should have cared more than I did.

I didn't even go home to visit my family until Christmas night, because I was sure Curtis would call or come by or something. He didn't.

Time at home for Christmas wasn't the ideal situation either. I wonder is it ever, for anybody. Too many nosy folks, and too much drama. Kinfolk asking me why I haven't managed to catch a boyfriend or husband with "all those men" in the army, my mom lamenting about how all of her friends have grandkids, a random cousin fighting with a baby's mama or baby's daddy, a random belligerent drunk friend of somebody's making rounds before moving on to the next house. I just told them that I had to work. I'm in the army. They always believe that.

Chapter Eighteen – Good Intentions

I didn't kid myself into saying that this new year, 2001, would be my year. Last year hadn't been great, so this year couldn't get any lower. That's what I thought until I had to bring in the New Year doing remedial PT. But remedial PT is the price you pay for failing a PT test.

After the first couple of days, getting up with Lopez at 3:30 in the morning 3 days a week, running—well, okay, dragging at first—over three miles a day, left me too tired to do much thinking about Curtis. I was on a three-month remedial program. He could have made it five days, but he said he thought I could do it in three, and for those three days a week, Lopez and those three miles were kicking my ass. As far as he was concerned, the longer the better. The colder, the wetter the better. "Love that army rain," he said.

Shit. Love it? While he was loving it, I was thinking to myself, *This is some bullshit. I can't believe what I gave up to be doing this. I could have long been married-ever-after, laying up in the bed right now with a man. Fucking Army. Fucking college.* There's nothing more depressing than army rain. It falls harder and wetter than regular rain. It's heavier when it hits you, and clings to every inch of your body so that you feel the weight of it with every step. It always smells like a storm, even if it's just a drizzle. You can smell it coming before you're out the door. Shhheeeit! How did I get stuck with this crazy son-of-a-bitch?

Come rain, thunder or lightning, this fool still wanted to run. I guess he meant well. But you know what they say about good intentions and where they lead.

Hell was opened for business at 3:30 in the morning on Monday, Wednesday and Friday. Hell was a three-mile stretch of dirt and asphalt that ran all over Fort McPherson. And I swear, it rained every Monday, Wednesday and Friday in January. But I kept running. The only thing good about that workout was that for the first time in over a year, I could sleep soundly at night when Curtis wasn't around. I was too tired not to.

And every Monday, Wednesday and Friday, Lopez always looked at me smiling. Now he smiles? Now I can count one time I've seen him smile sober— when he's amusing himself with my Stupid Stare.

"I don't know why you looking at me like that S'arnt, but you better get it out of your system now."

I scowled in silence, staring off into nothingness. *I'm looking at you like this because it's cold, it's early and I'm sleepy, motherfucker. If you had any sense, you'd be looking like this too.*

The Stupid Stare is what people get at times like this. This is not to be confused with the Thousand-Mile Stare, the one that says, *I've been to hell and back and I don't want to talk about it.* The Stupid Stare is just that early in the morning, wish I was somewhere else stare. Your eyes get all watery and glassy and you just look around at nothing. Your face is pretty much expressionless, not really frowning, but damn sure not smiling, as you think to yourself, *What the hell was I thinking when I came here,* or, *Who did I piss off to get here?*

It's not a look I'd had too often in my army career. That pre-PT, pre-FTX—field training exercise—or pre-road march look. I'd only had it in basic training, Air Assault School, the primary leadership course, and now.

There's that miniscule percentage of people who get the Stupid Stare with a twist. They're the ones who believe in being positive and optimistic about every damn thing, no matter the circumstances. They're usually out there in formation hung-over or still drunk. They'd smile if they could manage it, but mostly all they get out is sort of a painful-looking grimace.

It's one of those times when all you can do to console yourself is remember that it's a temporary existence. It's got to end sometime, even if it does seem like a lifetime.

After I was about a month into the program, over a month since he'd punched my door and walked out on me, Curtis started calling me again. He didn't even ask me to explain the situation with me and his wife. I guess he realized I was telling the truth when she never brought it up.

He showed up one day and just said, "Hey," when I opened the door.

"Hey, what?"

"I missed you."

Really? "And it took you a month and a half to figure that out?"

Elliott opened his door, carrying a bag of garbage. He brushed past Curtis and nodded a hello.

Elliott always seemed to be going in or coming out of his apartment whenever Curtis was at my doorstep.

Curtis nodded hello back, as if Elliott were speaking to him. Elliott doesn't even like him.

"It's not like that, Sweetheart," Curtis said. "I've been doing a lot of thinking, and I miss us."

"You miss the sex." I did, too.

He smiled. I didn't.

"Yes, I miss us being together," he said. "But things just got messed up."

"You have no idea."

"I miss how you know me. How you get me."

"But I don't get you, Curtis. And you don't get me. And no matter what's been going on, I'm always an afterthought. I'm never first. Ever."

"You will be," he said. "I promise."

"Don't promise me. Just do it." I started to close the door, and he blocked it with his foot.

"How?"

"Figure it out," I said, pushing the door so hard he had to move his foot to keep me from squishing it.

Every day for the next nine days, I found one of his business cards in my door, with *I miss you – Please call me* scribbled on the back.

On the tenth day, I called back, tired of pretending that I didn't miss him, too. A part of me felt like I needed to talk to let a load off my chest, and be angry, and slap and punch him until I got tired. But when I saw him standing at my door, looking good, smelling good, talking good about how lucky he is that I chose him when I could have chosen anybody else, appealing to what I wanted to hear, I reaffirmed to myself that talking about it wouldn't change the past. So I slipped into an uneasy denial and right back into him arms. I aimed to refocus my mind on my future. Period.

I guess it was easier than it should have been, but it felt right to be reconnected to him. And it wasn't just about sex, because at first there was no sex. It was just like having another Raphael around, except now that I had more of Curtis around, I was just fine with having less of Raphael around. Curtis and I were just easing back into our relationship. There was just me and Curtis being together and me being glad about it. And so there was no real reason to hang out with Raphael as much. Raphael understood that. That's part of what made him so cool.

After a couple of weeks, I started missing PT, one or two days a week. I would call Lopez the night before or the morning of, and make up some shit about back problems or cramps, which I'm sure he didn't buy, but he didn't snitch on me to the first sergeant, either. Finally, one morning, when I did show up, he was at the parking lot, leaning on his car, waiting for me. In the rain.

I was thinking, *Shit. I really don't want to hear his mouth*, but I was due at least a verbal counseling, and I knew I had it coming. I got out of my car and walked to him, ready to get it over with.

All he said was, "Just because I don't gossip, don't mean that I don't know."

I just looked at him. I almost wish he had told on me instead of giving me the disappointed drill sergeant look.

Then he said, "Come on, S'arnt, let's go."

And then he made me run four miles. If I could've caught that bastard, I'd've kicked him. He trotted up ahead of me like it was just a stroll. He'd run back and pace the ground ahead of me, and then run backwards in front me, saying stuff like, "Come on, High Speed," and singing the "Up in the mornin', 'fo day!" cadence, which I really hated because it was so true. "I don't like it, no way!"

I could barely get out, "Go to hell." I huffed and wheezed and grit my teeth so hard, I could've broken a filling. But he made his point.

"Come on S'arnt! Bring your ass!"

The best I could do was, "Shut the hell up," grunted through my nose.

Anyway, that following Sunday night when Curtis showed up at my door, at nearly 10 o'clock at night—I'd already been asleep for an hour—I told him I couldn't see him on Sundays, Tuesdays and Thursdays.

"What the hell is that about?" he asked. "Why the hell not?"

I told him that my new work schedule was a little rough, that I was taking time to get used to it. It was sort of true, but mostly I was too embarrassed to tell him that I'd failed my PT test run and I had to get up for PT at clock-nothing.

I would've thought he bought that work schedule bullshit, but then he turned around and called me. It must have been right at midnight.

"What's up?"

"Baby, I'm sleeping," I said. He knew that.

"I know that," he said. "What's really up?"

"Nothing," I said. "Just sleeping."

"Well, I'm coming back," he said. "Now."

I spent the next two or three minutes telling him no, until I thought I'd finally convinced him that I wouldn't open the door and he'd just be wasting his time.

"I'll see you tomorrow, though. Okay?"

"Whatever," he said, and hung up.

I thought, *Good*.

I think that's when he first started acting funny with me. He'd gotten the idea that if I didn't want to see him, I must be seeing somebody else. Men can be so stupid that way. And sometimes they can do stupid things, just to be stupid.

He showed up that night, true to his word, banging on the door until I let him in. By then, it was at least 12:30 or one o'clock in the morning. When he realized I really was asleep and alone, he almost looked disappointed that he didn't have something to raise hell about.

I got back into bed and he climbed in behind me, fully clothed. I turned toward him and rested my head on his chest. He held me in a sort of bear hug for a few seconds and then started rubbing my arms and legs. It was a pleasant distraction, but not enough to keep me from dozing back off.

"Let's make love," he whispered, kissing my ear. "I want you so bad.

It's been so long."

"Mmmm. Nuh-uh," I said back, pulling his arms around me. "I'm tired." I know he could feel me sleeping.

Then he stiffened up and said, "Tired?" He pulled his arms away from me. "You know, Sebrina," he said in full volume, wide awake voice. "I'm feeling like something's changed between us. I know I didn't come around for a while after that whole drama with the business card, but what am I missing? Is there something you need to tell me?"

My eyes popped open. Did he really want to have a conversation now?

"Really, Baby," I said. I moved closer to him and rubbed his face. "I can't do this now." I nestled my face in his chest and sighed.

"You can't even talk to me?" The volume was still on high.

"I don't want to talk about nothing now, Curtis. You can leave if you want to." I felt myself doze back off for the couple of seconds it took my words to sink in to him. "I'm so tired."

Then he asked, "What did you just say to me?"

My face wrinkled a little and I sighed again. If I was too tired to have sex, I was too tired to talk about it. Which part? "Um, I'm tired? You can leave if you want?"

He pushed my hand away from his face and held it. "I'm a grown-ass man. I can do whatever the hell I want to do."

"I know, Baby," I said trying to keep my eyes closed.

"Right now, I want to make love," he squeezed my hand.

I pulled my hand back and turned over away from him. "Well, I want to go to sleep." Sucks for you that's all that matters. Stop breaking my sleep. Of course, I said all that shit to myself, with that internal grumbling thing we do.

Then, after a few more seconds of nothing, I felt him slip his hand inside the front of my panties, rubbing me, then fingering me, one, then two, then three fingers at a time. And it felt really good, but I had to go to PT!

I rolled over onto my back and let it go on for a few more seconds, and then reluctantly told him to stop. When he didn't, I reached to pull his hand away, and repeated myself, "Mmmm. Stop, okay."

"No," he said. "You don't want me to stop."

He was right. I loved the way he touched me. It was almost like a feather gliding over me at first, just enough to raise the hairs on the back of my neck, or wherever he touched me. The way his fingers moved inside me made me want it more and more, but I couldn't help thinking about the sleep I'd be missing if this kept on.

Finally, I said it firmly. "Stop, Baby. I told you, I can't do this now."

"Stop me," he whispered back. He'd started using his thumb by now, pushing the right buttons, stroking the right spots, obviously enjoying the moaning sounds I made.

I reached for his hand again and he resisted again.

"You know what to do," he said. "Let me feel it."

"I—I can't," I said. "You have to stop," came out in sort of a whimper.

"All right then," I could hear him smiling, not making it any easier.

My mind said to pull myself back, move away and get some sleep, but I felt myself tighten up around his hand, and instead of moving away, I pushed myself toward him more. I decided to give up the fight.

We could make it quick, I thought, as I pulled at his belt buckle to unfasten his pants, and he pushed my hands away with his other hand. Then he sort of laughed. I was breathing so hard I could hardly ask him what he was doing. "I thought you wanted me to stop," he said again. "Go on, then."

He teased me with his hand, pulling it away from me as I pulled it back.

"I want it," I said. "Now."

"Oh, now you want it." He laughed. "How bad do you want this dick, Baby? Say it."

"Now," I tried to sound forceful. "Give it to me." I licked my lips and as I looked up to kiss him, he turned his head away. I turned toward him and put my arms around him, but he pulled them away.

"I know you do, Baby," he said.

I made a loud sigh and pouted at him. "What do you want me to do?" I asked, hardly able to speak at all.

"Make me stop, Baby," he said like he was teaching me. "Let me feel my baby cum. Come on."

"But I don't want this," not exactly meaning it the way I said it, gasping for air. "I mean, I want you." I wanted him so bad, I was shaking.

"Just me?" he asked, still not letting me kiss him or undress him.

"Uh huh," I said, not yet realizing what this was about. "Mmmm. Yes, Baby." How could he not know that he was all I ever wanted?

The more he asked me stuff like, "Is it just for me?" the more forceful his hand got, and it became apparent that a forceful hand would be the closest thing I'd get to sex from him that night. He said things like, "You're not giving my pussy away, are you? Tell me it's mine, Baby. Show me."

And no matter how much I said to reassure him, I knew I would be sore and worn out before it was over. It felt like he was trying to mark his territory on me, but my body wouldn't let me let him go. By the time he'd made me cum all over his hand, I was in tears. Then he just got up and left. Without saying anything, he just left me lying there all breathless, frustrated and sticky. He didn't even kiss me.

A couple of hours later, I was up dragging my ass around Fort McPherson. Sore, worn out and pissed off about the whole thing. "That's the last time I let him come see me on a PT night," I remember grumbling to myself. "I'll be so glad when this shit is over."

He tried the coming over in the middle of the night unannounced thing a few more times, but on PT nights, I managed to stay true to my word and ignore the banging on the door, which I'm sure really pissed him off. I was too tired to care how pissed off he was until the next couple of days went by and he didn't call. My body just could not take Curtis and a 4 a.m. run, one right after the other. And no matter how much I wanted him, my body wanted rest more.

At first, we just couldn't seem to get together at all, and I was surprisingly all right with that. He could stay mad for all I cared. He seemed to be pissed off on all the wrong days and cooled off on the wrong days. He'd call or come by when he should have been calling himself mad, and then not call or come by on the days I was off from PT, and missing him the most. One day, his mental clock finally got it right, I guess by either staying mad an extra day longer or cooling off a day sooner.

When it was all over, Lopez had helped me shave 5 minutes off my run time in less than 3 months. I hated his ass, but I was glad that I could make him proud of me for passing my PT test "with flying colors," as he put it.

The commander, a petite, Cuban female with blond hair, said something to him in Spanish and he responded. It was one of those times I wished I was fluent in something besides Ebonics, red-neck and hillbilly, but I didn't bother getting suspicious because they didn't say anything that sounded like a cuss word or an insult.

The commander was one of those women who made you feel like you had to tread lightly around her, because you never knew when she was going to blast you for something. When I got to MEPS, I was already a little skittish about meeting with her because her reputation preceded her. I sat down in her office, looking around, noticing that she, too, was an AKA.

Funny-Weird. I would never have guessed her for the sorority type, and much less an AKA, because they had a reputation for being elitists. Even funnier was the first thing she said to me. "Whatever it is, form your own opinions, not someone else's." To date, that's probably the best advice I've ever gotten from anybody. And other than this PT issue, I've never been on her hot seat, which Smitty liked to refer to as "The Upper Room" usually accompanied by his version of the Mahalia Jackson hum, because he said that whenever anybody went to see her or the first sergeant about an issue, that person was in serious need of prayer.

Lopez asked me if I would still be coming out to run with him even after I'd passed the test.

I told him, "Sure," really meaning it at the time.

He looked at me up and down like he wasn't buying it. Then he sighed hard, like he was about to drop a giant pearl of wisdom at my feet and said, "S'arnt, this army is full of say-ers and do-ers."

I just looked at him. I do that a lot. Just look at people. I didn't respond. I like to shoot looks at people just for effect. This was another one of those times.

"We'll see which one you are," he said.

"I'm a do-er, damnit," I said, resenting his implication. "I passed the test didn't I?"

He didn't smile or frown, but just repeated himself, "All right, S'arnt. We'll see."

"Yeah," I said, back. "We'll see."

That was the end of March. I was back on the PT track, my body was looking good, and I had my man back.

Chapter Nineteen – A Friend with Issues

By the second week in April, First Sergeant had managed to find another school date for me, which should have been a big deal to someone who gave a good damn about a promotion and keeping a career path on track, but I told him some kind of shit to get out of it.

The truth was, Curtis and I had settled into sort of a routine, and I didn't want to do anything to upset it. By then, I was back on the eleven-to-six, Sunday through Thursday schedule. Curtis and I started seeing each other two, maybe three days a week, not always on the same days of the week, for a few hours at a time, plus any time I happened to see him at one of the high schools or at the MEPS. I tried to always get on the calendar to test a school where he would likely be proctoring.

God knows, he was some kind of fineness, strutting around the room in those damn blue pants. And he knew it. He must have always known it. Did he know how I would stand there and sweat just thinking about him? Surely, he could feel something that intense, though I didn't spend more than a moment looking in his direction. It was almost electric when I stood next to him in that classroom or cafeteria or auditorium full of teenagers and other proctors, thinking how much I'd rather be lying next to him, or even better, underneath him, or straddled on top of him.

Sometimes, if I could cut the test short enough, there was just enough time for us to get together in the parking lot in the back seat of the GOV, or drive to my apartment, if it was close enough by. We even managed our occasional hook ups in the female locker room at the MEPS while he was waiting for an applicant to finish testing. Sex on a regular basis is something

I knew not to take for granted. And things were good between us. The past was in the past, and we were moving forward.

One Sunday night—or it could have been a Tuesday or Thursday—when Curtis had told his wife that he'd be working late at his station, but actually was with me, Sergeant Lopez called to remind me about PT the next morning. I was right in the middle of telling him one of my lame excuses when Curtis interrupted. He was more than a little curious to know who was interrupting his head and shoulder massage.

At first, he just asked, "Who is that?" in a really deep, fatherly tone. I think he could feel that it was a man, which is weird, because it might have just as easily been his wife calling, but I'd managed to wean myself away from her, too. I hadn't seen her since that day I took her to Don Janelle's salon to get her hair done, before Christmas.

I'd gotten rid of her cell phone number right after Curtis left me because of it. Every time she'd call, I'd screen the call and then not call her back. When she did happen to catch up with me, I'd keep the chats short and give her some sorry apology about how I was on a different schedule at work and I couldn't hang out shopping as much either because I'd put myself on a budget, but we'd definitely do something soon. Didn't she notice that I never called her? Well, I guess when you believe you're friends with somebody, it doesn't matter who calls whom, when or how often.

Anyway, I was glad it wasn't her calling, trying to set up one of those damn Girls Night Out things she'd been planning with one of her long lost sorority sisters.

But Curtis sensed it was a man, and he was right. I put my hand up to him and kept talking.

Then he broke out with, "Tell whoever the hell that is that you got company," loud enough for *whoever the hell that is* to hear for himself.

"Well, not tomorrow," I said to Lopez. "But I'll definitely start up again next week." My hand was still up. "Okay, thanks though. Yeah. Good looking out. Bye." I knew I wasn't going back to that 4 o'clock in the morning stuff. I was just a say-er, and I was okay with that. PT sucks. I had Curtis back, so it was an easy choice between early PT and no sleep, or good sex and sleeping in.

Curtis had detracted his attention away from the T.V. completely and sat up on the sofa, waiting for me to hang up. Then he lay back down.

I went and stood behind him, but just as I resumed massaging his temples, he grabbed both my wrists and squeezed them. "Now, who the hell was that?"

"Nobody," I said, trying to wriggle my hands free.

"Nobody?" he asked, not letting go.

"Just somebody from work," I said. "I run PT with him sometimes."

"Who is *him*?"

"Sergeant Lopez, from the Medical Section," I said.

"Oh," he said, letting go. "I can't stand that motherfucker."

"I didn't know y'all knew each other."

"I know that bastard goes out of his way to get people DQ'd."

"It's not really his decision, Baby," I said, not meaning to sound like I was defending him. "It's really the doctors. He's just the section chief."

"Whatever," Curtis said back. "I've lost more than one alpha, because of that motherfucker."

Alphas are what recruiters call applicants who ace the test, scoring a fifty or better. I guess sometimes it does seem like most of the people who end up DQ'd, disqualified, are alphas. But it's the nature of our business, to screen, qualify and sometimes disqualify.

I couldn't speak for the Marines, but we've got enough broke, as in broken, individuals in the Army who got broke from being in the Army, without letting in folks who are already broke all to hell in the first place. I didn't say any of that to Curtis. I just kept quiet and rubbed his head. Saying more would have started an argument. And we hadn't even had sex yet.

****

I swear my phone has a way of not ringing until I've got somebody in the house. It was about 3 o'clock in the morning, and now that I think about it, it must have been a Thursday night, because I'm off on Fridays, and I'm sure I would've been really pissed about my phone ringing that time of morning if I'd had to get up. Then again, my man was lying next to me, so that alone sedated my anger. I do remember thinking, *Hell, I might as well have gone to PT.*

Curtis pretended to turn over in his sleep when the phone rang, but I knew that really meant he heard the phone ringing and he would be listening to my end of the conversation.

When I answered, I barely got, "Hello," out when the voice on the other end just burst out crying.

I woke up completely and sat up in the bed, thinking it was somebody from home. Middle of the night phone calls from family are usually bad news, so I said, "Hey, what's wrong?"

But it was Al. Aw, Lord!

Right away she apologized for calling so late, but kept right on talking.

"I just can't take it no more," she bawled.

"Take what?" I asked, more agitated than concerned. But I knew what already.

Curtis was MIA, and it wasn't the first time she confided. Lately, when she called his cell phone, he wouldn't answer or wouldn't return her call. Then he'd show up at home in the middle of the night or just before day in the morning and go to bed without offering a decent explanation. "Busy with work, he says. He doesn't sleep with me."

"He doesn't? At all?" Wow.

"Says he's too tired from work." In between sniffs and nose blows, she repeated, "I just can't take this."

He doesn't sleep with her? My smile was slight, until she asked, "What do you do when Mack trips like this?"

As if I'd suddenly become an authority on men who act a fool. "Just—wait it out, I guess."

"Are you sure?"

No, I wasn't sure, and if she was going to ask me if I was sure, why the hell did she ask me?

"That's what I do," I said, as I turned and looked at Curtis lying on his stomach next to me, with his head facing the other way.

"I'm going to say something to him about it this time," she declared.

"Okay."

She went on to say how she'd heard or read somewhere that the first two years of marriage are the hardest. That if you could make it through them, you'd be okay. And here, I thought it was the first seven years. Guess I watch too many old movies.

She talked for another 20 or 30 minutes and I just said, "Well," and "Okay," occasionally, to let her know that I was still conscious and listening. Who was I to advise her? She reminded me of myself, rattling on about what I'd never put up with because of a man, what I'd never do to keep a man, and what I'd never take from a man right before I started taking it from this man lying next to me. She and I were just two opposite ends of the same candle.

I'd barely hung up when Curtis asked, "Who was that?" His voice partially muffled by the pillow.

"Just a friend of mine with issues," I said after a moment of thought. "She just needed to talk for a minute." I rolled my eyes at him in the darkness, as if he were the only one at fault.

He half turned his body and draped his arm over me. "Only women can find shit to talk about in the middle of the night." He pulled me close to him and settled back into his sleep.

That was the first of mine and Al's middle of the night, do you think he's really at work, chats. And every time was more like the last time, with, "I'm going to say something to him about it this time." So much for weaning myself away from her.

Chapter Twenty – Slipping Away

Al and I hung out and talked more now than before. This shit went on for months. Months! And I felt bad about it, mostly. But really, what the hell did she really have to complain about? She got damn near everything the man had to offer. She got the ring and his last name. She got a new car she wasn't making payments on.

She got all the holidays and birthdays. On my birthday, he was celebrating her damn anniversary. On Christmas and New Year's he wasn't speaking to me. I didn't even want to think about Valentine's Day. I wanted say, *Just shut up about it, already*, but that's not what you say to a friend who's pouring her heart out. But then, I shouldn't have been calling myself her friend. As a woman, she deserved better from me, and I knew all that, but it didn't change anything.

I liked Al, I guess. She was cool and all that, but the truth of it was that she was blocking my gateway to happiness. I didn't have the kind of time to keep starting over and waiting to see if something worked out. Being over 30 demanded that I look at things from a different perspective. I didn't want her to get hurt, but Curtis was meant to be mine.

Before I knew, another half a year had flashed before my eyes, and although Curtis and I hadn't made much progress toward the next level, I thought that the fact that he wasn't sleeping with her anymore was a very good sign. I'd invested so much in this relationship, sacrificed so much, it didn't seem right to just give up.

March, April, May and June had been great for Curtis and me, and now Al wanted to throw a wrench in everything. Calling, complaining and confiding in me, like I'm supposed to be her Rock of Gibraltar or something. Like I don't have enough of my own shit going on. Talking about how she can't take it anymore. She was tired of all his games. Games? Hell, if he was such a game runner, why the hell did she marry him? Even better, why won't she just leave?

A real bitch would have taken advantage of the situation and suggested it a time or two, tossing it in casually, like, "Have you thought about a trial separation?" But I wasn't a real bitch. Okay, maybe I was, but her life really wasn't so bad. If she was so miserable, why was she still there?

She'd gotten plenty of time with Curtis up until now. He still spent all the good holidays with her. What the hell was I going to do with him on Easter and Mother's and Father's Day? Not that I wasn't thankful to get him then, but it was on those days that I had to work even harder to train my brain to lock out the past.

I did get a small piece of him on the 4th of July, but she got him all on Labor Day Weekend. The more I thought about it, the more her whining made me sick.

The Friday after Labor Day, I agreed to meet her for lunch at the City Grill downtown. She was right about the raspberry lemonade. They were definitely on to something.

Eventually, the inevitable subject came up. Her so-called problems at home.

"I tried to be really calm and understanding about it," Al said. "Not trying to accuse him of anything, you know. Because they have been stressing him out on his job a lot, you know. Making him come in early and stay real late. A lot of times, he sleeps at his office."

"I know," I said.

Then she said, "I was like, 'Well, Baby, do you want to talk about it?'

And he was all like 'Baby, I've been talking to motherfuckers since 4 o'clock this morning. No, I don't want to talk about shit with you.' All hateful and stuff. I just sat there and cried."

"What'd he do then?" I asked, wondering if crying worked for her.

"At first he just walked off, but then he started making apologies and stuff, trying to act like he was sorry, and started saying stuff like he was tired of recruiting and the job was getting on his nerves."

He coddled her? That son-of-a-bitch.

"Well," I said, "maybe things will be better when he gets off of recruiting duty, or something." Son-Of-A-Bitch! What was I saying? I knew very well that better for her meant worse for me.

"Yeah, maybe," she said. "I'm just scared he'll do it again. I really want to believe him, but." She stopped like *but* was the end of the sentence.

I ordered another lemonade and wondered what the hell was taking the food so long. Food would give me something to focus on instead of her miserable face.

Something has got to give and fast. How did I get into this situation again? I can't just have a normal relationship. No, I've got to fuck around with him and get her as extra baggage too. Just when I thought some shit was going my way, some good sex and steady company, she got to come around playing the mistreated wife role, and fuck up my disposition. God, I felt like I was fucking both of them.

"I just don't know what to do," she whined and whined. "Sometimes I don't think it's ever going to get back to the way it was."

Well, I hope not.

"They've even got him working on his birthday."

Waa, waa.

"And I was going to do something special."

"Yeah," I said. "I'll bet."

It was all I could do to look sympathetic. She just shrugged a lot and picked over her food as she talked, hardly making any eye contact. She was nothing close to the blissfully ignorant, optimistic, person with all the answers to everybody's life who had out-drunk me on my birthday.

"Sometimes I think," she started, then clearly didn't know how to finish her thought. "Well, I don't know really."

"Me either."

"One day, I can't get him to say two words to me, and the next day, he'll start talking out of the blue about some stuff I could care less about, like I was there." Then she mumbled, "*Carmen Jones, Stormy Weather.*"

I looked at her intently. I love those movies.

"He gets in those moods to just talk about nothing," she continued. "And then he'll actually get pissed off because I don't know what he's talking about."

"Men are weird that way." I was still waiting for the part where I was supposed to feel sorry for her. This bitch had my life, and she was just shitting on it. She wants him to talk. She doesn't want him to talk. She needs to make up her mind. That's what I know.

"Do you think I could be losing him? I feel like he's slipping away from me."

"I don't know," I said, honestly. "Maybe. Relationships just evolve." Thank goodness. I wanted him to evolve my way.

"It's not that," she said. "I'm all for evolving, or whatever, but it's like more and more, he wants me to be somebody else altogether." Then she shrugged it off. "I'm just tripping, I guess."

"I'm sure it's not as bad as all that," I said. "But nobody stays exactly the same forever. I guess people have to change over time for the relationship to work."

"Oh yeah?" she asked with a hint of cynicism. "How has your man changed on you?"

First of all, who said my relationship was working? And how much did I really want to tell her? But I answered. "He hollers at me sometimes. A lot." I sighed. "He never used to do that. And I don't like it. And he doesn't call enough."

"Like the other night," she just threw in, like I hadn't said anything. "He comes home at 2 o'clock in the morning and wants me to watch some old movies. Said he needed to unwind." She shook her head. "And then talk me to death about them," she added as an afterthought.

There she goes again. She don't know what the hell she wants.

"Well, talking's good, right? They say a lot of what is wrong can be worked out by just talking." I cleared my throat. "Not that anything's wrong," I added quickly. "But they say talking helps." What the hell am I saying?

She looked blankly at me. "I don't want to talk about a movie at 2 o'clock in the morning, Sebrina. I want to talk about why he's not coming home until 2 o'clock in the morning."

Then my conscience crept up on me. "All I'm saying is that maybe love is about doing things you don't really want to do. Sometimes. Wasn't that you who said all that stuff about compromise not too long ago?"

She just huffed at me. "It's easy for you to say," she said. "You're not married. You can just leave it."

"And you can't?" Okay, she had definitely reached my sympathy threshold.

"I can't just keep do everything he wants when he wants," she said. "What? Do some stuff sometimes. Not other stuff other times? I already put school and my career on hold for him. And I swear, he's about to drive me crazy with all that 'when are we gonna have a baby' stuff.

"What's so bad about a baby?"

"I swear, if I'd known he was gonna worry the crap out of me about having babies..."

I waited for her to finish, but she didn't.

"Where do I draw the line?" she asked, looking at me like she expected an answer, but I barely understood what she was trying to say..

"You ever thought that maybe the reason you feel like you're losing him is because you don't give enough of yourself? Yeah, you put your career on hold, but watching movies and talking is such a small thing, when a relationship is concerned." It was at that point that I should have slapped myself. When the hell did I become her guiding light? Little selfish heifer. Let her figure it out.

"You ever thought that the reason you can't hold on to your man is because you give up too much of yourself?" she shot right back.

"Hmph," I said.

"Hmph," she said back. Right about here is where she might have been thinking that here's the difference between women with men and women who can't keep men. She'd say that women with men know how to tell them no and when to tell them no. Women with men figure out where the line is. Women without men don't even know the line exists. No, she didn't say any of that, but her manner of expression said it for her.

"Well touché, Madame Pussy Cat, but umm, I thought we were talking about you and your man," I said. Yeah, technically, it was the same man, but it was all I could think to say to reel her ass back in.

"I guess it sounds petty," she said, probably observing the unsympathetic look on my face. "But at least you don't have to worry about that."

"I do a lot of things I don't want to," I said, defensively, but she didn't notice.

****

Curtis' birthday was September 10th, and he was at work all right, just not the kind of work he'd told her about. We went on a date, on the South Side, out in Fayetteville, where nobody would be likely to know him. We saw a forgettable movie, ate a forgettable dinner and spent the whole night and most of the next morning in bed. While his phone and pager were blowing up on my night stand, and we were having the most explosive, earth shattering sex I'd ever known, the world as we knew it was about to come to a screeching halt.

By the time I got up that next morning, it was nearly ten o'clock. I logged onto my laptop just about the time he was checking the million messages on his phone.

By the time I focused on the picture on the screen and realized what I was seeing, all I remember getting out was, "Oh my God. What is that?"

About that same time, he was coming out of my bedroom saying, "Hey, I gotta go."

I went to work and it was like being in a movie. We all tried to act normal, business as usual, but it was anything but usual.

When I got back home, I was so sick about it that I threw up.

Chapter Twenty-One – Midnight and a Half

Sometime after midnight, the phone rang.

Some men just get it right. In my case, it was the wrong man, but then, they're the ones who usually get it. A phone call is everything.

Why in the fuck is that so hard for men like Curtis to understand? Just call, damnit. And leave a goddamn message. It doesn't matter what the message is, it's the sound of his voice saying it. *I got your message, I'm thinking about you, I'm on my way, I won't be there, I'm stuck at work, I miss you, I don't miss you, Happy fucking birthday*, or whatever the hell. It can be a 30 second conversation or a 5 second message. Sometimes it's exactly what you need. Other times, like today, it's like putting a band-aid on a gun shot wound. But it's always, always, ALWAYS the right thing to do. Just fucking call.

I was lying on my back in bed with nothing on except a black Victoria's Secret® bra and white Hanes Her Way® panties when the phone rang. Mismatched all to hell, but if there was ever a cotton underwear day, this was it. I guess I must have really sounded out of it when I answered the phone because when I said, "Hello. May I speak to Sebrina?" It was Raphael.

I cleared my throat and tried to sound like I thought I should sound. "Hey, you."

"Hey, Ma. What you doin'?"

"Aw, nothing," I said back. "Just sitting around feeling like shit." Before he could say anything, I continued. "Hey, look. You wanna come by for a while and maybe talk, or something?" I didn't even bother to try to use my midnight sexy voice, the one that suggests I'm trying to get a man over to have sex, but without actually saying I want to have sex. Instead, I sounded more like I was asking him over to come help unclog the sink.

It was one of those times when you feel like a good fuck would get your mind back right. When all you want to do is get some sense of balance from somewhere, and if the right man leaned too closely in your direction at the right time, he just might get lucky. Good sex might not change the world or what was happening in it, but it just might have changed my disposition. For a little while, anyway.

When he didn't say *Yes* or *No*, I got embarrassed. "You know what? Never mind. I'm just tripping, okay? I don't know what I was thinking. Well, I know what I was thinking, but, you know, never mind."

"It's cool, Yo," he said, laughing. "Just my luck anyway to be nine hundred miles away when I do get the invite."

"Nine hundred miles?" I asked. "Where are you?"

"I'm at my mom's," he said. "I been on the road since 10 o'clock this morning and walked through the door a few minutes ago. I would've called to check on you earlier, but I was just trying to get here, you know?"

The fact that he even called meant he gave more of a damn about me than the bastard who should've been calling. "Thanks for thinking about me," I said, thinking about Curtis.

"Always," he said back. "So, where your man at tonight?"

Somewhere *not* thinking about me.

"Why he ain't there holding you right now?"

"Too busy holding onto somebody else, I guess." I knew.

"Well, if you feel like talking, I'm here, a'ight?"

I felt like more than talking, and I said as much. He just listened and said, "Mmmhm," once and a while. He told me that he'd been in South Carolina for work stuff when his dad called him this morning. His mom was sick with worrying and wouldn't rest until he and his other siblings were all under her roof together.

I felt my fingers gliding across my chest as he talked. "That's still one hell of a drive," I said.

"No doubt."

"Man, I barely made it home myself, and I only had to drive for fifteen minutes."

"Word?"

"Yeah," I told him. "I sat at a traffic light for a good ten minutes crying and shaking because I looked up and saw a flag flying at half-staff at a car dealership. If people were all blowing their horns and screaming at me, I couldn't even hear them."

I told Raphael how I just put the car in park like I'd forgotten how to drive and cried. I could hardly even see. I felt just like I did the day after my operation, only this time it was that full-on bawling, wailing out loud, acting up at a funeral crying.

"Trust me, Ma. It's going around. Just keep it together."

"I wish I knew how," I said.

I told him how I was having one of those feelings where you just want to do some shit you know you shouldn't be doing, and he just said, "DAaamn!" and we both laughed.

Just then, my phone beeped and I told him to hold on.

It was Al.

"Hey, girl," she said. I don't know if I was more pissed off that she was calling me or that Curtis wasn't.

"Hey, what's going on?"

She told me that she and Curtis had been in South Carolina most of the day with her parents, and that he was really shook up.

"Yeah," I said. "I guess everybody is."

"Yeah," she said. "You know the Lord works in mysterious ways, though."

I agreed. "Listen, I gotta—"

She went on to say how she was so upset all day, he didn't waste any time leaving work to spend the day holding her, telling her everything would be all right. Bet that's not all he did with her. She sounded way too damn happy to still be having a dry spell. She didn't have to say it. I could hear it in her chirpy-ass voice. When she told him she wanted to go be with her mama, he didn't hesitate to get in the car and drive to Beaufort.

"You know what, Al, that's really good, but I need to let you go. I got somebody on the other end."

"Oh, girl," she said. "Is it the bald Puerto Rican guy?" Like I couldn't have possibly had any other man interested in me since I met this guy almost a year ago. It could have been anybody.

"What makes you think it's him?"

"Well," she reminded me, "you said that Mack never calls, so I just assumed. So is it him?"

I didn't say he never calls. I said he didn't call enough. I hate a know-it-all somebody.

"Yep," I said. "He just called to check up on me. No big deal, but I don't want to be rude."

"Big deal?" she squeaked.

"Yeah," I said. "He's cute to death, but he ain't got sense worth a damn."

"Huh?" she asked. "Why you say that?"

"'Cause," I said with a hard huffing sigh. "He be all up on me, and know I don't want him like that. He knows I'm feeling somebody else, and he's still tryin' to—to—" "Shit, I don't know what he tryin' to do. So, no, it's no big deal, but I really do need to go. I'm being rude to him, and I don't want to do that."

"Girl, that is a big deal," she said, sounding pleased. "That guy must really care about—oh, hold on." I heard her take the phone away from her ear. Then she said something like, "Hey, Baby. You about to go to bed?"

He must have said, Yeah.

"Okay, I'm on my way." Then she got back on the phone and said, "Um, what was I saying?"

"I don't know," I lied. "Let me let you go, all right?"

"Oh yeah," she remembered. "That guy must really care about you. That's good." Then she asked, "Seen him naked, lately?"

While I was saying, "Nope, we're just friends," she took the phone away from her ear again and said, "Just one of my girls from Atlanta. I'm about to get off, now." Then she came back and had the nerve to rush me off the phone. "Okay, Sebrina, I'll talk to you when we get back. Bye, girl." *Click.*

Simple bitch.

I clicked back over and apologized to Raphael. "Look, sorry about that."

"No problem, Ma," he said real softly. We held the phone listening to each other breathe for a few seconds. Then he said, "Now why don't you go ahead and tell me about that shit you want to do that you shouldn't be doing."

"Never mind," I said, actually embarrassed for my thoughts. "I'm just talking." He put on his own midnight sexy voice, and said, "Then talk to me."

Suddenly, I got shy. "You know."

"I'm pretty sure I do," he said. "So, what's stopping you?"

"I never had phone sex," I admitted, with attitude, like it was his fault.

He laughed. "Don't worry about it, Ma. It's not like you can mess it up."

I didn't say anything.

"Just imagine me touching you," he said, softly. "Just think of me."

I got sentimental. "I'd rather think of you holding me."

And he said, "Well, you know I would if I could, Ma."

"Yeah," I said. "I know. I was just, you know, thinking."

"Well, then, do that. Just let me hold you for a minute. Now what else you thinking?"

"I smell you," I said, starting to enjoy the game. "You smell real good."

He laughed again. Damn, I suck at this.

"See, man," I said. "I told you I didn't know how to do this."

"Naw, Ma." He was clearly amused. "It's okay. Take your time. We got all night. Go ahead, Baby."

Maybe it was the way he called me Baby that turned me on, or maybe I just needed to feel alive, but I said, "Now, you kissing me. Mmm. Your lips are so soft, Baby."

"I love kissing you," he said.

"What else?" I whispered.

"I want you to feel my lips all over you."

"Like where?" I started to moan, as my hands slid down between my legs. I was actually wet from this nonsense.

"Mmmm." Then he said something in Spanish about a door. "I want you to open your pretty legs for me and let me touch that pretty pussy of yours."

I opened my legs and closed my eyes. "Oooh, that sounds nice."

"Rub it for me, Baby," he said. "Tell me how good it feels to have my fingers up in there."

I did what he said, and I told him it felt great.

"Rub that clit for me real fast, okay?"

"Ooookay", I heard myself saying. "And what are you doing for me?" I asked, not sure that I really cared what he was doing.

"Mmmm," he said. "I'm getting this hard dick ready for you."

"Mmmm," I said back, listening to the soft grunts he made, as I rubbed faster. "Is it ready yet, Baby? I wanna feel you put all of that—mmmm—hard, long," I started to slide two fingers inside.

"Joaquiiiiiin!" came a loud screech from the phone. My eyes snapped open and I heard it again. "Joaquin! Aye, dios mios!" or something like that. Then a few other words from a frantic Puerto-Rican-Mexican lady.

What the hell?

I heard the phone drop, and sound like it hit a table or the floor. "Mama! Aye! No— dios!" Something-something, and then just a click and a dial tone.

Damn, and I was just starting to get into this thing. Now, shit. Here I am, sexually frustrated all over again. Damn men make me sick. I tried to keep touching and fingering myself, imagining the sound of his voice, then the sound of Curtis' voice, then the sound of both of them at the same time. Hell, why not? Raphael's hands. Curtis' hands. My hands. I tried to imagine doing one or both of them at the same time. Curtis in the front. Raphael in the back. Me in the middle. Two good dicks. Hmph.

It didn't quite work for me. I needed more practice. But first, I needed a shower. Good thing about a hot shower is that it always tends to make me sleepy, so that worked out okay.

****

That Sunday, I went to church with my mom and I listened to a familiar message about forgiveness and redemption. It was standing room only, full like Easter Sunday, sad as a favorite uncle's funeral. My mom squeezed the circulation out of my hand through most of service. Then she got up at the end, just before altar call, and re-introduced me to my hometown, as her "daughter in the service." She wanted prayer for me. She cried a lot. I cried some, too. I definitely needed prayer.

After church, people wanted to walk up and hug me or say something to me, just for being a soldier. Stuff like, "Thank you," and "God bless you," from people I hardly even knew. Some of them didn't even know me at all. Some of them hadn't spoken to me since high school. Some of them didn't speak to me in high school. All that felt kind of funny, in a weird way. It was nice to be acknowledged for serving my country, but how much of it was sincere, and how much of it was just reflex.

Then I went back to Atlanta, I sat around some more and waited for the phone to ring. It was this point that I decided to be clearer with my prayer. "Dear God, if you're not going to make him love me, please make me stop loving him." All this time had passed, and my feelings were still the same. I didn't want to want him, but he was the one I wanted. God knew that, so why wasn't He doing something about it already?

Chapter Twenty-Two – Missing Pieces

By the time Curtis called, it had been six whole days later since I'd heard from him last. It was just about seven o'clock at night when he called. I hadn't heard from Raphael, either, and for some reason, that bothered me. He was probably doing family stuff, and it was just as well, because part of me knew I was taking advantage of his feelings for me, and that part of me felt kind of guilty.

I was just getting out of the shower and I almost missed Curtis' call. All he said was, "Hey," he said. "I'm about ten minutes away."

He'd hung up by the time I'd fixed my mouth to say, "Okay, Babe. See you in a minute." So I ended up saying that to myself.

It was okay though. I knew that he had shit on his mind. We all did. People were still missing and dying. People around the world were saying that Americans had suffered an incalculable loss brought on by our own fatal complacency. Fatal for some. Near-fatal for the rest of us.

Work had been hell for me for the past few days, so I was sure his day was just as fucked up. How do you recruit in the wake of this kind of disaster, on the eve of what's about to tear everybody's lives right down the middle? People who were alive a few days ago are dead, for no apparent reason. People who are alive this minute will be going off to die in the next. Sure, that's life. The way of the world and all that. People die every day. But not like this. Not here. My nerves had been shot to shit since it happened and the thought of it all made me want to throw up. Again.

I had just thrown on a U.S. Navy T-shirt and baggy pajama bottoms when my mom called and wouldn't get off the phone. The more I said, "Ma,

I gotta go," the more she said, "Okay, but let me tell you this," or, "Yeah, but what about that?"

Finally, Curtis' knock at the door rescued me. Before I could get to it, he knocked again. I felt good that he was anxious to see me too.

"Hey," I reached to hug him, but he blew past me and dropped his overnight bag on the floor. It looked like it was packed for a couple of days. For a second I was distracted, smiling, glad that he was planning to stay overnight.

"What took you so long to answer the damn door?"

"I—was getting off the phone with my Mama." I hesitated. "She's—you know." I was going to say she's worried about me and has been calling three or four times a day since last week, but he cut me off, which I hated.

"Why the hell didn't you have the door unlocked? I told you I was coming." He said all that without raising his voice, but it still came out cold and harsh.

"I don't know. I'm sorry."

"Yeah," he said, and went and sat on the sofa and clicked the T.V. on.

"And what the hell are you wearing?" he asked, as if he'd never seen me in baggy plaid pants.

"Uh, my pajamas?" I asked back.

"Why're you wearing that Navy shit? You ain't in no damn Navy."

I ain't in no damn Marines either, but he never complained when I wear that shit. "Baby, now, you know I work at the MEPS. Come on." I don't even know why I went into it with him. "I got a shirt from everybody but the Coast Guard. And I'm waiting on one of those."

"Fuck the Coast Guard," he mumbled. "Don't start that shit."

I shook it off and changed the subject. "Um, you hungry? I was about to order Chinese," I said. I took the menu from the table and handed it to him.

He grunted and half mumbled. "I don't want no Chinese. Can't you just cook?" I don't know why I felt like explaining myself, but I went into it with him again. "Curtis, I'm tired too. I've been at work all day too."

"So?" he asked as if that wasn't good enough.

"Babe, why are you giving me such a hard time, huh?"

He looked away from me at the T.V., saying nothing. He was in no hurry to answer, so I took the opportunity to vent.

"You've no idea what it's been like the past couple of days," I said, and my voice cracked a little. Hmph. Didn't know, and from the looks of him, he didn't want to know. "People been calling all day long, asking all kinds of crazy-ass questions about stuff we ain't got shit to do with. Parents can't get in the gate without an escort, kids no-showing to ship. We having to pull some kind of guard-damn duty at the hotel to make sure the kids that did show up don't change their minds and try to go AWOL and leave, I guess. And today!" I huffed, thinking it would make him look in my direction. "Today, some lady who finally did get escorted in the gate just missed her child shipping out, just broke down crying in my arms."

When he didn't look toward me, I started pacing back and forth, hoping to stay in his peripheral vision. "Right there in the middle of the lobby, right at the front counter. I'm trying to check people in for the test and she just busts out crying and ready to pass out in the floor. I gotta calm her down and explain to her that her daughter was just going to basic training, not to war."

I wasn't sure if he was listening, but I kept talking. "All this, and I got applicants waiting to take the test, and, and, and shit. Recruiters standing around, in the goddamn way, not helping shit. I threatened to put one of the testers out for having a bad attitude. I never do that. Then I told off a recruiter—who outranks me—'cause she standing up at the front counter going all off in front of the applicants when she should have had her ass waiting in her damn car or back in the lounge, talking shit about how she's so pissed off and ready to 'nuke 'em hard and nuke 'em deep', whatever the fuck that means."

I probably should have kept my mouth shut, but instead I heard myself mocking her so-called motivation.

She was going on about how she was from New York and *Ain't nobody from some other place gonna come to my town and do some crap like that and get away with it.*

I had said something really insensitive, like, *I guess it would have been alright if somebody from New York had done it, right?* I was getting pissed off again, just thinking about it.

"So I'm probably gonna get counseled for that, come tomorrow," I told him.

I was venting my ass off and he just stared straight ahead like I wasn't even there.

I felt a little more anger mixing in with the sadness. "You know," I said. "I could barely drive home Tuesday because I was shaking so damn bad."

I let him know one other thing. "And you know, when I got home, there was nobody here to hold me all night and rock me to sleep and tell me everything's gonna be all right. You didn't even fucking call me." And I hoped he knew I resented that. "You didn't even fucking call." Where was he for the last five or six days when my end of the candle needed to be lit? In South Carolina, lighting somebody else's fire, holding and protecting the one he really gave a damn about.

"So?"

"So?" I needed my fire lit and stoked, and you were somewhere else, you son-of-a-bitch.

"So what?" he said. "You're in the damn army. You ain't no damn baby. We're in the military for a reason. To go to war. To kill people. That's what we do."

Now he gives me the *I'm a trained killer* speech? All that, *What makes the grass grow? Blood, blood, blood! Marines make the blood flow* bullshit at a time like this?

"Curtis, I'm not one of your applicants. Save the 'that's what we do' shit. That's what you do, maybe."

"Naw-uhn," he said back, a combination of *No* and *Uhn uh*. "You save it. You're the one walking around crying and shaking," he pretended to shake as he spoke, "and being sad. Then cussing people out for no reason. You ought to get counseled for disrespecting a senior NCO. I always knew your smart-ass mouth would get you in trouble."

"Curtis, can you be on my damn side, please? I mean, especially since you 'bout to get in my bed, can you just get on my damn side just a little bit? You're all acting like it don't hurt you, or scare you, or nothing. What's wrong with admitting that?"

"I ain't got to admit shit to nobody," he said calmly. "Okay, yeah. I'm hurting. I might even be scared. But I'm mad too. When are you planning on getting mad? How can you call yourself a soldier and not be pissed off right now?"

No this motherfucker didn't just insult me. "I call myself a damn soldier the same way you call yourself a Marine. What the fuck is that supposed to mean?" I was mad all right. I just couldn't straighten it out in my head who I was mad at. "Can I take a fucking minute to grieve about the motherfuckers who just died before I jump on some fake-ass band wagon talking about killing more people who didn't have shit to do with it?" I felt tears gathering in my eyes and he was going to see them fall.

"Sebrina," he said, like his kettle was about to come to a boil, "it's like those motherfuckers just walked right into your house and slapped your fucking mama. So, what? You just gonna sit around and cry, or go out and do something about it? Pay back the bastards who did that shit?"

"They're already dead, Curtis."

I must have hit that nerve just right, because he stood up and shouted at me. "So the fuck what?! Somebody needs to pay for what the hell just happened. I say go over there and squeeze every one of those motherfuckers until they give up that bin Laden bitch. Kill whoever we have to."

"Look," I huffed up at him. "Don't be hollering at me in my own damn house!" I shouted back. Then I dropped my shoulders. What the hell was I shouting about? I know he didn't mean that. He was just tired and hurting and mad, like everybody else. But who the fuck was he screaming on? "I bet I'll knock you the fuck out." Damn, did I say that?

He must have been thinking the exact same thing, because he looked down at me and asked, "What?"

It occurred to me that I could try to remain the voice of reason, so I tried to diffuse him. "Babe, can we not talk about that?"

"You started it." He sat down just as calmly as he'd been before.

"Right," I said. "And I'm sorry. I'm just a little shook up, you know? Just blowing off steam, I guess." I turned the tables on myself. "You know, I'm just feeling a little off balance right now. I got equilibrium issues, okay?" I pretended to laugh at myself. Did I say a little off balance? One minute I was ready to punch him, the next minute all I wanted to do was hold him.

I sat down next to him and wrapped by arms around him. He sighed and I sighed. Then I told him, "I just missed you so much. I just thought maybe we could chill out a little bit. You know. Be together."

"So all that's a no." he said.

I was confused and I guess it showed. He stood up and pushed the menu back at me.

"Like I really needed to hear all that shit when you could have just said, 'Naw, Curtis, I don't feel like cooking.'" He made a *Hmph, I'm so disgusted* sound and grumbled, "I don't need this shit."

I tried to think of what to say, as he started pulling clothes off.

"I'm gonna take a shower," he said.

He walked past me, going to the bedroom. I thought about trying explain that I didn't have anything thawed out, or I hadn't planned to cook, but instead I followed him in silence and watched him take off his clothes. I needed to say something. "So how was your day?" What a dumb-ass question.

He ignored me, so I tried again. "Uh, I came down on assignment today."

He didn't say anything, so I carried the conversation like he'd acknowledged me.

"Yeah. I'll probably get orders sometime next month."

Still nothing.

"Japan," I said. "You've been to Japan, right?" I rambled on about how everybody thinks the Army is going to initiate a stop movement and stop loss of personnel, so my orders probably wouldn't get cut.

He thoroughly ignored me and went into the bathroom and closed the door.

I decided not to push it. I went to the kitchen and got on the phone. I ordered a large beef and broccoli, shrimp and broccoli, the house lo mein and a couple of egg rolls. "Twenty minutes," the guy on the phone promised.

Yeah, right.

I turned the lights down and changed the channel on the T.V. *Law & Order* had already started. Just when it got to the part where they were about to arrest somebody, the phone rang.

I picked it up, assuming it was my Mama again. "Hello," I sang.

"Hey, Ma. What's up?"

"Oh, hey," I said, trying not to sound short. It was Raphael, with bad timing.

"How you doing? Okay?"

"Hey. Yeah," I said. "I'm good, thanks."

"Okay, cool. I just called to check on you."

"Oh, cool. Thanks," I said in sort of a whisper even though the shower was still running. "But, listen, I can't talk right now, okay?"

"It's cool, Yo. I just thought you might want to know that my moms didn't kill me or have a heart attack or nothing the other night for me talking that shit on the phone with you. She's from that old school that believes it gives you cancer." he laughed. "Called to see what you're up to tonight."

I laughed back, thinking of his mom screeching as she yelled at him in Spanish. A grown-ass man getting chastised by his mama for talking dirty over the phone. Lesson learned. Don't get caught jerking off in your parents' house. "Well, that's good." I leaned against the wall. "I ain't up to nothing much, but really, I gotta go. I got company right now and he's not in the best mood."

"A'ight then," he said. "Where company at now?"

"He's in the shower," I said turning around. "And I really gotta—Oooh, shit." I looked up, and Curtis was standing in front of me naked, dripping.

"You gotta go shit?" Raphael laughed on the other end of the phone. "Well tell that motherfucker to hurry up." I kept my eyes on Curtis as he listened to the male laughter coming out of the phone.

I didn't respond, but stood there gripping the phone. He pulled it out of my hand and started talking into it.

"What's up, motherfucker!" Still dripping on my carpet.

Curtis barked into the receiver. "Don't call here no damn more."

Raphael must have asked where I was.

"Don't worry about where the fuck she is. Don't call her no damn more!"

Then I heard, "Put Sebrina back on the phone! Fuck you!"

"How about I put my foot in your ass," Curtis said back.

Raphael must have said back some stuff Curtis didn't quite catch, because all Curtis could say was, "What! Motherfucker, what? What'd you say about my Mama? You Puerto-Rican bitch, I bet I'll—,"

I guessed Raphael must have said something like, "Ni Madre" or "Chenga tu Madre," which roughly means, "Hell no," or "Fuck you." Raphael must have hung up on Curtis because Curtis was left saying a few of his own bad words to a dial tone before he hung up. Then he just looked at me.

Why was I still standing there?

"What the hell was that about?"

I tried to step around him again, but he wouldn't let me. Shit. I drew a blank. "Nothing," I said. "Why is the shower still running? Why are you standing there with no clothes on?"

"Don't walk away from me," he said, stepping in front of me every way I stepped. "And don't fucking lie to me." He grabbed my face with one of his hands and squeezed it so tight my lips puckered.

"I'm not lying," I said through puckered lips.

He let me go.

Then I asked again. "Why the hell didn't you put on a towel or something?"

"You didn't give me one," he said. "I was coming out here to get one."

"You couldn't just ask for one without coming all out here, getting the carpet all wet?"

"I did ask for one," he said, crossing his arms and looking away from me at the phone. "I guess you were so busy giggling with your boyfriend to hear me. And where the hell is the food?!"

"Baby, I can't make the man get here no faster with the food 'cause you mad."

"I said I was hungry," he said back, looking at me again, and then back down at the phone.

"I heard you the first time," I smart-mouthed back at him. "What you want me to do? Cut my arm off and fry it?"

I swear I could hear him thinking as he reached to pick up the phone. He wanted to read the names and numbers in the Caller ID.

Just when he picked it up, it rang again. He just clicked it on and said, "What's up?" Then he stuttered a little bit. "Oh—yeah—I mean, yes ma'am. Hold on. Here she is." I stepped around him as I took the phone, and before I could get "Hello," out good, my mama was making her inquiry.

"What's going on?"

"Nothing, Mama. What's wrong now?"

"I wanna know what's going on. I heard that Bush done declared war." The way she said it reminded me of the card game we used to play when I was little. And why was she always calling him *that Bush*? I guess she was still mad about the election.

She was referring to the headlines that declared the *Global War on Terrorism* had begun, but she didn't know the difference. I didn't feel like explaining, so I said, "Ma, it's all right. Nothing's happening."

"Well, on the CNN," she started.

"Ma!" I said firmly. "What's going on is that a whole lot of people who are alive right now are gonna be dead real soon. Some of the people going over there ain't coming back. I don't know who. I don't know when, okay?"

Then she got real quiet.

Shit. "Ma, I didn't mean that. Just turn the T.V. off." I don't know how she kept getting something new on CNN when all I'd ever seen them do was show the same stuff every twenty minutes. "I promise, it'll be all right." God help us. I was never cut out for the hard-driving, kill, kill, kill attitude that people expect to be ingrained into the military consciousness. Knowing the reality doesn't make it easy to accept. People who talk shit like it is are just talking shit.

Or maybe I was failing the poster image in some way. My conduct as of late was certainly unbecoming, but I was hurt. I was tired. I was scared for what was to come. My mama didn't deserve the outburst though. "I'm sorry, Ma."

"Uhn huh," she said suspiciously. "You wouldn't tell me anyway."

"Probably not," I agreed. She'd worry regardless.

She clamored on for another minute or so, while I stood there leaned against the wall, and Curtis stood there next to me, still naked, like he was guarding me.

Nobody's as theatrical as my mama. Everything is the end of the world, though in this case, I wasn't sure that she was that far off. Every few words, I managed to repeat, "Ma, it's all right."

"Well," finally she changed the subject. "Who's that boy answering your phone like that?"

"Ma, I gotta go okay."

"Don't you start letting no man answer your phone. He don't pay no bills there, do he?"

"Bye, Mama, Bye. I love you. Bye."

"Bye, yourself," she said. "Call me back."

I waited for her to hang up. Then I clicked off and cleared all the numbers in the Caller ID before I put the phone down.

The shower was still running, so I went into the bathroom to turn it off. It was one of those bathrooms hardly big enough for one person to stand and turn around in, but as I leaned over into the tub to turn off the water, there Curtis was, standing over me.

"Will you move?" I tried to push him back and nearly fell back into the tub. Now I was wet and agitated. I turned the water off and stood up and turned around. He kept stepping and moving in front of me trying not to let me pass, like it was a game.

"Move!" I shoved him really hard, frowning and stomped past him, full speed, face first into the corner of the door. "Got—," my mind was saying, *to be more careful, to be more careful*, but my mouth said, "Damn!"

Damn near knocking myself out, I bounced back and stumbled into him, holding my face. He caught me, holding me up. That bone under my right eye was hurting and it felt like my nose was broken. It stung all the way from the bridge of my nose up to the middle of my forehead. The fuck?

"Aw, shit, let me see it," he said.

I pulled away from him and slapped him in the chest.

He pulled me back. "Let me see it."

I stood still and he held my face in both hands and looked toward my eyes. My hurt eye was half shut, but from what I could see out of the other one, he looked genuinely concerned. Then he lifted my head up and touched my nose. "It's okay," he said. "It's not broken."

"How the fuck do you know?"

Then he kissed it. "It's not even bleeding."

"Good," I said pouting and squinting up at him.

Then someone knocked on the door.

"Aw, what now?!" he said. "Put some ice on that," he told me. "I'll get it."

Suddenly I thought about my mama. If she didn't want me letting a man answer my phone, she sure wouldn't want me letting him answer my door.

"I'll get it myself!" I pulled away from him, being more careful this time to get straight out of the door.

He walked out behind me and pulled me back. He held me by the underarm and led me to the kitchen. "Put some ice on it," he said.

"Put on a towel," I said back.

Then the knocking repeated.

"I'm coming, goddamnit!" he shouted. He grabbed a towel from the linen shelf in the laundry room and wrapped it around his waist. He gave me a wash cloth to wrap the ice in and then went to the door.

I put a few cubes of ice in the cloth and went to the sink to wet it. What would my mama say? Then it occurred to me I didn't really care what she would say. I'm a grown ass woman.

I must have hit my nose a little harder on that door than I thought. Why was I tripping about Curtis answering the door?

The Chinese delivery guy was standing there, probably mouthing some bad words in Chinese. Then he repeated the total, as if he didn't want to let go of the food until he had his money.

"Okay, man. Hold on," Curtis told him and went to the bedroom to get his wallet.

The delivery guy put the food on the table and looked across the bar at me standing at the sink. When Curtis came back and handed him a twenty, I guess the delivery guy noticed that I was fully clothed and dripping wet and that Curtis was nearly dry standing in a towel. The guy could hardly take his eyes off of me long enough to try and make change. He was too busy looking at me looking at him looking at me with a rag on my face.

"Oh, just keep it, man," Curtis said, motioning the little guy toward the door.

I went back into the bathroom to look at myself in the mirror, halfway afraid of looking at what I'd see when I moved the iced pack. That place under my right eye was already starting to bruise and my nose still hurt, but not as much. I stood in there for a few minutes just looking. I could hardly stand to look at myself in the mirror, and yet, I couldn't stop looking. Suffice it to say that it was not a pretty sight.

When I went back into the living room, Curtis was sitting on the sofa, already eating. He had set up a plate and fork for me, and the boxes of food were open on the coffee table. I put some food on my plate and sat on the floor leaned against his leg with my legs crossed under the table. After a few minutes of eating in silence, he moved away from me toward the edge of the sofa and patted his lap. I got up onto the sofa and then lay my head in his lap facing the T.V., but not really watching what was on.

He touched my face gently and then kissed the palm of his hand and rubbed across the place where my eye was bruised. He caressed my face for a few more minutes like that and then said, "Sit up for me." I sat up and he got up and stood up and stood in front of me.

"Come here, Baby," he said, opening his arms.

I sat up on my knees and then reached up and hugged him around his neck. I lay my head on his shoulders and he rubbed the back of my head. He picked me up and I wrapped my legs around his back and he carried me to the bedroom.

He lay me on the bed and then just stood over me, just looking at me. Then he said, "You know, you are really beautiful."

I sat up and just kind of looked away. I wasn't feeling really beautiful with a black eye and a hurt nose.

"You don't have to say that, you know," I said, sitting up and pulling my shirt over my head.

"I know," he said and dropped his towel. "But you are."

I lay back again as he pulled off my pajama bottoms and socks and started to kiss my feet. He kept kissing me all the way up my body until he reached my neck. Then he rolled over onto his back and pulled me over on top of him.

"I ever tell you, you have the softest ass?"

Only all the time, I thought. Then I said, "Once or twice."

"Well, you do," he said squeezing like he was testing the Charmin®.

"Well, thank you." I pulled his arms up around my back.

I lay still on top on him, holding him, him holding me, and everything was okay.

Then the fucking phone rang again.

"Damn Grand Central Station, tonight," I said. "I swear, if I was here by myself, nobody'd be calling." Then I stretched over and picked up the phone and then slammed it back down. I turned the ringer off and then resumed my position on top of him. "It's probably just my mama again." I tried to pull his arms back around me.

"Probably?"

"Yeah," I said. "Ready to fuss about 'I thought I told you to call me back.' You know."

Then he pushed me off of him and crossed his arms, my signal not to try and remount him. "So why didn't you answer it?"

"'Cause I wanna be with you. Right now," I said, rubbing his chest. "Just want to be with you." This probably wasn't the best time to say it, but I said, "It's just that I love you so much."

"Since when did you start loving me?"

"Are you serious? Since always," I told him against my better judgment. Hell, life is short. This was as good a time as any to say it. "I just want to be with you."

"'Cause you miss me so much," he said, pushing my hand away.

"Yes, I do," I answered and propped myself up on my elbows just to look at him. I missed him so much I was aching for him. It was torture being so close to him, but not close enough. Even touching him was painful, but I just needed to feel him.

"Say it," he said.

"Say what?"

"Say it, like you mean it."

"I miss you?" I asked.

He squinted his eyes at me.

"Of course, I miss you," I repeated. I rubbed my face against his side. "Babe, I miss you so much. Just let me be with you." He sat up, saying nothing.

I touched him cautiously at first, like he might push my hand away again. When he didn't, I touched him again. And then with both hands. Then I climbed back on top of him slowly and rubbed my hands everywhere on his body. I kissed him wherever my hands touched. His face. Hip lips. His nose. His neck. His chest. His arms.

The more I kissed him, the more I wanted to taste him. I licked his shoulders, his stomach, his navel and his sides. I got into a kneeling position facing partially away from him, toward his side, and arched my back with my ass in the air, so that he could finger me from behind, the way he liked to do and I loved for him to do, and he could see my face as he worked. I nibbled gently on his hips, going from side to side, trying to excite him, as I moved in closer to my target.

At first I thought it must have worked too well because he suddenly grabbed my hair. I stopped nibbling him and started back kissing him, but he gripped my hair tighter.

"Say you want it," he said, gritting his teeth, as his fingers continued to work their magic.

"Oh, I want it, Baby," I said. "I want it so bad."

Then he said, "Say it again," pushing my head down with one hand, and fondling me with the other.

So I said it again. "Mmmm, I want it, Baby. Just you, Baby. Just this dick. It's my dick, right Baby?" But that didn't help either. He wasn't just pushing my head. He was forcing it. "Curtis," I stopped kissing him and started trying to loosen his hand from my hair. "Don't hold me so tight."

Then he pulled my hair back and jerked my head up to look at him.

"Stop it," I said. "Now." But he acted like he didn't hear me. He kept working his other hand, fingers stirring inside me, like I hadn't said anything.

"You want it so bad, beg for it," he said. "Beg for this dick."

"What?" I asked, my head still tilted up at him, my ass still in the air. Was he kidding? "This is not funny, Curtis. Now let me go."

I moved my bottom half out of his reach, but my head was still in his lap. I kept trying to pull his hand out of my hair with one hand, while trying to push myself off of him with the other. He gripped my hair tighter and pushed my head back down.

"Beg for it," he repeated. "Say, 'Curtis, please put it in my mouth'".

I shook my head, "Uhn uh."

"Say it!"

"I won't," I said, still struggling to get up. "What is the matter with you? Are you fucking crazy?"

"Then how about, 'Curtis, please fuck me'?"

"No," I told him. "Let me go!"

"Fine," he said, letting me go. "Telling me no. Then get off of me." He pushed me off of him again. I rolled over onto my side and looked at him. I was breathing hard and wiping the hair out of my face, pouting, waiting for him to look at me.

When he didn't, I took a deep breath and waited for him to speak. He just stared up at the ceiling.

Finally I asked, "Baby, why are you doing this to me?" I felt myself starting to shake, so I started patting my feet on the bed instead. "Talk to me. What's wrong? Why are you doing this?"

"I guess you don't miss me like you say you do," he said, coldly.

"I'm not a dog, Curtis," I said back. "I don't have to beg you for f— for nothing."

"No, you don't," he said. Then he turned over onto his side facing away from me.

I looked at him for a few seconds and then said, "Baby, let's not fight, okay?" I was about to touch him on the back when he half turned to look at me.

"So do you want to or not?"

"Of course, I do," I said. I pulled him over onto his back, climbed on top of him again and then stretched to reach and open the top drawer in the night stand. Then my heart started beating faster because of something I wanted to talk about before we got to bed, but I never had time to bring it up. I pulled out one of the small packages from the brown paper bag and rolled off of him back onto the bed. I lay on my back and held the bag in my hand as I cleared my throat.

He turned over towards me and was propped up on his side with his elbow dug into the pillow. He looked at me like he was looking through me. Then I blinked away, sort of looking down. I licked me lips and breathed through my nose.

"What?" he asked.

"I got these a couple of weeks ago from the gynecologist after my last pap smear."

"Yeah," he said.

These, was a little bag full of individually wrapped multi-colored latex condoms that the OB-GYN seemed compelled to give out like it was a trick-or-treat goody bag. I had been keeping them in the night stand, waiting for a good time to bring up using them, preferably not right before sex, but that's the way it seemed to be happening.

"Baby, I was wondering," I started, not intending to stop in mid sentence.

"What?" he asked again. "What is it?"

"I think we should use condoms again," I said, feeling really clumsy. "You know, like before, back in the day, when we first started. You know."

"What the fuck?" he asked, not moving.

I couldn't think of any of the words I'd planned on using earlier.

"Sebrina, what are you talking about?"

"I don't know." Why did I say I don't know? "I mean, I want you to use one. When you're with me." I felt my mouth getting dry, but all I could do was lick my lips. "Okay?" This was coming out sounding like shit and I knew it. And I could still barely make eye contact. "Will you just do that for me?"

"No," he said bluntly, still in the same propped up position. "Now what? Do you want to or not?"

What? What kind of answer is no? "Of course, I want to."

"Then what's this condom shit all of a sudden? Suddenly you don't trust me?"

"It's not that," I said, sitting up. "I just think we should be smart about it. Don't you?" I asked, trying to lead him into a nod.

"I'm smart all right," he said. "Smart enough to know when some shit has changed."

"No, Baby. I just don't want to get pregnant or something."

"Or something?"

I should have left off the something. He had a strange talent for latching on to the wrong words and not hearing the important ones.

"The something is, either you don't trust me, or you're fucking around on me and you know I'll kill you if you bring me some shit."

Fucking around on him? Hold up. Kill me? What the hell did I just miss?

"Curtis, who do you think you're talking to?" I moved to climb over him and get out of the bed.

"Who do *you* think I'm talking to?" He put his knee up to try and block me, but I climbed over him anyway. I was almost to the doorway when he got up and stopped me. "You think I don't know this is about that bastard on the phone? You think I'm fucking stupid now? If it was about getting pregnant, you could just take the pills."

"I already told you I don't want to take those pills because they make me fat, and it's harder for me to lose weight than it used to be." Yes, it was vanity, but I wasn't 21 anymore. That whole metabolism thing wasn't working in my favor. He knew that!

I stood with my back to him, a few inches from the door. I just shook my head. The more we fussed and argued, the more off balance I felt.

Maybe this was a bad time to bring up using condoms again. It wasn't about not trusting him, or fucking around, or not really about fear of getting pregnant again, which I now knew I could never tell him about. I was just missing the man I fell in love with, the one who cared enough about me to use a condom, even when I was a virgin. I guess this whole thing had been about me trying to recreate a relationship that was long gone. I started a fight for nothing.

Then after a few seconds I spoke. "I trust you, Baby. I just thought we could stand to be a little more careful. You know, like before." I knew that he knew that I referred to the college days.

"Before," he said, "you used to trust me with your life."

"Before, I didn't have to share you with a wife." Having a condom between us seemed like a way for me not to be sharing so much of him, like he wouldn't be bringing any of her to me, or more importantly, taking any part of what he shared with me back to her. I just wanted him to myself, but I wouldn't ever be able to make any sense of that to him. The more I thought about it, the less it made sense to me.

"Oh, so now you gone turn this shit on me?"

I shrugged and sighed, now standing at an angle, able to see him out of the corner of my eye. "Baby, I don't feel like fighting. Do you?" I just wanted to be with him. At that point, it didn't matter how, or with or without a condom. Would he really rather be standing there fighting? Didn't he want to make love to me?

Then he shrugged and sighed, as if to match my movements. "I feel like fucking. Do you?"

Not quite the response I was hoping for, but I had my answer. "Look," I said, barely moving at first. "It's my body. I care about protecting it, even if you don't." I turned around and brushed past him and went and got back in the bed. "Either use a condom, or, or—," Oh my God, I was about to give him an ultimatum.

He stood there looking at me, waiting.

What was it about this man that made me so afraid to tell him no? Fuck if I know. He certainly had no problem telling me no.

Then I chickened out. "Oh, just forget it," I said. Who was I kidding?

I rolled over and wrapped myself in the covers, wondering if he would get back in bed or not, and I hoped he would. He got back in the bed and turned away from me. I lay there on my side looking at his back for the longest time, thinking about how his back always smelled and tasted so sweet.

I was only a few inches away and I could feel the heat from his body. I knew he wanted me as bad as I wanted him, but I could play the waiting game better than he could. He'd made me an expert at it. I should have been mad at him, but I missed him more than I was mad.

I turned over to my other side away from him and tried to fall asleep. I even tried to imagine him touching me. I tried to touch myself the way Raphael had told me to, hoping the sound of me purring and moaning would turn Curtis on to me, but it wasn't working. I couldn't help but get a little turned on at the fact that I was imagining Raphael's hands touching me while I was lying next to Curtis. That had never happened, and it didn't last. I really couldn't get into it as much as I wanted to, because he wasn't watching or listening. Finally, I went to sleep.

Chapter Twenty-Three – Broken Sleep

I swear it must be some kind of special turn on for a man to wake a woman up in the middle of the night just to have sex. It was as if he could sense when I was slipping into a comfortable state of unconsciousness. I didn't resist when he touched me because this was one time I didn't mind a little broken sleep. In fact, I was looking forward to it.

When he first touched me on my neck, my eyes popped open. He wrapped his hand around the side of my neck and stroked the side of my face with his thumb. I closed my eyes again like I was still asleep.

He slipped his arm underneath me and pulled me back into him. He swept my hair off the back of my neck and kissed me there and it was nice. He kissed me harder, like he was biting me. I thought about telling him he was kissing too hard, but it didn't really hurt.

He grunted and breathed really heavily through his nose as he pressed his body against mine. He was wearing it! Good boy.

I turned my head toward him and whispered, "Thank you, Baby," but he didn't even acknowledge me. I bent my knees and opened my legs to make it easy for him, and as I reached back to guide him, he pushed my hand away. Then he pushed into me as hard as he could, like he was trying to knock me off of the bed.

I found myself reaching for something to grip onto just to hold on and try and keep up with his rough rhythm. I held on to the edge of the mattress until he pulled my hand away and turned me from my side to my stomach. I tried to get up into a kneeling position, but he kept pushing me back down, grumbling at me, pumping and grinding himself into me.

He kissed and gnawed and sucked all over my back and neck and shoulders, and he was handling me a little rougher than I needed him to be. He flipped me up and down and sideways, like I was some kind of rag doll. One minute he wanted me flat on my stomach, the next minute up on my knees and pressed against the headboard, the next up on all fours, the next turned onto my side with one or both of my legs pinned in the air or over his shoulders or some other contorted position.

Then, without even breaking his stride, he turned and pushed me face down on the bed. Did he forget my nose was hurt? It seemed like he had me that way for a long time, like he really wanted me to think about the position I was in, and a part of me resented the implication, but if letting him do me that way was going to give me my equilibrium back, it was worth it. He could turn me on my head and hang me by my ankles from the ceiling fan as long as he hit the right spot. And because I knew that he wanted it just as much as I needed it, I was glad to take everything he threw at me. It was so good to me that I moaned loud enough to wake the neighbors.

"Mmmm, Baby, just like that," I told him. "You feel so good."

But that wasn't what he wanted to hear. The sound of me enjoying it pissed him off, and he needed to be rougher and faster, until finally, I was just gasping and moaning, and then screaming so hard, I couldn't even make words, just noises.

"You want it like this, don't you?" he said , as if he didn't know I couldn't form the words to answer. "How does that feel?" and "You like that? You like the way I'm fucking you? Whose pussy is this?"

I just nodded and moaned. I tried to say, "Yours Baby," but I couldn't manage the words quickly enough.

"Say it, then." He slowed down just enough to let me catch my breath. "Say it!"

I screamed out something that could have passed for "Yes! Yes, Baby. Don't stop!" It didn't seem to matter to him that I was crying at that point, but because the way he talked at me hurt my feelings, not because he was physically hurting me.

"Again," he said.

And I screamed everything he told me to, as much as he wanted me to. I don't even remember all the things he had me saying. The more he knocked me around, the more he wanted to talk to me. Why do men always ask stupid questions during sex? I mean, at first it was a turn on, but when I have to think about the answers, it's just too much work.

"Who else is hitting it like this?" He grunted, going faster again.

All I could do was shake my head, which should have been enough

"Who, damnit?!"

"Nobody else, Baby," I managed to get out. "Just you."

"Damn right, nobody," he said, thrusting and grunting, dripping sweat on my back.

Then he came really hard, and collapsed on top of me. He wiped back my hair from the side of my neck and kissed me in my ear. But just when he thought he'd stop to catch his breath, I pushed him off of me onto his back and pinned his arms down with my knees.

The look of surprise in his eyes excited me. Before he knew what was happening, I had him locked down, and he was helpless to do anything except what I wanted done, making sounds that I caused and commanded.

I held onto the headboard and rocked into sort of a Kimchi squat just above his head, but before I could spread my legs into a full Chinese split, he pulled me down onto his face and shoved his tongue inside. I rolled my hips around in small circles, and he held my thighs down with his arms, licking and nibbling and stroking until I felt like I was floating. Then I felt him pushing his fingers inside of me, and he said something like, "Mmmm. That's my girl. Come on down. Let me feel it."

Oh, no you don't. I caught myself and pulled away from him, despite how turned on I was. I sat on his chest, as I reached for another condom on the night stand and tore it open with my teeth. I slid down and straddled the tip of the Devil Dog, and rolled the condom on. He just grinned at me, saying, "So, you're still hungry?

"Don't talk to me," I said back, as I pushed it in with a single thrust. I gasped a short breath, at taking it all at once. "Just fuck me."

I rode him as hard as I could, so hard that it actually hurt, but I didn't stop. Up and down, harder and harder, until he was begging. When he grunted, "Awww, Sebrina!" and actually squealed out, "Yeeees, Baby," he reached for my waist to hold me down, but I pushed his hands away. Hmph. He could moan and scream just as loud as I could.

I was clamped down on him like a vice, loosening, then tightening, then loosening my grip again. I rocked back a little like I was about to get up, but all he said, was, "Ohhh, God!" He grabbed my waist again, and kept repeating, "Oh, God, Oh, God! Oh, God," in every key from alto to soprano and back. He was biting his lip, unable to make up his mind between slapping my ass or squeezing it. He licked his lips as my sweat dripped down onto his face.

I leaned down to kiss the sweat off of his face. "You want me to stop?" I whispered, as I rocked back again.

He grabbed the back of my head with both hands, and kissed me like he was stealing it. His mouth was all over my face. "Nunh, uh," he whispered back. "Don't stop."

I smiled at how helpless he was, as I pretended to start getting up again. He pulled me back down urgently by my waist. "Don't," he repeated, sweating and gasping for breath.

"You want to put it in my mouth, don't you?" I teased him. "Ain't that what you wanted, Baby?" He just grunted again, not letting go. "Well, I have to stop, then don't I?"

He just held onto me, and pressing his fingers into my back.

"Don't ever stop," he moaned.

"I can't hear you, Baby," I said, testing him again.

He heaved a sigh, and wrapped his arms around my waist forcefully. "I said, d—don't. Don't stop."

Oh! He felt so good. With that, I stopped pretending that I wasn't feeling him just as much as he was feeling me. I don't know about *ever*, but I was sure ready and willing to take it for as long as he could give it.

The more he moaned, the more I wanted to hear. The more I heard, the more excited I got, enjoying his violent throbbing inside me. I couldn't let go at that moment, if I'd wanted to, and I didn't want to. I did everything I could think of until my body completely drained his.

As I leaned forward to relieve my back, he grabbed both my breasts and pulled them toward his mouth. Then he sat up with his back against the headboard, careful not to let me slip off of him. He palmed both my breasts in one hand, squeezing them together and licking the nipples, biting the right one a little too hard, and kept his other hand pressed into my back. He let go of my breasts, and pulling me toward him by the back of my head, he slid back down onto his back again.

He hugged me around my neck and then pushed my face into the side of his neck as I listened to him grit his teeth, urging me to, "Ride it harder, Baby. I—love—Oooh! God, don't stop!"

"It's good, Baby?" I stuck my tongue in his ear, as I humped him. "Mmmm. Didn't I tell you to shut up?"

I loved the way he couldn't help himself, saying, "It's so good, Baby. Mmmhmm!" Then he just grunted, "I love you, Baby. Love you, Baby," in short breaths, and that made me go harder and faster. "Oooh, God—Damn! Mmmm. So good. Oooh! Jesus, don't ever stop."

And even with my aching back, I didn't want to stop. I tried to sit up for a moment, but he held me down, and I imagined his eyes closed tightly, as he begged for it, trying to squeeze back the tears that were already welled up and ready to fall. I don't know if it was the intensity of his exploding inside me, or the sound of him screaming like someone had just punched him in the gut, but when he exhaled, "Awwwwwgh!" sounding like he was calling God, I screamed too. Whooohooo! Did I scream.

Then I just rolled off of him, thoroughly spent, my sweat happily mixed with his. I lay on my back with my arms raised over my head, trying to breathe through my mouth and nose at the same time. He lay there on his back, looking at me, and I lay there just smiling back at him.

"Hey," I said.

"Hey," he said back, half smiling. "You feeling okay?"

I nodded, feeling pretty well balanced. A few more days of this, and I'll be just fine. "You?"

"I'm cool," he said.

I slid down to lay my head on his chest. His heartbeat was fast at first, then it slowed. His chest heaved up and down like he was about to say something but kept deciding not to. I slid down further and kissed his navel. Then I rested my head on his stomach as he breathed.

Finally, I asked, "What is it, Baby?" I expected him to say that it was nothing or tell me something about work.

"You're dangerous," he said.

My face was turned away from him and I smiled at what I took to be a compliment. Damn! Was it that good?

"Dangerous, huh?" I ran my hand lightly down his thigh and rubbed my fingers gently across his knee. Damn, he was good and sprung. Good sex never made him trip like this. I am the shit! And that heifer ain't got shit on me.

"Mmhmm."

"How's that?" I asked, fishing for more.

"A man would kill for you, and you wouldn't even give a damn, would you?"

I sat up, and looked at him.

Then he smiled at me like he was only kidding. "Yeah, you."

"Oh, whatever."

"Whatever, my ass," he said.

"What man would kill for me?"

"Any man stupid enough to really love you."

Okay, that was no compliment. "Excuse me?"

"I mean, any motherfucker fool enough to keep loving you," he said, as if that sounded any better.

Oh. Was that his way of saying he really doesn't give fuck about me? I searched his face for a look that made sense. Then I said, "Well, guess that counts you out, right?"

He just looked at me.

"I mean, no worries there, huh?" I tried to look and sound like I didn't care.

For a second I wondered what I wanted him to say next. *Yes* and *No* would have both been the wrong answer.

"And you better be glad," he said back, and sat up. "If it was me, more than one motherfucker would be dead by now."

Talk about a back-handed, fucked-up way of putting things. We both sat there for a few seconds looking at each other. Which dead motherfucker was he referring to? Was he talking suicide or homicide? Where in the hell was all that coming from? I didn't know whether to be insulted or relieved. He got up and went to the bathroom.

I shook my head and propped my hands on my pillow and lay my face on my hands and closed my eyes waiting for him to come back and lie down next to me. The toilet flushed and then a few seconds later, the sound of his belt clinking made me open my eyes.

"Hey," I said, raising my head from the pillow, watching him thread the belt through the loops of his pants.

"Hey."

I sat up on my knees. "Uh, what are you doing?"

"What does it look like I'm doing?" He buckled his belt.

I rocked back on my knees and just watched him, feeling stupid for asking such a silly question. It seemed as though my watching him in silence bothered him more than the silly question.

"What?!" he asked, tucking in his already tucked shirt. I hated when he said *what* like that.

"Nothing," I said back. His face was blank.

"I'm going home," he said, matter of factly.

My eyes got wide and watery. My mouth opened, but nothing came out. Then out came, "I just thought—I mean, what's up?"

"Nothing," he said.

I thought about his overnight bag in the other room. "I was hoping," I stopped myself and sighed. Why was he leaving? All this because I asked him to use a condom? "I don't understand, Baby. Please talk to me.

"Please, huh? What?" he asked, kneeling to tie his shoes. "Now, you wanna beg? Feel like beggin' now?"

I rolled my eyes toward the ceiling and lay down and plopped my head down on the pillow and looked the other way. I wanted to do whatever it took to make him stay and hold me like it meant something. To balance me, like he didn't mean to be mean, the way he was acting. My heart was beating faster and I was running out of time. I didn't want him to go. That's as much as I knew.

"Well?" he asked, expecting.

I propped up on my elbows. I sniffed and swallowed hard and stared at him. "Would it make a difference?" I asked, widening my eyes more as if that would hold in the tears.

"Don't know," he crossed his arms. "Try me."

I looked away and stared down at the designs on the sheet. I can't believe I'm even considering this. I shook my head at the thought. Tears dropped down and I wiped my eyes and then across my nose with the back f my fist.

"Look, Sebrina," he said all impatiently, "I told you all about all that crying shit ain't even necessary. Turn it off."

So I wiped my face again and rolled over on my back and then held the pillow with both hands across the top of my chest. "I was wondering," I said, looking more at the ceiling than at him, "will you?"

"That's it?" he scoffed. "Hmph. Look at me."

I looked at him and tried again. "I mean, I—would like it very much—if you would stay. Here. With me." I bit my lip and breathed through my nose. "Tonight." I put my hand up to my mouth and chewed at my thumbnail. I blinked away and said, "Please," barely above a whisper. "I'm asking you not to go."

"Take your hand out your mouth and look at me," he said.

I took my hand down and tried to maintain eye contact. "Please, Curtis, damnit. It would really mean a lot. To me." Then I couldn't shut up. "I need you to." I could feel him tipping the scales on me with every word I struggled to get out. "Please. Okay? We could talk or something. I just really miss you. I love you so much." At this rate, I was going to end up feeling even worse than before we had sex. God, please let him stay. That's all I need to stay on balance. Just let him stay. It wouldn't even have to be all night. Just for a couple of hours.

"Nah, I don't think so," he said bluntly.

"Huh?"

He kind of smirked at me. "I got an early day tomorrow, and uh, I just want to sleep in my own bed. You know?" Then he smiled and his dimples peeked out.

I kind of smirked back at him, taking for granted that he was kidding me. "Man, what kind of bitch-ass excuse is that? Come here."

"That's funny, huh?" he laughed back. "Well, how about this? I'm a recruiter in the motherfucking Marine Corps."

"Okay," I said back, absorbing his seriousness.

"And that's more important than this—bullshit you trying to put me through."

Bullshit? I looked around like there was someone else in the room. What I'm trying to put him through? "I know what the hell you do for a living. I'm just asking you to stay the night. How is that hurting your job?"

He wasn't buying it, so I switched gears. Back up. Don't want to fight, remember? Want him to stay. I searched his eyes for some place I could reach.

"Baby, I said, 'please'. Okay? Let's just talk a little bit. I feel like there's pieces of me missing lately, and I need you to help me fill 'em back in, you know?"

"You be wanting too much from me," he said, not making any damn sense. "Then you want to play these games and shit. I got a stressful ass job. I got a new goddamn car payment. I got a wife."

Suddenly, I went from reverse to overdrive, firing off on him just like he'd started on me. "Man, I know you got a fucking wife. I know you got a damn job. And I know you're in the motherfucking Marine Corps!"

I grit my teeth and squeezed the pillow to keep from flinging it at him. What the hell did I ever ask him for to *be wanting too much shit* from him? What games? And what the hell was he so stressed about? He had his fucking cake and all that extra shit too. "And God knows, I know that comes first. But how the hell long do you expect me to put up with all this back and forth from woman to woman bullshit?"

"Woman to woman?" he asked, like I'd meant something else.

"You know what the fuck I mean," I said. "Are you sleeping with her, Curtis? Are you?!"

When he didn't answer, I said, "You know what? Keep playing stupid. Fuck it." I turned over again and didn't look at him. I was hoping he would say something back so I could say something else.

"Fuck you," he said, a predictable, weak-ass response. "Fuck you and that motherfucker on the phone too."

"Fuck you!" I shouted. "Get the hell out, then!" My eyes closed and my head was starting to hurt from the way this night had turned out.

"I'll get the hell out, then," he said. "I gotta go call my wife anyway."

Shit, now. My heart sank as I tried to pretend like I didn't hear him. He was probing for a nerve and I wasn't going to give him the satisfaction.

He knew I knew she was out of town because he was there when she called me from her parents' house. He'd probably overheard her asking me about the Puerto-Rican guy and had I seen him naked lately, and all that other shit. Still, I wanted to pretend our conversation wasn't ending this way. I wanted to clear my throat and deepen my voice and look straight into his eyes and ask again, *So will you stay or not?* I wanted to try to explain all the stuff I knew he didn't understand. But I didn't. I didn't say anything. I lay there on the bed, looking the other way, crying inside, pissed off outside.

Then I grumbled something like, "And I gotta go get somebody who wants hold my 'peer-ness' open once in a while." I didn't care that he couldn't speak Spanish or that what I'd said was barely audible. I didn't even know that what I was trying to say was "piernas" which didn't mean what I thought it meant at the time. Then I spoke up. "I'm tired of being treated like I'm not good enough."

"You know what I'm tired of?" he asked. "I'm tired of thinking one thing and finding out something else."

"You don't have to think," I said, still facing the wall. "You know everything there is to know about me."

"I doubt it," he snapped.

"Then I don't know what to tell you," I snapped back.

"Look me in the face," he said like he was daring me. "And tell me you're not fucking him."

I turned over and looked straight at him. "I'm not," I said. "Now what?"

"Whatever," he said. Then he walked out of the bedroom. He called to me as he walked out and closed the door behind him, "You wanna come and get this door?"

I just lay there like I didn't hear him. What did he care? Someone could come in and get me, rob me, beat me, kill me for all he cared. He didn't even wait to see if I was coming to lock the door behind him. Bastard.

After a few more minutes of being pissed on the outside, eventually, I got up and locked the door. I walked past the open containers and half eaten plates of Chinese food on the table in front of the still on T.V. I turned the T.V. off and left the food sitting there. I went back to the bedroom, glanced down at the floor at the place where his bag had been, and suddenly, I had that dumb bitch feeling. The feeling that says you just got fucked and you still have to sleep alone.

I just stood there looking at the bed. It looked lonely. Too big. It would smell like his sweat. I was worn out and tired, but I didn't want the bed. Then I went back to the living room and closed up the food containers and threw them into the refrigerator. I went to the bathroom and looked in the mirror and my eye was completely black around the outside, bloodshot yellow and red on the inside. Ugh. The sight of it broke through my resolve.

I flung myself down on the bedroom floor and cried. Hard crying and hard shaking like I was going through some kind of sexual detox withdrawal, having one of those Delirium Tremens fits, like it wasn't even me. I heard myself praying long and hard and out loud, between sharp deep breaths and big snotty tears. This can't keep happening like this.

Oh, God. He is toxic. Some kind of poison to me, and the tears weren't pushing it out fast enough. This is gonna kill me or drive me crazy. It felt like my head would just explode right there in the middle of another crying fit.

I lay there on that damn scratchy-ass carpet and prayed and cried for what I knew I wasn't supposed to want, and tried to want to not want it. "Why won't he love me, Lord? God, please! This can't be what you meant for me. What did I do that was so wrong that nobody else ain't already done?" That bitch, for one. But I didn't say that to God. Yes, I know He knew I was thinking it anyway.

I lay there pleading and snotting all over myself. I felt like even if my eyes fell out right then, I couldn't hurt any worse. "Why won't you make me stop loving him? Make it stop. God, I just want him here. Oh, Jesus. Please, make it stop." I really felt like it was worse this time than the first time, and I couldn't make it stop.

As my DTs subsided, and my head stopped pounding, I lay on the floor, not so much struggling to breathe, but struggling with the person I'd let myself become. Pathetic and sleeping on the floor, and actually giving space in my head to think about how I was in for an extra long get-none stretch, and that I'd brought it on myself. That damn Raphael, calling me. I couldn't wait to cuss his ass out the next time I talked to him.

Chapter Twenty-Four – Conduct Unbecoming

I got up early the next morning, because the floor was hard, and the bed still literally nauseated me. I couldn't help throwing up, and sleeping in was not an option. As this was a *feeling really fucked up* day, I went for a PT run. Hell, I figured with all the shit that had happened in the past week, coupled with my own insignificant-but-significant-to-me shit, I had at least three or four miles in me.

I knew myself better than that, but sometimes that motivational army *hooah* mentality creeps up and takes over, and you experience a temporary lapse in sanity. It must have been those equilibrium issues. I had taken the 5K route through the woods and dirt roads, instead of just running the regular, sane, 1-mile track a couple of times. Running the 5K ensured that I would do at least three miles, because once you go so far on that course, it's easier to finish it than to turn back.

Before the end of the first mile, I was tired as hell, and I was long over that *running clears your mind* theory, which I've never fully subscribed to anyway. What the hell was I thinking? I had just had marathon sex the night before, and I thought I could run a 5K? But I had to keep going because the faster I got back, the faster the shit would be over.

To make a fucked up day worse, on the way to the second hill, I ran up on a puddle that stretched across the entire dirt road. Instead of running through what I knew to be a shallow puddle, I decided to run around it into the edge of the wood line, which meant that I had to cross the ditch twice, once at the narrow part to get to the wood line, and then again, at the wider part to get back onto the road. What can I say? The simple way made too much sense, I guess.

I guess I underestimated the width of the ditch or overestimated my ability to jump my tired ass across it, because I leapt and slid right into a puddle of neck-deep muddy water. All I could think was, *Goddamnit, now it's going to take me even longer to get back.* Not, *Oh my God, I can't swim!* Or *There could be water moccasins in here!* but *Goddamnit, I got to keep running in these heavy, wet-ass clothes!* Thank God, I was too pissed off to panic, because my dumb ass would have probably drowned.

All I could think when I got back to the MEPS and into the side door was, *Ain't this a bitch? This shit is not cool. The fuck am I doing?* I was soaked from head to toe and looked, felt and probably smelled like a wet cat. The locker room was on the other side of the MEPS and that particular side door was locked, so I had to stomp and scowl past a few bewildered applicants and nosy MEPS personnel at the front counter to get there. My feet were squishing and tracking water in my shoes all down the hallway. My sweats were dripping and dragging off my ass, and my weave was soaked with dirty ditch water.

The spray of the usually cold-ass shower in the female locker room was just warm enough to make me sleepy. I couldn't help thinking about the last time Curtis and I had sex in that very stall. I felt sick again. Nauseas, in fact. I couldn't keep up this mess with him and keep my sanity. And where was God with my sign?

Nauseas as I was, I managed to get the lead out of my ass and get dressed anyway. Even with the extra fifteen or twenty minutes it took to blow dry my hair, I walked into my shop, smiling and loud talking somewhere between thirty and forty-five minutes early. Yes, I was overcompensating for feeling like crap.

I'd gone to work that day thinking about the way I was fucking up my situation, as if there was ever anything about my situation that was un-fucked up. My grip was slipping by the second.

Tubbs was packing his stuff for a road trip up to Rome High. It's a small school, a one TA session. He was just finishing up counting his answer sheets and binding up a stack of scratch paper with a rubber band. He and Mitchell, who was on his way to a school down south, were divy-ing up some test materials.

It's always entertaining to watch Tubbs pack for a test. He's a fucking picture of control. His books are color-coded, pre-sorted and separated. His scratch paper and answer sheets are counted out exactly. Even his extras are counted out. His pencils are always new or nearly new and sharpened, boxed and rubber banded tightly. All of his materials fit perfectly into his carrying cases and trunks. He always has his map handy and his directions plotted. If anybody was ever made for this job, it's him. He's so neat and meticulous, while the rest of us just usually want to make sure we have enough for what we need to do. And there's no worse day or less excusable disaster than coming up short on answer sheets, because those are easy numbers just carelessly thrown away.

Testing is all about the numbers. It only takes one time to fuck that one up. It's that same feeling you get about a speeding ticket or a bounced check. You could just kick yourself for throwing that money away, saying to yourself you'll never do that stupid shit again.

All of a sudden, Tubbs and Mitch broke into a debate about the pencils.

"Hey man," Tubbs started. "What's up with this raggedy box?"

Mitch had taken all the new boxes of pencils and left the dull, raggedy or stubbly ones for Tubbs.

"What? Man, that's good enough. Just sharpen the pencils and tape up the box."

"Man, I don't want this raggedy box!" Tubbs flung the box on the floor. "Look at this shit."

Mitch picked up the box and started putting more tape on the tape that was already holding the box together.

They sounded like two kids arguing over crayons.

As far as Tubbs was concerned there were three cardinal rules of testing. Number One: Never be late. Number Two: Never get caught unprepared. And Three: Never, ever, lose your cool. You lose your cool, you lose control of the situation, and that can't happen.

But Tubbs was about to lose his cool over that ratty box of old pencils. He had a fed-up look in his eye, and his jaw tensed up. Mitch was about to get it, and I had the best seat in the house to see it.

I smiled at the two of them, waiting for what was coming next. That was the moment Tubbs saw my face and forgot about the raggedy pencil box. "So, uh, Cooper, what the hell happened to you?"

It was as if the radio went to dead air silence. Mr. A., Mitch, even Sergeant B. back in her office waited for my reply.

"I ran into the door, okay," I said, putting my head down. "I wasn't paying attention, and—"

"And the door hauled off and smacked you in the face," Tubbs interrupted.

"Something like that," I said, and then looked down look like I was studying the pile of papers on my desk.

"That the same door that put that big-ass hickie on your neck?" Mitch chimed in from the cubicle behind me.

I reached up and rubbed the back of my neck, as if I could rub it off. "How about none of your damn business?" I sounded more agitated than I meant to.

"How about none of your damn business?" He mimicked me in a whiny voice. "Don't be twisting your mouth all up at me, because you wearing your business on your neck."

"Fuck you." I shook my head and flipped my finger up at him, not looking up. "And what about your business?" I asked, nearly crossing a line. "Don't you get it twisted."

"Yeah," Tubbs said, to keep it going. "You know, we don't play that shit. Just let us know what's up."

"Goddamn," I said. "I said I ran into the damn door. It's stupid, but that's what happened." Shit. "Don't start treating me like my name is Anna Mae or Miss Celie or somebody." I rolled my eyes up at Tubbs and flipped Mitch another bird before he had a chance to comment.

"All right, it's cool, if you say it's cool," Tubbs said, backing up. The concern was still on his face.

"It's cool," I said.

Then Mr. A. said, "Um, excuse me there, Coop,"

"Yes, sir," I said, in a tone that was meant to let him know I wasn't in the mood for a lecture. I slapped my hands on the desk and spun my chair around to look at him, awaiting his two cents.

"Did you get your proctor support sheet back for that school in Paulding County yet?"

Oh shit. I forgot all about it. And I felt like shit for snapping at Mr. A. for no reason. "No, sir," I said. "I'll get it back this morning."

He just smiled and said okay.

Finally, it was Sergeant B.'s turn. "Sergeant Cooper," she called me like she was Mother-May-I. I went into her office and closed the door.

"What's up?" she asked.

"Nothing."

"Heard you came down on assignment. You taking it?"

"Why wouldn't I?" I asked. "It's about that time ain't it?"

She shrugged. "Everything cool?"

"Yep," I assured her. "I really did run into the door. You know these busters make a big deal out of everything."

"Yeah," she said, not sounding convinced. "You think you can manage to be more careful the next time?"

"Got to," I said back, waiting for her to drop it.

Then she got familiar on me. "Look, Sebrina. Is there something you want to tell me?" She asked it like she already had all the answers, but I knew she didn't know shit about it.

I wasn't going there at all. I was cool with Sergeant B. and all that, but if I wasn't in the mood to hear it from the guys, I was definitely not in the mood for the *just keep me informed, don't let me hear it from somebody else* speech, so I said, "S'arnt I got it." I stood there looking at her, waiting for something else.

"Okay." She shook her head. "Go fix that," she said, referring to my business on my neck. "That's it."

I walked out and went straight to the bathroom to pull my bun down to cover the back of my neck. It took a while to get it to stay above my collar.

I managed to get from the bathroom back to my desk without running into anyone else who'd feel compelled to get in my business. I rummaged through the clutter on my desk and found my copy of the proctor support form I'd faxed to the recruiting station a couple of weeks ago. I can't believe I dropped the ball on this one. That's so not like me. I picked up the phone and dialed the Marine Recruiting Station in Douglasville.

"Marines, Gunny Curtis." He'd answered with the speakerphone. I could tell by the funny sound of his voice.

Anyone who answered the phone could have helped me, but I was so glad it was him. I wanted to speak to him so bad, my throat got tight and my voice cracked.

"Hey," I said. "Um, Gunny Curtis, this is Sergeant Cooper from the MEPS. Hi."

He picked up the receiver. "Yeah," he said dryly.

"Um," I said again. "I was calling because I noticed we haven't received our proctor support form back from y'all yet and we got the test in a couple of days."

"Yeah."

"Well," I cleared my throat. "We need it." I threw in, "Today," just to add a little edge. I'm usually really edgy with recruiters. That probably would have been sufficient enough to convince my co-workers that everything was normal, until I said, "Please," a little softer than I should have to be making a demand.

"We'll get it to you," he said back.

"S'arnt I hate to rush you, but—"

"Gunnery Sergeant, damnit."

I felt like I wanted to apologize or something. I wanted to hear him talk. If not talk, just listen to him breathe. It was stupid, but that's how I felt. I managed to say, "I just need the form back today. You got our fax number, right? Um, it's 4-0-4—"

"Look," he said like he was about to rush me off the phone.

"If you could just get with the other recruiters, and um, get us some proctors on there and fax it back that would be great." I was being way too soft on him. The proctor support form is due back to us two weeks before the test date, not two days. I couldn't lose control of the situation, and certainly not in front of the people in my shop, who were probably starting to notice the call was taking too long. He didn't say anything. I guess he noticed I was prolonging the call too.

"Um, sometime today would be great," I said. Then I remembered what I'd just told Mr. A. "This morning, okay?"

He didn't say anything.

"Hello?"

Then he went back to, "Yeah."

"Yeah," I said, relieved that he was still there. "So I guess I'll see you there."

"I guess you won't," he said back.

All I could get out was, "Um. Oh."

"Staff Sergeant Finley, you got that school on Thursday," he said, talking away from the receiver.

I could hear Finley mumble in the background.

I heard Curtis reply, "Get some names and phone numbers on this shit and fax it back over there today." Then he spoke back into the phone to me, saying, "Staff Sergeant Finley'll fax it back today. That it?"

Before I could say, "Yeah, thanks," he had already hung up. I just said, "Okay, thanks. Bye," to the dial tone and hung up like I hadn't been hung up on first. That shit wasn't cool.

Chapter Twenty-Five – Something Else

Two days later, we were running late, and we needed to unload those books and get set up in less than 15 minutes.

Mitch was driving. And if it wasn't for the fact that he was a speed limit driver, on I-20 of all places, and a few unexpected turn-offs to the boondocks— I'm not the best navigator—we might have arrived on time at least, instead of 10 minutes before the test was supposed to start. Mitch didn't have the sense of direction that Tubbs did. So there we were, lost and late. In that order.

Visitor parking was down a hill and several sets of steps away from the school. We drove up and hoped for a few up front visitor spaces, but we weren't having the beginnings of a lucky day, so the next few minutes just followed suit.

"Okay, Coop," he offered. "Let's just park and walk. We're already running late."

He had a point, but I didn't feel like walking.

"Naw, man," I said. "Just pull in right here in front. Don't turn it off. I'll unload the trunk right quick. Then you go park. I'll get set up."

We pulled into one of the spots right in front of the main doors. Of any of the three or four vacant spots we could have pulled into for a few seconds, we pulled into the wrong one.

Just after Mitch had popped the trunk of the GOV and I was pulling out the hand-truck, a squeaky-voiced blonde lady in a red sports car pulled up behind me. She wasn't in a position like she was waiting for us to back out. It was more like she would have driven right past us, but then changed her mind and came to a dead halt, like she'd discovered something she overlooked.

I didn't notice her until I'd turned and noticed my beeline to the sidewalk was blocked by the front of her car. I dropped my shoulders in a huff and propped the toe of my pump against the back of the hand-truck.

"Excuse me," she said, not really meaning it. "Excuse me. You can't park there. You're in my spot."

"Yes, Ma'am," I said. I would have called her pretty if her attitude hadn't preceded her. "We're just unloading."

Mitch turned to look at her from behind the wheel. "We just want to unload our books. We're giving the ASVAB test." He smiled as he talked. Mitch had a smile that most people would have found charming.

"Well, you're still going to have to move!" she said. "That's my spot, and you can't park there," she repeated like we didn't understand the first time.

"Yes, Ma'am," he continued to debate. "We're just running a little behind."

"Move your car, now!" What the hell was up with this wench?

Mitch tightened his lip and put the car in reverse. As he looked for me in the rear view mirror, I had walked up beside him on the driver's side.

"Put the car back in park," I said as calmly as I could. "The trunk is already popped. She can wait a minute. I swear, if it ain't one thing, it's something else."

"Coop, it's not worth it," he said. "I'll just park right there. He referred to the spot right next to the one we were in.

"Park the goddamn car! Ally McBeal can wait."

The squeaky blonde lady huffed and said, "Look, I don't know who you think you are, but if you don't move that car right now, I'm going to have you towed."

I was thinking to myself, *Fine with me. By the time the tow truck gets here, we'll be moved, and you'll look like crap for mistreating the military.*

By this time, we were holding up at least one bus behind us and a hand full of onlookers had gathered on the sidewalk. I charged right over to her car while she was in mid-sentence and said, "Ma'am, this morning has been a little rough. And, something else, in case you haven't noticed, the past few days have been a little rough! And yet," I talked over her attempt to interject, "I am prepared to give my LIFE in your defense, do you understand me?"

She stuttered a little, probably less out of embarrassment and shame of her behavior and more because I had taken somewhat of a threatening stance.

"We," I said back. "Him over there," I pointed at Mitch, "and me, are prepared to do that. For you. Now like it or not, I'm unloading this car. Right now."

She looked stunned, and she should have.

"My life ought to be worth at least the 30 seconds it's going to take me to get my books out of this car and onto the damn sidewalk. Hmph."

I shook my head and walked back to the trunk of the car. My life for 30 seconds. I wish she would. Gonna do something. You're gonna what? She's *going* to get cussed out if she ain't careful.

I must have calmed down a little too much, because she blinked bold at me and said, "You can just park down there in visitors parking." She pointed down the hill where I was not about to go. "I am not about to be late because of your poor planning."

I looked down the hill and then looked back at her, thinking, *Bitch, do you want to get slapped?* I know I had to be just about seeing red, but she seemed to be in the mood to make a point. Maybe she was going through a long stretch too. Or maybe she'd just lost a friend or loved one on September 11th and she was still lashing out. Or maybe she was just a selfish bitch who just wanted her designated parking space.

There we were, military members in uniform, decked out in ribbons even, barely a week after, and she was bitching at us about a parking spot. The flag in front of the school was still at half-staff for goodness sake. And she was probably playing Lee Greenwood or Bruce Springsteen on the way to work. Fake-ass, bandwagon-jumping bastards had just about grated on my last nerve, and here was one more to deal with. It didn't occur to me that with a spot right in the front of the building she must have been somebody important, to the school anyway.

I pretended to ignore her as I steadied the hand-truck and snatched what is usually a heavy footlocker full of books from the trunk of the car and plopped it down onto the hand-truck.

"Lady, I am not about lug these books across a parking lot and up umpteen stairs just because you don't have enough appreciation for the people who guard your country and your damn snotty-ass way of life to give a soldier a break."

"Well, I'll—"

"You will just wait and like it," I grumbled, not really caring whether or not she heard me.

And wait she did, though it's a safe bet that she was not liking it. Mitch didn't move the car until I'd given him the signal. He mouthed, "Thank you," to Squeaky as he pulled out and drove down to the visitors' lot. I waited on the sidewalk for him to park the car and then we went into the school together.

Starting a test late makes me anything but mellow, but it's not the end of the world. Running through the instructions and combining the last three parts of the test usually make up for any lost time. So I was cool.

When we wheeled our stuff into the cafeteria, the sorry-ass recruiters, including Staff Sergeant Finley, were standing around smoking and joking with the kids. Finley was just the beginning of the nightmare. Standing too close to him to be professional was Squeaky, the parking lot Gestapo, flirting her narrow ass off. She peeled her eyes away from him long enough to notice us, and then she gave us that played out gesture of looking at her watch.

"Good morning, again," she said to Mitch, sounding surprisingly sincere. "We're on a tight schedule here, so we really need to get started." She smiled up at him, but he was obviously still smarting a little from the parking spot incident too.

"Ma'am, Sergeant Cooper is the lead test administrator," he said directing his eyes to me. "She's got this one." He looked over her head and motioned for the recruiters to come over, get their briefing, and help us start passing out test materials. Finley strolled over with the others and they stood there ready.

At first Squeaky just answered, "Oh?" and then recovered with, "Oh. Well, let me know if you need any help." She gazed at Finley as she talked to me. "Pencils, paper or anything like that."

With the kind of month it had been already, and the kind of day it had started to be, I should have known better than being a smart ass, but that's what I was feeling. I turned my back on her to open my carrying case. I said, "Thanks, Ma'am. We have everything we need."

There were a total of seven recruiters. We expected to have somewhere between 250 and 280 students. So we brought 300 books. We're supposed to plan for at least 20 possible over what we expect. We ended up with 265 students, but unfortunately, we only had 200-and-too-few answer sheets. We were low on scratch paper too. I looked and felt like shit as a TA.

It was bad enough that I had to send one of the proctors to ask Squeaky for some additional scratch paper, but when I had to turn away the last two rows of tables full of kids because I didn't have enough answer sheets, hell could have opened up and swallowed me. Squeaky came in and stood at the door. I managed to get through 2 ½ hours of, *Your score on this test will be based on the number of questions you answer correctly. You should try to answer every question. However, do not spend too much time on any one question,* etc., etc., by the sheer grace of God.

I thought I felt enough like shit for having to turn people away at random. Some of those kids probably got there and were seated before others, but I had no other way of doing it. That was poor preparation and there was no excuse for it. Plus, we were late. The reason was plain old bad traffic and Mitch drives like he's chauffeuring Miss Daisy. And being a Marine makes him unable to ask for directions, I guess. Or maybe that's just any man. I had once been late for a test because Curtis had spent the night and we'd had some not-so-quick sex that morning. I had used the bad traffic excuse. And I had plenty of materials on me that time. Today, I just fucked up for no reason.

And then there was a poor Air Force recruiter from Hiram, who was nothing but helpful, who ended up on the receiving end of his unfair share of my Curtis-induced crankiness. Crankiness that should have been directed at somebody like Finley, or Squeaky, or Curtis himself, to tell the truth about it. But there I was, breaking the third cardinal rule of testing. Never let a recruiter see you lose your cool. I could feel the blood rushing to my head because my ears got hot and I stumbled over a few modules of the test before Mitch took over for me. I was going to MEPS hell when I got back and I knew it. Tubbs and Mr. A. were going to be so disappointed.

To hear those snotty school counselors tell it, you'd think I'd never administered a test before, like I'd lost a book or something. I'm sure they'd've had me fired, if there was such a thing in the Army. All because of a few answer sheets, and having to turn away 25 kids from the test.

Immediately following the test, Squeaky had the nerve to chastise me in front of all of my recruiter-proctors and then tell me how she'd done me a favor by cooling off, because she was, in her own words, "pissed" about the whole situation.

Then she started going all off about how every one of the students in the school could easily score a 50 or better on the test, and how *they* were doing *us* a favor by letting us in to test them in the first place, as if every kid in that school had a college scholarship in his back pocket or something. The Lord was sure holding my tongue that morning because I actually thanked her when I really felt like pointing out, *Bitch, I scored a 99 on the test. So what?* She could stow all that garbage about them doing us a favor by letting us in that raggedy-ass school, when we were the ones there to give their students other career options. What a crock of shit. Then again, me pointing out the career options part would have had me putting too much of a recruiter slant to the whole thing. And I was really hating all recruiters just then.

Whether I deserved a private ass-chewing or not—and I did—for recruiters to see you falter and get chewed out about a job you know you know, is intolerable because when it does, your power base as the person in charge slips away from you. And not just any recruiters; no, it had to be Finley's talking ass. Not to mention the irreparable damage it does to your credibility. After that fiasco, I was sure I'd never give another high school test again. So I just stood there and took it. Then I thanked her for her professionalism.

I waited in the school's administration office outside the head counselor's door for twenty minutes hoping to extend a verbal apology for the screw up. Mitch stood there patiently beside me, like a walking cane in the corner, in case I needed him. The office aide and the receptionist glanced toward us periodically and smiled weakly like we were a couple of kids in trouble, waiting for the principal to give us detention. Finley stood outside in the hallway, occasionally looking in at us, shooting the breeze with whoever'd stop to pay him any attention in his dress blues. He did look good.

Just when Mitch and I were about to call it lunchtime, in walked a sight for sore eyes. I must have been some kind of distracted because I didn't even see him walk in, but I looked up and there stood Raphael. Good-looking, smiling Raphael. And if that wasn't enough to turn the tide, he was being escorted by my old high school classmate, Floyd, who happened to be one of the assistant football coaches for Raggedy High.

"Hey, Miss," Raphael smiled. "How you doin'?"

"Hey," I said back. "What are you doing here? I haven't seen you since—well, since… "

"Since the last time you could fit me into your schedule," he said with a smile. "I been thinking about you. How you doin'?"

I forgot that I meant to cuss him out for getting Curtis mad at me. I was just about ready to lie and tell him I was fine, when I noticed Floyd standing at the desk, getting a visitor's badge for Raphael.

"Hey!" I said again. "I didn't know you worked here." I immediately thought about Curtis. Wait until I told him who I'd run into. I had all but forgotten why we were sitting in there.

Floyd brought me back to reality. "Hey! What's up girl? What are you doing here?"

I just answered, "Work."

Just when I was making the introductions to Mitch, when out of the office comes Squeaky, better known as Bitch Number One, sent to tell me that Bitch Number Two didn't have anything to say to me, that she'd say it to my commander, in writing. I didn't want her fat-ass to do any talking anyway. I was there to apologize, but she had the audacity not to even see me.

I thanked Squeaky's fake-smiling ass over my embarrassment and Mitch and I got our stuff together to walk out. Floyd and Raphael happened to be headed to the cafeteria for lunch, but I decided that I'd spent about as much time in that school as anyone should have to stand. A part of me wanted to stick around and have the *Guess who else is in ATL?* conversation with Floyd, but then I remembered my discretion. We exchanged email addresses in the hallway, and then Raphael walked with me and Mitch outside to get the car.

Mitch was cool enough to let me stand at the sidewalk with the footlocker and carrying case while he went to get the car. Waiting on curb service gave me a couple of minutes to find out that Raphael was there scouting football players for UGA, looking over a few hopefuls. "So, do you see anything you like?" I asked.

"Of course, I do," he answered. Then he did the over-exaggerated leering me up and down move. "Not bad at all." He winked at me, and I bumped him with my hip and stuck out my tongue.

Then along came Finley, walking up pretending to be helpful.

He started by completely ignoring Raphael standing there and asked if I needed help loading our books into the car. Where the fuck was he this morning?

"No thanks, s'arnt, we got it."

"Staff Sergeant," he said, like a true Marine.

"Okay," I said back. "We still got it."

"So what's up with the tests? Are we going to be able to use them?" he asked all in one breath. That was what he really wanted to know anyway. He made me sick. "Are they going to let us back into the school?"

"I don't know, Finley," I said, looking at Raphael. "You've been in there all morning kissing ass. You'd know better than me."

He cleared his throat and said, "My bad, big sarge. Am I interrupting something?" He rolled his eyes at Raphael. "What up, Money?"

There he goes, practicing his homeboy talk, like ebonics was a foreign language. What the hell was taking Mitch so long with the car?

Raphael answered something like, "What up, Yo?" or whatever the hell, as they both pretended to be cordial to each other. At that point, I wouldn't have put it past Finley to say something stupid and obnoxious such as, "Yo quiero Taco Bell," but he didn't.

Not wanting to afford him the opportunity to be a more obvious cock-blocking jerk, I interrupted them and asked Finley to excuse himself from our company, to which he reluctantly obliged.

As he walked off, I paraphrased the testing debacle from that morning. "I was just about to be exiled from the premises when you and Floyd came in and rescued me."

"Anytime, Ma. You know how we do." and even opened the door for me when Mitch pulled up to the curb. I got in and he closed the door. Mitch sat there waiting as if he knew not to pull off until he'd given Raphael time enough to say, "I'll give you a call tonight, a'ight?"

"All right," I said back.

For the first time that day, I felt lighter. I felt like whatever else happened, I could shake it off and keep it moving. I was glad that Raphael had that effect on me. I was glad I hadn't cussed him out for getting Curtis mad at me the other night.

Chapter Twenty-Six – Messengers

By the time we got back to the MEPS, of course, the counselors had already called ahead and expressed their extreme disappointment in my incompetence. I'm sure my commander was seeing red, but Mr. A. pulled me out of that frying pan and managed to diffuse the bitch squad by coordinating another test, at a date to be determined by the school. By the time he'd finished, Raggedy High graciously agreed to *let* us come back the next week, specifically requesting Staff Sergeant Mitchell, and would be willing to consider allowing us to return the next year, provided I didn't come back as one of the TAs. Oooh! Those bitches.

That afternoon, as I thought a bad day was finally drawing to a close, I was finishing up QRP and getting ready for night test check-in. I organized my clipboards on the counter and waited for 2 o'clock. I was chilling at the front counter with Petty Officer Morrison Smith, who we all call just Mo or Smitty, or even Red, because of his complexion. God had decided to smile on me. I guess He knew that I needed a break, and being around Smitty always put me in a good mood. Smitty was always doing or saying something to make people laugh, and he was charming as hell. And nobody can wear those Navy white pants quite like he can. Some of the females around the MEPS call him The Ice Cream Man, which he gets a kick out of too.

We were joking around and laughing, and the chaos of that morning was melting away. Unfortunately, the break was short-lived, because I looked up from my clipboards to see the last person I wanted to see that day:

Finley. I didn't want to see him, hear him, and certainly not talk to him. I knew Smitty had my back.

I cued Smitty with a nod in Finley's direction, so he could head him off before he got to the counter. Smitty started, "Recruiters to the lounge," song and dance he'd made up to emphasize the point that recruiters should not be on the floor with applicants. It was a sort of Bankhead Bouncy-James Brown sliding type of thing set to music only he could hear. It really did the trick, embarrassing the hell out of recruiters and amusing the rest of us. "Recruiters to the lounge," he sang over and over, "Recruiters to the lounge," and motioned Finley away from the counter, sliding, bouncing and pointing toward the recruiter's lounge.

"Yeah, man. I got it," Finley said. I pretended not to notice he was looking at me as he spoke. "Can I talk to you outside for a minute?" I started to roll my eyes at him and then he added, "I got a message for you."

Smitty continued his dance and modified his song to, "Recruiters to the lounge, or take it outside. Recruiters to the lounge, or take it outside."

I fell for the message bait, and walked outside with Finley to his GOV.

I sat there for a second, trying not to act anxious, but I the more I listened to him playing "Living for the City", the more agitated I got. I looked at the CD player and then rolled my eyes at him, not saying anything. What the hell could he possibly know about hard-time Mississippi?

"So, what's up?"

"Why don't you have lunch with me sometime," he smiled.

"The message," I insisted.

"The message is, you look, um, hungry."

"Well, I'm not," I said. "You didn't have a message, did you?" I was genuinely disappointed and I know it showed. I reached for the door handle to get out. "Very funny."

"Come eat with me anyway," he persisted. "Dinner. Maybe a movie." He winked and smiled.

I looked at him like he must have been suddenly deaf. So I said it again. "No."

He leaned over and licked his lips like he was about to kiss me.

"And back up," I said, staring at him dead on. "I said, no. Thanks."

"Okay, I'll eat," he smirked. "You just, um, cum."

I should have slapped him, but I just said, "Whatever." I was used to guys like Finley making passes, aggressive flirting that bordered on harassment, and I was used to dealing with it. Standing your ground and putting them in their place is infinitely more effective than cowering behind an EO complaint. I squinted my eyes and twisted my lips at him. "Why would I?"

He just smiled at me with a look like he thought I was considering it. He was close enough for me to smell the flavor of the gum he was chewing.

"Look, B.J.," I said. "I gotta get back to work. It's almost time for me to start check-in." I pretended not be affected by how he was invading my personal space.

"I just want to put my mouth on it," he said.

"Back up," I said, pushing him away. "Do I look like I'm in the mood to put up with this bullshit?"

"You're still sitting here," he reasoned. "What would your boy think about that?"

"Fuck you," I said, opening my door.

"Anytime," he said.

I stopped and turned to him before I got out. "Like you really thought I would fall for that weak-ass come on, so you could run back and tell some dumb shit, right?"

"You know what's up," he said.

"Yeah, I know you call yourself trying me. I thought we were better than that, but I guess not," I said. "You trifling bastard. You make me sick."

At first he looked wounded before trying to cover it up. "I'm trifling?" He pretended to laugh.

"Yeah, you," I said. "Smiling all up in his face, flunkying around for him, pretending to have his back with all that *Band of Brothers* bullshit." Then I added, "Oooh! You're such a fake."

"I'm a fake?" he asked. "You're so-called friends with his wife. What does that make you?"

Okay. Touché, for real, because I did not see that one coming. My mouth fell partially open, and I looked away, trying to regroup. I got out of the car and turned to push the door shut. I leaned at him through the window and asked, "Does he know you're all up in my face right now trying to get your head between my legs?"

"Maybe," he said after a pause. "Does he know I've already been there?"

I wondered when he was going to play that old ass card.

"Maybe," I lied, without pausing.

"From what he says, it's better than I remember. Does he even know about me?"

I just stood there looking at him enjoy his moment. Why is he even talking to him about me?

"Does he know I'm better at it than he is?"

"No, he doesn't," I said, blinking away.

"I didn't think so," he said, smugly.

"Hmph," I smiled at him and said, "I didn't think so, either," as I pushed away from the door with both hands. I didn't wait for his expression before I turned and walked away, but I hoped his face was cracked and falling right into his lap. That cocky son-of-a-bitch.

I resisted the urge to turn around. I was sure he was still looking at me, watching me walk away from him. He probably had on those dark sunglasses that he always wore, which I'm sure are out of Marine Corps regulations, so why he wore them was a mystery to me. But then, he did lots of shit I didn't understand, shit that he wouldn't explain and I couldn't get past.

Like how he always went out of his way to portray himself as something or somebody other than whom he really was. He probably had his radio set on a country station right now, but he wanted to make sure I heard him playing Stevie Wonder, to show his versatility, I guess. He also has a motivational recruiting song, the rap song about the ballers and shot-callers and Impalas. I'm glad I got out of the car before he started playing that one.

Curtis and the other recruiters call him Fin. I nicknamed him B.J. for Barrett Jonathan. Since then, I've noticed he always signs his 714s *B.J. Finley*. Nothing ever really happened between us. Remember, I don't count oral sex as sex. We went out a few times, months before Curtis came to ATL and became the station commander at Finley's station, but that's it. On our first date, he was playing Tim McGraw and Travis Tritt, but when I mentioned that Outkast and Ludacris were two of my favorites, suddenly he's versatile, eclectic. What a piece of work.

I'd say the best thing the Marine Corps ever did for Finley was show him how to pull off that swagger, the one that says *I am sure*, even when you're not. At least that fit him well enough.

All I knew for sure about Finley is that whatever he and I had was definitely in the past. And I was definitely glad about it. Besides being confused as hell, he has to be the bitchiest Marine I've ever met in my life. Does the training make them so hard core that they have to be such bitches about it?

When I met Finley, I was doing what we spend most of our afternoons doing at the MEPS: Putting recruiters in their places, usually somewhere outside. I'd just given him one of my best verbal lashings when he walked up to the counter and asked if he could speak to me outside. I said yes.

We went down the sidewalk, away from the door and then he presumed to chastise me for challenging him with my choice of words. He said that I was being confrontational. Talk about tender nerves.

"You know what?" I didn't give him a chance to answer. "Shut up." I started to walk off, but instead of blowing him completely off, something made me ask, "Uh, are you all right?"

"I'm fine. Why?"

"If you weren't so cute, I'd cuss your ass out right now."

"I don't get that often."

"What? Cussed out?"

"Talked to like that," he said.

He had a nice smile, so I kept it going with, "Yeah, well that's probably what's wrong with you."

After the initial confrontation, we hit it off okay. He started off like they all did, shooting the breeze, flirting a little bit, then working his way around to asking for early test scores because we were on cordial terms.

So when he asked me out, I thought, *what the hell?* He's cute and he's paying. And he was really good at what he did. I wouldn't have expected anything less. I mean, white boys invented it, didn't they?

He was so good at going down on me that I could have fainted right there in the bed, except I didn't want to pass out and miss something. I would just lie there and hold on to whatever was handy when he was at work. And even though I'd be completely out of breath when he was done, he did it in a way that I never wanted him to stop. If he was doing it while I was standing up, I'd collapse right on top of him. If he was doing it while I was sitting down, I'd unfold flat out like a broken lawn chair. Nobody had ever had my body convulsing the way B.J. did.

The first time he did it, we were in the balcony in the back of a near-empty movie theater. What the hell was the name of that movie? Maybe it'll come to me later. Mmph! He really was better at it than Curtis, but neither of them will ever know that.

One thing I'm sure of is that they're not sharing notes. At least, Finley's not. Curtis trusts Finley and Finley feels connected to Curtis in some strange way. Both their dads being preachers makes them think they have some special bond, I guess. More of that *Band of Brothers* mentality or whatever.

After a few dates, Finley revealed his issues, issues that he didn't share with me until he'd already taken me to the movies. His dad didn't approve of race-mixing, and he knew he could never take me home. So basically, he couldn't decide whether or not he really gave a damn about me. It's weird, because he said that thought he was in love with me. "We still have the Confederate Flag hanging in our front window," he once told me. Well damn. Just when I thought the white boy might have some potential to be The One.

I told him we could be cool, but we couldn't go out anymore. That I couldn't see myself with any man who didn't think I was good enough to meet his mama. The truth was, I wasn't cool with it. The situation didn't do my self-esteem any favors.

Then one night, he showed up at my door, high as a Georgia pine. Whatever he was on had those pretty eyes on fire. Somehow, he was too high to drive home, but not too high to find his way to my apartment. And, he was driving a GOV. I let him sleep it off on my sofa and then read him the riot act the next morning. He slept until damn near noon.

All he had to say was, "I thought you of all people would be able to relate."

"Me?" I felt insulted. "Why the fuck would I be able to relate to you being a dope head?" I asked, disgusted. "If they gave you a piss test today, your ass would be out. You're hot as cayenne pepper."

He had a shadow already growing on his face. The purple haze was disappearing slowly, and the blue was fading back into his eyes.

"I just thought," he said, "the way you drink—,"

"The way I drink?" I cut him off. "And just how do I drink? What the hell are you trying to say?" Sure, I liked my fair share of spirits, and I kept a bottle or two handy in the pantry, but so what?

"All I'm saying," he continued, "is that you know what it's like to have shit on your mind."

"Mmmm."

"I just thought maybe you understood what it's like to miss me as much as I miss you," he said. "And not be able to do shit about it."

"Look, B.J.," I told him, "I'm not the one with the redneck daddy. I could take you home now—high, hung over, drunk or sober, sick, or well."

I handed him the glass of raw egg and hot sauce I'd concocted for him. "Or damn near dead in your case—and my family wouldn't give a damn about nothing, if they thought you made me happy."

He couldn't even look at me. He took a gulp from his glass and set it down on the floor by his foot. The eggs might have been a little old, but served him right.

"And right now, you don't make me happy," I lectured. "You're lucky you didn't run into a tree or a ditch or somebody's child. In a goddamn GOV! Shame on you. You're acting like a fucking coward."

I must have a talent for striking Marine nerves, because he jumped up, knocking over the half-full glass. "I'm a goddamn United States Marine. I'm no fucking coward!"

Oh no, he didn't just goddamn raise his voice at me in my house. He was going to get it, now. "I know you didn't just kick that shit over on my carpet." Pushing my hand up against his face, I asked, "And who the fuck are you hollering at?"

He didn't move, didn't try to knock my hand away. He looked so pathetic that I found myself calming down.

"I know you're a '*goddamn* Marine', B.J. But you got to get your shit and get out of here."

He started with the *Baby, I'm sorry's*, but I wasn't hearing it.

"I won't do this with you, B.J." I was so firm. "I'm not the sneaking around type."

"But I never been with anybody the way I have with you," he claimed. "I've done things with you I've never done with anybody."

I doubted that. Anyway, the answer was still no. He had to go. So he left and that was that.

After that, we hardly spoke at all. And then, when he and Curtis became buddies, he hasn't had more than two words for me. Until today.

I took a moment to contemplate the fact that I'm in the same fucking pattern with Curtis that I was with Finley. "What the hell am I doing?"

I went back inside and stood at the counter. Naturally, Smitty was curious. "What's up with that crumb? What did he want?"

"Wanted to walk in a tester, of course," I lied. That was the typical reason that recruiters want to discuss something outside. "Promised me a sweat suit."

"Word?"

"Full of shit, like the rest of them. What the fuck would I do with a Marine's sweat suit? I told his ass to get back here before five like everybody else walking in."

Smitty believed me, and went to take care of some other business. I stood there at the front counter, thinking about that whole B.J. situation, refusing to acknowledge its similarities to my situation with Curtis.

Chapter Twenty-Seven – Misunderstandings

Later that same day, about forty minutes or so into night test check-in, going on three o'clock in the afternoon, when one of the shuttle drivers showed up to take the shippers to the airport. Other drivers were dropping off applicants to take the night test. Plus, there were still applicants coming up to pick up contracts for ceremony briefings.

Recruiters started to trickle in, leaning against the walls, hoping to go unnoticed, until their applicants either checked in, shipped out, or were sent into the enlistment ceremony. Smitty sang and danced them toward the recruiter lounge or back out the door. The front counter traffic was getting a little hectic, but it was no more of a fuster cluck than typical for that time of day.

I spotted one of the new army recruiters who wasn't as new as he pretended to be. I'd dealt with him a few times during the night test check-in and had worked a high school test with him over in Jonesboro. He had a small talent for pretending not to know any better, but I guessed it was just a skill they all developed eventually.

He walked in and semi-paused in mid stride, as if he expected to be stopped. He was almost to the door leading to the liaison offices and applicant waiting area before Smitty stopped him.

"Hey, hey, partna," Smitty waved at him.

When partna kept going, Smitty looked at me like I was the one slipping, and I said, "I got it."

I put my command voice on and said, "Excuse me. S'arnt." When he stopped, I said, "Yeah, you, S'arnt."

He turned around and walked up and leaned on the counter with his arms crossed. His muscles filled out the shirt like it was made for him.

"Hey," he said, smiling. "How you doin' big sarge?"

"I'm good, thanks." I smiled back.

"Are you?" he asked. I ignored what could have been easily passed for a come on line.

He was wearing baggy Tommy Hilfiger jeans and a black Army polo shirt with the recruiter logo on it, the type the recruiters wear on their down days.

"You know you're not supposed to be in here out of uniform, right?"

"What?" he asked, feigning innocence. "This is my uniform of the day."

"Then this is a day you should've sent somebody else down here to do your MEPS business. Right?"

He didn't answer, but had that guilty look on his face.

Smitty said, "Mmmhmm."

"We can't have recruiters running in and out of here looking like applicants," I continued.

"Oh," he said. "So you puttin' me out?"

"Not this time," I said. "Just do the right thing, okay?"

"Right," he said. "I'm going straight to the lounge. I won't talk to nobody except—"

"Except nobody, Sarge," I interrupted. "Come on, now. You're already in the wrong."

I guess he could tell I didn't have it in me to be hard on him, and I guess he decided not to press his luck with Smitty.

"All right," he said, still smiling. "I ain't talking to nobody until I'm outta here." Recruiters knew that we couldn't allow them to be hanging out in any applicant areas because we couldn't risk any undue influence on applicants' processing, including interviews, exams or job selection. Some recruiters have been known to try and "steal" applicants away from other recruiters in order to make their own numbers.

Yeah, right, I thought, but I just waved him off toward the back. I went back to checking in the next tester, and Smitty went back to directing traffic.

Not five minutes later, in came Curtis, walking straight toward me. No applicant in tow, no walk-in test request, no 714 form, just some shit waiting to hit the fan. I got that same flushed feeling that I got when I was losing my power base at Raggedy High. As far as I knew, he could have been watching me and the army recruiter from outside the whole time. I pretended I was too busy to notice him. I *was* too busy, but I'd never be too busy to notice him.

"Staff Sergeant, can I talk to you for a minute?" He just walked up to the counter and stood there like he expected me to stop and drop everything I was juggling. I was in mid-sentence of checking in a test applicant, waiting for the results of a SSN pull request on my computer, and on hold with another MEPS who had called us asking for something, and I needed an extra pair of hands and legs to go follow up in the files room.

Besides test applicants, who were to line up two-by-two around the corner, there were kids just now coming out of the morning physical, kids waiting to pick up contracts to get sworn in. Mrs. Harris—a civilian who was already working at the MEPS way back when I first came in the army—stood a few inches away from me at another terminal. She was handing out contracts and calling names for the next swearing in ceremony. Holding up the other side of the counter were the Ops O, who seemed to always be looking for something to do, and the first sergeant, looking for his unit clerk, who was probably outside on an extended smoke break. Smitty was conspicuously absent, and so was my good mood.

Also filling this small space on my side of the counter was Mr. A., who was filling in as the travel clerk, lining up his shippers to get shuttled off to the airport for basic training.

Where the hell is Smitty when I need him? Then I remembered Smitty was in the ceremony briefing room, preparing applicants for the ceremony.

"Is there a problem, Gunny?" the Ops O asked him. God, bless him. He looked like he was wearing the same Air Force uniform that he got issued in ROTC. I just shook my head, thinking surely his wife doesn't tell him that tight shit is sexy.

Curtis ignored him. "Right now, Sebrina."

I cleared my throat and pretended not to notice all the noses that were suddenly pointed in my direction. "Sure," I said. "Be right with you." I looked down at the 714 and told the applicant I was checking in to have a seat and wait until we called him to go back to the test room. Mr. A. offered to take over at the desk while I excused myself.

At first Curtis and I stood outside the first set of double doors in sort of a breeze-way area, just before the double doors that lead outside. People could see us, but they couldn't hear us.

"What the hell kind of clown are you trying to take me for?" he asked, louder than he should have.

"Who said I was trying to take you for any kind of clown?" I asked, but I already knew who'd been telling shit wrong again. Finley spurned, stirring up shit. People were steadily walked in and out of these doors as we stood in their way, so I suggested, "Let's go outside."

"Let's go," he said, pushing open one of the doors leading outside, almost hitting a recruiter who was coming in.

I followed him down the walk, and when he turned to me, I said, "First of all, we shouldn't be having this conversation."

"Why not?" he demanded.

"Because I'm at work. And we damn sure shouldn't be having it here, at the front door of Peyton Place."

"Do I look like I give a fuck?" He didn't look like he gave a fuck, but I did, and he should have. "And you can cut the 'first-of-all' shit," he said. "Fin already told me about your little meeting with your little boyfriend out at the school."

"What?" I asked, not really surprised. "Fin?" That hater. That bitch-ass hater.

"Yeah," he said. "Some pretty motherfucker in a suit, macking you out by your car."

Oh great.

In afterthought, he added, "And who's that other motherfucker you're exchanging numbers with in the cafeteria?"

He was talking about Floyd. "Oh, yeah."

"Oh, yeah?" he repeated.

What? Had Finley called himself, giving Curtis the play-by-play? That simple bastard was probably back at the station right now, listening to country music, ready to flip the station whenever Curtis or one of the other guys came back in the office. Leave it to Finley to tell it wrong. It was in the hallway, not the cafeteria. And it was email, not phone numbers. I tried to set it straight. "Listen, Baby. You—"

"Don't fucking 'Baby' me," he snapped.

"Curtis, you got it all wrong."

"Do I?"

"Yeah, you do," I said. "That guy was a friend of mine from high school. He coaches football over there now. I didn't even know," I said, trying to lead him into asking who it was. I just smiled and shook my head, thinking how stupid he was going to feel when I told him it was Floyd.

"Yeah? And what the fuck are you smiling about?"

"Because I was going to tell you anyway." I said. "You'll never guess—"

"Just shut up," he cut me off. "You're lying."

That *shut up, you're a liar* thing kind of threw me off track.

"I'm not lying," I said back. "I haven't seen him in years."

"So?"

"So," I said. "You know who it is? It's—"

"So, if you ain't talked to his ass in years, what you got to talk to him about now? What?"

At that point, I started thinking about what people must have been saying inside and what people must have been saying passing by. "You know what? I don't know. Nothing, really. Forget it, Babe. I'll tell you when you feel like listening." I thought that would cut the interrogation short.

"What?" he kept going. "You gonna talk about old times and all that *bull*shit?"

Curtis was completely off track, and he wouldn't let me get a word in. Floyd was his boy, or so he'd said. Not to mention a guy I'd grown up with. Floyd was cool, but to him, I was just a friend's little cousin from the neighborhood.

"Anyway," I said, "he's married."

"Is that supposed to mean something to me?" he asked.

After a momentary reality check, I said, "No, I guess it wouldn't."

Just then, applicants started filing out of the building on their way to the van.

One of Curtis' applicants recognized him as he was walking out and said, "What's up, Gunny?"

Curtis turned around and shook hands with the kid and said something about making sure he stayed focused at boot camp. The kid held up his bible and Curtis' agitation with me seemed to break instantly. He smiled. "Stay motivated," he said, putting on that typical, two-faced recruiter enthusiasm.

"You know it," the kid said back, and smiled at me as he turned to get in the van. I knew the kid. Young Mr. Madison. I nodded and smiled.

As the van pulled away from the curb, I said, "I see he stuck with you after all this time, huh?" to Curtis, referring to the fact that the kid was only a sophomore in high school the first time I'd met him at the night test.

"Yeah, he did," he said dryly.

"Well, I guess you have that effect on people, huh?" I added, trying to get him to lighten up. He didn't say anything back to that.

After we watched the van drive away, he stood there looking at me with his arms crossed like he was waiting for something.

"Look," I said finally. "I wouldn't—"

"Wouldn't what?" he asked. "What?! You friends with his wife too, I guess."

Now this is the second man I should have slapped today, but I guess I stepped right into that one. Then it triggered a thought. "Why did you tell Finley that I knew *her*? Why did you even tell him about us?"

"What us?" he said back.

"I gotta go back to work." I turned to walk away, but this man has had a thing for grabbing my arm since I met him, so I should have expected it.

"I already told you, don't walk away from me," he said, pulling me back.

"Don't make a bigger scene than this already is," I said. "You don't think people are looking at us right now?" I didn't want to add to the gossip and speculation about why some married recruiter was snatching and jerking on me like I was his child.

He let me go and said, "All right, fuck it."

Before I could stop myself, I mumbled, "That's your answer to everything. When are you gonna mean it?" as I turned and walked toward the door to go inside.

"Sooner than you think," he snapped back as he started to walk off.

I turned around and walked toward him like I was ready to jump. "You know what? You're confusing the shit out of me. Just leave me alone, okay?"

He stopped and started walking back to me. "What?"

"I'm sick of all this, this—sneaking around shit anyway," I poked him in the chest with every other word I spoke.

He poked me back once, saying, "Don't fucking poke me."

I straightened my shirt and cleared my throat. "If I wanted to put up with all that, I might as well be with B—" I stopped.

"Well?"

"Be by myself," I said, backtracking. That's what I feel like most of the time, anyway."

Did I mean that? Well, hell, it was too late. I'd already said it. I just meant that I wanted to be able to do anything for the sake of somebody, and have that somebody treat it like it meant something. Whatever it was. "I just don't want to keep regretting everything I do."

Then he just looked at me with that same wounded look Finley had given me. "Consider yourself left," he said. Then he walked off toward the parking lot.

What?! I stood there for a second, holding the door open. What was that? Only a man would break off a relationship like that. I hated when he left me hanging like that. What a fucking coward.

I went inside and took over the check in from Mr. A., thinking to myself, *I know why people drink in the middle of the work day*. This was one of those days, and at that moment, I wished I was one of those people who brought mine to work and poured it in a McDonald's cup. I think vodka would do nicely.

With the shippers gone, and an enlistment ceremony underway, the crowd at the front counter had thinned out. Only Mrs. Harris was still up front with me. I used to talk to her sometimes about my dates with B.J. Since she was married to a white guy, I thought maybe she had some insight on the odds of it working out, and maybe something here and there about how they'd made it work for them all those years. I didn't tell her anything about Curtis though.

"A misunderstanding?" she asked after a few minutes.

"A lot of them," I replied.

"He looked pretty upset."

"He's a jerk," I said back. "Just another one of them, wanting something for nothing." I rubbed my chest. Damn, that poking shit does hurt.

"Mmmm," she said. "He sure does have a pretty bald head though."

He sure does. "He's a jerk," I repeated. "Plus, he's married."

"Oh, well," she said. "No harm in flirting, I guess."

I just kind of smiled at her, because I knew there could damn well be a lot of harm in it. "Yeah."

****

After work, I decided to call Raphael and take him up on his offer to hang out again. I needed to get out. I needed male company. He was available.

As I left my apartment, wearing jeans and a sleeveless top, Elliott was coming out of his door.

"What's up with the gladrags? Must be going somewhere special," he observed, pretending to marvel at the fact that I wasn't wearing sweats and a white T-shirt.

"Hmmm. Very funny," I said. "Just to a dollar movie with a friend."

"Big spender, is he?"

"He's a friend," I stressed. "It's not a date. It's a—non—date."

"You seem to have a lot of those. The non dates, I mean."

"Do I?" With your nosy ass. "Since when did you start watching my comings and goings?"

"Don't look at me like that," he said. "All I'm saying is that you spend more time with him than with—what's his name. Don't you?"

"It's not like that," I assured him. "We just hang out sometimes, you know. What's the big deal? It's every blue moon. Good grief."

"I know," he said. "But have you ever thought that maybe—"

"It's. Not. A. Date. Okay?" And then I changed the subject. "So where are you headed?"

He slung the bags over his shoulder. "Going to see my parents for a little while."

"In Chicago?" I guess the look on my face amused him.

He looked shocked back at me and said, "What? Did they up and move back to Alabama without telling me?" and then smiled. Just then, his phone rang. He pulled his phone out of his jacket pocket and answered it.

He looked at me as he talked. "Oh, hey Daddy," he said.

Just like most people who are country folk at heart, his dad was a loud cell phone talker. He called Elliott by what must have been his nickname as a kid. Loudly.

I was glad he'd mended fences with his father, who didn't approve of Elliott's choices, but under the circumstances, the recent reminder of how short and precious life is, I could see how they'd reevaluated their priorities.

"Yep. Leaving right now," he repeated. "Love you too." Then after a pause, he clicked off without saying good-bye.

"Jerry?" I asked.

"Short for Jeremiah," he clarified.

"As in the prophet?"

He shrugged. "Or the bullfrog." Then he smirked and winked. "Well, I guess I'm off," he sighed, patting his pockets and tugging his bags.

When Raphael came up the steps and saw us standing there, he seemed pleased that I was ready and waiting at the door. "I'm on my way down," I told him, and he turned to go back to the car.

Elliott and I started down the steps together. "Now that's a tall drink of chocolate milk," he smirked.

I ignored him. When we got to the bottom of the steps, I gave him a hug and said, "Be safe."

Chapter Twenty-Eight – Man Stuff

I had a good time with Raphael. He made no demands. He didn't trip. Ever. At the end of our non-date, Raphael and I sat in my living room and talked. And talked. And somehow, the talk turned to me, and what I wanted. What I was hoping to find. What I would like for a man to do for me.

He sat up on the sofa, and I lay across his lap, looking in his face as we talked. He rubbed his thumb across my right eyebrow as he listened to me go into a rant. "Hell," I said. "Just man stuff. That would be fine with me. A man who's around to do man stuff. Period."

"You make it sound simple," he said, smoothing the other brow with the same thumb.

"Well, isn't it?" It isn't?

"Just what is 'man stuff'?" he asked, like he shouldn't have already known. He shook his leg to make my head bounce up on his lap. I rolled my eyes at him and started to sit up. He laughed and said, "Okay, I'll stop," then shook his leg one more time.

"Man stuff," I said. "Take out the trash, wash the car, change the oil, change a few light bulbs, put stuff together, fix stuff, you know. Carry that heavy shit up the stairs. Man stuff."

"Is that all?" he asked.

"Not much to ask, I don't think," I said, and then I added, "And know a good mechanic if you can't be one."

"Oh yeah," he said, kind of laughing.

"I mean, I'll cook and wash dishes, clean up the house… Well, maybe not clean up the house too much. But I'll pick up the dry cleaning and stuff like that."

"And you're telling me, you've been in ATL for almost three years, and you haven't run across one brother who can do any of that?"

"None available," I said. "If they're not old, ugly or gay, they're all married or committed or should be committed. And those are the main ones always stepping up in my face. It's fucking ridiculous. Like I got 'Unavailable men, please approach me' stamped on my damn forehead."

"Don't take it too serious, Ma," he said. "Brothers just like to flirt sometimes. Take it as a compliment."

"A married man flirting with me is not flattering," I said, defensively. I thought about how innocently and naively I used to look at it back in the day.

"Well, what is it then?"

"It's a fucking insult, and it's disrespectful."

"Really?"

"Yeah," I said. "Married bastards need to act married. Make me fucking sick."

"I can tell," he said. "But really, it's not that deep, unless you let it be."

"I'm starting to think that marriage is my Never-Never Land. Marriage, kids, somebody who actually gives a damn about me."

"Mmm," he said softly. "Well, Ma, it might help if you had some idea of what you're looking for in a man."

"I thought we already had that conversation. Plus, who said I was looking anyway?"

"You're right about that. Nobody could ever accuse you of looking."

I turned my head away from him and stared at the wall. His lap was firm, but comfortable.

"Share that thought, Baby Girl," he said.

"Who says I'm thinking anything?" I said back. "Maybe I'm just listening."

"Maybe you're just stalling," he suggested.

"Maybe I'm wondering what makes you such a brain-picker all of a sudden." I still didn't look at him. I took the opportunity to turn the conversation in another direction. "I mean, it's not like you're, you know, not seeing other women, when we're not hanging out, right?"

"Yeah. That's right," he said, after I'd barely gotten the question out. "I spend time with other women. I actually call them dates, though." I pretended like I didn't feel him looking at me. Smart ass. "But that doesn't mean I don't look forward to the time we spend together. And I'm not even sleeping with you."

"Does that mean you're sleeping with them?" I asked.

He shook his leg again. "Do you really want to know?"

"Hmmm," I said. "Guess I got my answer." I tried not to let on that I was a tinge jealous. "Even though I really don't care who you sleep with. It's not me."

"It's okay, Ma," he said. "It's cool. Whatever."

Damnit. There he goes being all agreeable and shit. "I'm thinking you'll probably think I'm crazy if I tell you what I'm thinking."

"You're far from crazy," he said. We both laughed as he tried to turn my head to look at him. I kind of resisted, but not really. He did have a pretty face.

"Hmph. I'm plenty crazy. I just hide it from you. How'm I doing?" I laughed again, but he didn't laugh with me.

"Whatever, Ma. It's cool." For the first time since I'd known him, he didn't look like it was cool. He looked on the verge of fed up with my ass, but hadn't quite gotten there yet. Whatever. I wasn't making his ass come around me.

Then, for as crazy as I knew it sounded, I told him. "I just feel like every time he cuts himself off from me, I'm in the throes of grief."

"Throes of grief, huh?" He smirked.

"Shut up," I said. "Do you want to hear this or not?"

"Of course," he said, seriously.

"Well, okay," I felt like stalling again, but I kept going, not exactly sure why I cared about his opinion. "See, you're laughing, but it really hurts. I feel like I can almost hear our children crying to me, and if I don't hold on, or do something about whatever it takes to hold on to him, they're slipping away from me. They won't be born. That's what I mean by grieving."

"How do you know those are his children you're grieving for?"

"I just know," I said. That moment was the first time since we met that I felt like I couldn't tell Raphael something, actually wondering about what he'd think of me if he knew about my operation. "Let's not talk about it anymore."

"If you say so." He looked at me like he was thinking about trying lean forward to kiss me, and I was thinking I just might let him. Just then, the phone rang. I jumped up to answer it. "Hey!" Al said.

It was Al. "Hey, girl!"

"Oh, hey," I said, with a sigh of disappointment. If this heifer would stop calling me, then maybe my damn conscience wouldn't keep nagging me.

"Hey," she repeated.

I looked over at Raphael and shook my head, as I spoke. He shook his head back at me, and I could tell he thought it was sad how quick I was to jump at the thought of Curtis. "Hey girl, what's up?"

"I'm just calling to see what's going on with you," she said.

Oh, damn. Why couldn't she just leave me alone? Where was Curtis? Maybe sitting right next to her. Maybe he really is at work this time. I said, "I'm cool. I got company right now, though. Can I call you back?"

"Oh," she said, like I shouldn't have company. "Well, no problem. Anyway, I was just calling to see if you wanted to go out this weekend."

"Uh,"

"Friday," she added. "With me and my soror I told you about," she continued.

"Tomorrow?"

"Oh, yeah, I guess it is tomorrow." She laughed like something was funny.

"Uh, I don't know" I said. "I'm not really into clubbing anymore."

"Naw. We're not going clubbing. Just to a restaurant or something. And I meant to say next Friday. I got a hot date with my husband tomorrow night," she offered happily.

Hot date? That definitely sounded a lot like somebody who was getting some, or somebody who expected to get some. He was fucking her again. He didn't have to admit it. I just knew it.

"Where?" I asked. Then before she could tell me something I didn't want to hear about her hot date, I quickly added, "I mean, where do y'all want to go next Friday?"

"I was thinking somewhere downtown," she said. "We could meet up and have a girls' night."

"Oh yeah, right. I'm with that."

"About seven thirty or eight," she said, lingering.

"Uh, yeah. Yeah, that's good too. But hey, I really gotta go. I'll get the details later." I really didn't have to go. It was just Raphael, but I really wanted to go.

"Oh, okay," she said, like I was supposed to change my mind about getting off the phone. Hell, call your soror and whine on her nerves for a little while.

"Oookay," I said. "Bye." I hung up. I couldn't believe she took all that damn time to say nothing. I couldn't believe I agreed to meet them. "Can you believe I just agreed to meet them?" I asked Raphael.

"Do your thing, Ma." He didn't smile the way he usually did.

Before I could make myself comfortable in his lap again, he stood up and told me that he was going to take off. I didn't get my usual lingering goodbye hug, either. It was more of a quick hug-pat on the back.

"Well, thank you for the movie," I said.

"No problem, Sebrina." Sebrina? What happened to Baby Girl? Ma? Yo?

"I had a really good time. Maybe we could do it again sometime, soon."

"Yep. I'll call you," he said, in a *don't call me first* tone of voice.

Well, okay. I admit that I didn't see that coming, but t didn't bother me. Much. I was going to be leaving Atlanta in a couple of months for a new assignment anyway. But it bothered me a little bit that he was the one who suggested the space thing. As cool as he had always been, I was started to feel like he might start tripping like I owed him something. Whatever.

Chapter Twenty-Nine – Happy Hour

There's a place in Midtown called the Shark Bar. It's one of those nicely decorated, trendy places with large windows, strategically moderate lighting, contemporary artwork on the walls, and hardwood floors in the dining area. The bartenders and wait staff wore white shirts with crisp collars, and they carried the trays like they'd been trained in charm school. The music was a mellow mix of R&B favorites and newer tunes.

That's where I met up with Al and one of her sorority sisters that she'd run track with way back when. We were supposed to meet outside the front door on the sidewalk.

I parked near the Fox Theater and walked the short distance to the bar. I saw Al standing there with her hair and make up all done up like she'd been to the salon. She wore a beautiful pewter silk one-shoulder blouse with a black skirt and pointy-toed pumps. She didn't look like she was even trying to hide extra pounds though. Her face was fuller and her arms were definitely healthier. And she had the swollen fingers I'd once imagined on her.

I'd had my eyebrows done but that was it. Okay, and a manicure and pedicure. My hair was pulled back into a ponytail. We stood there for a minute while I complimented on what I believed to be Phyllis' handy work. Then she noticed that her sorority sister was standing just inside the door waiting for us.

They greeted each other with a simultaneous, "Heeey" and hugged. Then Al said, "Soror, this is my girl, Sebrina. Sebrina, this is my Soror,

Alice."

Alice. She didn't look like someone who'd be named Alice, the girl-next-door, pretty, unpretentious librarian type. My guess is that somewhere between high school and college was when she discovered her femininity, scarce though it was. Nor did she look like a former track star. Apparently, she and Al had been close once upon a time. They were in each other's weddings, and then sort of been out of touch since. They ran into each other recently at the mall or somewhere and decided to get they'd get together. Lucky me, I was invited to come along for an official girls' night out.

Alice had long enough legs that she could have been a decent hurdler once upon a time, but she looked more like one of those girls who was probably great at basketball or softball back in the day. Girls who slumped a lot because they thought they were too tall, who had to work at being a girl because they'd spent most of their adolescence competing with or outdoing all the boys. She looked like one of those girls who someone had told she should try modeling because she had long legs and a thin nose. She looked a little too butch-ish to be a model, but I was sure she'd been to her share of modeling convention things trying to get discovered. She had a look of disappointment and unfulfilled aspirations in her eyes.

Now, Alice's hips had spread significantly, and she was wearing matronly jeans that came up over her stomach way over her navel. She looked like a cow covered in denim.

I didn't like something about her right off, and the way we exchanged the standard, "Hey, how you doing?" pleasantries, neither of us extending for a handshake, just confirmed it. She wasn't very friendly.

Alice eyed me up and down before she started a fake compliment about my outfit and then cut it short like she'd decided it wasn't worth her breath.

She ended up saying something like, "Oh, that's a cute...pair of shoes. Nice to meet you."

"Rich's half-off sale last week. Nice to meet you too," I said back.

We couldn't have picked a more crowded night to be in the Shark Bar. Damn near everybody inside looked like they were hoping to impress somebody, but looked totally unimpressed with everybody they saw around them. We decided to stay there for a couple of drinks and maybe some food, then decide whether to check out the happenings downstairs in that matchbox they used for dancing. We lucked up on a table that probably should have been used for a larger party, but it was just far enough from the door and close enough to the bar to suit all three of us, so we sat down.

We were working on our first round of drinks, and Alice and Al had just ordered something from the menu, when Alice's phone rang. She looked down at it and ignored the call. I didn't order anything to eat because I was there to get as fucked up as I could.

"Whew, girl. Y'all wouldn't believe the week I've had," Alice bellowed out. "Just, run, run, run, nonstop."

I know it was just a figure of speech, but whatever. From the looks of her thighs, I doubt if she's run anywhere in years.

"Honey, I swear, if it wasn't for my birth control pills, some days I wouldn't even know what day it is."

"I know what you mean," Al chimed in.

Birth control pills? "Why are you on birth control pills and you're married?" I asked Alice. I knew why Al was on the pill. Compromise.

"Because me and my husband decided we didn't want anymore kids," Alice answered. "Two is enough. I still haven't gotten my body back from pushing out babies."

"*You* and your husband decided? I see."

Alice's phone rang again. She took forever to answer it and it was getting on my nerves. Finally she picked it up and grunted a few times into it. "Hello. What's up? Mmmhmm. Yep. Yes. Okay." Then she just hung up.

"I'm just checking in, Babe," she whined, repeating what he'd said.

"Well? What so wrong with that?" I asked.

"She's just tripping," Al said. "She thinks he's checking up on her. Not checking in."

Like somebody would need to check up on her frumpy ass.

"They've been together since high school," Al went on. "She followed him to college," she said and winked, apparently trying to get a reaction from Alice. "And that was that."

"That's cool," I said.

"Whatever. I did not follow him to college," Alice said, and then turned it on Al. "Can't believe old Mack Daddy let you out tonight anyway."

"Girl, please," Al said back. "My man trusts me. And don't call him that. I've always hated that nickname."

I just kept drinking my watered down Cosmopolitan. I noticed their matching AKA pins and matching double chins as they sat in profile.

"Aw, that's sweet," Alice said. "Where he at now, then? Still at work?"

"He's always working hard, right?" Al said, pretending to be serious and then added, "Not!"

They both laughed. Then Al said, "He's somewhere hanging out with the guys at his station." She laughed. "They're probably in the office with the door locked, getting toasted."

I wondered where he really was, but instead of pretending to nurse my drink, I slipped and said, "He doesn't drink." When they both turned on me with a H*ow would you know?* look, I added "Right? I mean, I thought you said he didn't drink."

"Yeah, maybe I did," Al said, but not looking convinced. "But he likes to stay around and make sure his guys get home okay on nights like this."

I stuck my nose in my glass and took a big gulp.

Al continued with, "It's a thing he does ever since one of his recruiters got in a wreck in one of the military cars last year," Al continued. "Driving drunk and stuff. It was a big deal, so he likes to be careful."

"Oh, that's cool," I said.

"So, Sebrina," Alice asked, "Where's your man tonight? You got a man?"

"Um, not really," I said quietly, even though it was too noisy to be speaking softly. "We kind of broke up."

"Kind of? Oh. I guess it's complicated, right?"

"Well," I said. "You know how it goes. There's a chance we'll get back together. If it's meant to be."

"For what?" she asked, like she was judging me. "Broke up is broke up. I don't see how any woman could make herself latch on to some man when he obviously don't want her no more."

What was she trying to say? And how the hell would she know who left whom? Just assuming that I got dumped. Heifer didn't know me like that, and I was just about to tell her as much. Then her phone rang again.

With an exasperated grunt, she answered, "What?!"

I swear I hate when people say *what* like that. That shit just irks me.

"Yes, Alfred. I know. I told you that this morning. Yes, it's okay. Why wouldn't it be? Bye."

She hung up and noticed me and Al looking at her.

"What's up?" Al asked. "Twice in the last five minutes."

"Nothing," Alice said. "Something about Alicia spending the night with some little girl down the street. She said I said it was okay, and he wanted to know before he let the little girl's mama pick Alicia up."

"He can't do nothing without you, huh, girl?" Al teased.

Alice, Alfred, Alicia. Mmph. I'll bet they had a son named Alex or Alfred Jr.

"I swear," Alice said, putting the phone back in her purse. "Sometimes he gets on my fucking nerves."

"I think you're really lucky," I told her. And I meant it.

"Lucky, huh?" She sounded like she didn't believe me.

"Blessed really," I rephrased and smiled at her. "I really admire that."

"What's so—blessed about it?"

I didn't even have to think about it to answer. "To never have to be alone," I said. "To have someone to go home to. You know, like at night, sleeping next to somebody. Just the thought that you got somebody to hold on to in the middle of the night. Tell stuff to. You know."

She looked blank back at me, like she was thinking, *Oh, that's right. You ain't got no man.*

"Regular sex." Al backed me up without looking up from her drink.

"Yeah, that, too" I said. "And you've been together so long."

"You got that right," she said, as if everything else I'd said was bullshit. She rolled her eyes over at Al, as if they were members of some kind of *Woes of the Married Women Club*, and I couldn't possibly understand their plight.

"Don't look at me, Soror," Al said. "I ain't in this."

"That's 'cause you just got married," Alice said, dismissing her. "He still calling you the love of his life, I bet."

Al smiled as she stirred in her drink.

Alice grunted. "Trust me. That high school-college sweetheart stuff don't stay sweet for long."

"I love stories like yours," I said. Alice looked at me like I was crazy, but I didn't care. The alcohol loosened my lips, and I felt like talking. I can't wait until I have someone who loves me like that."

"Oh, stop complaining," Alice said. "Just give it time, and let it happen for you. Enjoy what you got before you get stuck in a marriage. Having a man around ain't everything you think it is."

"First of all, I wasn't complaining," I said. "I was just speaking my mind," I said. "I can't help how I feel."

She let out a hiss and then repeated, "Complaining."

Now that pissed me off. I was so sick of married people trying to act like they know shit about the single life when they don't. Sick to death.

"Don't sit there and talk to me like you know, 'cause you don't."

"Hey now," she started. She looked at Al as if to ask, *Where'd you get the chick with the short fuse?* "I'm just saying."

"Don't—tell me nothing about it. Can't no married somebody, especially, married with children, especially any bitch married before 30, tell me shit about what it's like to be single. *Especially* after 30. I'd give anything to be married as long as you have."

Al interjected again, trying to make peace. "Don't worry about it, Sebrina. She's just messing with you."

"Make me sick," I mumbled.

"Excuse me?" Alice asked, as if I'd stuttered.

"I said, I'm sick of it," I snapped. Hell, I'm grown. I ain't scared of repeating myself. "Tell me this, what do you have to be unhappy about? Talking about 'stuck in a marriage'. Give me a damn break."

Then Alice answered, "I know that being married, with or without children, don't necessarily mean you're going to be happy. And that's something y'all single heifers can't appreciate. Maybe single people," she said with conviction, "need to appreciate being single instead of being in such a hurry for something they don't know shit about."

"I know it takes a whole hell of a lot of being single to appreciate being married," I responded without missing a beat. "Bitch, you ain't never been me."

"Bitch?" she asked, like she'd misheard me.

"When's the last time you spent years, that's right, years without being in a relationship? Not being held onto or even kissed?" That's speaking as someone who's selective about who she kisses. "When's the last time you had some fool groping at you like he was doing you a favor for expressing some interest in you when you knew you didn't want to be bothered with his ass?"

"I got a fool at home," she said. I wasn't even surprised by that response. Ungrateful bitch just wanted to have something to say.

"When's the last time you went over a year without sex? And I ain't talking about holding out. I'm talking about going without? For real."

Surprise. She had no answer.

"When's the last time you had to wonder if you done missed your chance to get married, or if you'll ever have kids? Or even find a baby daddy, let alone a husband?"

They both sat there silent, which I guess they'd figured out was good for them.

"Oh yeah, that's right," I said. "Never. Because you got a man. And kids. So you'll never be me. Or anybody like me."

"I ain't got to be you to know," was Alice's weak ass comeback.

"You don't know shit about it, and you never will, because any bitch at your age with a man and/*or* kids will never know what it's like to be the bitch at my age without 'em. You don't know what we go through, or what we gave up trying to wait our damn turn. You don't ever have to think about what it might be like to have to grow old by your damn self. Time ain't standing still, so don't tell me to wait and let it happen."

"She's a foul mouth little somebody, huh, Soror?" I guess Alice decided to direct her comments directly to Al since I was perched high on my soapbox beyond her range of condescension.

I took a breath and said, "And another thing. If you didn't want the man you married, or to have his babies, then maybe you shouldn't have married him. Hell, maybe you should have kept appreciating being single and let him marry somebody else. Naw. 'Cause the truth is you didn't want risk it. In the back bottom of your heart, you'd rather be with somebody than risk being without somebody. And now you act like you got some right to complain." Selfish bitch.

"You know," she said.

"I know what?!" I snapped back, ready to argue.

"You remind me so much of this girl that comes to my church."

"Oh, Lord," Al said. "Soror, don't go there."

Soror went there anyway. "No, really."

So I asked, "How's that?"

"Always got something to say about some shit."

"Oh?" I wanted to hear more.

"Always standing up testifying about being thankful for what God has done for her, which is always the same shit every Sunday, and then in the next breath counting somebody else's blessings and trying to pray for somebody. Be the main one all up in the singles ministry with a nerve to talk about waiting on God to send her good man, when she probably got a man somewhere breaking his neck to be good to her, but she really wanna be with somebody else who ain't even thinking about being good." She rolled her eyes. "Yes, I lead the New Providence Baptist Singles Ministry," she said, which left me wondering why in the hell an obviously unhappily married person was put in charge of a singles ministry.

"And I? Remind you of her?" I asked, still not knowing where she was going.

"Yes, Lord," she said. "Praying for single parents, and married couples and acting like she really gives a damn about somebody besides herself."

I didn't say anything, but I was looking at her just waiting for the right wrong word to come out of her mouth so that I could knock her on her ass.

"Okay, Soror, just drop it," Al said. "Nobody's after your husband."

"She's after everybody's husband," Alice insisted. "And constantly in somebody's face smiling and wanting to hug on them and leaning over talking to folks children, calling them sweetie and angel and other fake shit."

"Okay," I said. "So why the sister got to be fake?"

She didn't answer, but said, "And I get that same vibe from you."

"A vibe," I said. "You get a vibe that all single sisters are fake if they admire what you got. A husband or kids or a family or something like that." I wanted to be sure I was understanding her. Guess some women just don't know how to appreciate married-ever-after.

"Mmmhmm," she said. "And this same sister is always, I mean *always*, rolling up in there late, sitting all up in the front, and acting like she glad to see everybody. Always got to be the first one to greet the new faces and scope out their husbands, too."

It would have been so easy to question her motives for going to church at this point. Instead, I asked, "So, why does she have to be there to be after somebody's husband? Maybe she's at church for the same reason other folks go to church."

"People go to church for different reasons," Al offered. "Lots of different reasons."

"Mmmhmm," Alice repeated. "Like what?"

"Oh, forget it," Al said. "You just feel like arguing. Everybody ain't after your husband. I thought you would have outgrown that insecure shit by now." She drained her glass and then motioned for another drink at the waiter who was carrying food to another table. "Some people might go to church looking for a husband, but you don't even know that girl. And I'm sure she's not looking for yours. God, Alice. You can be so insecure."

"Then what, Soror?" she asked. "You tell me what the hell else she could be up in there looking for, if not a man?"

Smug-faced sisters like her just make me sick. Like they know every damn thing. Who's to say that just because a man is in the church that he's some special catch?

Curtis was raised in the church. B.J. was raised in the church. Elliott even, raised in the church. Raphael, raised in the church to believe that masturbation causes cancer. Going to church doesn't guarantee people will live a certain lifestyle or behave a certain way outside of it.

My experience with church-going men had been nothing to brag about. Men are just men, regardless of what the so-called happily attached, prayed-up sisters try to tell you. Some nice church-going men fart freely in your direction while sitting next to you at the movies. They think it's refreshing to be so comfortable around you that they can be that open and honest, when honestly, they should get up and go the bathroom or wait until they out in some open air.

Other nice, church-going boys just want to fuck you, preferably in the ass, and then want you to shit on them. Literally. And they're so comfortable around you that they feel they can share this fantasy with you on a first date. What in the hell, right? And then there are some who just bore you to a point beyond description. Whatever God means for me, He certainly does not mean that bullshit.

And I for sure ain't trying to be no man's last chance at redemption. Falling all up on me trying to make amends for the bullshit he put some other woman through. Now, he's desperately trying not to be the old man in the club. Or some man trying to latch onto me because the last one he latched onto was a chicken head, or crack head, or some woman he knew was crazy when he hooked up with her, or some woman he had a hand in making crazy. As if being with a good woman will absolve him from whatever association he had with a woman he's decided wasn't good enough.

Spare me the ones who are too quick to tell the story about how they survived tragic brief encounters, accidental conceptions, and ill-advised relationships with women with issues, issues which they'd probably gotten from these same men. Lord, save me from all that extra nonsense. I've enough to deal with the nonsense I've already gotten myself into. With a man who just happens to be a church-going man. Send some peace my way, any time now, Jesus.

"Maybe the sister just wants some peace," I finally said. "A novel concept to some folks I guess, but some folks have been known to find peace in the church. Maybe she just wants peace."

"Yeah," Alice said back. "Maybe a piece of my husband."

"Or fellowship," Al said. "Or friendship."

"A piece of married dick," Alice rephrased.

"Whatever," I said. "Everybody you think is against you ain't against you."

"Whatever," Alice said back. "And everybody you think is for you, ain't for you either."

This bitch just wanted to have the last word, no matter what. Where in the hell was the food? Or at least another drink?

"I'm just saying how I feel," Alice said, mocking me. Then she turned away towards the middle of the floor. That was my cue.

"You 'bout to feel more than that," I muttered as I leaned and reached for the glass ashtray on the table, ready to connect it to the side of her smug face.

"Sebrina!" Al grabbed my hand and pulled it back down to the table.

Alice turned around slowly like she was only half interested in what was going on. She glanced at the ashtray and then looked back out toward the floor as if she was looking for somebody.

"Girl," Al said, clearing her throat, "I thought you said you quit smoking." She pushed the ashtray away from my hand as she spoke.

It was one of those, *Miss Celie, that razor sho' look dull to me* moments. It would've been laughable, if I hadn't been so pissed off. What the hell got into me, just then?

"Ewww," Alice turned back toward me and scrunched up her fat face. "You smoke?" She didn't even look at me long enough to wait for any answer.

Okay, this shit was a trip. I had really sat there and let this Alice heifer push my buttons. Buttons I didn't even know I had until now. Was I drunk enough to start a club fight? And with this big-ass bitch? I've never been in a fight in my life, and now I was ready to tear something up in here because this bitch just called me fake.

I needed a cigarette all right, and I didn't even smoke. So I just sat there pissed off at her for talking down about somebody I didn't even know.

And she just sat there, smug as can be, like she thought she had something somebody wanted. Track star. Hmph. Glory days had certainly passed her by. She and the sorors obviously spend way too much time reminiscing and not enough time exercising. Meanwhile, her butt's getting bigger, hips getting wider, stomach's getting pudgier, arms getting flabbier. Look at her now, round as an inner tube and wide as the front doorframe. Track star one day, a fat sluggish, tub of lard the next. A sow in a silk blouse. It was lucky for Al that they did lose touch for a while, or she'd probably be looking the same way, and from the looks of Al, she didn't need any help in that direction.

I should have at least cussed Alice out, but I just sat there and shook my head like it wasn't worth it. That had been my cue to lay my fist upside her head, but I'd missed it.

I got up and walked to the door. I'd stand outside for a minute and pretend to be smoking. Some guy offered me a cigarette, but I declined.

Men and their offers. Smitty once told me that men offer the dick on many different levels, whether it's moving a couch or opening a door. It's the art of the offer. "It's very subtle," he'd told me. I smiled, thinking about Smitty and his philosophies. I smiled harder thinking about his ass in those white pants.

About a minute later, Al came out to find me. It was kind of sweet of her to try, but it was also her bitchy friend who drove me out here in the first place.

"She's always been a fusser," Al said, apologetically. "You know the type. Just ain't happy unless they're fussing about something."

"Yeah," I said. "Come to family gatherings just to get the fussing started."

"That should have been her line name, The Fusser. If she wasn't fussing about something, she was getting a vibe about something."

She laughed and I laughed and then I stopped before she noticed.

"Oh, girl, don't worry about her vibes. Half the time, they ain't worth a damn either. She had a so-called bad vibe about Curtis, and look how that turned out."

"Yeah," I said back. Too bad Alice had been right about that one.

Al looked at me and suddenly I couldn't look her in the face. She kind of chuckled again and then asked, "What's up? You got all this extra energy and um, hostility toward my girl, and y'all just met. I know she can be a little much, but—"

I shook my head and said, "It's—a lot of stuff."

She attempted to read my mind. "Girl, fuck that motherfucker."

I half rolled my eyes at her. If she only know how ill-advised her words were. "Forget it," I said. "I'll figure it out."

"No, really," she said. "What you need to forget is that bastard that's got your face dragging the ground. Let his ass go."

"Just like that?"

"Yeah," she said. "Let his ass go get on somebody else's nerves for a while."

Then I sighed and said, "I'm pregnant." Before she could say anything back, I just said, "Fuck. Before I knew about this baby, I was planning to just let it go, but now? A baby complicates shit. This is so not how I figured my life would be at this age."

"Does he know?" she asked.

"Nobody knows except you," I said. "I guess at this point it's all too little, too late, but just thought I should tell you."

"Well," she said, dragging. "But, the father. You need to tell him. Right?"

"He's married," I said.

"Oh shit."

"Exactly," I said.

"Well," she said again. "I did notice your face looks a little fuller than usual."

"Really," I said in a sort of *Is that the pot calling the kettle black?* tone of voice.

Then she cleared her throat. "When are you planning on telling him?"

"He's been tripping a lot lately. I really don't know."

"Mmph," she said back. "Mmph, mmph, mmph."

"I'll figure it out," I said.

"How long?"

"It can't be that long," I said. "I was just at the OB-GYN a couple of months ago, and she didn't say anything."

"Oh."

"Just gave me a big ass bag of condoms. A day late and a dollar short."

"Yep," she said.

I calculated in my head. "Maybe a couple of months."

She kept saying, "Hmmm."

"I've been throwing up and stuff, but I just thought I was shook up because of the World Trade Center stuff. You know."

She missed her cue, so I kept going. "I took a test this morning."

"Well," she said, as if *well* and *hmmm* were the extent of her vocabulary. "I guess that explains the hostility."

There she goes, practicing her psychology on me, not helping at all. I was really wishing she wasn't being so nice to me.

"I'll figure it out," I said again, trying to convince myself at the same time as her.

A few more minutes passed, and I decided I was cool. When we got back inside, the food had come to the table, and Alice had started without us.

Alice talked and ate as if a quiet table made her uncomfortable or something. As if the bustle and music in the room wasn't enough noise. She just talked. Mostly to Al about people and things that she knew I couldn't relate to. Then about her soap operas. She couldn't get enough of *The Young and the Restless*.

"I've been watching that show since college," she said loyally. As if I needed another reason for the contempt I was feeling. She talked about it like the people were real, and it's always gotten on my nerves when people did that. I know it's all fantasy and fluff. Nobody's that rich. Nobody's that beautiful. Nobody's that unhappy. But people like Alice just took all the fun out of it. You'd think she could feel her blood pressure rising just talking about it, worrying her empty ass life about a whole bunch of made up people with made up problems that didn't even exist. Ooh, please shut up! Talk about something else, for God's sake.

Then suddenly she switched. "Guess who else is living in ATL?" she said, obviously not to me.

Al looked at her with raised eyebrow as if to ask, *Who*? She had a mouth full of food at the time.

"Melissa Franklin," she said, like it was somebody famous.

Al's eyebrows wrinkled at first, and then she said, "Oh. Mel. Really?"

I just kept drinking.

"Yeah," Alice said. "Mel Franklin."

"That was your girl back in the day wasn't she?" Al asked.

"Still my girl, as far as I'm concerned," she said. "With her crazy self," she acted like she was laughing, and then said, "We just haven't been in touch in a while, you know. Kind of like me and you. But you're still my girl."

"I know," Al said. "You still my girl too."

I just sat there in my chair against the wall, looking at the two of them, and feeling like I had been pushed off into a corner. I just made sure the waitress and I kept eye contact.

Alice started reminiscing about a time when her and this Melissa-Mel person had had the nerve to go to some guy's house and confront his girlfriend about an affair he was having with Melissa-Mel. She chuckled pretty hard as she talked at first, until she realized Al wasn't laughing so hard, and I wasn't laughing at all.

"Melissa was wrong, Soror," Al said. "And then to just take old boy's drawers and just drop them at old girl's feet like that."

Alice couldn't help but laugh, apparently.

Al said, "That just wasn't cool."

Then Alice looked almost apologetic. "I guess it was pretty thoughtless," she said. "Just immature, I guess."

"Yep," Al agreed.

"I guess," I said, still drinking.

Thoughtless, she said. Thoughtless? Talk about an understatement. I think this is just a little worse than re-giving a gift to someone at a party when the someone who gave it to you is at the same party. I'd done that. That was thoughtless. It wasn't on purpose, but still. I digress.

I stirred my drink and looked out around the floor for the waitress.

"I'll never get over the look on that stupid girl's face though," Alice said, clearly more amused than apologetic. "The way she just picked up his drawers and just looked at us."

"I'll bet," I said.

"So, I asked her," Alice said, "'Doesn't that bother you? As a woman?'"

"And what did she say?" I asked, because someone had to.

"She didn't say shit," Alice said like she'd just won an argument. "She just looked stupid and shut the door in our face."

I stared her, waiting for the part that made sense. Al just kept eating. We both sat there, waiting for the rest of the story, then I asked myself how would it make me feel as a woman to have some raggedy bitch come knocking on my man's door just to tell me that she's been sleeping with him? And to have her partner standing there with her, as the agitator. How high school can you get? And these were so-called educated, college women? The more I thought about it, the more agitated I got at my own situation.

I wanted to ask her what the hell else happened, but I could guess the answer was nothing. If something else worth mentioning had happened, she would have said so. Instead, she just asked us both again. "Wouldn't that make you feel bad as a woman? I mean, doesn't it make her look like the biggest fool?"

"Look," I said, trying to break it down to the simplest terms. "You talk like she just danced naked on stage at a Hot Boys concert or something. *She didn't do shit wrong.* Your girl is one stuck out there with her face cracked 'cause she slept with that woman's man and he didn't want her silly ass no more."

"Whatever," Alice mumbled. "That was Mel's way of letting old girl know she was through with his ass."

"And you the one who looked stupid standing there with her," I said. "You should've been asking your soror how she felt as a woman while she was getting the door slammed in her face."

"First of all," Alice said, "she didn't slam the door."

"Whatever," I said.

"And plus, he left that pitiful bitch and went back to Mel, anyway."

"Oh," I said dryly. "Guess she wasn't through with him."

"Really," she said emphatically, looking over at Al like there was definitely something else not being told. I didn't know what it was, didn't know if I wanted to find out.

"Well," Al mumbled through her chewing, "didn't he end up marrying old girl though?"

"Yeah," Alice said. "Her dumb ass married him knowing he was in love with somebody else. With Mel."

"Well, hell," I said. "Why didn't he marry Mel?"

Nobody said anything.

"In love. Right." I continued. "He was in something, all right. Deeply."

Alice had heard enough from me. "How you gone sit there and judge somebody like you perfect?"

"Excuse me? I never said I was perfect. I'm just agreeing with your girl." I nodded toward Al. "Melissa-Mel, or whatever the hell her name is, was wrong. Period."

"You ain't lived on her side of the street to know what was going on," Alice said. She was mad now, and I didn't care.

"You don't know where I've lived. And *you* ain't never lived on my side," I said. "Or on the side of the single girls at your church. Or any other side but your own side, so you can just get up off me."

"Oh, sweetie," she said, "I ain't began to get on you, yet. Something in your wash ain't clean. Not at all."

What the fuck? What in the fuck? This heifer's vibes must have been working overtime. I was ready to grab that ash tray again and clock her square in the mouth, which was indication to me that I wasn't drinking enough.

"Something in your grass ain't green either. Sweetie." And I ain't your goddamn sweetie, either.

"You know what?" she asked.

"Naw, what?" I said, hand on the ash tray.

Al interjected again. "Soror, you need to let it go. Sebrina's right, and you know it. Mel was all the way wrong. So let it go. It ain't even that deep for you to be picking a fight. We supposed to be having fun, y'all. Come on, now."

"Never mind," Alice said back. As she put some more food in her big-ass mouth, I couldn't tell if she said, "It ain't even worth it," or "You ain't even worth it."

Nobody said anything.

And what was that saying about me? I'm the old-ass 30-plus version of Melissa-Mel's simple ass, minus the drawers on the front porch. I kind of wondered what Mel was doing now, but I just kept quiet.

Chapter Thirty – Another Side

I noticed Al giving me a sort of disapproving look, every time I tilted up my glass, but I just kept drinking.

Once the drinks got rolling, we all got a little more mellow. Even Alice's uptight ass. Hell, once she got a few drinks in her, she wasn't at all bad. Or maybe I had enough drinks in me by that time not to notice. Or maybe it was the food that she inhaled like she thought somebody would ask her for some that improved her disposition. By then she couldn't say enough about Alfred. Alfred this, Alfred that. "Do you want to see a picture of my baby?"

Not really, I thought. "We got a choice?"

Al just shrugged and nodded into her drink.

"Here's my baby," Alice bragged, pushing the wallet in my face.

It was a picture of a big, muscular, light-skinned guy, with big brown eyes and long eyelashes, standing next to a kid in a little league baseball outfit. The man had his baseball cap turned around backwards and he and the kid had identical flashing smiles. Little Alfred, I suspected.

"My big baby and my little baby," Alice went on.

Damn! He was fine. Now, I'm more than half drunk, so you can just about imagine how I was looking at Alice at this point. How the hell did he end up with her?

As I looked at her she just grinned. "I know what you're thinking."

"Hmmm, naw you don't," I said back, with an attitude, my lips twisted at her. Why do these bitches always think they know what somebody is thinking? Make me sick, but I was still stuck on the how in the hell did she end up with him part. *How? In The Hell? Did You? End up with him?*

"You're wondering what I did to get him," Alice said, not missing a beat.

Well, shit. I nodded without really smiling. I pushed the wallet back to her with no expression or comment.

"I didn't suck his dick until we got married," she said, proudly.

"Okaaay! That's enough," I said. "Not my business, Sis. You can keep that one." What is it about food and alcohol that gets these heifers all loose-lipped?

"Soror!" Al laughed, embarrassed, as she tried to reel Alice back in.

"Well, hell," Alice continued. "With all those dumb broads out there sucking and fucking like nobody's business, I had to save something special for my man on our wedding night."

"Wooo!" I reached for the closest drink on the table.

"Slick, sloppy bitches," Alice said. "Knew he had a woman and still trying to get at him." She smiled and shook her head. "But I still got him, 'cause he knew I was worth the wait."

And I sat there amazed at how this is the same woman who just thought it was funny as hell that she and some other wench dropped panties on another woman's doorstep. "Yeah, okay," I said. "Okay."

Al laughed, but kept her nagging eye on my glass. "Well, I guess it was a gamble that paid off."

"Damn right," Alice said. "He the first, last and only that I done had these babies wrapped around." She smacked her lips.

Then somebody got the idea in their head to play the Picture Men Naked game, a notch up from picturing them in their underwear. I knew I had to be careful, because as loaded as I was getting, my imagination was more vivid than usual, and I really did not want to visualize some sagging-ass man with ashy knees and a shriveled dick. And just as I expected, the Picture Men Naked game got boring after a while of looking at more sorry-asses than pretty ones.

Alice sucked on hot wings and ribs and swilled down cognac, savoring every drop as she ate and drank. "Mmmph! Oooh! This is so good," she moaned like she had a man hidden under the table. "Oooh! Mmmm, Mmph!" She went on and on like the last of barbeque sauce in the place was stuck to her fingers.

At first I just looked at her like she was crazy. Then I just had to smile. Maybe Alfred ain't all that after all, if this is how she acts over a few pieces of chicken, a baked potato, and a couple of shots of Martell. Maybe all that fineness wrapped up in that pretty package is no guarantee of a good pussy pounding. Well, I'll be damned.

"It's so good to be satisfied, ain't it y'all?" She looked at me and Al and then back at me again, smiling the first genuine smile I'd seen on her face all night.

"Apparently," I said back.

"Apparently," Al agreed, smiling, "the best feeling of all time."

Then suddenly, Alice had to go. And she had to go like she'd been holding it, so she just shot up from the table and said, "I'll be right back. Order me another thing of wings."

Alice left the table and Al and I ordered more food and drinks. She ordered more food. I ordered more drinks.

While she was gone, I said, "Your girl is really a trip, huh?"

"She can be," she said smiling. "Like I said, pay her no mind."

"She doesn't like me very much, does she? I mean, not to even know me."

"Sebrina, stop sweating that. When people who don't like you for no reason, usually it's because they don't like something about themselves."

"More psychology?" This girl really needed to get her ass back in school.

"Alice is probably jealous a little bit because you're single, and she got married right out of college," Al explained. "She's only been with one man her whole life. Now, she thinks she's missing something."

I shrugged. "Mmph." She ain't missing shit. I wondered what it was about me that gave Alice the apparent impression that just because I'm single that I'd been with a lot of men. I'd been on my share of dates, but to whom does dating automatically equate to sex? Alice is an idiot, and an ungrateful cow.

"She really is a good person, though."

"Yeah," I said. "And what's up with your girl, Melissa, or Mel, or whatever? She one of your sorors too?"

"Yep," she said, as her smiled disappeared. "She's the roommate I told you about that called me homely," she said just as she took a drink. "And old boy in her room that night was the same one who ended up marrying old girl."

"Oh," I said.

"But you couldn't tell her trifling ass that she wasn't all that."

"Yeah," I said.

"That bitch got played just as much as the rest of us. She's probably just as stuck up as she ever was."

With that, I just said, "Damn." I could gather there was no love lost between Al and Melissa-Mel.

While Alice was still gone, Al took the opportunity to revisit the baby subject. "You know, you're drinking like your mind is already made up. What's up with that?"

"I didn't say my mind was made up," I said. "And I'm not drinking that much."

"Oh, you're drinking like a fish, Sebrina. I'm just saying."

"Well, don't say," I suggested. "I appreciate your concern, but I'm cool."

Neither of us said anything else until Alice came back to the table with a person they both apparently knew.

"Hey, Sis," she said to Al, who was concentrating on her drink. She nodded toward me in a gesture to say hello, and I got an awkward feeling like I knew her, too. She actually looked familiar.

"Well, hey!" Al jumped up with a smile.

Just when Al was getting up to throw her arms around her sister-in-law, "Esther?" just kind of slipped out of my mouth?

"Excuse me?" she said with a noticeably stronger tone. "What'd you just call me?" She gave me one of those *Do I know you* looks. Naw, she didn't know me from Adam, and I was slipping tripping for real.

"Um...?" I quickly turned my eyes toward Alice. "I mean, umm. Is—there? Is there? Yeah. A line in the bathroom? I kind of have to go."

"Naw, chick, go on," Alice said, as if she needed to give me person to excuse myself.

I stayed gone long enough for what I'd hope would be time for them to catch up or whatever, and then sister-in-law would keep it moving. I actually felt kind of stupid for making such a dumbass impression on Curtis' sister. Must have definitely been the liquor making me give a damn. She would have liked me if she'd known me first. I wondered if while I was gone, they were calling me stupid or spacey, or if Alice was giving Al the *watch your back around that shady chick* vibe.

When I returned to the table, sister-in-law was gone and the *Soror, this,* and *Soror, that* cackle fest was over. Al attempted to explain who she was and what she was in town for, but she couldn't quite catch on that I wasn't interested.

I wasn't interested in sister-in-law/Soror, nor their pledge-and-stir solidarity, even if a small part of me envied it. Sure, I threw out the window a side of sisterhood that respects boundaries, and feelings, and supports decisions, dreams and visions and all that. I realize that I sacrificed it to focus on my own myopic view of my objectives.

But this same sisterhood escapes so many women because we fool ourselves into believing that genuine solidarity is inherent in blood relatives, sorority sisters, roommates, in-laws, or hastily hand-picked friends, instead of recognizing it for the cultivated and nurtured process that it really is. Some women don't have the patience or inclination to cultivate such relationships because we're on the fast track to getting what we want. Yep. By my own actions, I had let myself become one of *those* women. But back to sisterhood, I wondered if those heifers would even be friends if they weren't "sisters".

Alice, running on empty and ready to start over, had been thinking, or perhaps vibing, in the bathroom about all of our issues, and in the ten five minutes, she'd found just the way to fix them all. Somewhere she'd read or heard that writing down your feelings is a good thing, therapeutic and all that. Something about focusing on the good shit in your life.

Who the hell felt like making a list? Al must have been thinking the same thing because she spoke up with, "Well, I don't have anything to write on, Soror."

But Soror wouldn't be deterred. She kept her train of thought like Al hadn't said anything. "So, I'll start a list until the food comes," she said. "A good shit list. Kind of like a brainstorming thing." She pulled a napkin out of the dispenser and a pen out of her purse and starting writing. She called it, the Top Ten Greatest Feelings of All Time.

"I'll start with number 10," she said. "Being able to empty my bladder at will."

That's it? I wondered. Then I humored her. "Especially when you're in a tight," I said. She definitely needed to get out more.

"Yeah," she said. "Especially then. But that's still number ten."

"A raspberry lemonade slush on a hot day," Al joined in. She needed to get out more, too.

"Okay," I said. "Number eight is, hearing the man I love call me *Baby.*"

Then it was Alice's turn again. "Sleeping late on an unexpected day off." To watch soap operas, no doubt. She *would* come up with something that had to do with sleeping. Lazy cow. That's why she's so big now.

"Your turn, soror," Alice said. "What's number six?"

"Waking up next to the man I love."

Waking up next to the man *I* love was more like it, Pudgy. I tried to play it off with a smile as I came up with number five. "Climbing into a warm bed on a cold night."

Alice surprised me again, with, "More like, climbing onto a warm body on a cold night."

"Now that's more like it," I said.

Then she said, "Good hard sex after a hard day at work. That's four." Maybe Alfred was hitting it right. Or maybe she used the words hard sex and food synonymously.

Al smiled and then said, "Cuddling up with to someone who means it."

"How about making love to someone who really means it?" I suggested.

Alice kept a tally on her napkin. "Nunh uh," she said. "Same thing. Same thing. That's still number three," she said. "I like that better, but it's still number three. Beats the hell out of cuddling, don't it y'all?" I think it shocked us both a little bit to be in agreement. "Anyway," she said, "you still gotta come up with a number two, now."

"Okay," I said, "A real good—"

"Fuck," she said. "I already said that," she looked at the napkin to be sure. "In number four."

I smiled at her because I don't even think she knew how drunk she was. Then I said, "I was going to say a good sneeze."

Al laughed out loud. "That's pretty good. Alright, soror, what's number one?"

I didn't know what to expect, but I was sure it was going to have something to do with food.

Then she said, "A really good kiss."

Damn, that was good. I think we all agreed.

That seemed to work pretty well. It did put me in a better mood for a minute. I started thinking of more stuff, kind of creating an Honorable Mentions List in my head. They didn't add up to be a total of ten, but what the hell.

In no particular order:

A good perm after taking the braids out.

When the person who shampoos my hair scratches my scalp in all the right places, preferably a man.

A warm bath right before bed, preferably, with a man.

The cool down after a good Brazilian wax, right before getting with my man.

The "after" of a good tooth cleaning. Nothing like a clean mouth and fresh breath, to kiss a man.

Leftovers the day after Thanksgiving, Christmas or Easter. Alice would like that one.

A good pedicure, when the water stays warm and bubbly the whole time and a paraffin wax is included.

Finishing a long run, finishing, being the key word.

I could only come up with eight, but it started to get good to me, so I kept going. That's when I realized how bored I was. I was supposed to be having a night out and I was making lists in my head. I couldn't believe that someone actually makes money on *Letterman* doing this stuff. So while they babbled and ate, I sat there drinking mostly, and nibbling a little bit in between to quiet the rumbling in my stomach.

I'll bet it'll be great, I thought, to carry a baby and behold my healthy newborn for the first time. I'll bet it's great to hear *I love you* first from someone you love back already.

Then Alice blurted out, "I feel like dancing! Y'all feel like dancing yet?"

She broke my train of thought and Al just looked at her. That's when I started getting mushy, and the feelings kept coming out. I called it the It Sucks List.

It sucks to have to get into and start a cold car on a cold morning when you're already late for work. It sucks to change a tire in the rain. More than that, it sucks to be stranded on the side of the highway. It sucks to have to depend on somebody else for transportation when you don't have any. Even more than that, it sucks to carry all the heavy shit up the stairs and into the house by yourself. Oh yeah, and to actually endure a bikini wax that leaves hair bumps, or peeling or burn scars, like the one I'd paid for at a place in Peachtree City before I found Don Janelle's. I was glad the check bounced.

Alice squirmed around in her chair like she had to go again. She still felt like dancing, but nobody else was moving. Al kept drinking, and I kept thinking.

How about, it sucks to have to get up early on your day off? That's really shitty. And none of that is as shitty as running on a cold day. Even worse, running early on a cold day.

I looked over at them reminiscing and laughing and eating, and observed how Alice's butt was spilling over the sides of her chair. It must really suck to go to bed wearing a size 6 and wake up wearing a size 16. Poor Alice, how she must have felt like shit to go to bed one size and wake up twice as big. It's hell to stand in front of a mirror and discover for the first time that your thighs and ass are not what they used to be in high school, but damn, wasn't she doing anything besides eating and having babies?

And Al wasn't far behind her, maybe a plate or two away from fat herself. Oh well. Sitting on her ass behind a counter every day and taking two hour lunches was bound to catch up with her sometime. Maybe she already knew that she'd be one of those women who never get their figure back after a baby.

My mouth was getting dry. I waved at the waitress. It sucks to be thirsty. Alice was still scarfing down whatever was in front of her. It sucks to be hungry. She'd be sorry later, because it also sucks to overeat. And I'd a feeling what she was really craving wasn't going to come out of that kitchen on a plate.

How long would it be this time before Curtis spoke to me again? Maybe this was the beginning of the end. Was I prepared to be a single mom? I know people make it work every day, but that's got to suck. Nobody chooses to be a single mom, just like nobody really chooses to be single, not on this side of thirty anyway. No regular man, no regular sex.

It definitely sucks to be without sex. That one goes at the top, right after it sucks to be lonely, especially on a cold night. Or maybe somewhere between having bad sex or having sex and still being lonely. God, I missed him. I missed him like somebody sleeping in the rain. And I'd slept in the rain. And that was misery.

Maybe list-making wasn't my calling. I tried to cheer myself up by thinking about people worse off than me, namely the two sad bitches sitting at the table with me.

I'll bet it sucks to be married to someone who cheats on you, or would cheat if he had the chance. If it were any other situation besides mine and Curtis', I'd feel sorry for a woman with issues like that.

I bet Alfred had a mistress too. One hard look at Alice, and I was sure of it. Ha. At some point, I guess dick sucking ain't enough. And I felt sorry for Alice. Sort of. That's probably why she ate so much. She wasn't getting any at home. But look at her. She was a walking hunk of sausage.

I'll bet she knew he was cheating too, and that's got to suck. To be married to someone who cheats and you know it, or in her case, I'll bet it was more a case of being married to someone who cheats on you, you know it, they know you know it, and you pretend you don't mind.

And poor Alfred. It must hurt like hell not to love the person you married. And poor Curtis too.

And then there was Al, sitting across the table from me, oblivious that she was at the very, very top of the It Sucks List. To not be loved by the person you married. But I still didn't feel sorry for her. She ought to pay more attention to what's going on around her, instead of whatever the hell she was doing, thinking that he was really working all those times. Talking herself into it was more like it. It's one thing to be blind, but a whole other thing to gouge your own eyes out. Dumb ass.

I didn't feel sorry for him either, once I thought about it. Poor Curtis, hell! I must have been tripping. Poor Sebrina, was more like it.

Yeah, I get it. I was wrong. Period. But if he really loved her really, he would never have been with me. And if she'd had any sense, then she'd have never married him. Alice was right. Stupid bitches shouldn't marry men they know don't really want them. Wait a minute. Alice is right? Now I know I was tripping.

But back to Stupid. All that space before the wedding garbage was her sign from God that they weren't meant to be together. It's her own stupid fault for not seeing it. Serves her right. Sure, if I was really her friend, I wouldn't be sleeping with her husband. But I never claimed to be her friend, did I? Come to think of it, every time we talked, she was calling me. That should have told her something. She clung to me. She called me on my cell phone and left a message and started all that shit.

Aw, hell! Why does my life have to be a journey to doing the right thing? I sure was taking the long way around. And look at the mess I was making. Pregnant, again. And my baby's daddy is my friend's husband. Now that's just not fair.

When will it be my turn, Lord? When will all this waiting stuff stop? Sure, I took a few liberties with some red lights, but for what? Just to end up waiting at another red light? How long will I have to put up with what really sucks? All this fucking waiting. And why is it that most of what's really great I have to work so damn hard for and wait so long for? When is the good stuff coming my way?

Even in the meantime, God knows how much hell it is finding someone who can give a really good perm, head-scratching shampoo, pedicure, and Brazilian wax with no bumps. It's nothing short of a minor miracle to get all of this in the same salon. And with no waiting. Okay, that's a fantasy. But then, most of the time, so is sleeping late.

Do I always have to get a triple shot of what *Sucks* with a half a shot of what's *Great* served up like a watered-down martini? If *Sucks* is some kind of chaser to keep me from getting sauced up on *Great*, then can I have a few shots of *Great* straight once in a while?

The best I could think to do is load up on as many number nines as I stand. And then at least a number ten is inevitable. Oh goody. To pee at will. What a bleak, dismal outlook for someone who started out with the best of intentions. Lord, can this be right?

"You know what?" I popped back into the conversation. I pulled $30 out of my wallet and put it on the table. That should be enough to cover my share of the bill and a tip. "I gotta go." If I hadn't had to go around Alice to get up from the table, I doubt they'd've noticed.

Al said something like, "Call me later," as I headed toward the door.

Yes, I drove home drunk. I knew better, but doing the wrong thing was becoming an easy habit. It wasn't really that far from Midtown to College Park. A few minutes on 85 South and I was home. It was about 12:30, still pretty early, but I'd had about as much of girls' night as I could stand. I left the sisters at the bar to close the place down if they wanted. I'd had about enough of both of them.

Chapter Thirty-One – Forth and Back

I stumbled up the stairs. Just as I reached the door, I heard Curtis say, "Hey." I didn't even hear him walk up behind me.

I was full enough already to pee in my pants and him sneaking up on me almost did the trick. "Hey," I said back. "Where the hell did you come from?"

Just then, Elliott peaked out like he thought someone had knocked on his door.

"What's up, Georgie," Curtis said.

Elliott squinted his eyes, cracked a fake smile and immediately shut the door.

I sighed and said, "I told you, his name is Elliott."

"My mom was a Rod Stewart fan back in the day," he said. "Don't play."

"Don't be a jerk," I said back, as I fumbled to find my keys and unlock the door. "Anyway, what are you doing here? Where'd you come from?"

"I was sitting in my car," he said. He walked through the door behind me as I bee-lined to the bathroom. When I came out, he was sitting on the sofa.

"What do you want?" I asked, going to the bedroom to get undressed. I knew he was expecting me to jump into his arms, but I managed to not to. I threw on last night's T-shirt—this one said, *ARMY*, in big yellow letters—and pajama bottoms as he spoke from the other room.

"Where you been?"

I came out of the bedroom and headed to the kitchen. He was still sitting. He repeated, "Where you been?"

"You know where I've been," I said looking in the refrigerator as if I didn't already know what was in there. "And no, we didn't talk about you." Not really, anyway. I pulled out a single cheese slice and unwrapped it. "Where have *you* been?" I asked as I folded the cheese in half and started eating.

"Sitting in my car," he said again. "Just—in my car."

"All night?" I asked. "Here? Just— sitting? For what?"

"Just sitting," he said.

"Hmph." I walked to the bar. "Well, how long you plan on sitting—right there?"

He didn't answer.

This was about the time I thought about dropping the baby bomb on him, but I changed my mind. I told myself that I really should be thinking with a clear head before having that conversation. Hell, he'd rather get his information about me from somewhere else anyway, let's see if he hears about this from somewhere else.

"Met your sister," I tossed out.

"My sister?"

"Yeah. Taller than you, ain't she? Like a freakin' Amazon."

"Um, yeah."

"Pretty, though," I said. I didn't drop the fact that she looked at me like she wanted to kick my ass for calling her by her baptismal name. "Parents got an anniversary or something coming next weekend, huh?"

"Yeah," he said. "That's right."

"Cool." I went back into the refrigerator for another piece of cheese, unwrapped it, folded it, and started eating.

"So, uh, how's Finley?" I asked, not really expecting a conversation to come out of it.

"Fin's on some personal shit, I guess," he said. "He's been tripping, but I just ignore his ass and let the rest of them deal with it."

"Mmph," I said. I can imagine.

"He came in the other day and started playing some country shit."

"Really?" I smiled as I leaned on the bar. Well, I guess I was wrong about flipping the stations.

"Yeah," he said. "And him and Chatman almost got into it 'cause Chat said we didn't feel like listening to the Grand Ol' Opry, or some shit like that."

I kept smiling, but Curtis didn't notice because he was looking straight ahead, as usual.

"I just went in my office and shut the door."

"Mmph," I repeated. As amusing as all that was, I couldn't manage to stay interested. "All right," I said, sounding as nonchalant as I could. I leaned on the bar and looked at him, waiting for him to say or do something. He didn't move, just kept staring straight ahead at the T.V., which was not even on.

I can't believe I let myself get pregnant by this man again. I can't do this. But I can't go through that again. What does he want from me?

Then I asked, "Curtis, what do I mean to you?"

I wasn't really surprised that he didn't answer.

"I used to be somebody you loved, but what am I now?"

Still nothing.

"Come on, man," I said. "Can I get some words from you tonight? I mean, even though they never mean shit. Something?" I sighed. "I can't keep doing this with you."

"You're somebody who's got my head all fucked up," he said. "I don't know whether I'm coming or going with you."

"Damnit." I guess I will be figuring this out by myself. Again.

"Baby, why are we fighting?"

Hell, I didn't know we were fighting. I thought I was just left. Again. But if I'd been sober enough to think it through, I would have probably said something like, *Because you're married and I'm not your wife* or *Because you believe what other motherfuckers say before you listen to me*. But instead, I said, "Babe, I don't know."

"Me either," he said, still not looking toward me.

"Well, me either, either." And frankly, I was a little too tired and too drunk to try to figure it out tonight. "But I think..." I took a breath. "I think I'm ready to let it go. I'm just tired, and this is just too hard."

"But what if it's not what I want?"

When he didn't say anything else, and I'd finished my piece of cheese, I said, "Well, let yourself out." I headed toward the bedroom, flipping off lights as I went.

"I was thinking I'd just stay," he said, which stopped me in mid step. I turned and looked at him. He was still sitting, holding his face in his hands. "If it's okay, I thought I'd stay tonight."

Okay, he got me. All I could say was, "Okay." It was okay for me, but his wife wasn't out of town. She was in Midtown, with her fat sorority sister, and presumably, her mean sister-in-law who's in town for the next week.

Why was it okay for him? I decided I didn't care. And so I said, "Sure."

I went in my room and fell into the bed. It didn't take long for me to doze off. I don't know how long I'd been asleep when I turned over onto my stomach and threw my arm across the bed. My eyes popped open because I half scared myself when my arm landed on Curtis' chest. He was still fully dressed, lying there, stiff, like he'd been afraid to move. I pulled him toward me and scooted closer to him. He put his arms around me and held me.

A few minutes later, I woke up again and asked, "Your mama was a Rod Stewart fan?"

He just lay there and said, "Mmmhmm," and squeezed me tighter. "She probably still is. She just don't let Daddy hear her playing it." I felt his chest jump as he chuckled about it.

I pictured his parents at home alone dancing in the middle of the living room floor to some secular Sam Cooke music, like *We're Having a Party* or *Somebody Have Mercy*. "Yeah, I'll bet," I said. "They've probably just got y'all fooled."

I felt him shrug.

Then I kind of laughed, "Wonder if your dad—?"

"Shhhhh," he said to quiet me.

This felt so easy and right.

Right then and there I prayed, "Thank you, God." And I held Curtis tighter. And he held me tighter back. "I'm so thankful to God that you found me again. I do love you."

"Me, too, Baby," he whispered back. "Now, shhhhh."

"Baby, can I tell you something?"

"No," he said, squeezing me. "Sleep."

Then I dozed off again.

Chapter Thirty-Two – The Wake Up Call

I was up too early the next morning to suit my hang over, but Curtis had to be up for a pool meeting with his recruits, which meant he'd spend a good half a day giving pep talks and doing little training tasks to help prepare them for basic training. A pool meeting basically fucked up the absolute best sleeping day of the week to have my man in bed next to me. So when Al called, I agreed to meet her at the downtown at the Underground. I told myself that maybe it was time to come clean. Things were looking to me like Curtis was making up his mind in my favor, and God was making that clear to me now. At the same time, I felt like not saying anything. I thought she must have been on her shopping kick again, but we grabbed some food and a couple of drinks and sat down and talked.

"I don't understand him," she said.

"Me either," I mumbled. "Men are stupid." I added.

"He swears he loves me, and then he does stuff like this."

I just sighed. It's my own damn fault. I'm so damn sleepy.

"He comes in at damn near eight o'clock in the damn morning, long enough to take a shower and change clothes, and then leaves back out talking about going to another pool meeting, whatever the hell that's supposed to mean."

I didn't even consider telling her what a pool meeting is. She's married to him. Why didn't she ever ask what a pool meeting is, for goodness' sake.

"I mean, does he mean it or not?" she asked.

"I wish I knew," I said. "You know, they say the first two years of marriage are the hardest."

"I told you that," she said and sort of smiled.

"Oh. Yeah," I said back. When the fuck did I become her best friend? Where was her soror when she needed to talk about this shit? Her fat ass was probably hung over too, but she had sense enough to stay in the bed with Alfred. Where's Esther's mean-looking ass? I am so damn sleepy!

My problem was I was always available. I was always available. Too readily available. For anybody. I think people must sense that or something. That's the problem. I'm everybody's damn girlfriend.

I should have been at home drinking an egg and hot sauce or something. I had to work this shit a different way, and soon. I had enough of my own stuff to deal with.

Then again, she didn't deserve to be wrung out like this. For the first time since I met her, I was glad I wasn't in her shoes. Especially now that she had a husband with a pregnant mistress. Then again, what the fuck did I care about what she deserved? I didn't deserve to be a pregnant mistress, but the shit happened.

"I don't want to lose him," she said, as if she was about to try the crying trick on me.

I didn't even look at her. I just said, "Yeah." Then I kind of wiped down the front of my shirt, like I was pressing out the wrinkles.

It was like she was reading my mind when she asked, "So, have you thought anymore about telling him?"

"No," I said. "I started to last night, but—"

"Last night?" she asked. "I thought you broke up."

"Well, yeah. But he came by. I still didn't tell him. I guess I was scared he'd trip again, and I wasn't—I just didn't."

"Well, could you blame him?"

"Where's that coming from?"

"All I'm saying," she said. "I just thought you were smarter than that."

"Smarter than what?"

"Look," she said, glaring up at me and then back down. "The man is married, for God's sake. What were you thinking?"

"Excuse me?" Did she forget that she told me that she fucked her married department head in college?

Then she stiffened up completely with, "Forget I said anything. It's none of my business anyway."

Why was she being such a bitch? She was the one who called me out of bed on a Saturday morning. Did I mention, a rainy ass Saturday morning? Now, for once, because the conversation is not all about her, she thinks she can fucking insult me? "Look," I said. "You're making me sorry I even told you."

"So, why did you?" That was really a good ass question.

"I guess I just needed to tell somebody," I said. "I mean, it's not like I really knew where the relationship was going, you know. All that back and forth stuff."

"Of course not," she said, and I wasn't sure if she was being sympathetic or sarcastic, but it didn't matter.

Maybe it was my hormones starting to clown on me again, but all at once it just got to be too much. "I just need some help, is all I'm saying."

"Help?" She looked annoyed.

"I just need something to be about me for a change, you know?"

"Not really, no. I don't know." She just sat there giving me the Alice look. The one where she rolled her eyes and pursed her lips like she was having another bad vibe.

"I didn't want to go through this by myself again, I guess."

"Again?"

Then I sighed and confessed about the last time. She sat there listening in silence with raised eyebrow while I poured out my heart. I shrugged and said, "I made a mistake. I know you really don't get most of what I'm talking about, but I'm just trying to do the right thing." I felt myself actually about to cry, and I didn't want to cry in front of this heifer. "I'm telling you, now, because I'm tired. You don't even know how tired. I feel like I'm losing—something. And it hurts a little bit, damnit. It hurts!" Did I just put myself on blast? I did. I took a deep breath and wiped my face. "I made a mistake," I repeated calmly.

"Sounds like two mistakes to me," she said. "And what's that, the right thing? The right thing for who?"

"I don't know," I said. "But I'm really thinking I should keep this baby, because I don't know if I'm ever going to have the chance to have babies again. I think things are going to be different now. I don't mean for anybody to get hurt. I just want to be happy, too. You know? But right now, a baby just complicates everything. I just want to be more sure about where this relationship is going."

"Relationsh—" she started to say. Then she hissed, "Shhhit."

"Yeah," I said.

"It's going nowhere, Sebrina" she said, with as much blunt force as she could deliver. "The man is married! You're not in a relationship. You're in a situation. And a pretty fucked up one, if you ask me."

Well, ain't nobody asked you.

"Are you sure it's even his? I mean, you got down with the Puerto-Rican guy from the bar, right?"

"I'm sure," I said. "I told you that was just that one time."

"I guess."

"Where is all this cold shoulder shit coming from, Al? I'm opening up to you, and this is what I get back?"

She looked at me like she wanted to tell me to stop calling her that.

"You know," I said, composing myself, "you starting to sound a lot like your girl from last night," hoping to snap her back into herself.

"What the hell makes you think you're different from any other piece on the side running after a married man?" she snapped.

"I'm not some piece on the side," I snapped back, almost raising my voice again. "I really get him. He gets me. I know it doesn't seem fair, but all's fair in love and war and that other bullshit, and I loved him first, damnit!"

I think I must have shook her a little bit, and some of the few of the other people sitting around us, because she leaned back in her chair and changed her tone, but not her attitude.

"You're right," she said.

"I am?"

"It's not fair. You are wrong. Period."

"Fair?" I asked. "What are you, ten? Fair is for kids. Grow up. No grown ass person should be whining about what's fair, and I damn sure can't worry about it at my age."

"We're not talking about dividing marbles on the freaking playground, Sebrina. You're playing with wrecking somebody's marriage."

"Al," I said, "*Fair* walked out the door the day this man walked back into my life, and *Fucked Up* moved in and set up house."

"You're doing some really dumb stuff for your age," she said. "You should really think more of yourself by now."

"You know what?" I said. "It's really not a good time for you to be judging me, or psycho-analyzing me, or whatever you call yourself doing. I'm not you, and you're not your mama, calling yourself chastising me."

"And I was eighteen. You're thirty-something years old, and you really think all this is okay?" She talked to me like I was a child, out of my league. Then she scoffed and chuckled as she looked down into her drink. "You can wake up anytime now."

Wake up? Wake up?! So, now she's Spike Lee?

"Look, Al," I said. "I don't know what else to say. He loves me, and I know he does. I don't know how else to put it. He loves me, and this is my second chance."

"You're acting like it's your last chance."

"Maybe it is," I said.

"Or maybe, you're just being a selfish—person."

Selfish? Yeah, okay. This was my perfect chance to be selfish, and tell her that Mack and Curtis were the same man, if I ever was going to, but I decided that I'd let him break it down to her. She was already in full Alice mode, and I couldn't get through to her anyway. "I'm not making excuses for it."

"No?" she asked, looking right at me.

"You can stop that, okay?"

"I'm just trying to tell you for your own good, as a friend," she said.

"I never asked you to be my friend," I said, meaning to be cold.

"What kind of friends do you have, that you have to ask them to be your friends? Whatever."

"Look," I said, "I admit I didn't put enough thought into this situation, but life just happens the way it happens, you know?"

She kind of sucked her teeth at me and hissed back. "And this last chance is important enough to you that you'd wreck a marriage?"

"It's important enough for me to do what it takes." I looked her in the eyes, and her eyes glazed over slightly as she held her stare with me.

I didn't know what to say back to her after that.

"Whatever. Like I said," she repeated, as she looked away, "It's none my business anyway."

"Right," I said.

"Right," she said back.

"Well, all right! Shit." I said, meaning to get the last word on it. "Fuck it. I won't say shit else to you about it."

She looked at me like she wanted to say, *Good*, but then decided to let me have the last word after all.

"Look," I said softly. "I'm gonna go. I'm feeling a little tired. I can't believe I came out in the rain with you for this."

She thinks she's so smart. All right then. Tell me how I ought to live my life. Judge me? Hmph. I'm going right home and call him right now! I'll show your judgmental bitch ass. Right after I take a nap.

Chapter Thirty-Three – Second to Last Chances

I got home just as it was starting to rain, thinking how nice it would have been if Curtis had still been there in my bed, but it was okay that he wasn't, because his scent lingered well enough to suit me. I lay down and breathed it in as if I could feel his arms wrapped around me, and I fell asleep pretending I was safe and happy in our life together.

I slept for a three or four hours. Then I called him. And paged him. When he finally called me back, it was one of his famous, short, I'll-be-there-in-a-minute *Click* calls. Maybe I should have known something was up, but I didn't think about it. I was thinking about telling him about our baby, and to hell with everything and everybody else.

I stood on the balcony, watching cars come and go from the parking lot. It was raining pretty hard with cool, wet breezes occasionally blowing through the screen. I started feeling really excited when I saw his car come through the gate.

I opened the door and stepped outside bare-footed, waiting for him to come up the stairs. He was wearing one of those red Marine Corps sweat suits. He got soaked from the short walk from his car to my door, but I threw my arms around him anyway, and pressed my face against his chest. "It's raining like crazy out there, huh."

"Yep," he said, as he hugged me back with noticeably less enthusiasm. "I'm wet," he pointed out, and he started to loosen himself from me.

"Hey," I said, looking up and expecting, not letting him go. "I missed you today." He leaned over and gave me a get-it-over-with kiss, like he had something on his mind.

"Let me go, now," he said in kind of a question.

I let him go and rubbed down his arms. "I can dry this for you," I suggested as I started to unzip his jacket.

"I'm cool," he said, stopping my hands.

"I don't mind, Baby. I want to do it for you," I said, trying to unzip it again, but his hands didn't move. "Okay," I said, and kind of patted him on the wet chest before I let him go. "Okay, Baby."

He looked down at me for a long couple of seconds. I smiled at him, waiting for him to smile back. He did, finally. Then he walked over to the sofa and sat down, and I stood in place, just smiling at his every move.

I took a deep breath. Baby, I want to tell you something." When he didn't look at me, I said, "Baby, you're making me uncomfortable when you do that. Something wrong?"

"Nope," he said. "Everything's perfect."

I pretended not to notice the sarcasm, but I felt clumsy saying, "I'm so glad you're here," and even more clumsy asking, "Want a drink or something?"

"Yeah," he said. "I'll take a drink."

I went to the refrigerator and pulled out a Coke®. I opened it and poured it over a glass of ice and took it over to him.

I sat down next to him. "You know, I really want to tell you something." I felt the excitement building, eager to see the look on his face when I told him about our baby.

He turned up the glass and drank all of it in one swallow, saying "Ahhh," really loudly as he finished. "Got anything else?"

"Um, sure, Baby," I said, starting to get up.

"No, Babe, I'll get it." He patted me on the knee as he got up with his glass and then walked to the kitchen.

I sighed, and twirled my hair in my fingers. "I really want to tell you something, but you need to be still."

"Hope it's something good," he said. He stood in the middle of the kitchen and locked his eyes on mine.

I nodded. "Yeah. Hurry up and sit down."

"Something worth celebrating?" He smiled back.

I bit my lip as I looked at him. "Yeah," I said. "Come on, now, silly."

"Oh, wait then." He went to the pantry. There was about a half a bottle of Bicardi® and a bottle of Absolut® that hadn't been opened that he pulled out and set on the counter. Then he reached back in and got what was left of a corner of Crown Royal® and set it on the counter. After rifling through the rest of the shelves and finding nothing, he stood there smiling like a cross between a bar tender and a mad scientist.

Now I was really getting uncomfortable, but I played it off. "What's the joke, Baby?"

"Nothing," he said. "I'm having what you're having, right?" He mixed the rum and vodka together as he poured them one after the other into the glass.

Okay, whatever was on his mind wasn't funny, so I said, "No, that's not right. I'm not drinking right now anyway." I meant not anymore, since I'd made up my mind to tell him about the baby.

"No?" he asked with an obvious attitude. "Since when?"

Before I could think of how to phrase my answer he said, "That's cool. I can drink enough for two, right?" He untwisted the cap on the Bicardi and poured it into his glass. "That's what you do, right? Drink enough for two?"

As my mouth fell open, I felt a flutter in my stomach that told me he knew I knew he knew.

He turned up the glass and gulped it down, struggling a little more to get out the "Ahhh," which sounded more like an "Ughh." Then he said, "Close your mouth." He did the same thing, and again with the corner of Crown.

I sat there with my eyes bucked open, mouth closed, for a few seconds.

"What's the matter?" He had nerve to be asking me. "Want one?" He poured and drank, remarkably steady.

"Nunh uh," I said, barely above a whisper, shaking my head. "Thank you." I don't even know what the hell to call that, but even I wouldn't mix all three of them.

"Sure? We're celebrating, right?" He walked over to me with a half full glass. "Oh yeah, that's right." He pretended to remember suddenly. "You're not drinking now."

"That's right." I nodded at him.

"So when's the last time?" he asked as he leaned against the wall over me, still holding the glass. "When's the last time you had a drink?"

I shrugged. "A couple of weeks, I guess. I'm not really sure," I whispered.

He looked around the room like he was looking for someone and then leaned over and whispered back, "Not counting last night, right?"

I tried to keep my thoughts straight. Then I said, "Yeah, last night."

"We're looking at two, maybe three months gone, right?" he asked, turning up his lip, his eyes actually watering.

"Don't do this," I said.

"Right?!" he asked again, voice raised.

"Almost. I mean, I guess," I said. I didn't look at him anymore. What was happening? I felt sick and nervous.

"So basically, you've been poisoning my baby for three months."

I didn't say anything.

"Is that about right?" he asked. I heard him swishing the ice around in the glass.

"It wasn't even like that," I said.

Then the glass flew across the room and hit the wall, breaking. I jumped as I waited for the screaming to come, but his tone was the exact same. "So tell me what it was like."

"I love you," I said.

"Not an answer." He shook his head.

But I couldn't think of anything else to say. "I love you, Curtis."

"Try again," he said, walking over to the counter and picking up the Bicardi bottle.

I wasn't sure if he was planning to turn it up or throw it, so I tried to say something else.

"I think I was scared about you leaving me again." I found myself actually trying to explain. "I wasn't thinking straight at the time." I never really thought about it at all until this second.

He just looked at me.

"I just love you so much."

"Did you love me the other time too?"

Suddenly, I felt a bitter taste in my mouth. He knew everything.

"Mmmhmm. See, she talks to me too," he said. "I get home with my mind all on some other shit, and she gets at me with this yang about the stupid drunk-ass friend of hers fucking around with some married bastard that's got her ready to have a second abortion."

"I never said it like that," I said. She called me a stupid drunk?

"But I guess this way is cheaper, right?" he said, holding up the bottle and putting it back down. "Tell me something? Why the fuck does she know more about our business than I do?"

"You got this all wrong," I said, trying desperately to get control of the conversation. "It's not even like that."

"Every time I think I can trust you, I'm all wrong about that too, I guess."

I shook my head and tried to say, "No," as tears started down my face.

"And don't start, okay?" he said, like I was a spontaneous cryer.

"Oh," I said. "But it works for her, right? Just not for me?" I wiped my face.

"When were you gonna tell me?"

"I was gonna tell you, but you said I was left, and I didn't want to call because—well, because."

"Because, what?"

I didn't know because what, but I continued anyway. "And then last night, you kept telling me to shush, and I was gonna tell you today. That's why I called you. I really was."

He looked at me for a moment, like he was really trying to process what I'd just said. "This is so fucked up." He picked the bottle up again like he was thinking about throwing it and then set it back down. "I gotta go."

"Hey," I said, looking at the floor as he walked to the door. "Please help me with this." I started wringing my hands like a person with bad nerves. I went to him and just grabbed him and hugged him as tight as I could, wet clothes and all. I didn't care. "I want this baby, Curtis. I do. I want us to be together. Please, can we talk? Please can we talk? Please can we talk?" It came out at least three times before I realized I was babbling. The tears kept coming.

"Let go of me," he said calmly. So calmly, I actually let go. He stood there motionless, looking at me.

"Baby, please don't do this to me, now," I said. I stood with my arms down by my side, not sure what to do with myself.

"You can be pretty good at that *please* stuff when you want to be, huh?" I stood like I was stuck to my floor and watched his feet reach the threshold. When he turned the knob, I sprung after him. If he left this time, he might never come back.

"Hey!" I grabbed him by the shoulder. He pulled away from me and kept walking.

The rain was still pouring, and for about a second, I stood bare-footed on the doorsill calling him to come back. He kept walking.

So I ran after him. "Baby, wait a minute, please listen. I'll do anything to make it right. I'll do anything to make it work."

I'd do anything to keep him with me. All he needed was for me to reassure him that I wanted him as much as he wanted me, that I wanted our baby as much as he did. He needed to know that I was ready to give him a baby, even if his selfish wife wasn't. That had to be it.

He was planning on leaving her, finally, and Al was just jealous and tired and trifling. Throwing salt at me 'cause she couldn't hold her damn marriage together. I knew that was it. How dare that bitch twist my words like that.

I ran after him down the steps. My foot slipped on the second or third step and I couldn't catch myself. I fell forward and landed with my face on the curb at the bottom of the steps. *Schlick! Skrrrrrr. Boo-doo-boop-boop. Boop.*

It really is like falling in slow motion, and when you land in whatever unflattering position you end up, it's like waking up from a dream you can't remember all the parts to, like you blacked out on the way down.

I sat up and ran my tongue across my teeth. My lip was bleeding a little. I covered my mouth, thinking I was otherwise okay, until I started to stand up and couldn't. I saw blood coming from a gash on my forehead. Suddenly,

I couldn't see, I couldn't breathe, pain was shooting all up and through my body, and my chest was about to explode.

I felt myself slipping in and out of consciousness just as Curtis was scooping me off the sidewalk and carrying me toward his GOV.

As he loaded me into the back seat, other thoughts like, *God, please don't let him leave me* went through my head. Hell, I might have even said those things out loud, for all I know. *God, please don't take my baby. Oh, God, I promise. I'll do right. I promise I'll be a good mama. God, please don't take my baby. I promise, I promise, I promise.* But I guess God didn't think so. And no matter how much I prayed to God to make it be undone, please let this be a dream too, I felt my baby slipping away from me by the second. Just like that.

Chapter Thirty-Four – Figuring It Out

When I woke up, I was left with seven stitches in my forehead, a cracked rib, and a chipped tooth.

A not-so-young doctor and a middle-aged looking nurse tried to sound and look sympathetic. She may have even said something like, "I'm sorry."

Once they were done stitching, stuffing, patching and wrapping me, they packed me with a few pain killers and sent me on my way. "Your boyfriend and your sister are waiting for you." I guess she noticed that I wasn't wearing a ring.

My sister? I assumed and confirmed the worst, as her voice echoed some other instructions about taking it easy or taking medicine or taking or not taking the bandages off, and something else about following up. On the other side of the double doors were my boyfriend, Curtis, and my sister, Al.

We all looked at each other, consumed by the awkward silence. I couldn't tell if Curtis was grieving for our baby or his marriage, but the loss was all over him. I could only guess that Al was torn somewhere between her completely obliterated sense of trust and the demise of a friendship she tried so hard to create. She looked at me as if her eyes were too full to take in anymore and then turned around and left. I was completely empty.

Curtis looked like he couldn't seem to fix his gaze on me. He looked exhausted. Then he said, barely above a whisper, "I'll get the car."

As he was driving me home, I finally managed to look over at him, and it was like he heard the question I was thinking.

He just said, "I didn't know what else to do."

I looked blankly at him and then straight ahead again. "You didn't know what else to do?"

He said nothing.

"So you called your wife?" He really is crazy.

"I've never been so scared in my life," he offered what I guessed was supposed to explain it. "She's the first person I thought of, and I guess—"

"You guess?" I asked with an edge.

"Look, I was losing my baby, and I just needed to have the closest person to me close to me," he said, like that made sense. I must have had a really fucked up look on my face because then he sighed and said, "I know it don't make sense to you, but I was hurting and I just lost it for a second."

I thought to myself, You've lost it all right. All of it. And for more than a second.

"I'm hurting more than I ever thought I could," he said.

I didn't know what to say to that. Selfish son-of-a-bitch.

"I never thought something like this would happen to me." He paused like he was thinking about it. "Never," he said, as if this were something that was just happening to him. Happening to him? Like he was the only one hurting from the inside out.

"Welcome to my world," I said back.

"I just wanted it to be over," he said, and didn't say anything the rest of the drive home. I just sat there, trying to absorb what he'd just said to me and everything it meant. What did he want to be over? Us? His marriage?

"I just wanted the lies to be over," he said, reading my mind again.

Let me get this straight. He's scared. He's hurting. And the first person he thinks to call is his wife. Never mind that another woman is in the other room miscarrying his baby. I heard myself refer to myself as another woman. Why couldn't I get it in my head before now that that's all I would ever amount to? "Were you ever going to choose me?"

"Choosing you is what got us into this situation. Considering our history, I should have known better." Funny how he had no trouble recognizing it as a *situation*. I guess that's all it ever was for him. "Were you ever going to trust me?" he asked.

"Trusting you is what got us into this situation," I answered. "I should have known better."

He pulled into a parking space closest to my steps and turned the car off. I got out.

He got out, too, and hurried around the car after me as if he thought I'd collapse on my way up the stairs. He walked behind me, not really holding me, but keeping his hands on or near the small of my back. When we got to the door, I said something like, "Thanks. I got it." He stood behind me as I turned the key and went inside.

"Can I do something? I mean, do you need anything?"

I just shrugged and said, "Naw, I got it."

He looked lost for words. I waited until he said, "Do you want me to come in?"

I did. I wanted him to come in and hold me and never let go. But that wasn't going to happen "I'm all right." I'm always all right.

As I was closing the door, he put his hand against it and asked, "Listen, could I come by later? Just to talk or something."

I agreed. "Call me later."

****

Not only didn't he call later, Curtis didn't come by, either. But was I really surprised? He didn't set foot in the MEPS. Five weeks and three days went by before I even heard from him. The end of fall was coming, and the leaves weren't the only thing turning. Amazingly, I didn't call him, either.

And just maybe, that's when God started to finally pull him off of me.

I can't lie and say my spirit was at ease, but nobody was holding a weight on my chest, either, and it got a little bit easier to breathe without indulging my habit of calling him. Thirty-eight days of breaking a bad habit, and I was on a roll, I suppose. Whatever.

In that time, I packed and shipped my household goods, threw away my glasses and bought contact lenses, threw away my contact lenses and got new glasses, and made an appointment to get my tooth fixed. I even went out and bought a Spanish language CD and learned something besides the bad words for a change. Why did I even waste my disappointment on him? Every day that he didn't call, I thought about him. Missed him. Some days more, and other days not as much.

He can't pick up the phone to give me a passing thought? What is that? What man who loves me would do that? And every day that I let it, it sunk in a little bit more, and hurt a little bit less. Still felt like shit, but one day, I stopped crying. And then, I was unable to remember the last day I cried.

I told myself that the only way to feel better was to look better. I could hardly stand looking at myself in the mirror, and not just because my eyebrows were way past due for some maintenance. I needed to get out and have someone other than myself for company and a trip to the salon was just the thing. With the fall season being on its way out, what better excuse was there for me to change my hair? I latched onto the idea of changing with the seasons, and tried to embrace my own new season.

Two hundred and twenty-seven dollars lighter on the debit card, I walked past the mirror on my way out and half smiled. I had most of my hair cut off and had what was left twisted into short brown coils. It was cute on me, thank God, and I looked good, but that was all.

In the back of the reflection I saw a face looking at me. She was sitting in the waiting area, holding a chunky, shiny-faced, chocolate baby on her lap with little fuzzy tufts of hair on his head. If I had to guess, I'd say he was about four or five months old. I found myself smiling at the baby, not really acknowledging the mom, but when I made eye contact with her again I turned around to get a focused look at her. Oh my God. My heart ached a little bit when I realized that it was the girl I remembered as Sarah sitting next to me that day at the doctor's office late last year.

I stiffened my lip, put on a smile, and took a step toward her. "Wow. What a cutie he is."

"Thank you," she said, shifting him on her lap. "This is Ethan." Sarah and Ethan were waiting to pick up her sister who was there getting her hair done. I took what I thought was a slick moment to notice that Sarah still wasn't wearing a wedding ring. But at least she had little shiny-faced Ethan, and that was more than I had. Sarah and I didn't exchange any more words. I just nodded and did the baby-bye-bye wave at Ethan before heading back toward the exit.

As I pushed open the door and stepped out of the salon, I noticed Al getting out of her car and heading toward the salon from a different direction. She, from the distance, looked as shitty as I'm sure she was feeling. I made eye contact with her not meaning to, and I tried to fast-step in the direction of my car.

"Oh, now you just gonna walk past me like you don't see me," she said in ghetto fashion I didn't know she had in her. "And not say shit to me about nothing, I guess."

All I could think was, *Really, Lord? Really?!*

"Look," I stopped and turned around to face her. She really did look like shit, like a sad cocker spaniel. Her hair was flat, droopy and greasy-looking, like floppy ears, and her eyes were sunken into their sockets with dark, dark circles around them. Her light skin really brought out her acne and emphasized the circles.

"What do you want me to say? I'm sorry?" I asked. "Okay. I'm—sorry. Damn." Then I breathed out slowly and tried again. "I'm sorry."

She snapped back as if she'd been rehearsing a conversation of her own. "Yeah, you're sorry all right." She walked toward me. "Always have been, always will be. Sorry for the rest of your sorry life. Or haven't you figured that out yet?"

I took that and tried not to show the sting I felt. I know I must be a sorry somebody. Of all the trifling heifers in this world, without a conscience or a lick of sense, God considered me and said, "Nope. I won't even give this fool a baby." And I know some super sorry, too many baby-getting, multiple baby daddy-having, non-working, ignorant, misguided, chicken-headed tripes, trollops and hoe-bags out there, and God chose to tell me no. *You're not even as good as them.*

I tightened my lips and nodded and started to walk away again. Then she reached out and grabbed at my arm. I could just guess where she picked up that little habit, but she was about to catch an elbow in her mouth.

"I know you're not walking away from me," she said.

I tugged my arm out of her grip, and said, "Al, I know—"

She cut me off with, "Don't you call me Al, bitch."

At that point, I was calmer than most women I know would have been, but my conscience was working over time to keep my temper in check. Bitch, I am really trying to take the high road, but you are pushing it.

"Okay. Andra-Lyn. Peggy. Whatever. I know you think you want to fight me."

To which she quickly replied, "Damn right."

She stared at me like she was willing to try me, so I stared back at her.

The hurt in her eyes wasn't as amusing as I'd once imagined it would be. She clinched her fist once and then loosened her hand as if she'd suddenly remembered she was above fighting in parking lots. Then she had a strange look like she would have been content if she could just slap me real hard and get away with it.

I breathed hard through my nose as my eyes stayed on hers. "I don't really want to fight your ass, but come on," I said. I dropped my bag off my shoulder and tried to prepare myself for the inevitable.

Then she threw her bag to the ground and screamed, "Biiiitch!" in a really long exhaustive breath. Then she sort of flung herself toward me, lunging at me with both fists upraised. Out of reflex, I stepped back, with my left arm up to block her and my right arm drawn back with a fist. She just stopped herself in mid-lunge and dropped down on the ground, in the perfect position for me to kick, actually. I kept my eyes on her for a couple of seconds, with my shoulders hunched up, waiting. Then I dropped my shoulders and then lowered my arms and unclenched my fists.

"Shit, I'm sorry," I said again. "But that's all I got."

She didn't say anything back.

"But I'm not some bad person. I made some bad choices and people got hurt."

"And that makes you a bad person," she said, not looking up.

Did she really think it was that simple? That the only difference between good girls and bad girls is that bad girls make bad choices? It was so simple it almost made sense to me, too. The only difference between bad girls and good girls are the choices we make. Hmph. I wouldn't bet a senior thesis on it.

"If there was any justice in this world, I really *deserve* to have you kick my ass, but please don't try me." In a split second scene I imagined her cold-cocking me with a hammer-style left hook up side my head with that heavy-ass-looking purse she was carrying. Like something out of the footage from an old Ali fight. The kind that looks like it stuns the hell out of you and hurts all the way across the middle of your face.

"Don't you stand there and talk to me about justice," she spoke up, as she sat still. "You pretended to be my friend while you were fucking my husband. If there was any justice," she added, "the ground would open up and swallow your ass right now."

"Aw, give me a damn break. Your ass shouldn't have married him. He shouldn't have married you. Then, he wouldn't have been *your* husband." It suddenly occurred to me that I really wasn't making much sense. "I just lost my baby," I said, pissed off at everybody. "And no, he hasn't called me. He hasn't been to see me. I don't know where the hell his head is. Are you happy?"

She just glared at me with a *Do I look happy?* look.

"I'm not the only one who ever did dirt, and look at you."

"You give me a damn break," she looked up, determined that I wouldn't see her cry. "I just lost my whole life." Then she squinted her eyes at me. "Yeah, I did dirt once. But who made you queen of justice? You were my friend!" Her voice broke and then she looked away. "Esther a fucking line in the bathroom? Sex with popsicles. 'Life just happens the way it happens.' You sorry bitch. Thanks."

"I didn't mean to—" I stopped myself. What could I say? I never meant to hurt you? I never meant to make a fool out of you? I never meant to fuck your husband? I meant to do all that, and I meant to enjoy doing it. But I never meant to be her friend. I never meant to give a damn, but I did.

I didn't want to stand there and watch her cry and hate me and then come to a boil again about the whole damn thing, but I didn't move.

"And don't keep fucking saying you're sorry like you expect me to forgive you or something. It's not like you didn't know," she said, composed but simmering up a little bit. "You knew and just didn't give a damn." She just looked up at me, as if she was waiting. Then she got up and left me standing there.

She had every right to say everything she said. She had a right to say more. She could have done more. She could have hauled off and slapped the shit out of me and chances are my conscience would have made me take it. Okay, maybe not that. She could have hung my ass out to dry with the Army, but not without putting Curtis' ass in a sling along with mine. I guess she loved him too much, or something. She shouldn't have loved him so much, but I guess in a fucked up way, it's lucky for me that she did.

****

I got home and checked my messages and there were none that I wanted to hear. I sat at the dining table and ran my hands through my freshly styled hair, wishing they were somebody else's hands. Even Raphael's hands.

When the phone rang, I wasn't surprised at the voice on the other end. "What's up, Ma?"

"Hey, Good looking," I said. "I was just thinking about you."

"Hey yourself, Baby Girl. Just wanted to give you a call before things got too crazy," he said. "I know we had talked about that whole space thing, especially with you moving, but you've been on my mind lately."

"Crazy?" I asked. "What's up?"

"Looks like I'm moving on, too," he said and kind of laughed. "I hate moving. Crazy, like I can't find shit when they start packing shit, and I need to put my hands on it. Crazy, like time getting away from me before I let you know I've been thinking about you."

"Great," I said, not believing my luck. "Let me guess. You're getting married."

"Naw, Ma," he laughed. "Nothing like that."

For some reason, I sighed, relieved and glad in a selfish sort of way.

"I got that job at USC. I've been thinking about it for a while, and I'm taking it."

"Oh," I said. "That's cool."

"Yeah," he said, clearing his throat, but saying nothing else.

"Hope they pay you more than sorry ass UGA."

He laughed sexy. "It's all good. It's all good. So, what's up with you?"

"Trying to get some shit out my life," I said. "You know, getting rid of old clothes and stuff. Trying to lighten my luggage."

"Yeah, Ma, that's cool," he said. "The less baggage, the better when you're trying to move on, right?"

Just then my phone beeped and I told him to hold on. Before I could even say hello, I heard, "Is now a good time?"

"Uh, sure," I said back. Now that was new. Curtis never cared about timing before. "Hold on, okay." I clicked back over and told Raphael I had to take the call.

Of course, he was okay with that. "Handle your business."

We listened to each other breathe for a couple of seconds and then I said, "Um, good luck with all that."

He just said, "Yeah, Ma. You too."

Then I stalled. "You know, before I let you go, I really should tell you I'm sorry for dragging you into some bullshit. I mean, if I hadn't already said so. And I'm sorry." He'd been really great about everything. "Anyway, that's all."

"That's all?" he asked.

"Well, what I mean is, maybe, we could keep in touch, if you wanted to.

You know, emails, whatever."

"A'ight, bet," he said brightly. "That's sounds good."

"That's not to say I'm trying to start something," I said.

"Right."

"I don't have a whole lot of faith in long distance relationships, you know," I explained. "Hell, I don't have a whole lot of faith in relationships period, right now."

"That's cool, Yo," he said.

"Like I said, I'm sorry for pulling you into that bullshit."

"It's cool, Ma, for real."

I kept talking. I told him about the whole hospital scene and how I hadn't heard from Curtis in the whole month and change since it happened, until now, and about my chipped front tooth and how it took forever to get an appointment to fix it, because it wasn't considered an emergency. "No pain, just ugly," I told him. "So, to them it's not an emergency."

He laughed. "It's probably not near as bad as you think."

"Either way, I won't be smiling for another three days. That's if they fill it with the right color." That's all I need is two-toned front teeth.

"Well, if that's old boy on the phone and you need to go, I can get at you later."

"No," I said, surprising myself. "He ain't called in all this time, whatever he has to say can wait a few more minutes." I knew I was taking a chance that he'd just hang up and not call back for another month. But something told me he'd wait, so I kept him holding. Plus, in another month, I'd be gone and it wouldn't matter as much.

I imagined Raphael smiling through the phone and his perfectly straight pretty white teeth. "I just think you've been cooler than most men would have been through this whole thing. And I appreciate you not being crazy and stuff."

"Well, I'm cooler than most," he said. "And you're welcome." We laughed together. Then he said, "I'm just sorry I couldn't be the one to play your song for you."

"Yeah," I said.

"But hey," he said back. "You never know, right."

"I guess not"

He was quiet again.

I asked about his new job and he told me about it. How much he'd been working all these years just to get to that point, and now he was there. "A dream job," he said. "All I had to do was wait for it."

We talked a few more minutes about the job, my new assignment and exchanged email addresses.

"Make sure you send me your phone number and stuff when you get settled," I said. "And I'll send you mine. Just make sure you get the time zones right in your head before you start calling to Japan in the middle of the night."

"No doubt," he said. Suddenly, I realized I would miss the sound of his voice and that sexy dialect.

"Oh yeah," I said. "And I know what all that 'me gustaria tocar tus piernas otra ves' really means."

He just laughed. "Well, it's about time." Then he said, "Like I said, you never know. How about we talk about it over dinner? After you get your tooth fixed."

"Sounds good," I said. "Call me back." At least I knew he would.

I finally clicked back over to Curtis and said, "Hey, what's up?"

"I need to come over," he said. I was amazed that he was still holding, and even more amazed that he didn't start a fight about being kept on hold.

"Now, if that's okay." Funny. He never cared before about when and if it was okay, but now he was actually asking for permission and waiting for it.

Chapter Thirty-Five – Barely Sane

I opened the door and let him in. The floor was covered with piles of stuff that needed to be boxed up and given away or thrown out or returned to wherever I'd borrowed it from. I didn't bother to acknowledge that he probably had something he wanted to say.

"Watch your step," I said as I went back to sitting on the floor sorting and packing.

"What's up?" he asked to my back. "How you doing?"

How the fuck did I look like I was doing? I was straining so hard that the thoughts bumping around inside my head even made my eyelids hurt. My ears throbbed like somebody had been trying to wring them off of my face. Even the circles under my eyes hurt.

Finally, I said, "What's up?" still sorting.

When he started with, "Uh," I turned and rolled my eyes up at him.

"I could use something to drink," he suggested. He rubbed his hand across the top of my head, but didn't comment on the new style.

"I quit drinking," I said immediately. "Ain't got nothing." I jerked my head away.

"Nothing?" he asked, like he just knew I was lying.

But it was the truth. I hadn't had a drink since I woke up in the hospital almost two months ago. And I was leaving soon. Why would I have anything?

"Come on, Sebrina," he said like this was really about something to drink.

For a hard couple of seconds, I thought about what I had left in my refrigerator. Jello. A half a jar of pickles. Maybe some butter. "How about some pickle juice," I said. "Do you want that? 'Cause that's all I got."

He didn't say anything.

"But you'll have to drink it from the jar, 'cause all my glasses are packed and gone too." I thought a little bit more. "And you can take them raggedy-ass Oreos® in the pantry, too. I don't even like them damn things. Only reason I bought 'em is because you like 'em. And they make your teeth black. Yeah. Please take them, too."

"She's leaving," he said, speaking of gone.

"Mmph," was all I had to say. I could have said I didn't blame her or something smart like that, but I wasn't feeling that salty for some reason. I'd helped fuck up her life and I wasn't as proud of that as I thought I'd be. I just kept walking through the apartment back and forth from the bedroom to the living room, darting in and out of his sight, packing stuff and throwing stuff into different piles.

He didn't seem to appreciate not having my undivided attention, so he said, "Can you just stop and talk to me?"

I stopped and looked at him before tossing something else in the throw away pile. A pair of jeans I thought I'd lose weight enough to fit back into two years ago.

"I need you," he said when we made eye contact.

"So, where you been all this time?"

He didn't answer.

"Sitting in your car thinking? Sleeping in the car, I guess. Sleeping at the station? Sleeping on the couch?"

He still didn't answer.

"Curtis, you just lost the love of your life and you need me?" I shook my head at him and continued to sort through stuff. "Didn't you just lose the love of your life? The closest person to you?" I asked stopping to stare into his eyes. "You called her that didn't you?" My heart sank a little more. I'd lost two babies and a good chunk of one of my original teeth in all this. I refused to feel sorry for either of them at this point.

He looked at me as if I was speaking English for the first time.

"Did you or didn't you?" I raised my voice at him.

He stammered and all he managed to get out was "I—"

"You told me you were in love!"

"I was," he said. "I am. With you."

"Shhh," I said. "All you *am* is confused."

"I'm not confused, Sebrina."

"Is that right?" I said, not asking. "Since when?"

"I've always loved you." That was the best he could do.

"Well, then, goddamnit, you should have married me. I like poetry too."

"Didn't you hear what I said? She's leaving me."

"I heard you the first time," I said. "That's—really too bad, I guess." That was probably where I should have added I'm sorry, but hell, I wasn't sorry, and *too bad* was pushing it.

He sighed like he wanted to say something but couldn't think of what.

So I asked, "Does that surprise you or something?"

"I guess not," he said softly. Then he spoke up. "Baby, I can't change the past. I should have done a lot of things differently."

"You got that shit right."

"Well," he tried to sound thoughtful. "Maybe this was a test for us."

"A test?" I repeated. "For us?"

"Yeah," he said. "To see if we were really meant to be." He leaned with his back against the door and half smiled as if he thought I was buying that garbage.

Well, of all the sorry shit I'd ever heard in my life! "Yeah. Maybe," I said back calmly. "Or maybe you just wasted a whole fucking lot of my time!" I threw an old T-shirt at him that only floated half way across the room. He's been fucking with my head since I met him. "You've been fucking with my head since I met you. And I'm actually pissed off at myself for taking all this time to figure out that God wasn't testing me. He was telling me to leave you the hell alone."

"Baby, I don't understand," he said. He picked up the T-shirt and walked over to me, dropping it in the wrong pile.

"Look at me," I said. "I'm leaving. I'm sleeping on an air mattress and living out of two suitcases. Eating take out and Cup-o-Noodles® until I fly out of here. Don't you think that—among other things—makes this conversation just a little bit late?"

"So, what are you saying?" he asked.

"I'm telling you that I can feel myself turning into a crazy person," I said back. "And maybe I deserve it because I brought it on myself. But you helped."

"Why are you making this so hard?" he asked, as if I'd just put myself on assignment and cut my own orders. "I'm asking you for a chance. I want to be with you."

A chance to get her left-overs? Hmph. No damn thanks. Suddenly that old Millie Jackson song pushed its way into my already crowded head. *All ya' getting' is my leftovers. Picking at love I done picked over...*

God must have been playing a joke on me. He didn't leave her for me. Hell, he didn't do the leaving at all. He had chance after chance to leave, but he didn't take it. *She* left him!

"Hard?" I asked. "A chance to do what? I ain't got no more heart for you to break. You don't know hard. And stop calling me Baby." I felt myself getting wound up again. "Hard is having to accept the fact that you, who supposedly loved me, married somebody else. You fucking married her, Curtis. Whoso findeth a wife findeth a good thing, right?"

He looked at me like he couldn't believe I'd taken it there, but said nothing in response.

"And you *knew* I loved you." I shook my head, feeling exhausted, defeated, drained of any more emotion.

"Yeah, after I was already married," he snapped back. "Good goddamn timing."

Timing? That was enough to summon a sudden emotional flare up. "Motherfucker, you fucked me the month before you got married! What the fuck did you think that was about?"

"Uh, fucking," he said like I was just plain stupid.

"Yeah, I guess you would," I said, feeling just plain stupid. "I'll tell what's really hard, Curtis," I said, getting back on the calm track.

"Babe—I,"

"Curtis, shut up." I felt like I'd waited my whole life to give him this speech, and I wasn't about to let him make me lose my train of thought again. He'd turned me into someone I didn't like and I'd let him. I hadn't had that much contempt for myself since I was a homely college virgin.

"Hard is you knew me first, and you still chose somebody else. And even harder than that, is that you had the chance not to do it and you did it anyway. And you've always loved me?" This time I was expecting an answer.

"Yes," he answered.

"Well, I can't tell," I said. "And if this is love, it sure ain't happiness. I'm as unhappy as anybody has ever been. And I know that much about what I don't want." I felt the grief churning in my stomach at that moment.

I waited for him to say something else, but I guess he wasn't ready. Then I said, "I don't know what you want, but I know it ain't me."

"I'm here, ain't I?" he asked. Looking good, as usual. But this time, not good enough.

"Not when it counts," I said back. "When it counts, you run. When it counts, you cut me off, like I don't exist or don't matter. When it counts, you choose her, not me. And what's really fucked up about it is that she's so much like me, I almost understand it. Hell, she's damn near me, but better, right? If she hadn't left first, you wouldn't even be here now, would you?"

"It wasn't like that," he said back to me.

"Bullshit."

"So?" he asked. "Now what?"

"So, nothing."

"In other words, you're throwing away our chance to be together," he concluded.

"Bull. Shit. You threw it away a long time ago. Now what? You want me to dig it up try and recycle it or something like that? We tried that already. That's how we got here, so, uh, no thanks."

"Sign a dec or whatever. Get out. Marry me," he said, as easy as 1-2-3.

If I hadn't already been sitting on the floor, I would have fallen over. I looked up at him like I was about to be sick. Sign a declination of service, refuse my assignment, un-ship my shit, which should have been already halfway across the Pacific by now, get out of the army, and marry him. I went back to trying to sort through my stuff like I'd heard him wrong. I couldn't tell which pile was which, but I acted like I did.

"We could be happy," he said. "Isn't this what you wanted?"

Damn. This is exactly what I wanted. Hmm. God and His sense of humor. "Happy?" I asked. "Have you lost your mind?"

Curtis rubbed his fingers across his eyebrows as if his head hurt. "I'm getting there fast," like he was the only one.

Hmph. Yeah, well, join the club. I could hardly believe what came out of my mouth next. Without thinking about it, I closed my eyes and sighed, "And you're gonna take care of me?"

"Yes, I will," he said, exactly the way I've always wanted to hear him say it, sounding so sweet I'd swear it had an echo. For a second, I almost smiled. For another second, I almost thought about it.

Then I said, "I doubt it." Back to the reality that was my life.

He persisted. "How about it?"

"It took you two years and two babies to get to this point, and I'm supposed to make up my mind in two seconds? Okay. How about, no?"

"No?" he said. "Just, no?"

I considered saying *how about, just get the hell out*, but then I thought of something better. "Curtis, you're not the man I fell in love with," I said, finally stopping and giving him my full attention. "How about you're not the prize you used to be." Hell, maybe he never was. "You're a man who cheats."

He blinked at me like I was in error. Then he opened his mouth like he was about to set the record straight. "Are you really going to sit there like you didn't have as much to do with this as I did?"

"Sure, I did."

"Like you weren't the other half of this situation?" There. He said it again. *Situation*.

"Sure, I was."

"Like you're not just as…"

"I'm not," I said quickly.

"Not what?"

"I am not the kind of person who does what we did and thinks it's all right. I tried to be, but I'm not."

"You are," he said. "You and all that talk about signs from God."

God was giving me signs all right. I was just misreading them, and taking hella detours.

"Yeah, yeah. I did. I was. And I'm not."

"You say that, but…" He stopped short of what he was saying and walked toward me.

"I'm not, I'm not, I am not! And I ain't gon' sit here and goddamn argue with you about it."

I know I did wrong, but I was a good girl who deserved better. Guys like him have a thing for finding the good girls. I was good. She was good. The next one will be good. "I've a feeling you'll be just fine. For some reason, you really do have God's favor." He'll be one of those who goes out and gets redeemed by a good woman. He'd always end up with a good woman. It'll probably even be her again, taking her ass back to him. In a few weeks, maybe a month or so, she'd go back to him. Hell, it wouldn't surprise me if they were reconciled by Thanksgiving. Time enough for me to get the hell out of the way. Sure, she would go back, but maybe this time, I can manage to have moved on with my own life, and not be jealous of what I think she has, and know she doesn't.

He knelt behind me and gently placed his hand on my neck, moving it slowly to my shoulder.

"Don't do that." I pulled away from him.

"Do what?"

"Touch me like somebody who has the right to be touching me should be touching me. Don't do that."

"I just—"

Whatever. He was just testing me, and it wasn't going to work. Not today. "Baby, just go fix your thing, 'cause I will not spend another Christmas, birthday and—other days waiting on something from you that you'll never have to give. You need to be somewhere begging her."

He seemed genuinely perplexed by my reasoning.

"But me and you?" I continued. "We got about as much chance of being happy as I got of winning the Georgia Lottery."

"What? Do you think you'll find someone who loves you more than me?"

"I sure won't find anybody who loves me less." There must be somebody out there better for me than him. "And I won't have to look for him. He'll find me."

Then he gave me a bullshit look and asked, "And what are you planning on doing in the meantime?"

"That's just it," I said. "I guess it does all really boils down to a matter of timing."

"Really?"

"Yeah. I used to wonder what it was about her that made her the so-called one when I wasn't. I know now that I'm as much as, and as good as anything you ever saw in her, but I get it now. That's just how men do it."

"Do it? What *it*?"

"Men choose to get married, and then choose the woman. For y'all, marriage is a matter of timing. And you and me ended up back together because of timing. No matter how many good women you overlook or step over in the meantime. Men get married on your own time."

I was so ready to be in love and be loved, and I wanted so much for this second time around thing to be God's timing, thinking he could be the man I loved so much then, and dismissing that he was still the man who hurt me so much back then. I'd've sworn that this was it. Loving Curtis for the man I thought he had the potential to be. "And it wasn't until I lost my baby that I realized that I loved you way too much for anybody's own good. I wish I loved myself half as much as I loved you, at least long enough to see that love doesn't treat people the way you treated me. And rather than believe that you all along meant to be the bastard that you are, I've decided that it was just bad timing and bad decisions. I refuse to love you anymore based on your potential."

Clearly, my brain had just worked overtime trying to make sense of this mess, and after I'd so eloquently laid it all out, the best he could come up with was, "I kinda see what you're saying, but hey…"

"But hey?" I waited, but nothing else came out of his mouth. "But hey, what?"

Still nothing.

"Look," I said finally. "I got all this shit I got to wade through, so— unless there's something else." I nodded toward the door and then turned away.

"It's cool," he said, backing toward the door. Before opening it, he added, softly at first, "You never know. Small world. Timing."

Not small enough. I said, "I know that." I also knew that with every passing year, hell, every passing minute, chances grew slimmer and slimmer that I would ever get married. I've heard of statistics saying that the chances are damn near astronomical. What was I doing? Was I about to resolve that I was okay with the possibility of being alone the rest of my life? A spinster? An old maid? Just for the record, Lord, I'm not okay with that.

"Well, I'll see you around." Something in the look in his eyes told me that he still thought I was weak. That he knew to himself that I would always be weak for him. Like he expected that when and if I saw him again, he was sure I'd just fall back into bed with him, as long as enough time had passed.

"Hmph. Not if I see you first," I said. I pretended to go back to my sorting and waited for the sound of the closing door.

This time I was through for real. No more of those school-girl theories of romance and tests of time and long lost loves. All the romantic bullshit like that helped me get my heart beat to a pulp, hung out to dry, grounded into dust, and any other over-used metaphor I couldn't think of at the time. All I had was a head full of worthless memories that were good for nothing except driving me crazy. I should have run from his ass when I had the chance the first time.

I placed so much value on him, invested so much of my self-worth in him, that didn't want to risk losing him. The fear of losing my last chance at a normal life was crippling me. To be somebody's wife, somebody's mom. All because of an unnecessary, self-imposed timeline. Way behind schedule, and flat out convinced that I couldn't do any better.

Al was right. I had it twisted. Instead of feeling like I was too old to think so much of myself, I was too damn old to be thinking so little of myself. If anything, the other side of thirty is when you stop settling for bullshit, afterthoughts and leftovers. I was too damn old not to think so much of myself. On the other side of thirty, you're old enough to know better. Damn, I really hope she gets back in school with that psychology stuff. She's certainly got no reason to wait, now.

Knowing better doesn't necessarily mean we'll do better. We want what we want, whether it's good, bad, or indifferent to us. Knowing that we can't control what other people choose to do or not do, anymore than we can manipulate time doesn't incline us to take more risks.

But I suppose that taking risks is the only way to confront and possibly overcome the fear. And I guess that's what I was doing now. Scared shitless.

The door still wasn't closing. But I kept my back turned. I could look unaffected as long as I didn't have to look him in the face.

When I heard the door open a little more, I popped off, with, "You know, your boy Snake is in town, right?"

"Snake?" he asked weakly. "Yeah?"

"Mmmhmm," I said. "He coaches over at one of your schools out in Paulding County. You should look him up when you get a chance."

"Yeah," he said again. "I'll do that."

"Yep," I said back. "That'd be good."

He didn't have to know how broken my spirit was, nor about my fear of spending the rest of my life in an empty bed. He didn't have to know that a year from now, maybe even a week from now, I could be regretting that I took this risk, and let him walk out of my life. Again.

Maybe he was right about everything. Maybe I just thought I was another woman. Maybe I was as weak as he thought I was. But today, I'll be strong. And that's all he needed to see.

Finally, the door closed.

Chapter Thirty-Six – All That I Can Be

I got up the next morning and checked my seldom-checked Army Knowledge Online email and almost choked. What in the fuck? It was an electronic notification telling me that my assignment had been cancelled, and to contact my assignments branch if I had any questions. If?

When I finally got someone on the line who knew what I was talking about, the first thing he had to say to me was, "Congratulations, S'arnt. You're on your way to the trail." That's what we call drill sergeant duty.

Trail? Oh, shit no. I spoke up with, "Whoa, S'arnt, I think there's been a mistake. I gotta get away from here."

"You're getting away from there, S'arnt," he confirmed. "Straight to Fort Jackson."

"That's sounds real good and everything, but, all those hard-headed recruits? Do you know I'm just now leaving a MEPS? I know what drill sergeants have to deal with."

"We know that, S'arnt," he said. "We looked your records."

"And unhh!" I whined. "All that damn running. Early in the morning. In the rain." Then I took a breath. "S'arnt, tell me you're kidding, right."

He had no sympathy. "S'arnt Cooper, as a 71L, where did you think your career path was taking you?"

"To Japan. In less than two weeks." I said. "S'arnt, I already shipped my stuff."

"Un-ship it, S'arnt."

I stifled a sigh. This was not an argument I wanted to waste my time having. I couldn't win it. After all, he was right. It was time to soldier up. To do something with my life that I could be proud of for the next few years. Actually, that kind of turned me on.

"You're right, S'arnt. I know I can be good at this," I said. "I want to make soldiers out of people who never thought they'd be soldiers, I guess. Kind of like me. Besides that," I added, "I want to see what it feels like to run in the rain and be good at it again." I thought about the look on Sergeant Lopez' face. His motivated sense of purpose. His entire aura.

It kind of reminded me of Curtis when I'd first met him. I wanted that aura. It occurred to me that that's what I'd wanted all the time, or so I told myself. Maybe being in special assignments had given me a near-fatal complacency. Maybe his coming back into my life was a part of that. Maybe that was the sign I misread so miserably. Maybe I'd forgotten why I joined the army in the first place. To get my own stuff.

Maybe Curtis had started all that all those years ago. Started me wanting something he had, and not just the sex. That sure-footedness, or whatever it was. But now, I didn't want it from Curtis. And I didn't want to spend my life just admiring people like Lopez, wishing I had what they had, and going after it the wrong way. I wanted my own.

"I can do this," I said to reassure myself more than him. Frankly, the thought of it scared the shit out of me.

"S'arnt, I know you don't think you're the only one who hates PT in the rain," he said, knowingly. "Early mornings and all that. I can see from your records, you started out on the fast track. Air Assault. Master Fitness."

"I was young," I sighed into the phone.

"And you've been a pogue for the last two assignments."

"Yeah. So?" I said back. "Pogue and proud of it."

A pogue soldier is one who's only been in office-type environments. I wasn't so proud of that part, but he didn't know me like that. It's one thing to be called out by your buddies, but from somebody who's just looking at you on paper, it's too close to an insult.

"I don't know if you got it in you no more than you do," he continued. "But you're a single, no-dependents, female NCO, and that's what we're looking for right now. You can get ready to hate it or get ready to love it. Either way, suck it up."

"All right, S'arnt, you're right." Jerk.

Just as he was saying, "Good," I was hanging up on him.

****

School was everything I expected. Hard as hell. And too much damn rain. Funny thing though, about army rain. The PT still sucked, but there's something about being a genuine motivator and being genuinely motivated.

Having somebody else running alongside you or waiting for you at the finish, getting soaked all to hell and not caring because all they want to do is see you make it, gives the rain an almost sweet smell at the end, and a taste that you don't mind wetting your lips. It's something that you sort of wear like a badge, however wet and heavy or soaked with sweat. Something you don't mind wearing a little bit longer, that you almost hate to take off, because you want other people to know what you've been through without having to tell them.

Do you ever wish you could blink and some things would just not be true, that you could fade them out of memory of everyone who was even there? I wish I could blink away the lies that I told, undo all the easy sins I committed.

Maybe dangerous fits me. But not because some man would kill for me and I wouldn't even care, as Curtis had put it. But because of what I was willing to do and had done, and he hadn't even noticed. I not only let parts of me die to get him, but I killed parts of myself for the sake of being with him.

And I'm not just talking about my babies. My beautiful babies for the transgressions of my soul.

I'm talking about how I smothered pieces of my spirit just trying to keep them quiet while I went after what I thought I wanted. Big pieces of the person I was died. And what I didn't kill, I ignored. Compromised. And I willfully snuffed out parts of other people in the process, including Al's trusting heart that she'll never get back. Now she's one of those who will never really trust another female. I guess women get as many issues from each other as we get from men.

The real shame of that is that it didn't have to be that way, if I had treated her like the sister she tried to be to me.

Maybe I should have stopped and looked around me before doing some dangerous shit that got me where ended up, even if it did put me where I said I wanted to be, in a position to take the man I loved. Maybe calling it love isn't good enough to make it all right, but I can't go back to who I used to be, or thought I was, or what I thought I knew.

Dignity, integrity, honor, loyalty, self-respect, and little more empathy might have been worth holding on to, rather than casting off as dead weight that was just slowing me down on my way to trying to make better time, because they too much on my conscience. Those things probably should have mattered more to me than my need to matter more to him.

When it mattered, really mattered, he clung to the things that mattered to him, not to the things that should have mattered, or wanted to matter, but to the things that did. And what does that really say about the person you say you love and what he values, if it turns out that you're not among those mattering things? I mean, whether you're married or not, what does it say, and are you willing to hear it? And when I consider all the things of real value that I let go of because I wanted to be counted among those things, it makes me want to tell somebody, anybody else to be more careful of what you cling to and what you throw away, even if you finally get what you said you wanted. Because it ain't all green on the other side. Because sometimes, what you think is love is really just a lesson. Even if that lesson is only to be more careful of the glass houses you condemn.

****

Funny thing about God and His plans. In my second week of drill sergeant school, I fell off of the podium while leading a PT session, busted my left knee and got dropped from the course. Just when I was feeling like I was exactly where I needed to be, God said, "Nope!" Again. So much for that, I guess. Whatever the plan, God must really love me to spend so much time on me.

I thought to myself that my branch managers would put me back on the attaché assignment in Japan. I was rather looking forward to it, until I somehow ended up staying right where I was. Just when I was ready to be pissed off for being left at Fort Jackson, South Carolina as a "turtle"—that's someone who works with the other drill sergeants to get the experience while preparing to go (or go back) to drill sergeant school—I thought about how Raphael was nearby at USC. And I thought maybe I should give him a call.